COMPLICATED HEARTS

BOOK TWO

ASHLEY JADE

This story is strange and unconventional. It's everything you hate.
If you're looking for perfect characters and a perfect story...this
book isn't for you.

To those who need the reminder that love is too beautiful to be concealed...
This one's for you.

PROLOGUE
BRESLIN

Five years earlier...

My lungs burn as I continue running through the storm with only one goal in mind.

Make sure Asher Holden doesn't see where I live.

I take a deep breath that seems near impossible due to the heavy rain. Shivers zip up and down my spine and my feet keep slipping in the mud as I reach the once dirt road turned pseudo lake leading up to the trailer park.

But I don't let up, I'm so close to being in the clear I can almost taste it.

"Breslin," a deep voice shouts in the distance. I take a sharp right and surge forward. Adrenaline holds my body hostage and my chest rises and falls as I suck in as much air as I can.

My teeth chatter, God, I'm so cold. It's the end of fall and Mother Nature seems to be taking no prisoners with this storm.

Lightning flashes through the sky and I run faster and faster. I just need to make it home before he sees me.

He's on a razor scooter, idiot—I remind myself before fear pummels me and I nearly trip over a fallen tree branch.

It's dangerous as hell for him to be riding that stupid thing right now.

Great, you're going to be responsible for committing homicide on your 16th birthday. *Way to go, Breslin.* Reach for those stars.

I look around...I'm already past the gates. The dirt land filled with dingy double-wide trailers that reek of poverty a glaring reminder.

My father couldn't even spring the extra 20 bucks a month for the nicer park.

I close my eyes and tilt my chin toward the rain...waiting for the inevitable.

It's not like it matters anyway. I'm not a princess...and my life sure as hell won't ever be a fairy tale. Why I thought meeting Asher Holden and him setting his eyes on me a few weeks ago would change all that is anyone's guess.

And his family. God his family in their million-dollar house with *real* silver spoons, looking at their son like he had a temporary bout with sanity for bringing me home for dinner.

The only person who didn't look at me with disdain was his brother Preston, but that's only because he was so busy stuffing his face and looking at the stock market on his phone. What 14-year-old is interested in the stock market anyway?

Oh, that's right. Rich 14-year-olds whose families are loaded.

And then his mother...the look of horror she shot me when she asked what my favorite kind of cake was so we could celebrate my birthday and I said, 'The yellow kind from a box' like an idiot.

I never even knew what Crème Brûlée was before tonight. And to be perfectly honest, to me it tasted like burnt dog shit—but I have manners and didn't want to insult their chef or their hospitality; so I just smiled and thanked them profusely for it.

I look down at my poor excuse for a dress and slam my palm against my forehead.

Good Lord, there's not only a small hole, but a stain smack dab in the middle of my chest. How did I overlook that?

I guess that's what I get for shopping at Goodwill for this outfit and taking advantage of their two for one sale. Because that's exactly what I've got.

"Breslin," Asher shouts again, his voice much closer now. Any minute he'll be rounding the corner.

I could probably meet him halfway and pretend I got lost and that I don't really live here.

Well, I could have before tonight when Asher's dad told me immediately after dinner ended that he would drive me home, and I said there was no need because my father was waiting out front—and then before I could stop him—Asher ran out after me to say goodbye and quickly figured out my father wasn't anywhere to be seen.

Because—*Yeah, right.* My father doing something fatherly?

No, my father wouldn't waste the time or effort picking his teenage daughter up from some boy's house. On her 16th birthday no less.

Not only did he not wish me a happy birthday as I was fishing him a cold one before I left for school this morning, I doubt he even realizes that I'm gone now. In the middle of a rainstorm, shaking and shivering my ass off.

Waiting for Asher Holden to discover the girl that he—for reasons I'll never fathom—thinks is worth getting to know.

I squeeze my eyes shut and curse the rain. Silently wishing it would wash away this bleak life and give me any other one. As if hearing my prayer, the rain slows to a mist. *Mother Nature is such a bitch.*

I hear the vroom of Asher's scooter approaching and grit my teeth.

I mean what is he playing at anyway? Why is he being nice to me? No one else ever is.

He's only been in school a few short weeks but he can have any girl he wants. Something he *must* be acutely aware of given that everyone's eyes follow him and stay on him whenever he walks into a room.

Not that I can blame them...the guy is hands down the hottest guy I've ever seen in my life.

Admittedly I haven't seen wallops of hot guys in my short 16 years...but he's way hotter than those celebrities gracing the covers of tabloids and fashion magazines.

Which only further makes me wonder—just what in the hell does he want with *me*? I'm a plain Jane at best. Sloppy and 'this close' to being chubby at worst.

I pop my eyes open and my heart jumps to my throat. Because blue eyes nicer than any ocean in the Caribbean are staring right at me.

I expect him to be mad. I mean, he should be, my behavior was strange. Borderline rude even.

But he isn't. Instead, he swings his backpack over his shoulder, retrieves his jersey, and offers it to me.

I want to laugh, because if Marcy Bush was here witnessing him hand me his jersey right now, the bitch would have a coronary.

When I decline, he frowns. "You're shivering, Breslin."

Probably because my clothes have holes in them, you blind fool— I want to shout, but I don't. I begrudgingly slip his jersey over my head and hold out my arms. "Happy? The only thing you've managed to accomplish was making your jersey wet. I'm still shivering. It's still raining...*nothing* has changed."

Because I'm still a poor girl from the trailer park. And he's Asher Holden...destined for the kind of greatness I can't even wrap my head around.

You ain't meant for boys like him—my father's voice taunts me.

He's gonna leave you as soon as he figures out you ain't good enough.
Just like your Mama left us.

I walk over to the large log holding one side of the trailer park gate open and sit down.

I can feel his eyes on me and when I look up, the light from the dimming street light shows me the somber expression on his face. "I'm sorry. I know my family was rude to you tonight. I know my mom's a space cadet and my dad can be an asshole."

Wait, he's apologizing for his family?

"That's not why I ran off," I say before I can stop myself. I smooth my hair out of my face and take a deep breath. Might as well get this over with now. "I live here, Asher."

He circles around and points to the ground. "Right here?" He walks over to the log I'm sitting on and taps on it. "One hell of a hard bed, Breslin."

I laugh and shake my head. It's not funny, but the way he's trying to make light of the situation for my betterment makes him even more endearing to me.

"I—uh." I rest my shaking hands on my thighs. "I was embarrassed. I didn't want you and your dad to see where I lived. That's why I ran off like I did."

He plops down next to me. "I get it."

I snort. "Yeah right. You're rich."

"No," he corrects. "My parents are rich. Big difference." He grins and flips the inside pockets of his sweatpants out, showing me they're empty. "See? I have no money. We're the same."

"We are not the same," I argue. "And just because you don't have money on you doesn't mean you don't have access to it. Your family is well off." I circle my finger in the air. "This is pretty much my destiny."

"Says who?"

"I don't know...the universe? Society?" I look up at the night sky. Now that the storm has passed the stars above are twinkling bright.

"You're dangerous for me," I whisper and my heart pangs. "And I'm no good for you."

"That's not—"

I turn to look at him. "What do you want with me, Asher? Because I've got nothing to give you."

"That's where you're wrong." I gasp when he reaches for my hand and places two fingers over the spot where my pulse is pounding rapidly. "Because I want this." He brings my wrist up to his lips. "I want *you*, Breslin Rae."

I swallow hard, both my mind and body spinning out because neither knew they were capable of feeling so much at the same time.

"My mother liked to paint," I blurt, wishing I could take the words back.

"She left when I was just a baby, but my dad said she left behind her favorite paint set for me."

I leave out the part where my dad sold them to a neighbor so he could buy a 40 ounce.

"In her note, she told me to always chase my dreams." My voice cracks, I'm a second away from breaking out into sobs.

Concern pulls on his features. "Is that what you think being with me will do? Stunt your dreams?"

"No." I look at him and a tear slips down my cheek. "That's what I'm afraid I'll do to you." I gesture between us. "If we do this...I'm going to fuck up your life." I draw my knees up to my chest. "I'm not the girl you should be with, Asher. I'm not the girl you can show off. I'm not the girl you can take to dances. I'm not the girl who fits in your future, period."

I stand up. "I'm not the girl who will propel you forward, I'm the girl who will keep you here. Just like my dad did to my mom...until she finally had enough and left."

Leaving me to deal with the mess left behind.

I start to walk away but his hand wraps around my wrist, holding me in place. His other hand pulls out his cell phone and I hear the first few bars of *Glycerine* by Bush start to play.

Before I can question him, he pulls me close and starts swaying.

"W-what are you doing?" I choke out, the stuttering in my voice no longer because I'm cold.

"You said you're not the girl I could take to dances," he proclaims. "So, we'll have our own dances."

I shake my head but he lifts my chin to look at him. "You said you don't fit in my future." His eyes turn hard with determination. "Let me prove you wrong."

I open my mouth but rain starts to fall again, heavier than before.

Of course, Mother Nature would choose the worst moment to grant my previous wish.

He brushes my hair out of my face and thunder booms above us. "I'm gonna prove you wrong about everything, Breslin Rae. And I'm gonna love you harder than anyone ever has before," he shouts above the rain. "The only thing you have to do is let me."

Tears prickle my eyes, my vision becoming hazy, the soft guitar strings from the music plucking my heart.

"We're gonna go down in flames," I argue.

He leans in. "Then let's make one hell of an explosion."

I open my mouth again, but he closes the distance between our lips. There's no room for protest, because all I can feel is myself free-falling. The kind of fall that doesn't feel a thing like falling...because my heart no longer belongs to me. It's Asher's. And it's soaring so high in his atmosphere, there's no way I'll ever get it back.

He smiles. "So, what do you say, Breslin?"

I nod, happiness and warmth coating my heart as he leans down to kiss me again and I feel myself float higher and higher.

But that's the thing about falling...

Sooner or later you're bound to hit something.

And there's no way of knowing what the damage from the impact will be until it happens.

And there are some falls—you just can't recover from.

CHAPTER 1

BRESLIN

Present Day

This. Can't. Be. Happening.

I shake my head, convinced that this entire scene before me is a mirage of some sort caused by jet lag.

Because why else would I be seeing Landon on the bed *naked*...and a stark-naked *Asher* hovering above him.

"*Breslin?*" Asher chokes out, and that does it.

Everything in my body locks up, because there's no mistaking that it is him now.

There's no mistaking that I just walked straight into something that not even my worst nightmare could conjure up.

I try to take a breath, but I can't. Oh, God. I. Can't. Fucking. Breathe.

I turn, my stomach flips and my vision is blurry, and I'm certain I'm a mere second away from passing out due to shock. But I can't, because I need to get out. I *have* to get out of here, every nerve in my body is screaming for me to run.

So I do.

For the briefest of moments, I consider going to my apartment and holing up in there, but I can't. Because I can already hear them scrambling off the bed.

The bed that they were...

I clutch my chest, bile rising in my throat, my vision becoming even more hazy.

I hike my bag up my shoulder and snatch my luggage that's propped out in the hall. And then I'm running down the stairs and out to the lobby as fast as my shaky legs can carry me.

I hear someone shout my name behind me but I don't know who, because everything is blending together and I can't form a cohesive thought right now to save my life.

I throw my bag in the car and jump into the driver's seat. I don't know where I'm going, but anywhere is better than here.

Tears are clogging my eyes, streaming down my face faster than my cheeks can catch them as I grasp the steering wheel and turn the key. I feel like I've been thrown into one of the circles of hell...the *worst* one.

The last time I saw Asher Holden is burned into the back of my mind and I can't help but choke out another sob as I press on the gas. Back then I thought *that* betrayal was the worst, but how wrong I was.

What I don't understand is *why?*

Why is he here? Why is he with Landon? Why is Landon with *him?* Just what kind of sick and cruel joke is this?

Whose idea was it to pull the rug out from under my feet like this?

I'm sobbing so hard I have to pull over. I want to call Kit; because I've never needed my best friend more than in this moment. But then I remember that she's proposing to Becca soon and I'd hate myself for ruining her happiness.

I wipe my face with the back of my hands, but fresh tears continue to fall. It's like they won't ever stop, taunting me just like the memory of finding them in bed together.

I need to figure out a plan, because there's no way in hell I'm going back to that death trap that is the apartment complex. I can't go to a hotel because I'm low on funds—because I spent my money trying to come back here to make things right with Landon.

But he was with *Asher*.

That thought pings around the walls of my skull and I scream.

Anger needles my insides, prickling my skin with tiny bolts of rage that are on the verge of taking over my entire body. I honestly don't know which one I'm angrier with.

Actually, that's not right, because when I think about Landon...there's a swell of sadness.

But when I think about Asher?

Oh...I want to tear his beating heart out of his chest right before I shove it down his throat and watch him choke on it like he did to me.

I rest my head on the steering wheel and draw in a breath. Where the hell am I going to sleep tonight?

The thought hits me, and I'd almost smile if it wasn't for feeling so miserable. The dorm.

I had forgotten on account that every student on tour was granted an extension, but it's official check-in day today. And although Kit had talked about wanting to rent the apartment for the rest of the year, I told her no because I couldn't afford it.

Of course, she offered to pay, but I wouldn't let her. So we registered for a dorm again, and Kit being Kit; threw some extra money the school's way to ensure we'd be roommates this year. I mean, *now* I'm guessing she and Becca will move into the apartment together, but I can go to the dorm tonight.

I don't have to go back to the hell hole.

I drive toward the college, refusing to let myself think about what will happen when classes start in a few days. For the first time in my life, I'm thankful Landon and I have different majors, because there's no chance I'll see him around campus.

And hopefully, that means I'll never have to see Asher again, either.

But Landon. God, fuck my heart and the way it pangs. Was this his way of getting back at me for hurting him? Tracking down my ex and...hooking up with him?

I know what I did was wrong. I know I hurt him. But I'm pretty sure I don't deserve this amount of hatred thrown my way.

But who knows...because I sure as hell don't feel like I know Landon anymore.

Or Asher.

Or myself.

I know *nothing*. Nothing but this unbearable pain seeping and settling in my chest.

I pull up to the school parking lot which is semi-packed due to students officially checking in the weekend before classes start, and I silently pray there isn't a long line.

I reach for my sunglasses and tug my luggage out, cursing the sun the entire time for having the audacity to shine bright and warm when there's nothing but a gray force-field enclosing my heart.

I force my mind to go blank as I stand in line, force myself to pretend like my life didn't just fall to complete and utter shit for the *second* time because of *him*.

When I reach the check-in table, I plaster a fake smile on my face and take a breath past the ache in my ribs.

Thankfully the girl at the table checks me in without question and without any hiccups.

I lug my bags into the elevator and press the button for the senior co-ed floor, telling myself to just keep it together for a few more minutes.

I stride past the blonde knocking incessantly on someone's door and curse when I realize the door she's knocking on is the door next to mine. She's got about two more knocks left before I hit her with a dose of reality and inform her that the person on the other side is either ignoring her or not in their dorm.

She turns to face me right when I stick my key in. "Have you seen him?"

I have no clue who *him* is and right now I don't care to. I give a shake of my head and mutter a curt, "Nope." which makes her huff and walk away.

As soon as I let myself in and toss my bags inside, I fall against the wall.

And finally, I let myself break. Let myself shatter.

Let the pain swallow me whole and pray that I'll somehow get through this for a second time. Because right now? I'm not so sure that I will.

CHAPTER 2
ASHER

"Breslin!" I yell, my voice sounding like heavy glass shattering as I watch her flee to the parking lot.

Emotions, all kinds of fucking emotions grip me by the throat as I run after her. Some woman in the lobby gives me a weird look that I'm positive is due to my bare feet, no shirt, and what I'm sure is my dick flopping out of my unzipped jeans, but I don't care.

I need to get to her. I need to...

Tires screech in the distance and my heart folds in on itself because there is *nothing* worse than watching Breslin Rae run right out of my life for the second time.

What kind of weird twist of fate is this? Just what in the actual fuck is going on?

I spin around when I hear footsteps behind me, because I know who they belong to. And boy, do I have some questions for Landon fucking Parker right now that I expect some fucking answers to.

However, what I don't expect—is a punch that rocks my jaw the second his eyes lock with mine.

I throw a punch back in his direction, smiling wide when my fist connects with skin.

It's a smile that wipes clean off my face when I see him stagger back and look at me again.

He looks just as hurt and confused as I am, which doesn't make any sense.

"*You*," he grinds out, low and deadly. "You're him, aren't you?"

I open my mouth to say— what, I'm not sure—but he spits blood on the ground and walks away.

I don't follow him, not only because it's clear he doesn't want me to, but because I need to wrap my head around this entire situation myself.

I also don't want to be responsible for *murdering* the guy I have serious feelings for because it turns out he was shacking up with *my* Breslin.

Because she will always be *mine*. Even when I fucking hate her...

I grind my jaw and fight the urge to march back up to his apartment and beat him to a bloody pulp.

The woman who witnessed the entire exchange widens her eyes and shakes her head as she looks me up and down. "Need a ride?"

I nod, hoping she can understand that while I need the ride, I'm not exactly in the mood for chit-chat during the journey.

Thankfully the campus is such a short distance away, it doesn't give us time to talk.

When I thank her and step outside of the car, a few students look at me and their nervous and cheery expressions drop.

Of course, this shit would go down when it's check-in day.

My dick is, for the most part; safely tucked back inside my pants, but considering my overall appearance at the moment, I can't blame them for looking at me like I'm insane. I'm one hell of a sight for these poor freshmen to be taking in.

Barging past, I brush them off and make my way to my dorm

room, feeling and looking more exposed to these goddamn people than I ever wanted to.

I inwardly groan when I find O'Conner's girlfriend rapping on my door.

I am not in the mood for her bullshit right now, I have more than my fair share presently.

She smiles brightly when she sees me, and on some level, I should probably feel bad that I'm about to burst that bubble she's blown up for herself, but I don't.

"Theo. He's gone." she says, looking at me in wonder.

I nod, because I'm not sure what else I'm supposed to say or why the fuck she's here.

The second I stick my key in the lock she presses herself flush against me. "I can't believe you wanted to be with me so bad you got him expelled," she says breathlessly against my back.

Awe, hell. Just when I think it can't get any worse, it does.

"He got expelled because he attacked a student," I grunt. "I had nothing to do with it."

"Yeah, but someone on the football team said—"

"Said what? That I went through the trouble of getting him expelled for *you?*" I snort. "Sorry, sweetheart, but your pussy wasn't that great. Mediocre at best."

She gasps, cries out that I'm an asshole, and slaps me hard across the cheek.

I relish the physical sting, it's on the tip of my tongue to ask her for another. Because it's so much better than the emotional one I'm feeling currently.

Her face twists and she mutters that the only reason I didn't like her pussy was because I'm a faggot.

I tell her how original her insult was and slam the door in her face.

Then I give in to this crushing weight that's like a bomb going off inside my chest and I slink down the wall.

Breslin.

My fucking Breslin...*here.*

Or rather, she was; before she ran off to God only knows where.

Pressure tightens against my ribs, making it harder and harder to breathe with every beat of my heart.

A heart that can't tell if it's beating so painfully because it's longing for the girl that it *always* has and needs another hit of her— or a warning to my system because she destroyed the fucking organ once already and it won't be able to survive the next hit.

Christ, I equally love and hate the way Breslin fits inside my heart and soul in a way no one else will ever be able to.

The back of my head hits the wall and I force myself to breathe and tell myself to stop being a pussy. But there's no point...because all I can think about is her.

What the fuck is she doing at Woodside of all places anyway? She was supposed to be at Falcon, pursuing some bullshit career in architecture instead of *art* like her talent warrants.

I close my eyes, my head spinning out of control...and that's when I hear it.

The sound of someone sobbing, rather intensely, on the other side of the wall.

It's so muffled and raw I can't make out who it is, especially given that I've never met the person on the other side of the wall— but I can't help but feel a sort of kinship with them considering the way my life just fell apart today too.

And although I'm certain that my circumstances are a hundred times worse than their feelings about being homesick or missing their boyfriend back home, I shift and place my hand on the wall anyway.

"You're going to be okay," I whisper, knowing that they probably can't even hear me and it's pointless. "I know it seems bad right now...but you're gonna get through this."

I stuff down the ball working its way up my own throat, because I'm not so sure who it is that I'm trying to comfort anymore.

My chest squeezes and I stop talking, instead choosing to listen to their uncontrollable sobbing.

And that's what I continue doing for the rest of the night...listen to them cry their heart out, because I can't.

CHAPTER 3

LANDON

I try and focus on the music, try and lose myself in it, but I can't. It's been 24 hours since Breslin ran in here and ran out, with Asher following suit.

My feelings are all kinds of fucked up. I have so many questions for the both of them. But for the first time; I can't seem to bring myself to pick up the phone.

Just like I can't seem to play music.

Because I can't escape these overwhelming emotions that are holding me hostage.

I touch the ivory keys again, begging for some clarity or relief from this prison.

The universe is cruel. So fucking cruel.

I never really planned how I would tell Breslin about Asher when she got back, but her finding me in bed with her ex-boyfriend didn't even make the top 100 on my list of ways to tell her.

Christ, she must be devastated.

Kind of like how I felt when she left and ignored me. I swallow the bitterness rising in my throat and attempt to play again.

The shakiness of my right hand due to low blood sugar throws me off and I can't help but notice the abrasion on my knuckle.

The one that's there because I punched Asher. And fuck if I can pinpoint my reason behind it. One moment I was blind with rage over the fact that *he* was the divide between us. The reason I couldn't have *her*. And the next? I was hurt that he ran after Breslin like he was on fire and she was the only source of water for miles.

Less than 24 hours after I...after *we*...

God, what the hell have I gotten myself into?

My heart beats out a painful rhythm, making me even more aware of the raging war within it. A war that's battling right down the middle, ripping me to shreds in the process. A war that I'm not quite sure how to deal with because it's something I've never experienced before.

I grind my molars and slam the piano. Thoughts of Breslin *and* Asher swirling through my head. The emptiness that I feel now strangling me. Because I lost them...both. And there's no way in hell this shit is going to work itself out.

This situation is far past complicated...it's completely fucked. I'm probably best off staying far away from them entirely.

Besides, there's only one way this can end, and it just did.

CHAPTER 4

BRESLIN

"Breslin," Kit whispers and I roll over, the ache due to not using my muscles and lying in bed for four—no make that five—straight days, becoming annoying now.

But it's so much better than the alternative. Because I can't face the outside world just yet. Not without cracking and breaking into a thousand tiny pieces.

"You've already missed the first two days of classes," she reminds me and I shrug my shoulders from underneath the blankets.

Kit was able to put together what happened after she came back, went to the apartment—realized I wasn't there—and tracked me down here. Smack dab in the middle of my incoherent crying session.

My mind flits back to late last night when she held me and basically force-fed me a granola bar while making me take sips of water since I hadn't eaten in days. Which is probably not such a bad thing now that I think about it, considering the 5 lbs. I'd put on in Europe. Maybe my jeans will fit better.

Provided I ever walk out that door again that is.

And with the way I'm still feeling? It isn't likely.

"Get up," she yells and I curl into both myself and my pillow.

"Breslin you are on a scholarship!" she screams. "You only have a limited number of days you can miss."

"So, let them expel me," I murmur.

Let them throw me right on out of here. Because I just don't care anymore.

"Your painting class is on the schedule for today. You've been looking forward to it since you signed up for it," she says and I squeeze my eyes shut. Which is a bad idea, because all I see is *them*. Together. My past and present rolling around in sheets.

"You have exactly one minute to get your ass in the shower or I'm throwing you in there myself."

Silence is my answer. The crushing weight in my chest and the heaviness in my heart a reminder of why I can't.

There's tugging on my right leg and I kick in protest. "Stop it, Kit," I yell, but she goes for the other leg and tugs harder.

I grip the sheets, but they slip off the mattress.

"You are not fucking up your life because of that douche canoe," she grunts. "Either of them."

"How does something like this happen not once, but twice in my life, Kit?" The cracking and quivering in my voice causes her to drop my legs and rush over to me.

"Bre—"

I sit up and swing my legs over the bed. "Am I not attractive enough? Or interesting enough? Do I suck in bed?" I shake my head. "There has to be something inherently wrong with me. You know the saying... fool me once shame on you...but fool me twice —" I bury my head in my hands. "I wish I never went to Europe. I wish I hadn't ignored Landon while I was there. None of this would have happened."

I can hear Kit's sharp intake of breath before she utters, "Do you think it would have made a difference?" When my mouth hangs open she quickly says, "What I mean is...sooner or later you would have figured out Landon was into guys, right?"

"Are you saying I should just excuse what he did? All because he had some kind of come to Jesus moment?"

She chews on her thumbnail. "Do you want the standard best friend response first, or the truth?"

"Truth first."

She faces me on the bed. "Sometimes you have connections with people. Connections you never expect and no matter what...you can't prevent them from happening—because it's too strong to fight. And as strange as it sounds, maybe that was the case for Landon. For all you know, maybe Asher played him all along."

She squeezes my hand. "Because I honestly don't think Landon intentionally tried to hurt you. I think he was hurt over what you did...but I just don't think he's the type of person who would willingly hurt another. He doesn't have a vindictive bone in his body." Her eyes narrow. "Now, Asher? Yeah, you and I already know he would willingly hurt you because he's done it before."

She tips my chin up. "And I think when you're ready to handle the truth, you need to talk to Landon. It won't change what happened, but I think it will help. Hear his side of things, because you'll be wallowing in all these unanswered questions and 'what-ifs' if you don't."

She stands up. "But right now? You need to get your ass to class, B. I love you, which means I will straight up murder Asher Holden if he stops you from graduating. Hell, I may even do the same to Landon if he's not careful." She gestures to the bathroom. "Your class starts in 25 minutes. Go take a shower. I'll have coffee and an outfit waiting for you when you get out. All you have to do is show up. Even if your head isn't there today, your body has to be."

I nod, pushing to my feet. "Okay," I say before I throw my arms around her. "Thank you, Kit."

I don't feel better and I'm not sure if I'm going to take her advice...but without Kit...my life would be even worse. I know that for a fact.

Best friends like her...*people* like her are a rarity.

"You're my person," I whisper, squeezing her tighter.

She squeezes me back. "Are we really having a *Grey's* moment right now?"

"Shut up and take my love."

At this, she laughs and I start walking to the bathroom. I pause when my foot hits the cold tile. "Random, but do you have any idea who the person next door is?"

She thinks about this for a moment and shrugs. "No idea. I've been in here with you for the last couple of days. Why?"

I return her shrug, thinking back to that night. "I don't know. I mean it's not that big a deal I guess."

"What's not?"

I look down at the polish on my toenails. "The first night I was here, I was an uncontrollable sobbing mess. And I guess I didn't realize how loud I was being until I heard murmuring on the other side of the wall. I couldn't hear what he was saying, but I assume it's a guy because of how deep the tone of their voice was." I pull on my bottom lip. "They didn't yell or bang on the wall and tell me to be quiet, though. In fact, I think they were trying to soothe me in some weird way. I thought maybe I would thank them and let them see that I'm not some mental case."

Just a girl with a broken heart who's trying to find the will to breathe again.

She turns to my dresser and opens one of the drawers. "Yeah, I don't know who he is, but I'm sure we're bound to run into him sooner or later." Sadness crosses over her face. "Well, you more than me because I'll be at the apartment."

"You're still staying there?" I ask with more bite than I intended to.

She looks like a deer caught in headlights. "It's not like I want to but I signed a six-month lease before I left for Europe."

I rub my forehead, guilt crawling up my spine because I have absolutely no right to be mad at her. I should be happy that she's happy. Becca obviously said yes, and instead of celebrating like she should be, Kit's been here with me. "God, I'm a shit friend."

She waves a hand. "No, you're just a little battered and bruised. But you'll be okay. You're the strongest person I know, B."

She gestures around the room. "I already told Becca I'd be here with you for a few days and that we'll start moving her things in after." She grins. "However, we are meeting for lunch later today." She places a finger on her lips, pretending to think. "Or rather, she'll be eating lunch and I'll be eating her for lunch."

I hide behind the door, toss my dirty shirt over my head, and throw it at her. "You're such a perv, I swear."

She giggles. "You say it like it's a bad thing."

I crack a smile—the first one in what feels like weeks—and roll my eyes before I close the bathroom door and step in the shower.

"What do you mean I'm not signed up? I specifically remember signing up for the Women's Study class."

I recall what the professor said about me not being on the roster and the class already being full and I grit my teeth.

When the adviser starts to protest again I say, "It's the *last* Social Science class that I need to graduate. There's no way I would *not* sign up for it. Something is wrong with your computer. Please check again."

She presses some keys and I try and steady my breathing. I don't know why the universe is shitting on me this week, but I've had all I can take of it.

"Sorry, Breslin but you didn't sign up for it." I open my mouth to argue again but she looks hopeful. "You did say you went to Europe on the study tour, right?"

I nod, I nod so damn hard my head is about to fall off.

She smiles and presses some more keys. "There might be a way we can get you that credit. Depending on what the Dean says—" Her expression falls and so does my stomach. "You withdrew?"

I can feel the color draining from my face. "I—well. Um, something came up and I had to leave. It was an emergency."

"An emergency? Well, if that's the case maybe—"

I stop her right there. "Not that kind of emergency. It was more of a personal emergency. My family is fine."

She raises an eyebrow and I know what she's thinking. Who in their right mind would leave Europe?

This idiot right here.

I drum my nails on the counter and swallow hard. "I know I don't have a right to ask you to help me out. But I really need to be in that class. I *have* to graduate on time."

She huffs out a breath. "The class is full. There's nothing I can do."

She taps a few more keys. "In fact, all of the Social Science classes are full."

My heart falls to the floor. This can't be happening. "Are you sure? Because I'll take anything. Even if it's five in the damn morning, I'll be there with bells on."

She starts to shake her head again but pauses. "Wait a minute...there's one spot open in the Intro to Ethics class."

I slap my hand on the counter. "I'll take it."

She glances at her watch, signs a sheet of paper, and hands it to me. "It's across campus and you're already 15 minutes late."

In a flash, I start sprinting, silently thanking Kit the whole time that she laid out a pair of leggings and an oversized shirt instead of something tight and constricting.

Despite the sweat dripping down my face, the poorly

constructed messy bun on top of my head, and the fact that I'm late, I breathe a sigh of relief and smile when I enter the classroom.

A smile that wipes clean off my face when I feel not one, but *two* sets of eyes burning holes into me and my stomach drops to what I'm sure must be the pits of hell.

My legs turn to jello. It's bad enough that Landon's seated at a small desk in the front of the room and he's what I presume must be the TA...but Asher?

Just what the fucking shit is he doing here? In a classroom.

He's supposed to be at Dukes. Correction—he's supposed to be anywhere but here.

I look up to the ceiling, refusing to cry. I'll save my tears for later, because Asher doesn't deserve one iota of them.

"Can I help you?" the professor questions, looking more than a little ticked off that I'm disrupting.

"I'm sorry for being late—" I quickly glance at her name on my sheet of paper before I hand it to her. "Mrs. Rogers, but I was just added to the roster a few minutes ago."

She looks down her nose at me "Take a seat, Ms. Rae. And don't make it a habit of showing up late to my class."

I nod, nearly salute; and scan the classroom for an empty seat. Which of course, because the universe is so fucking stellar lately; happens to be right next to the asshole himself.

I briefly debate telling Mrs. Rogers I came down with a bad case of Ebola; but don't want to press my luck.

My cheeks heat and I tell my heart to stop pounding as I take the seat next to him. I silently curse myself for wishing that I'd bothered to put on makeup this morning, because I shouldn't care what Asher Holden or what Landon Parker think about me or my appearance.

I straighten my spine and pull out my notebook, which stands out in comparison to all the other students with their laptops surrounding me.

But, oh well. They can take their silver spoons and shove them up their asses.

I root around in my bag for a pen, a pencil, anything; but come up empty. I'm usually prepared for class, but clearly not today on account of not planning to attend in the first place.

Out of the corner of my eye I see Landon snatch a pen off his desk at the same time Asher leans over and whispers, "Looking for one of these?"

The death glare I shoot him causes him to do a double-take. "Unless you want that driven through the heart that I'm certain you don't have, don't fucking talk to me," I sneer with enough bite that his eyes open wide.

Upon hearing my rebuttal, Landon quickly puts his pen down and the guy in front of me turns in his seat and hands me his pen. "Here, Buffy." I open my mouth to ask him what the fuck a *Buffy* is, but then I recall the television show and laugh as I take the pen from him. "Thanks."

He winks. "Don't mention it. Plenty more where that came from."

A sick satisfaction creeps up my spine and my heart beats double time when he turns back around and I feel both sets of eyes boring into me again.

I try my best not to smirk. And I really try my best not to look over at Landon, because my heart breaks all over again whenever I do.

Almost as much as it breaks for the other asshole sitting next to me. I take a deep breath, wishing that Asher would stop glaring at my every move like some kind of crazed stalker.

Landon's eyes narrow when he tracks his movements and it throws me for such a loop I almost don't hear when the Professor calls my name. "What is the definition of morality, Ms. Rae?"

"Um—" I swallow. She knows damn well that I didn't do whatever assignment was given out.

Luckily, it's a fairly easy question and I'm fairly smart. "The distinction between right and wrong or good and bad behavior. You know, common decency. Not going out of your way to hurt another person."

I can't help but look at Landon when I say that—because I sure as hell won't look at Asher—and he blanches.

Mrs. Rogers dismisses me with a curt sniff and a nod and I go back to taking notes.

I ignore Asher when he hangs back after class ends and stands at the door. I have absolutely nothing to say to him. Now or *ever*. Hell, I'm pretty sure if I could get away with it, I'd run him over with my damn car.

I'm about to charge right through him, but a touch to my elbow stops me. "I need to talk to you," Landon whispers.

Asher's jaw tics and I can practically see the hairs on his neck raise.

"Well, I don't want to talk to *you*," I grind out, hiking my bag up my shoulder.

Landon averts his gaze. "Mrs. Rogers had to go home so she asked me to stay back and give you the assignment that you missed."

"Oh," I say, my voice suddenly small now.

I grimace when I notice that Asher is still standing by the door glaring at us.

"Don't you have to get to practice?" Landon growls in his direction and I don't know whether to laugh or cry because at least I know what Asher's doing here now.

Sort of. Woodside's football team sucks. Why the hell would he come here to play?

Not that I should care. Because I don't.

Asher makes a noise in the back of his throat. Somewhere between a throaty groan and a hiss before he checks his watch, mutters a curse, and leaves, slamming the door behind him so loud I jump.

Landon closes his eyes briefly before he leans against the desk and hands me a piece of paper. "The assignment's pretty standard stuff, just terms and definitions. Overall, it's an intro class so it won't be too heavy."

I look down at the syllabus and nod my understanding. "Thanks."

I make the mistake of looking up at him and my heart pulls.

Three weeks ago, everything was perfect with us.

Three years ago, everything was perfect with you and Asher—my mind reminds me bitterly.

Only with Asher...I know I was a good girlfriend.

But I can't say the same about Landon. He tried so hard...for *months.* Put his heart on the line for me time and time again. Had the patience of a damn saint with me and my bullshit...all while I treated him like he was second string.

"I'm sorry," I whisper.

His brows draw together, confusion swirling in those warm brown eyes of his. "What? Bre, you have nothing to be sorry about. If anything, it's me—"

I take a step forward and cut him off. "I hurt you."

His eyes cut to the floor. "You did. But it doesn't excuse—I didn't know who he was. I didn't know that it was him."

Now I'm the one who's confused, until he says, "You never told me your ex's name, or what town you lived in. You never even told me what high school you went to. You never told me much about yourself, so I never connected the dots."

My heart twists, for two reasons. One—because hearing him talk about Asher is making me sick. And two—he's right. I never opened up to him.

I take another step forward, closing the space between us.

Because even though I'm so hurt and upset with him...I'm also upset with myself.

Because I could have had this amazing man standing before me. But I blew it. All because of Asher.

I reach up and run my hand along the stubble on his cheek. "Would it have made a difference?" When he gives me a look, I say, "If you knew who he was, would it have made a difference? Would you still have—" I can't bring myself to finish that sentence.

"No, of course not." There's a long silence that almost stops my heart before he whispers, "I don't know." His eyes turn hard and he pulls my hand away. "You not ignoring me and giving us a try *would* have made a difference, though." There's a coldness to his tone that causes me to wince. I've never seen him so angry.

Before I can stop myself, I grab both his cheeks and force him to look at me. "I'm sorry," I repeat, because it's the truth. "But I came back. I realized my mistake and I came back for you." My voice cracks on the last word. I'm a razor's edge away from breaking down, but when I look up at him again...the energy between us shifts entirely.

I lean into him and he exhales sharply, a storm brewing on his face. And when I adjust my stance and step between his legs, I can feel his cock hardening in his pants.

And in that singular moment, my emotions slice into two fragments. One part of me—is relieved that he still finds me attractive and wants him to fuck me so I know I'm desirable again.

But the other part of me; the most dangerous part, the part that's taking over—wants revenge.

Not against Landon.

But Asher.

And that's the driving force propelling me when I press my lips to his.

CHAPTER 5

LANDON

I t's funny how you can forget how potent an addiction is until you're indulging the substance again.

Like Breslin's lips. Her body. Those little whimpers she makes when I teasingly brush the sides of her breasts.

My cock jerks and I groan when Breslin sweeps her tongue inside my mouth, intentionally taunting me.

I can't help but give in. It's been so long since I've had my last fix, too long.

I reach down and grab a handful of her ass and she arches against me, driving me out of my goddamn mind.

But when I stand up, shift, and back her into the desk, she breaks the kiss. "God, Landon. I'm sorry—"

"Yeah, you said that already," I remind her as I graze my teeth along her neck.

"No, what I mean is—" Her breath catches and she moans when I bring my hand between her thighs and feel how wet she is through those leggings of hers.

She looks stunned and I can't tell if it's because of how forward

I'm acting, or because of what she witnessed in my bedroom a mere few days ago.

And for some reason I can't pin-point, that ticks me off. "Look, if you're having second thoughts about me fucking you on this desk in the next minute, I suggest you get the hell out."

Christ, even I almost wince due to how much of an asshole I'm being. But, I don't falter and I don't apologize, because every time I look at her now...all I remember is all those times I tried to get close to her. All the effort I put into our relationship that she never gave a shit about.

All the times she *hurt* me when she didn't return a call, a text, or showed up at 2 a.m. with some bullshit excuse about studying.

And call me crazy, but maybe this is my way of giving her a reminder of what she fucked up.

I'll never hate Breslin... I'm pretty sure I'm not capable of hating anyone. But I sure as hell can fuck her like I hate her right now.

I wait for her to protest, wait for her to walk right out that door — because she's so fucking good at that, but she doesn't.

Instead, she lays back on the desk and spreads her legs invitingly, antagonizingly. Like the little fucking temptress that she is.

I trail my fingers along her sex and her wetness pools through the fabric, saturating my fingertips.

When I come across a loose thread on my journey, I pull on it. She gasps when I tear open the crotch of her leggings a moment later, giving me a glimpse of her lacy purple panties.

Her chest rises and falls and I'm acutely aware of the way her nipples pucker through her shirt when I move those panties aside and expose her glistening pussy lips for me.

Bending down, I allow myself a moment of weakness—one taste of the sweetest pussy I've ever had when I slowly, languidly, lick a path from her opening all the way up to her clit and suckle it.

Breslin's head lolls back and her palms slap the desk, and

before she can draw in her next breath, I'm unzipping my pants and pushing my cock inside her.

I don't take my time, and I'm not gentle.

I fuck her rough and fast, driving myself so deep inside her I don't know where she ends and I begin.

She slides her hand around my neck, pulling me closer, and my balls draw tight. She feels so fucking good wrapped around me, like her body wasn't meant for anyone else but *me*. I look into her hooded green eyes and I know what she's thinking. Because I'm thinking it too.

This is without a doubt the hottest sex we've ever had.

It's carnal, savage. And so fucking *wrong* considering our strange circumstances.

But that's part of what makes it so fucking good right now. I need this release, I need to fuck her like she's mine...even if it's the last time.

Groaning her name, I pump into her hard. So hard, I have to grip her hair to make sure she doesn't slide off the desk. Spots form in front of my eyes and I don't know if it's because I haven't eaten, or because I'm so close to coming.

"Touch yourself." I sink my teeth into her neck and pull her shirt up so I can play with her tits. "I wanna see you get yourself off on my cock, right fucking now."

Her mouth opens in surprise and she quickly drops her hand between us. I stand up and yank her to the edge of the desk so I can get a better view of both the show and my dick sliding in and out of her.

She bites her lip and circles her clit. "Like this?"

I nod and swallow back a curse when she clenches around me. She's so close, I know she is. She might not have ever let me into her head, but I know her body better than I do my own.

I snatch her hand away and slam into her in one sharp thrust, stealing her breath. When she scratches her nails down my back, I repeat the movement and she goes crazy.

She bucks her hips and grips me tighter, so tight it's almost painful as she comes undone all over my cock.

I follow her, follow her down that tunnel of ecstasy that makes my entire body hum in the sweetest pleasure there is.

And that's when one singular thought hits me like a ton of bricks—*Did she come like this for Asher when he fucked her?*

It's such a messed up thought and I hate myself for thinking it. But I can't prevent the way it festers and grows. Just like I can't help the jealousy that burns in my chest like a hellfire. I'm just not sure if it's jealousy that's geared more toward her or him.

"Did he fuck you nice and hard too?" I rasp before I can take the words back.

Her breath stutters in her chest and she gapes at me.

And similar to the way the air around us changed before...it does again. Only this time, it transforms into something dark and threatening. There's so much pain in her eyes, my stomach rolls and I immediately regret what I said...or rather, I regret the look of utter heartache on her face.

"Get off me," she croaks, slapping my chest. "Get the fuck *off* me."

I push off her almost instantly, the remorse I feel now twisting my guts. I don't know what the hell is wrong with me or why I'm letting this vicious envy I feel chew me up and spit me out like this.

She jumps off the desk. "You really have some nerve, especially considering the circumstances."

The impact of her words hit me right in the chest and I cup her face in my hands. "I'm sorry, Bre. I'm so fucking sorry."

And I am. Even though I know the truth about what happened with her and Asher. Or should I say, *his* side of things—I know her side too. I know how much he hurt her.

I know I hurt her, too.

She turns her head away, like she can't bear to look at me and that only makes this feeling worse. "Let me go, Landon."

There are tears in her eyes as I back up and I swear to God, I've never felt like more of an asshole in my life.

She pulls her shirt back down and runs to the door, but not before she turns around to look at me. "And to answer your question. Yeah, he fucked me hard." There's a pause that I feel all the way down to my bones before she whispers, "So hard I broke."

CHAPTER 6

ASHER

"Holden."

I freeze at the sound of Dragoni's voice and watch as my teammates shuffle out of the locker room, leaving me in the dust.

I stay put, refusing to turn around, because I already know what he's going to say.

Hell, the look of disappointment and disgust in Coach Cranes' eyes before he shook his head and walked off the field was enough to tell me how much I royally sucked during practice today.

Not only did I miss *three* practice plays—I also threw to a lowly second-string receiver with a *serious* case of butterfingers. Not to mention, my arm didn't pack half the punch that it usually does.

Because there was only one thing on my mind while I was out on that field.

Breslin.

I *have* to find a way to talk to her.

Dragoni grabs my arm, and before I have time to react; I'm being slammed up against a locker.

"What the fuck was that bullshit you pulled on the field today?" he grits through his cigarette stained teeth.

I open my mouth to answer, but the knife he takes out of his pocket and holds up to my neck causes any snide remark to die on my lips.

It's not so much that I'm scared of a knife, because I know I can take him, it's the power he's connected to and the damage he can do to Preston that has me yielding.

"You are on thin ice, Holden," he spews. "I have a lot of money riding on your sorry ass this year."

I lift my chin and glare at him, but that only causes him to dig the dull side of the knife into my collarbone. "If I were you, I'd start thinking about whose bones you want to see break first."

My body tenses. "*What?*"

His other hand wraps around my neck. "You want to watch your brother beg for mercy first, or that tutor of yours?"

My eyes damn near bug out of my head and that only causes him to laugh. "It's real obvious you two are fucking, which means he makes great collateral." He snickers. "But I'll tell you what, maybe we'll cut off his dick so you can have it as a keepsake before we bury him six feet under."

White spots form in front of my eyes and my heart compresses against my chest. Anger churns my guts, but there's not a damn thing I can do about it because I can't fight back. Not unless I want a grim outcome. And that messed up fact only makes me angrier.

After another moment, he finally releases me and I gasp for air. "First game is in nine days. Get your shit together. This is your last and *final* warning."

I cough and he gets close to my face. "You ain't here to have fun, Holden. You're here to pay off your family's debt. Got it?"

When I nod, he slaps my back. "Glad we have an understanding. Now run along before you're late for class."

His laughter bounces off the walls of the locker room as he walks away.

I feel like I'm swallowing nails as I hike my gym bag up my shoulder and make my way to my final class for the day.

The one I'm least looking forward to. *That goddamn Art class.*

Not only is it a fairly late class, which always sucks; but rumor has it the teacher is a stickler for participation.

In other words, she *will* fail me. And I will lose my scholarship —over a fucking *Art* class.

Luckily, it's only scheduled for two days a week. I scrub a hand down my face and check my watch. I'm already ten minutes late and it's halfway across campus, so I start jogging.

When I reach the hall, I see what I presume to be Mrs. Kennedy closing the door to the art room. "Wait," I call out.

She purses her lips and appraises me up and down before she turns her head back to the classroom and says, "I guess luck is on your side, young lady. You have a partner for the semester after all."

Mrs. Kennedy's statement confuses and delights me for two reasons. On one hand, it's weird to have to be teamed up with a partner for an entire semester. But on the other? There's a possibility that my partner might be some kind of art guru and I won't fail this godforsaken class after all.

I'm all dimples as I enter the room, feeling like a weight has been lifted off my shoulders.

Until Breslin's narrowed eyes pierce mine and I notice the empty chair beside her.

A rush of satisfaction causes me to smirk at my new-found predicament as I walk over, because there's no way she can ignore me now. "Hey, beautiful."

It's cheesy, I know. But I can't help myself, for two reasons.

One—Breslin *is* fucking gorgeous. And two—it's how I've always greeted her. Maybe reminding her of our past will chisel the stone around her heart when it comes to me and she'll give me a chance to talk to her.

She folds her arms across her chest and I can't help but notice the way it pushes those glorious tits of hers together, giving me the perfect hint of perky cleavage.

Breslin Rae has certainly grown up over the last three years.

Not only are her tits even better than I remember, she's even more stunning.

And *feisty.*

Because fuck me—my kitty has quite the set of claws on her.

The smirk on my face spreads into a sly smile.

A sly smile that drops faster than a speeding bullet when I look up at her.

Because if looks could kill...I'm certain the one she's giving me would stop my damn heart.

CHAPTER 7

BRESLIN

A sher Holden has even bigger balls than I remember.

Why in the world is he not only acting like I owe him a conversation, but looking at me the way he is now?

Did the last 96 hours along with the last *three years* completely vanish from his memory?

When he finally peels his eyes from my tits and moves them up where they belong, I can't help but notice the cocky grin plastered on his stupid face.

His stupid gorgeous face.

A face that only seemed to get even more gorgeous over the years. Proving that Karma is not in fact a bitch, but a goddamn masochist.

I mean, is his jaw made of marble? And by God, if I stare too hard at those deep dimples or blue eyes of his any longer, I'll be in danger of melting into a puddle of goo just like all the other girls in the classroom.

But fortunately, or rather *unfortunately* for me—I know the poison that seeps from him.

I know what he can do to a person. His special brand of destruction that hurts worse than any physical scar ever will.

Therefore, I'm immune to his charm and looks.

I harden my gaze and steel every muscle in my body, silently warning him that if he says one stinking word to me I will kick him in the nads.

He clears his throat and takes the seat next to me and I honestly want to cry because this is the one class that I signed up for, for *me*. And somehow Asher Holden's managed to wreck that.

Just like he does everything else.

I cross my legs and his eyes follow, lingering on my exposed skin.

I'm now seriously regretting throwing on a dumb jean skirt when I went home to change between classes after the whole Landon event—but it was the only thing that was clean since I still haven't done laundry.

Because I was curled up in bed inconsolable for days...because of *him*.

I notice two girls staring at him and a light bulb clicks on. Turns out there's an easy solution to this whole debacle after all, because Mrs. Kennedy didn't say we weren't allowed to switch partners.

I lean over and give them both a sugary sweet smile. "Hey, would one of you mind switching with me?"

Shock crosses over their faces. "What? Why?" one of them ask dubiously, looking at me like I've lost my mind.

I ignore the look Asher gives me and shrug. "I'd just prefer to switch with one of you." I hike a thumb in his direction. "We don't really mesh well. Bad chemistry and all that."

Asher snorts and mutters something under his breath that I don't catch before he turns his head to look at them and sneers, "*No.*"

The dark tone in his voice has them sitting up straight in their seats and looking at one another.

And if that's not enough, Asher raises his hand. "Mrs. Kennedy?"

She stops in the middle of her lecture, looking only slightly ticked off as she glances down at the roster.

"It's Asher," he says before she can. "And we can't switch partners, right?"

She cocks her head to the side and adjusts her glasses. "Is there some sort of problem?"

"Yes," I shout at the same time he says, "Not at all."

She opens her mouth and then clamps it shut, looking confused as all hell.

Asher takes the opportunity to continue, "It's just, am I correct to assume with this being college and not high school, that it's time for some of us to learn to work with people and adapt?"

He gives her a smile, dimples and all before he adds, "Kind of like art, right? I mean, not only does art help teach us the concept of problem-solving, it's always changing and evolving. So, again, am I right to presume that an amazing teacher such as yourself would tell us that we aren't allowed to switch partners?"

Oh, good grief. Mrs. Kennedy practically grows a fucking hard-on at that and I swear I can see little cartoon hearts circling her head.

She beams at him. "You would be correct to assume that." She glares at me. "Whatever your issues are, young lady, I suggest you learn to deal with them outside of class. This is college, you are an adult. Please act like one."

"Burn," someone says from behind me and my cheeks turn hot.

I nod and she goes back to addressing the class—informing us about how our class time will be divided in half. The first half will be devoted to lecture; and the last half will be dedicated to focusing on our big project—a series of paintings that portray various depictions of love—which will count for half of our overall grade.

I blink back tears, sadness washing over me. This was supposed to be *my* time. I've been looking forward to this class for months...and now it's ruined.

When Mrs. Kennedy tells us that the rest of the class time is to be used to work on our projects, Asher cranes his head to look at me and his face falls. "Breslin."

My insides begin to tremble. I detest the sound of my name on his lips. Just like I loathe the fact that he's the only one who calls me by my full name and has never once wavered and shortened it like others do.

But mostly? I hate the tender swell of emotion that fills my chest when I hear it.

Almost as much as I hate the way he's looking at me like I'm the only person in the world who exists.

Because Asher Holden can take me down with a single blow and we both know it.

And if I give him an inch—he'll take a nautical mile; because a regular mile just wouldn't be enough for him.

Mrs. Kennedy announces that we're allowed to walk around the campus for inspiration, but that we must report back and sign out with her before class ends. I don't waste another second, I stand up and take a deep breath before I march out the door, grateful that I can finally be out of his atmosphere.

"Breslin," he calls out after me and I clench my hands into fists.

I will not let him see me cry. I refuse to.

I take a sharp left and continue charging down an abandoned hallway, looking for an exit sign, wishing his footsteps would fade instead of strengthening behind me.

When he has the audacity to try and reach for my hand, I stop short and face him. "What are you doing here, Asher?"

I curse the way my voice cracks on his name and the sadness in his eyes when he notices.

"Let's go somewhere to talk," he says. "Because I want to tell you. I *need* to tell you everything." He takes a step closer to me and attempts to reach for my hand again. "God, I've missed you so damn much, Breslin."

The sick feeling in my stomach intensifies and my throat locks up. He looks so sincere, it's palpable.

I back away, my body in full on self-preservation mode, because I won't go down this road again.

I have so many questions for him...so many things that need explaining. Starting with what he told me on Prom night. The night that plays over and over in my mind like a bad record skipping. Just like what I walked into the other day.

Even so—I'll sacrifice not knowing the answers for my sanity. Because it's the only way I know how to protect myself.

It's the only way I can cope with him standing in front of me.

Because I can't handle his truth. And I most definitely can't be sucked in again, I won't make it out alive this time around.

He searches my face, looking so innocent, so full of adoration and hope that I'm caught between wanting to wrap my arms around him and breathe him in like he's my only source of air—and wanting to rip his heart out of his chest and stomp on it.

God, I loved him so much. So damn much. I longed and prayed for him, I lived and breathed for him.

And every time I look at him, I'm reminded of that.

I know without a shadow of a doubt that I would have loved Asher Holden for the rest of my life if he let me. If he didn't break me.

Because there was a time that he was my alpha and my omega. My end and my beginning. My *everything*.

And the dangerous crushing ache in the center of my chest tells me that he still is.

But the overwhelming agony that rips through my heart, reminds me why he can't be.

"I don't want to know," I whisper, taking another step back.

"Breslin—"

I hold up my hand, cutting him off. "Did you ever really care about me?"

His face twists. "Of course, I did. I love you. I have always loved you. It never went away, and it's never going to. *You* were the one who walked away from us, not me."

I shake my head, because I can't bear to hear him try to rationalize everything and put his own spin on it when I know the truth. Because I live with the painful reminder every day.

And contrary to what he thinks—I didn't walk away because I wanted to. I walked away because *he* ripped us apart with his dishonesty and betrayal.

I should have been the *first* person he went to when he had feelings for anyone other than me. And Kyle should have been the *last* person he acted those feelings out with.

I raise my chin. "I don't know why you're here and I don't care to know. But if you ever really loved me like you claim...you'll do the right thing and leave Woodside."

He opens his mouth, but I press on. "I need you to leave," I whisper, and it sounds like a plea, because it is, from the very depths of my soul.

His face falls and he staggers back as if I hit him.

When he turns on his heels, I close my eyes and fill my lungs, relief washing over me.

That is until a force plows into me with enough horsepower to send me crashing into the wall behind me and lips capture mine.

"Not a fucking chance, Breslin. I just got you back," he grunts between deep, consuming kisses that penetrate me all the way down to my marrow.

I feel myself start to free fall and then float when he pries my mouth open and stakes his claim.

There's no finesse in his kiss, it's pure greed. It's so powerful, I can't help but whimper as I cling to him for dear life.

And that only makes him even more ravenous. His teeth nip at my bottom lip and I gasp for air. I've never needed a moment of lucidity like I do right now, but Asher won't grant me one. I scratch and slap the wall, fighting like hell to hold on to a firm foundation, torn between this fragile line of craving and complete disdain.

"You're kissing me back," he murmurs against my lips.

Before I can answer, he hitches my leg around his waist. Our hips brush and I can feel how hard he is for me through the denim of his jeans and desire, the traitorous bitch; pumps through my veins.

He plants a trail of kisses along my jaw, sucking and biting my skin. "Fuck, I missed you so much, baby."

Both the thick length of him nestled in between my thighs and his words zap me back to that night.

It's the exact reminder that I need to break the kiss and shove him away.

Too bad Asher Holden is made of granite and he doesn't budge.

Instead, he drops his head to the crook of my neck and inhales me.

"I love you bigger," he whispers and something inside me unhinges.

Tears prickle my eyes. I've missed his touch so much and the way it seems to bring all my nerves back to life. But not even my thirst can overshadow my haze of hate for him.

His big hand slides up my thigh, and my chest heaves against his hard one. Arousal licks at my skin, taunting me, making me its prisoner.

"Tell me you missed me too, Breslin," he rasps, his voice sounding strangled, desperate even.

"I'd tell you, but I'd probably choke trying to get the words out," I say deadpan, the bite in my tone a warning.

His jaw tics and he leans in, his lips caressing my earlobe. "Then why are you soaking my finger right now?"

I gasp when his knuckle brushes over my clit through my

panties, purposely emphasizing his statement.

Anger flares in my belly, coating the desire I feel. I refuse to let this happen and there's only one way I can think of to derail this crazy train that's already in motion.

Licking my lips, I reach down and move my panties aside.

I feel his cock jerk when his gaze travels downward and his eyes focus like lasers to where I'm unabashedly touching myself.

I smile then, but it isn't with humor; it's because I know exactly what it is that I need to do.

When his lips part, I remove my finger and slip it inside his mouth.

His eyes close and he groans as he tastes me.

And that's when I loop my arm around his neck, pull him close, and whisper, "I'm only wet because I'm full of Landon's come from when he fucked me on his desk earlier."

His jaw flexes and he bangs the wall beside my head, the look on his face is like nothing I've ever seen before.

I quickly maneuver out of his hold. "Leave me the fuck alone, Asher."

I glare at him. "Actually, leave us *both* the fuck alone."

Before you destroy him like you did me.

I try to dodge the curious look Kit shoots me when I walk in the door after classes end, but it doesn't work. "I don't remember laying that outfit out for you this morning."

My teeth sink into my bottom lip and my cheeks flush. "I had to come home and change. I uh—sort of had an accident."

Nearly two of them.

"Shit, are you okay? Need anything from the store?"

Before I can respond, she presses her hand to my forehead. "You don't feel warm."

"I had sex with Landon," I blurt out.

Her mouth hangs open and she blinks. "Like today?"

I nod and slink my way over to the bed. Since I value my hearing, I don't tell her about hooking up with Asher.

Plus, I'm positive I'll start bawling my eyes out if I do, so avoidance is key. I'll just pretend like it didn't happen and he doesn't exist.

She throws her hands in the air. "B, when I told you to talk to Landon—I meant with words, not your vagina."

When I make a face, she walks over to me. "Did it at least clear anything up? Do you feel better? Did you get some answers?"

I shake my head. "No, if anything it only made things worse. I don't understand, Kit. I'm so lost."

I fix the messy bun on top of my head and lean against the headboard, trying to gather the courage to ask her this. "How can he—" I look down at my hands. "Be so into me, but you know—suddenly be attracted to guys and stuff? I'm not trying to be offensive, I'm just trying to understand it all. Because today Landon and me—" I inhale a breath. "Well, we had the best sex we ever had...but how can that be possible when he's apparently...*you know?* How does it all work?"

I shrug helplessly. "Don't get me wrong, I have more serious issues I'm still processing and need to worry about, but I figure who better to ask than you about this one."

She chews on her thumbnail. "Well you should be asking Landon, but I get how it can be confusing to other people."

She takes out a notebook and a pen. "Think of sexuality like a scale."

"A scale?"

"Yes." She starts drawing a line on a piece of paper. "Now pay attention."

And I do. I sit back and listen as Kit does her best to educate me for the next two hours.

CHAPTER 8

ASHER

I'm going to kill him.

I'm not being dramatic, either.

I'm going to mutilate and maim the motherfucker. String his goddamn balls up like a set of Christmas lights.

He fucked her...he fucked *my* girl.

Right after we...

Christ, the asshole won't even give me the courtesy of showing up to our tutoring sessions this week, but he has no problem taking what's mine and bending her over a desk.

And Breslin...she won't even let me talk to her and set things right with us...but she has no problem fucking *him*.

Rage crawls up my gut and the pendulum my heart is swinging from can't seem to decide who or what it's madder at.

But I do know who my intended target is.

I pound on Landon's front door and I'm nearly ready to kick it down when he doesn't answer on the first knock.

When he opens the door after my second knock, I ignore the towel hanging off his hips and the beads of water trickling down his stomach and charge at him.

I throw, one, two, *three* punches at his face. My jabs are so quick, he barely has time to react as his glasses fly off.

"You fucked her." My voice comes out low, deadly even.

The adrenaline running through me picks up another notch and I take a swing at him again. This time, my fist lands near his kidney and he grunts, "Yeah, I did."

Finally, he starts defending himself and manages to land a punch to my jaw. I relish the burn. Hell, I want more of it.

I throw another punch, harder than my last few; and he stumbles back before he falls on the floor of the living room.

I'm so mad at him. So fucking mad, I honestly feel like I could tear him from limb to limb.

When I angle my leg, intending to sail it right into his rib cage and end the fight for good, I see a flash of panic on his face...and my heart squeezes.

Because no matter how many punches I throw his way...it will never change the fact that I have feelings for him.

It will never change the fact that Breslin or no Breslin—I ended up falling for Landon Parker.

I'm hopelessly and irrevocably in love with two people—and both have completely fucked me up and ruined me for anyone else.

I kneel down beside him and grab the nape of his neck, forcing him to look at me. "Do you regret what happened between us? Is that why you did it?"

He shakes his head. "No, that isn't why."

The definitive tone of his voice is absolute.

Tension locks my jaw. "Who do you want, Landon?"

My heart beats out of my chest—and I don't know if my stomach is knotting because I'm waiting for him to tell me that what we had was a mistake —or because I hate the fact that he fucked the girl I love more than life itself after she caught us in bed together.

I grind my molars as I wait for him to answer and my anger

accelerates. Breslin will forgive *him*...but not *me*. And fuck, if that doesn't make this jealousy smoldering inside me come to a head.

"I think you already know the answer to that," he says, wiping the blood from his now split lip.

My grip on his neck tightens. "No, I don't."

I don't know anything anymore.

He turns his head and spits blood on the floor. "My feelings haven't changed, I still want you both. But—"

I refuse to hear what his *but* entails, because I'm pretty sure I already know.

Right now, there's a storm brewing inside me—and since the girl who snuffs it out wants nothing to do with me—I need the other half of my heart to wade through it with me.

His gaze clashes with mine and I close the distance between us by bringing my mouth to his. Our kiss is angry and rough...and because I'm a dick and I want him to know what it feels like, I say, "She kissed me today," right before I take his mouth again.

The sharp sting of his teeth slicing into my lower lip sends my head spinning and all my blood rushing south.

He growls, actually growls; and snatches my hair forcefully. It's the exact reaction that I wanted to elicit from him. Because I need to feel his envy...I want to taste his bitterness.

I don't want to be alone in this. I'm always so fucking alone.

Before he knows what hit him—I turn him around, snatch off his towel, and sink my teeth into his neck. "Fucking hurts, doesn't it?"

He doesn't answer, instead he tips his head back and bites and sucks at my top lip, making my dick rock hard and evidently his as well.

I nudge him forward. "Bend over the coffee table for me, right fucking now."

He appears hesitant and I give him a look. I'm not in the mood for his apprehension, because the lust and ache plowing through me is enough to make me dizzy.

I grasp his jaw in my hand, giving him a peek at the vulnerability swirling inside me. "I need you, Landon."

You have no idea how much.

My heart's in my throat because I've never felt so goddamn fragile before.

Something passes in our gaze...and I know he feels it too. Our situation is so fucked up, it's borderline tragic. There's no way we're not going to come out of this unscathed. But there's no way to ignore our feelings for one another, either. We're far past the point of denying them.

I care about him and I want him. And the way my heart beats erratically whenever I look at him, along with the twinge of protectiveness in my chest—tells me that I love him.

He takes a breath, leans forward, and bends over the coffee table—raising that pert, tight ass of his in the air for me.

I slide my sweatpants down, spit on my hand, and give my cock a nice, long jerk as I kiss my way down his back. His skin is like heated satin, so fucking smooth. I love the way it ignites and contracts under my touch.

I see him reach over and open a drawer, rooting around for something before he pulls out a bottle of lube. He drags in a low, slow breath as he hands it to me.

Landon's nervous, there's no doubt about it, considering the way he's shaking right now. And yet, he still trusts me.

He trusts me to not only see how scared he is, but to let me take something from him that he's never given anyone else.

Landon's braver in a way I'm not sure I'll ever be, and there's something overwhelmingly alluring about that.

And equally heartbreaking...because now I can't help but think about Breslin and how much I royally fucked up.

COMPLICATED HEARTS   63

And if I could go back in time? I would change *everything* about that night.

I wouldn't have taken her virginity until she knew the truth, every single bit of it, and made the choice to give it to me. No wonder she hates me so much.

God, I hate myself. Deep down, I hate who I am and the things I can't deny.

I hate that I lost the love of my life because of it.

I look down at Landon and my breathing ceases. Because the only time I don't inherently hate who I am is when I look at *him*.

It's the only time I'm not ashamed of being attracted to men. The only time my disgust doesn't swallow me whole.

Because the feelings I have for him are stronger than any hate will ever be.

I squirt some lube on my finger and slip it inside him, letting him get used to the feeling.

When he takes a breath, I bring my other hand down and tease his taint, a spot that thanks to our last hookup, I know he's fond of.

His palms go flat against the coffee table and he juts his ass out at me. "Fuck."

I add another digit to the one in his ass and I can't help but smirk. "Oh, I plan on it."

When I feel him tense around my finger, I say, "You need to relax for me, otherwise it's going to hurt like hell."

He opens his mouth to say something, but I slip my now lubed up cock between his ass cheeks.

"You ready for me?"

He nods and I lower my head to kiss his neck as I position myself over him. I quickly add another squirt of lube to my cock and line myself up with that tight puckered hole of his and slowly press forward.

He pounds the coffee table and his entire body goes rigid. "Jesus."

I still myself, because I know I'm a lot to take, especially for someone who's never had anal before. "I'll go slow."

I lean my forehead against his back as I push in deeper, making him take me inch by inch. It's the sweetest torture I've ever experienced.

When I fill him up to the hilt, he exhales and looks over his shoulder at me.

And that's when I slide my cock out and push right back in. My balls clench and I groan. He's so fucking tight, so goddamn perfect.

"You have no idea how good this feels," I rasp as I pull back slightly and thrust into him again, relishing watching my cock glide in and out of him. "Fucking incredible."

"Then stop being a pussy and fuck me harder, *jock*."

When I look up at him there's a taunting grin on his face that sends another bolt of arousal right through my system.

Christ, Landon Parker might be my nerd in the library, but he's an addicting, uninhibited devil in the sac. Always pushing my buttons.

Always taking what's mine.

That thought elicits another bolt of wrath and I speed up my movements, ramming my dick into him so furiously I see stars. My balls slap against his ass repeatedly as I punish him with my dick. And despite the perpetual animosity, it feels so good, *too good*. There's no way in hell I'm gonna last much longer.

My balls tingle and I slam into him again. "Fuck, I'm gonna come."

When I hear Landon groan my name and he swivels that sweet ass against me, I come so hard I'm the one who's a shaking mess now.

I fall against him, inhaling his sweat-soaked skin.

He shifts underneath me. "That was—"

I don't give him a chance to finish, I yank him to the ground and cover his body with mine.

His muscles flex as I work my way down his torso, gradually inching my way toward my intended target.

That heavy dick of his that's bobbing right in front of my face, begging to be balls deep inside my mouth.

He sucks in a breath when my tongue trails down his pelvis, stopping only to slurp up the drop of precum that's collecting on his lower stomach.

I bite my lip and watch in satisfaction as a flush spreads across his face and over his chest.

"Please," he finally says, digging his fingers into the carpet. "I need your fucking mouth, Asher."

In a flash, I swallow his dick and he cries out my name. There are no teasing licks this time around, I suck him hard and fast, not even bothering to stop for air.

"Oh, God!" he screams, gripping my hair and gyrating his hips into my face.

I relax my throat and make room for him, taking him even deeper. When I start gagging, he grips my hair harder, holding my head in place as he fucks my mouth, giving me his own brand of punishment.

"Fucking hell," he grunts between thrusts, his eyes turning dark.

Five pumps later he's coming so fast inside my mouth he can't even call out a warning.

I swallow every morsel he shoots out and he damn near whimpers when I give him one long and hard suck before I release him with a loud plop.

I sit on my haunches and stare down at him, watching his chest rise and fall, waiting for his breathing to even out.

"You gonna fight for her?" I ask, fearing the answer.

The silence between us is as deep as the Pacific before he grinds out, "Yes."

He props himself up on his elbows and the muscle in his jaw works. "Are you?"

I lift my chin, refusing to break eye contact. "'Til the day I die."

And I mean it. Breslin has no idea what she unleashed by being back in my life again. Second chances don't come around often and I'm not going to ruin this one.

He looks around the room, irritation and a hint of sadness crosses over his face. "I guess this situation just got even more complicated then."

"It did." I lean down until my lips are ghosting over his ear. "Because I'm not only fighting for her now. I'm fighting for the both of you."

He cups my jaw and I honestly don't know what to make of the expression on his face, which is saying something; because he's usually an open book.

Right when I'm about to ask what he's thinking, he crushes his mouth against my lips, kissing me like I'm his lifeline.

He pulls back slightly and looks at me. "Good because there's no fucking way I can give you up. Either of you."

His expression shuts down. "Question is, now that we know where the other stands, what are we going to do about it? Does this make us lovers or enemies?"

"I don't know," I tell him honestly before I let out a bitter laugh. "But for what it's worth you're clearly in the lead. She doesn't want anything to do with me."

"That's because you hurt her, Asher." He closes his eyes. "We both did."

I stand up. "Trust me, I'm well aware of how much I hurt her."

He pushes to his feet and wraps his towel around his waist. "At the risk of giving you the upper hand—why don't you just tell her the truth about what happened back then?"

"Because she's not ready to hear it, yet." I rub the back of my neck. "And it won't make a difference anyway."

I slip my pants back up, choosing my next words carefully. "There are things you don't know about Breslin. About her home life and her upbringing." I pause, gathering my composure, because the tentacles of guilt are making it harder and harder to breathe again. "Things that will make it impossible for her to forgive me, whether or not she ever knows the truth about Kyle. The shit between us goes deeper than him."

The boy in me didn't understand it back then, but the man in me does now.

The man in me sees all the pain that's hidden behind Breslin's grown-up eyes. The real reason she never let Landon or any other guy in and pushed them away.

She can't move on because she's damaged. Thanks to me.

Not only did I end up giving credence to the fucked-up things her piece of shit father used to tell her when it came to our relationship. But I simultaneously validated that destructive inner voice of Breslin's that night, too.

In one singular moment, my actions and words proved to her that she wasn't enough for me.

And even though in the end she was the one who physically walked away, I was the one who sidelined her with my new-found feelings first.

I know exactly how much I hurt Breslin Rae...because I know her better than anyone.

I broke her trust by not being honest, and I betrayed her and what we had by keeping the biggest secret from her for months on end.

I did the one thing someone with her upbringing can't recover from. I internally checked out on her and left her behind.

Just like her mother did.

I was all she had. The *first* person who ever loved her, because her parents sure as fuck never did. And in the end, I emotionally abandoned my girl.

And unfortunately, I'm not sure there's a way to ever undo that or make her see that everything's not so black and white, because there's a lot of gray smearing our past. I don't know how to make her understand that just because my sexuality is fluid, my feelings for her never were.

She was always good enough for me.

She was *everything* to me.

I'm slowly coming to the realization that the only way to get Breslin back is to let her punish me. All while I keep pushing through those walls of hers over and over again, praying that one day a light bulb goes off and she realizes how much I fucking love her.

Because I'm not going anywhere and I'm sure as fuck not giving her up again.

And call me crazy, but I think deep down inside she doesn't want me to.

Because I know she still loves me. I felt it in that kiss earlier. Hell, I *feel* it every time she looks at me, and it's just as powerful as it ever was. Maybe even more thanks to the line of hate dividing us now.

I still have a piece of her heart, and that's the opening I need to bulldoze the rest of my way in. I'll fight her tooth and mother-fucking nail to reclaim my spot, because it's the only place I belong.

I look over at Landon and something inside my chest stirs.

Maybe not the only place.

"She never confided in me about her past," he whispers, distracting me from my thoughts.

The jealousy in his tone is evident and I can't deny the flicker of gratification it brings me.

A flicker that dims as soon as I see the dejection in his eyes and he lets out a soft scoff. "But then again, why would she? I'm not you."

I'm at a loss for words. On one hand, I almost want to comfort him. But on the other? I want to puff my chest out and smile.

Instead, I find myself throwing him a bone. "Back when we were 16 Breslin ended up finding a lost and abused puppy."

When he gives me a look I say, "I promise this story has a point."

He nods and I continue. "She basically spent most of the summer nurturing it back to health. Despite the protests from her father, she still found a way to take care of it. It was one of the most beautiful things I ever witnessed. It made me fall even more in love with her. She was so selfless, always putting that puppy before her own needs. Even giving it her own food which was usually scarce around her house."

I suck in a breath. "Then one day I showed up—I had purchased the little guy some food and toys—you know, wanting to help...but the puppy wasn't there."

"Why?"

A sad feeling simmers in my gut as I think back to that day. "Because she gave the puppy up. She ended up finding a good family with a little girl who desperately wanted it and off he went."

His brows draw together. "That was sweet of her."

I shake my head. "Yeah, but the thing is—Breslin loved that puppy more than anything. And when I asked her why she gave him up, she listed off a bunch of things, but it was all bullshit. She knew I would have helped her with whatever she needed and that she could have taken care of it."

I look him in the eyes. "In the end Breslin gave him up because she was afraid to hold on to something good. Because good things have never been a permanent thing for her. She's too scared to hold on to them, because she doesn't know when they'll disappear, just that they always do. So if she pushed you away? It was only because she cared about you."

The silence hangs in the air between us and I can see the

wheels in his head spinning before he says, "Thank you for telling me that."

I jut my chin out and head for the door. "I need to go. I have an early practice tomorrow morning."

He reaches for my arm, halting me. "You also have the big Shakespeare test tomorrow afternoon." He looks down at his feet. "I'm sorry I slacked on tutoring you this week. Meet me after practice ends and we can get in an hour or two before class starts, okay?"

I lick my lips and shrug. "That depends."

He puts his hands on his hips, I can tell he's getting ready to lay into me. "On what?"

I dip my head and press my lips to his Adam's apple. "On whether you're going to eat something, take your level, and your insulin." He starts to protest but I don't give him a chance. "Don't argue with me. Just do what you need to do and take care of yourself. Or the next time I see you, I'll be kicking your ass instead of fucking it."

"Asshole," he mutters under his breath.

I give him a sly grin and he opens his mouth, but then his gaze drops to my collarbone and his eyes turn hard. "Why do you have a bruise there?"

I think back to the exchange with Dragoni and stuff my hands in my pockets. "No reason." I lift a shoulder in a shrug. "Probably from practice."

His nostrils flare and he crosses his arms. "Don't lie to me, Asher."

It's not often that Landon is angry, and the tone in his voice right now tells me that he's livid.

"Dragoni threatened me after I fucked up during practice today." I fix the beanie on my head and avert my gaze. "On some level I deserved it, though. I was distracted on the field—I couldn't concentrate."

"Why?"

I step out of the doorway. "Why do you think?"

He sighs. "You had a certain fiery redhead on your mind."

I give him a curt nod and start walking down the hall. "See you tomorrow, *nerd*."

The corner of his mouth tugs up in a half-grin. "Don't be late, *jock*."

I feel a set of eyes appraising me up and down when I stick my key in the lock of my dorm room.

"Can I help you?" a voice behind me asks.

I spin around and come face to face with some short girl with blonde hair and bright pink tips, enough tattoos she could be featured in an art exhibit, and enough piercings to set a metal detector off.

Despite all the bling and distractions going on, though, she's attractive. Not that I'm interested in any other girl besides Breslin anymore, but I'm not blind, either.

"I'm pretty sure I should be the one asking you that." I point to the door. "This is my dorm."

She squints her eyes and purses her lips. "Haven't seen you around campus before."

"I just transferred over the summer."

She thinks about this for a moment before she sticks out her hand and says, "Well, any guy who helps out my best friend is all right by me. So, hi."

I have no idea what this girl is talking about, but I don't want to be rude so I shake her hand. "Hey, I'm Asher."

I barely have time to register the way her face falls, or the knee to my groin before white-hot pain sears into me and I keel over, grabbing my nuts which I'm certain are now on fire.

She goes to kick me again and I narrowly manage to dodge it. I have no idea what the hell this midget's—one who obviously has some kind of grudge against me— problem is, but she's out of her damn mind. "You fucking bitch."

I don't usually call women bitches, but when they attack my sac for no reason? Yeah, it's warranted.

She pulls something out of her purse and holds it up, ready to attack.

My mouth hangs open. "Holy shit, is that a shiv?"

Her eyes narrow. "Stay away from my best friend."

I blink, debate calling a mental facility, and stare at her. "I don't even know who your best friend is."

The sharp object goes sailing in front of my face, scarcely missing my nose before landing in the wood of the door. "Don't fuck with her, Holden, or I'll shove this down your throat."

Before I can object, she starts walking down the hall, pointing to her eyes the entire time. "I'm watching you."

When the crazy chick is out of my sight I open my door and pull out my cell phone.

Asher: Dude, I was just threatened and kicked in the balls by some maniac with pink hair.
Landon: Did you sleep with her?

I roll my eyes and type out my next text.

Asher: No. I've never met her before. But apparently she knows me because she told me she'd shove her shiv down my throat if I didn't stay away from her best friend.

The dots on the screen appear and then disappear before appearing again.

Landon: Pink hair you say?

Asher: Yeah, the ends of her hair. Some tattoos and piercings too.

Landon: Shit. That sounds like Kit.

Asher: What the hell is a Kit?

Landon: Breslin's best friend.

I groan and throw my phone on my bed. *Fucking perfect.*

CHAPTER 9

LANDON

My heart slams in my chest when I knock on the door.

A moment later it opens and red-rimmed eyes greet me. "What are you doing here, Landon?" Her brows knit together. "What happened to your cheek?"

I ignore her second question and focus on the first one, because it's the same thing I asked myself during the short drive over and again as I jogged up to the dorms.

There's only one answer I can seem to come up with. "I'm here because I think I owe you an explanation." I take a step in her direction. "But mostly? I'm here because I played a part in breaking something and I want to fix it."

She takes a step back, allowing me inside. I try like hell not to focus on the adorable freckles lining the delicate flesh of her shoulder or the sliver of smooth skin peeking out from the waistband of her sweatpants.

Sex isn't what I came here for. I'm here because I want something more. So much more.

I want what she refused to give me before. Everything that she gave him.

I want her heart.

And the way she's looking at me in this moment tells me I may actually have a piece of it. I just wish there wasn't so much pain and sadness clouding her feelings, but it's what I get.

Because beautiful things like her aren't meant to be broken...they're meant to be cherished. And Lord knows I'm partly at fault for the current state she's in.

"I'm sorry about how I acted earlier." I have to tuck my hands in my pockets to stop myself from touching her because I don't think I deserve that privilege anymore. "Fuck, I'm sorry about everything, Bre."

I suck in a breath when tears start falling down her cheeks. I've never seen Breslin cry before. I've never seen her so vulnerable, period. I'm torn between loving that she's falling apart in front of me, and hating myself because I know I'm the cause for her tears.

I take another step toward her, hoping like hell she doesn't push me away. When her head hits my chest, all my previous thoughts about not touching her go out the window. I pull her closer and kiss the top of her head. "I'm so sorry I hurt you. I swear it wasn't my intention."

Her tears soak my shirt and I scoop her up and walk us over to the bed, cradling her in my arms.

"Well, you got what you wanted," she chokes out. "You apologized and now you don't have to feel guilty or pity me anymore." She screws up her face and attempts to get out of my arms. "I think it's time for you to go."

I close my eyes and exhale, fighting the irritation that's rising. I need to wedge myself between her and this armor of hers before it goes back up again.

I trail my hands down her arms, holding her in place. "I don't want to leave. And I didn't apologize to absolve me of any guilt. I apologized because I love you and seeing you hurting like this kills me."

She lets out a frustrated sigh. "What do you want from me, Landon? Forgiveness? Sex? A clear conscience? Permission to be with my ex?"

"No. What I want is the same thing I've always wanted from you," I tell her. "Let me in. Even though I don't deserve it anymore, take the chain off your heart for me for once."

She shifts in my lap and I'm certain she's getting ready to kick me out again, but to my surprise she whispers, "I went to Truesdale High and I grew up in a trailer park."

I kiss her cheek and inhale her. "Tell me more," I murmur against her skin as I grip her tighter, scared she'll close up again. "Tell me everything, Bre. Because no matter what you tell me, I'm not going anywhere."

"My father is a drunk and he hates me." She sniffs. "I'm not just being dramatic, either. He actually hates me. No, worse than that—because hate would imply he gives a shit. He's indifferent toward me."

"He's an asshole," I bite out and she shakes her head.

"No. He's just grieving. He never recovered from when my mom walked out and broke his heart."

It's on the tip of my tongue to question why she's making excuses for him, but I don't want her to end the conversation.

I run my hand down her back in gentle circles and wait for her to speak again.

And when she finally does? It's everything I've always wanted from her. But it's also utterly heartbreaking.

CHAPTER 10

BRESLIN

There's something comforting and equally petrifying about showing someone your scars, letting them see you stripped down to the bone, raw and unveiled.

I bury my face in Landon's neck, attempting to hide the tears that I can't seem to stop. Telling him I grew up in a trailer park and that I used to work at a topless bar when we were together was the easy part.

Telling him how I was bullied for most of my life was a piece of cake.

But talking about my parents and my past? The things that haunt my soul whenever I look in the mirror or have a moment to myself. Things like—how much it truly hurts that my mother left me. Or about the remarks my drunk father would make when I was growing up. The same remarks he makes to this very day whenever the mood or rather, intoxication strikes him. Or about the agony that cuts like a knife whenever I think about Asher.

It hurts like hell.

"I get why she left him. I know all about how love isn't enough to make two people stay together and that things just fall apart. But

I don't know what I did to make her hate me and leave me, too. Why wasn't I enough for her? Why am I so unlovable?"

I rarely give into these feelings, usually I just hold them inside, refusing to burden anyone else with them, but letting Landon in tore the scab off and now I can't stop.

Landon cups the back of my neck, kisses my cheek, and holds me for dear life. "You're the exact opposite of unlovable. It was her loss. Believe me when I say that."

Resentment burns my insides and I exhale slowly. "Was it your loss too?"

His body goes rigid underneath me and I feel his heart start to race. "I guess I deserve that."

"And I deserve that explanation you said you were here to give me." The scene I walked in on replays in my head and my stomach starts reeling. "I came back from Europe open for you, ready to give you everything and you—" I swallow the words I can't bring myself to say. "You know what you did. But how? I mean, I know I told you to see other people but why *him*? Out of the seven billion people in the world...you chose *him*. Why would you do that to me?"

I twist out of his arms and sit up. "I never even knew you were attracted to guys, Landon. You could have told me. My feelings for you wouldn't have gone away and I wouldn't have judged you."

Even though Kit explained sexuality to me in detail and I understand it more than I ever have...it doesn't change where my anger with him stems from—because it doesn't change the situation. It doesn't change how gutted and bewildered I am over him and *Asher* sleeping together.

"I told you, I didn't do it to you on purpose," he whispers. "And before him, I wasn't attracted to guys, so there was nothing to tell you."

"Did you sleep with him because I hurt you? Was that why you turned to him? Looking for comfort?"

Rage bubbles in my chest and I start seething. "Did you ever stop to think that maybe he purposely sought you out. Used you and trapped you into—"

"Asher didn't know who I was either, Bre."

The fact that he's even trying to defend him causes my blood to boil. "You don't know that for sure. But of course you would stick up for him."

He shakes his head. "That's not what I'm doing."

He tucks a finger under my chin, forcing me to meet his gaze. "You want the truth?"

I give him a soft nod and wrap my arms around myself, preparing for the blow that's coming my way—because the last conversation I had like this ended up shredding my heart and I'm not so sure I can take another one in this lifetime.

The only reason I'm putting myself through this presently is because I can't help but feel like I played a part in ruining things between us.

I was the one who pushed Landon away in the first place. I was the one who ended things and ignored him while I was in Europe.

I was the one who gave him my heart a moment too late.

And for that? I'll always be sorry.

He squeezes my hand tightly, almost like he knows I'll bolt the second he opens his mouth.

"Despite being hurt over us...me falling in love with Asher had nothing to do with you, Bre."

I recoil, the impact of his statement smacking me in the chest. Sex is one thing—everyone has an itch to scratch I suppose, but hearing that he has actual *feelings* for him? That he *loves* him. That's a whole new level of pain and a blow to my heart that I'm not sure I can deal with. My first instinct is to run and my second instinct—the one I try like hell to ignore—is to tell him that *I* loved Asher Holden first; but Landon drops his forehead to mine and says, "Don't, Bre. Please don't leave me."

His voice is laced with so much emotion I'm surprised he isn't choking on it. When I look up at him there are tears in his eyes and my heart pulls.

If I thought I was lost and confused over this weird and fucked up situation...it's nothing compared to the way Landon looks right now.

Against my better judgment I cradle his face in my hands and will him to keep talking to me. Because no matter how much it may sting to hear it, I don't want Landon to keep everything bottled up inside. I don't want him hurting like this, because I do love him.

Despite the pain—the love still leaks through.

And call me crazy? But I believe him when he says he didn't hook up with Asher to intentionally hurt me and that he didn't know who Asher was when things happened between them.

And that right there is the difference between my past situation and my current one.

Asher cheated on me with an enemy, a bully who harmed me with his words time and time again. He didn't tell me about the feelings he was having until promises and bonds were already broken. He told me after he had already deluded and cheated on me.

Landon and I had no such promises or bonds...because of *me*. I pushed Landon away and ended things with him, leaving him free to do whatever he wanted.

But the biggest difference in all this?

I let Landon go out of fear, but I held on with everything I had to Asher and loved him with every part of myself. I had faith. I had hope. I trusted his love...our love.

Landon hurt me, but Asher shattered me.

I can forgive someone for hurting me. But I can't forgive someone for injuring me to the point of no repair—because broken things can't be put back together again, even with the toughest of glue.

Besides, I wouldn't even know the first step toward unraveling all the hate I've built up for Asher, anyway. The hate I have for him is my protection from ever letting him get close to me again and I'll be damned if I let my guard drop, especially given he's so close currently.

But this isn't about him right now. This is about me and Landon.

A man who I know cares about me. A man who looks so devastated and lost, I can't help but lean over and pull him close.

I know people wouldn't understand why I'm suddenly consoling a guy who only days ago was in bed with the guy who demolished my heart. And if I'm being honest with myself—I'm not so sure I do, either. All I know is that every instinct I have is gravitating to him. I want to be the balm to alleviate his torment.

"Tell me everything," I whisper, repeating his words from earlier. "Because no matter what you tell me, I'm not going anywhere right now. Just give me the truth, including the painful parts."

He wraps his arms around me, clutching my shirt. He's trembling and it only makes me hold on to him tighter. In a single moment, everything superficial and skin-deep about our former relationship has been washed away, the new tide bringing a depth to us that I never saw coming, our wounds blistering due to the layer of salt being poured over them in the exchange.

"I tried to ignore it, shove it down," he whispers into my skin.

"Ignore what?"

"The spark. The connection between us. But I couldn't. He's—"

"Impossible to ignore," I finish for him and he nods.

"He was like a freight train that crashed into me before I ever had a chance to realize what was happening. I couldn't even try to stop it—because by the time I recognized what I felt, it was too late."

My guts twist because I know exactly what he means. I know all about falling for Asher and his vortex that pulls you in.

His grip on the fabric tightens. "I didn't want to hurt you, I swear to God. I just couldn't fight my feelings for him. Just like I can't fight them for you."

I feel a tear roll down my neck and I run my hand down his back, attempting to soothe his anguish away. Landon's not a bad person, far from it. He's gentle and kind, sensitive to others. Regardless of the anger in my heart, it pains me to see him this way.

He pulls back and slides his thumb over my jaw, studying my face. "I love you, Breslin. Me falling for him didn't change that." He punches his chest. "You're still in here."

The look in his eyes combined with the twinge in my heart tells me every word is true.

When he cups my face, I turn to putty, unable to resist the pull. He skims his tongue along my lips, tasting me, and I open for him. Unlike Asher's kiss which was forceful and demanding, Landon's is sweet and soothing. He's making love to my mouth with a gentle caress and soft flick of his tongue, letting me know with every breath he takes how true his words are. Letting me know he won't let me shatter.

When his fingers curl into my hips, I snake my arm around his neck, tugging him even closer.

He reaches for the hem of my shirt and I raise my arms for him, allowing him to strip me bare. When his mouth finds mine again, my tears mingle in our kiss but he doesn't pull away. If anything, he deepens the kiss, assuring me he won't let me go. Telling me without words that the arms I'm in are safe, despite the strange chaos surrounding us.

I take off his shirt next and my thighs clench when I rake my gaze over his tattoos. Landon is beautiful. But not in the conventional, blond hair and blue eyes sense that Asher is. He's beautiful because he wears his heart on his sleeve and he's perceptive to others. He's beautiful because he'd be the kind of person who would take the hit over and over again if it meant absolving another person's suffering. His inner beauty surpasses the physical—not that he's bad to look at. Because those warm brown eyes, tall stature, adorable glasses, and toned body are enough to make anyone with a pulse swoon.

But the most beautiful thing about Landon Parker? He makes me forget my past and the tidal wave of heartache that constantly surrounds me. He makes everything better, just by being near.

And right now? I want to disappear in Landon. I want him to take me to that place that only he can. The place where the bad things can't reach me.

I need to get lost in his touch and escape in his desire for me. I reach down and stroke him through his jeans. "I need you inside me."

I repeat the movement and my heart races when he starts to thicken in my hand, ready for me.

That is until he draws back and shakes his head. "That's not why I came here."

I smile and unzip his jeans, refusing to break this connection, because I know what's waiting for me when I do.

Misery, pain, memories.

"It might not be why you came, but it can be why you stay." I reach for the string on my sweatpants and he halts me. "We have sex every time we're together."

I blink and swallow. "You say it like it's repulsive."

His face softens. "Are you kidding? Of course not. I love having sex with you." He gestures between us. "But I love what we have tonight even more. Don't check out on me because you're feeling too much. Because I'm right here with you." He reaches for my wrist. "I won't let you go, Bre. I'm here for as long as you want me. But don't use me as your escape from him." His eyebrows crash together. "Because I know that's what you did."

He frowns before he whispers, "Just like I know I'll always be second best in your heart."

My heart stops for several seconds and I open my mouth, intending to argue with him, but I can't...because he's right.

"I didn't realize I was using you all those months." Shame settles over me with the awareness. "I'm sorry, Landon."

But not nearly as sorry as I am that I gave my heart to someone else first.

He runs his nose along my ear. "I didn't realize I hurt you until you walked in on us."

"How could you think me seeing you with anyone who wasn't me wouldn't hurt?"

"Because I honest to God didn't think you cared," he says sharply. "Not only did you break up with me, but while you were in Europe I called you so many times I lost count. What was I supposed to think?"

The saying, *'sometimes the truth hurts'* has never been more prevalent than in this moment.

My stomach squeezes in protest. "I returned your call once while I was there but you blocked me."

"I didn't block you—" he starts to say before his mouth clamps shut and his eyes dart around the room.

"If you didn't block my number who did?" I gasp when I realize.

"Bre—"

"No," I interject. "Don't even sit there and try to defend him. Or you might as well walk right out that door and never come back."

I push my hair out of my face, willing myself to keep calm and not track him down. "How can you think he didn't seek you out intentionally or set you up, Landon? He went in your phone and blocked *my* number."

"It wasn't like that. I was...he thought he was helping a friend get over a girl who didn't want him. He had no idea it was you because I never told him your name and you're not stored in my phone under your name." He raises his hands. "But I don't want to talk about him anymore. Because you and he are like a pair of fucking boomerangs. No matter what, you'll just keep circling and coming back to one another somehow." He drops his head. "And I'm the one caught in the middle. Actually, worse than that. I'm the one you both ricochet off of and I hate it."

I glare at him. "Are you kidding? Do you really expect me to feel bad for you?"

His jaw flexes and he looks like he wants to protest but I don't let him. "The only reason you're caught in the middle is because you put yourself there."

His brow wrinkles and I look him in the eyes. I don't want to be in this situation with him any longer and there's only one way I can think of to get out of it.

"Do you love me?" I flinch as I wait for his response, despite knowing the answer.

He tips my chin up. "You know I do."

I can feel my guard lowering as I swallow and whisper, "Then choose me."

Fight for me because I want to fight for you. The way I should have fought for you.

Courage and determination crawls up my throat with my new-found resolve. "I won't mess it up this time. I'll love you the right way, Landon."

His face falls. "I—"

I don't give him the chance to answer because I fuse our mouths together, desperate to siphon every bit of him that I can while I still have the chance.

His breath is choppy and frantic when we break apart, a perfect parallel to the despair in his eyes.

"Don't make me choose—because I can't." He peppers kisses

over my jaw and along my cheek. "All I can promise is that I'll never lie to you." He hovers over my ear lobe. "All I can promise is that you're safe with me, because I won't let anyone hurt you again. Including him."

I give my head a shake, certain I misheard him because his words don't make sense to me. I don't know how he can make that kind of promise, all while in the same breath telling me that he can't choose between us and that he wants to date us both.

I clutch my chest. "I don't...I don't think I can stay with you while you're with *him*—" My exhale is heavy and loaded with sadness. I feel like he just physically took out my heart and stuck it on a stick before twirling it in a fire. "But I don't think I can give you up, either."

The gruesome feeling in my stomach grows. "I don't know what to say or where I stand. I don't know how I feel about this." My breath hitches and I feel dizzy. The room is spinning in one giant whirl, like I'm on a merry go round that malfunctioned and just keeps spiraling out of control, unable to stop.

How the hell am I actually in this situation right now?

Strong arms wrap me in an embrace before the merry go round tilts and I feel nothing but warm, buttery skin underneath me.

"You're okay," Landon whispers, running his hands up and down my back as I lie down on top of him. "Just breathe."

His hand curls around my hip, holding me in place. "Close your eyes, and sleep. I've got you. I didn't mean to make you freak out. We don't have to talk about this anymore."

I drag in a slow breath and my eyelids fall shut. I'm so exhausted, so drained from everything that occurred over the last week. But it's the last few hours that pushed me over the edge.

I sink into him, fighting thoughts of Asher the entire time but it's near impossible. He's always my last thought right before I fall asleep and the first thought I have when I wake up in the morning.

"I told him we would crash and burn," I mumble against Landon's chest. "I told him."

Panic grips me but Landon's lips brush the top of my head and his arms tighten around me. "Shhh."

His hand finds the spot above my heart—a heart that feels like it's beating out of my chest, and he kisses my temple. "Breathe, babe. Just breathe. Everything's gonna be okay."

My eyes burn with tears I refuse to shed. *He couldn't be more wrong about that.* Nothing about this predicament is okay. There's no way it will ever be.

A moment later he softly rocks me and starts singing the first few lines of my favorite song—*Colorblind,* by the Counting Crows.

I immediately relax, letting the deep, addicting timbre of his voice pacify and comfort me.

God, I missed his voice. I miss the way everything in the world is right again in his arms.

His fingers stroke my spine in gentle movements, and I clutch him, not wanting to let go. When he starts singing the part about no one getting to come in, my heart jams in my chest.

Because I want to let him in. I don't want to live in a world where everything is black and white...but I can't help it.

Because the gray parts are brutal. The gray parts are dangerous.

The gray parts always hurt so fucking much.

CHAPTER 11

LANDON

I watch her as she stirs in her sleep. The early morning sun is peeking through the small curtain—highlighting her long red hair, porcelain skin, and perfect curvy form.

Her brows draw together and her pouty lips part in a way that tells me that even when she's dreaming, she's still unsettled.

And I know I'm the reason for that.

I'm not the kind of man who hurts other people—especially those I love, and my heart plummets with the guilt and weight of the situation.

I've gone over things in my head non-stop, but I only seem to come back to one thought.

Trying to decide between them is a torture my heart can't bear.

And the only time I regret falling for one...is when I look at the other.

Making a decision and choosing one door over the other has never been my forte. Hell, it's probably why I'm a double major instead of pushing for music.

But unlike the situation with my education, I don't feel a pull guiding me more toward one of them. If I did, the decision would be easy instead of so fucking complicated.

But unfortunately for me, hell for *all* of us—both plowed into my heart with the same tenacity, jointly damaging me and making me feel whole in a way I didn't think was possible.

I never thought I'd find love with one person in this lifetime, let alone two.

Part of me wants to tell Breslin what Asher told me, but I don't, for two reasons.

One—it's not my place. The past is between them and as much as it hurts, I'm not part of that. Therefore, me opening that can of worms wouldn't be right. Plus, Breslin would assume I'm just taking Asher's side if I did. And as much as I get where he's coming from in regards to the past and can even empathize myself now given my feelings for him. It doesn't mean I can't understand where Breslin's coming from, or that I don't sympathize with the fact that she has every right to be hurt, angry, and upset over what happened.

For all intents and purposes—she believes she was cheated on and lied to. And no matter what struggles people may have with their sexuality...it doesn't excuse lying to those you love. And while the cheating is a gray area because he was blackmailed, him lying to her isn't something that even I can argue.

I watch as she shifts again on the bed and my heart slams against my ribcage.

The other reason for my silence? Is purely selfish.

I'm afraid of what will happen if Breslin forgives him. I'm afraid they'll move on without me.

Breslin might say she hates him...but she couldn't be more wrong.

She's still in love with him. The kind of love that never goes away or fades.

The kind of love that makes me second place. In *both* their hearts.

Maybe if I was a better person, I'd let them both go, but I'm not sure that would do any of us any good at this point. Or maybe I'm just unclear about what point logic and reason overshadow love. Because love is winning...love wants me to find a way to fix all the shattered pieces.

Love wants me to find a way to heal both of them.

I just don't know how to go about it without ripping my heart out in the process.

Then again, that's the thing about love...sometimes it fucking hurts.

But I love them both so I'm willing to sacrifice my own heart to fix theirs.

I just need to find a way to get Breslin on board without her falling apart at the mention of it. I need to get her to the place where she trusts that I'll be there every step of the way and I won't let her pain suck her under.

And I need to get Asher to the point where he trusts me enough that his jealousy takes a backseat and he agrees to the ultimate sacrifice.

Sharing Breslin.

With me.

Something that I know first-hand won't be easy, given my own jealousy that stirs in my blood at the thought.

I don't want to watch either of them with someone that's not me.

But the more I mull it over...I honest to fucking God think it's the only solution at our disposal.

The only way in which we don't get hurt—after the initial first few blows that is. Because it's sure as fuck going to hurt like hell in the beginning. Just like a wound that has to scab over before it can begin mending.

But I think we deserve to mend, despite all the mistakes we've made along the way.

Hell, I think everyone deserves a chance to rectify errors in their life. Fix what they had a part in breaking.

Although there's guaranteed to be some bumps and bruises along the road to redemption.

"I wish I'd told you yes when you said you'd wait for me while I was in Europe," she whispers in her sleep and my heart crumbles.

I glance at my watch. I really need to be getting out of here before the students on the floor wake up and see a TA sneaking out of a dorm at 6 a.m., but I drop to my knees beside the bed anyway.

"We can't change the past, Breslin." I bury my head against her stomach. "The only thing we can do is find a way to get past it."

Her eyes flutter open, glistening with unshed tears as she stares down at me. It's like another punch to the gut, seeing her wake up like this.

"I'm sorry," I whisper, because it's all I can seem to say to her as of late. "But if you can find a way to trust me, I'll find a way to make this right again."

Her hands comb through my hair and her chest rises on a deep inhale. "I don't see how."

I push up her tank top and kiss a path along her navel. "Don't give up just yet."

Concern pulls on her features. "You're shaking, Landon. When was the last time you ate something or checked your level?"

Now that she mentions it, I am a little woozy. "I guess I should get out of here." I give her a grin. "You know, before I end up having you for breakfast."

She bites her bottom lip and her nipples start to pebble underneath her shirt, and fuck me and the way my cock jerks at the sight.

I shift, intending to leave, but when I notice the damp spot on her little white panties and smell her arousal, I'm ready to pounce.

My conscience is gnawing at me, telling me this isn't right

because I haven't put my plan into motion yet and things are so screwed up it's not even funny, but the voice silences when I hook a finger into her panties and move them to the side, uncovering that holy grail between her legs.

She's so pretty and open for me. Before I can stop myself, I glide my tongue along her slit, allowing myself a taste of her. Just a little something to take the edge off.

That damn inner voice of mine won't shut the hell up though, not even when I stab at her with my tongue, scooping her up like she's the best flavor on earth, because as far as I'm concerned, she is.

"Landon," she breathes as she grips my hair.

My name on her lips brings me out of my haze and I pull back. It's not that I don't want her; I just don't want to complicate things even more and keep having sex with them both until I approach them with my idea.

I press a gentle kiss to her clit. "Can I take a rain check?"

Her mouth drops open and she looks at me like I'm insane, something I'm wondering myself because the amount of self-restraint it takes to walk away from her spread out for me like *this*...

I bite my knuckle and stand up, every cell in my body nearly weeping at the loss.

"I have to go before someone sees me coming out of your dorm."

It's not a lie, the amount of trouble I could face is something I don't even want to think about.

Her face pales. "Yeah, you're right." She fixes her panties. "See you later this afternoon, *teach*."

There's a playful yet taunting bite to her tone and I sigh heavily as I close the door behind me, wanting nothing more than to jump back in bed and devour her to the point we forget anything and everything.

Like the 6′4-inch guy with piercing blue eyes and a beanie

that's currently glaring at me like he's a nanosecond away from ripping my face off.

I thought the door next to Breslin's looked familiar, my thoughts were just in such a disarray last night I didn't really give it much thought.

Something I'm now regretting, because just like I don't want to hurt Breslin. I don't want to hurt Asher, either.

"It's not what you think," I start to say before he lunges at me, backing me into the wall behind me.

My hands clench at my sides, ready to defend myself. "I came here to talk to her last night. Not have sex with her."

He leans in close, his nostrils flaring. He still hasn't said a word, and I'm not sure whether or not to be thankful for it.

One thick arm lands on the wall beside my head and his eyes darken. I narrow mine in response and his jaw tics as he angles his head, getting close to my mouth.

Lust barrels into me, and despite me trying to fight the stubborn emotion and tell it that it's not a good time, it only grows stronger.

Especially when he slants his mouth over mine and sweeps his tongue inside. Something I soon realize is a mistake because he slams the wall beside my head and bites my lip so hard all I can taste is blood...instead of Breslin's pussy.

The fist that lands in the center of my chest before he pushes off me nearly brings me to my knees.

But it's nothing compared to the look on his face.

"Asher—"

His fist smashes into his door so hard it vibrates. "Don't fucking talk to me."

Two things happen at that moment.

One—Breslin's door opens and she gapes at Asher before she cries out, "What the fuck are you doing here?"

And two—Asher points to his door and growls, "I live here."

Before he focuses his attention on Kit and her girlfriend Becca walking up the steps and his eyes widen.

"You've got to be kidding me," Breslin yells before she slams her door shut.

Asher shakes his head and grunts before his focus turns back to Kit and Becca and his eyes linger on their adjoining hands.

"What the actual fuck?" he hisses, his gaze now on Becca.

Kit's head circles, much like a snake ready to kill its prey, before she takes a step forward. "What the hell is your problem, asshole?"

Becca quickly pulls Kit back. "It's nothing, baby doll. We're just old friends."

At that Asher snorts, the disgust more than evident on his face before he hikes his gym bag up his shoulder and strides past them.

Kit, ever the direct one, looks at Becca and says, "You fucked him. Didn't you? He's the reason you've been so distant over the last few weeks."

I open my mouth to interject, because I'm positive Asher and Becca aren't fucking, but Becca shakes her head profusely. "I would never cheat on you." She holds up her left hand and I can't help but notice a huge diamond on her ring finger. "This means everything to me."

I side-step them, because this conversation is none of my business, especially when their mouths come together and I hear the sounds of them gasping for air.

I march down the steps, deciding to grab a quick shower and a change of clothes before I head over to the football field.

Because just like I needed to talk to Breslin last night. I need to talk to Asher and make things right again.

Nerves barrel into me as I watch him get sacked for the second time during practice. Neither his heart nor his head are in the game right now. Which is alarming to say the least given the first game of the season is exactly one week away.

Coach Crane throws his ball cap on the ground in frustration. I've never seen the man so angry before. My eyes go to Dragoni who's chewing his toothpick with enough vigor it's going to become dust soon. His eyes stay focused on Asher. Hell, they haven't left him since practice started.

I have to tell Breslin the real reason he's here.

My stomach curdles with that thought, because again, it's not my place to tell her. However, I'm sure she doesn't want him dead.

I swallow. Pretty sure.

Fuck, this situation is such a mess.

"Off my field, Holden," Coach Crane shouts, loud enough that even I hear him all the way from my seat high up in the bleachers.

Everyone around him freezes as Asher takes off his helmet and throws it, looking so crushed, my own heart contracts.

Coach Crane walks over to him and grips him by the shoulder. He whispers something into his ear before he pats him on the back and Asher starts walking off.

Dragoni's eyes follow and when he stands up to go after him, I start walking down the bleachers. I'm not exactly sure what my plan is, but there's no way in hell I'm going to let him assault Asher again.

I quicken my steps when Dragoni disappears off the field.

And that's when Coach Crane's voice stops me in my tracks and he summons me over.

Every instinct in my body wants to tell him what's going on with his warped, mob-connected, assistant coach, but I can't— because it will lead to innocent people getting hurt. I'm in the worst catch-22 there is.

Correction—*second* worst.

"Wasn't aware you were a football fan," he says, his jaw working back and forth.

"I'm not," I start. "Asher has a test today so I figured we would catch up to study for a bit before class begins."

I grip the back of my neck. I suddenly feel like I'm under interrogation.

He looks ahead, focusing on the players plowing into one another. "I think I'm going to request another tutor."

It's on the tip of my tongue to defend myself, but I know better than to use the rope he's giving me to hang myself.

"Any reason why?" I ask, trying to remain unfazed.

That's when his eyes swivel to me. "He hasn't been in the right head space lately."

I'm a coward, because I know I'm partly responsible for Asher's current state, but my immediate response is, "Really? I haven't noticed. But then again I've been sick this week and haven't had a chance to tutor or talk to him."

Coach Crane looks surprised and my conscience punches me in the nuts.

Since when am I the type of person to lie to others? Just what kind of person am I turning into?

He looks sheepish. "I wasn't aware of that." He clears his throat. "I apologize for putting the cart before the horse."

I try hard not to correct that statement and give him a nod instead. "If it's all right with you, I really should be heading to the library."

He waves me off and blows his whistle so loud I find myself grateful I'm partially deaf in one ear.

As soon as I'm out of eyesight, I start running toward the locker room.

I breathe a sigh of relief when I pass through the doors and see Asher sitting on a bench.

A sigh of relief that I choke on when he lifts his head and I see his shiny new black eye.

I spin around, my hands forming fists.

"He's gone," Asher says gruffly. "Besides, there's nothing you can do about it anyway. Not unless you want to end up on the chopping block yourself."

"Well, someone has to do something. He can't keep beating you—"

He snorts. "Trust me, I'm used to it."

For a moment, I don't see the 21-year-old Asher Holden. I see the small boy that was beaten by his father and my heart sinks.

Lead fills my stomach. This can't keep happening, something's got to give.

He yanks me back the moment I reach the door. "No," Asher bites out. "Do you want to get yourself killed?"

I pivot, facing him. "No, but I don't want you to die, either."

"I've got it under control."

"Do you?" I scoff and his eyes turn hard. "Because even me, someone who doesn't know a lick about football can tell you blew it out there."

He stalks toward his locker and throws a t-shirt on. "Well pardon me, shit head. I guess I'm a little distracted by the fact that the guy I have feelings for is fucking the girl I'm in love with."

"I didn't have sex with her last night." It's a feeble attempt at defending myself because we both know that just a few hours prior, I did have sex with her.

Hell, the *both* of them.

Something which has to stop happening until I can talk to them about my plan.

He slams his locker shut so hard it rattles and barrels out of the locker room.

I hasten my footsteps to keep up with him. "Asher."

When I reach out and touch his arm, he stills. "You know, I've always wanted to taste her. Hell, I used to dream about it and jerk off to it." He shrugs. "Still do." He turns to look at me. "But not one of my fantasies ever involved another guy."

I bristle. "I—"

"No." His eyes narrow. "Don't argue. Don't defend. Don't say anything, Landon. Because as far as I'm concerned...we are done. I *can't* do this with you anymore."

He casts his eyes down. "I'm just not sure if it's because I'm heartbroken over you taking my girl." His eyes connect with mine. "Or because I'm heartbroken that you chose the easy choice."

He gestures between us. "But don't worry, bro, your little homo experiment is over for good. You get to have the white picket fence and the 2.5 kids." He rubs his chest, almost as if it hurts. "Take care of her. Give her everything I couldn't."

My heart stops when he takes a step away from me. This isn't supposed to be happening.

I don't think. I just act.

I shove him against the wall, and then I break another rule of mine, because I snatch his jaw and kiss him.

"Nothing about this is easy," I say before I take his lips again. "Because my choice is the both of you."

"Someone might catch us," Asher whispers, but I shut him up with my mouth again.

When we finally break apart, I glare at him. "I don't give a shit who sees us." I open my arms and circle the hallway. "I'm not afraid of my feelings for you. I'm—" I falter, trying to think of the right words to make him understand. "I don't know—accepting them."

I grip his collar. "What I'm afraid of is losing the two people I love."

He gives me a long stare. "Take it from me—you can't have your cake and eat it too."

"I know." I meet his gaze. "I just need you to put your trust in me while I sort everything out."

He gives me a strange look before he shrugs. "Fine. But the longer this goes on, the harder it gets...for all of us."

I rest my forehead against his. "I know it does." I kiss him again, because just like with Breslin earlier, I need something to take the edge off. "Don't give up on me, Asher. I'm gonna find a way to fix this."

His hand slides to my neck, his eyes penetrating mine before he gives me a soft nod. "Fine. But I think your hopes are too high. One of us is going to end up getting hurt."

"We're already hurting," I argue and he stays silent.

A moment later, I sling an arm around him and start walking down the hall. "But we can't focus on that right now. We have a test you have to pass in—" I glance at my watch. "Three hours."

He expels a breath. "Lead the way, nerd."

CHAPTER 12

ASHER

Landon peers at me from underneath those dark-rimmed glasses of his. "Okay, I think you're gonna be fine."

"I hope so," I tell him. "I was up half the night studying."

After I was threatened by a pink-haired head case while Landon was going to chow town on Breslin in the next room.

Irritation punches my gut with that thought and I shove my book into my bag and stand up.

"Where are you going? We still have another 45 minutes left before class starts."

"Food," I grumble and he lurches to his feet.

"I can go with you if you want."

"I don't want," I say, ignoring the way my heart kicks when he frowns. "Besides, I'm pretty sure you had enough to eat last night."

With that, I turn and start making my way out of the library.

"Whoa, hold up," he says behind me. "You just said you weren't gonna give up on us."

I huff out a sigh and pause. "Just because I'm not giving up on us doesn't mean I'm not angry, Landon." I tap his temple. "And if you can't understand that, you're not half as smart as your grades suggest you are."

He shuffles his feet. "I'm just—I'm sorry I hurt you. I'm going to do everything I can to make sure it doesn't happen again." He swallows. "To either of you."

I shake my head, because whatever endearing wheels are turning in Landon's head—they're not headed for a good destination. But the look in his eyes tells me he's relentless. And I care about him enough to let him sort his shit out...for a little while at least.

He draws in a breath and sticks his hands in his pockets. "Which is why I should probably tell you that I'm telling Breslin the truth about why you're here playing football."

An angry surge goes through me and I take a step forward. "No, you're not." I jab a finger in his chest. "Because number one— you promised me you wouldn't tell anyone. And number two—it's not your fucking place to tell her my shit."

He raises his chin. "I'm not letting you get killed, asshole. Maybe once she hears what's really going on she'll—"

"She'll what? Pity ride my dick and kiss all my boo-boos away?"

Jealousy crosses over his face and I inwardly smile.

"No. But maybe she'll be...I don't know, *nicer* to you."

"Breslin's not the same girl she once was," I whisper. "She no longer takes shit from people and I'm proud of her for that. Therefore, I deserve her hatred."

"The old you does—the douche bag who lied to her. But I'm not so sure the guy standing before me today does."

"Look, if you want us to still be—whatever the fuck it is we are —stay out of my past with Breslin." It's on the tip of my tongue to tell him to stay out of my future with her, too, but I don't. "And keep your mouth shut about Dragoni. I'll tell her when I'm ready."

"But you'll tell her?"

I blow out a breath. "Yeah. Eventually."

The relief on his face is more than apparent and it makes my heart jump. If I ever had any doubts that he cares about me, they don't exist anymore.

I take another step closer to him, reach down, and squeeze his hand briefly—the gesture is slight enough I know no one else in the courtyard caught it.

"One day, Asher," he whispers, looking around.

I nod, even though I'm not so sure that day will ever come. But I know in my heart that I want it to.

I want to hold his hand in public. I want to kiss him in public. I want to love him in public. I don't want to be his dirty little secret and I don't want him to be mine, either. I want to be brave enough for the world to see who I truly am without being ashamed.

He knocks my shoulder with his. "Come on, I'll buy you lunch."

I give him a grin. "You sure that's not against the school policy?"

He gives me a cocky grin of his own as we open the doors to the cafeteria. "Haven't you heard? I'm breaking all the rules lately."

I bite my bottom lip and pull out my phone, hoping the text I just got is my brother texting me back.

When I see his name flashing across the screen I pick up.

"Hey, Preston."

"What's up? I got your text earlier but I was in class. Everything okay?"

I look at Landon whose brows furrow as we stand in line for food and debate my next words carefully.

How exactly do you tell your brother that the girl he's just moved in with is cheating on him with someone else?

A pink-haired madwoman at that. One who's best friends with Breslin.

One thing's for sure, though—this is a conversation that needs to be had in person, not over the phone.

"You have any time in your schedule to hang out this week?"

There's a pause on the other end before he says, "Um. Yeah, sure. I can swing by your campus soon. I'll call you when I'm on my way so we can meet up."

"Sounds good. See you then," I say before I hang up and look at Landon who appears even more confused.

"My brother Preston and—" I start to say before I'm pushed forward.

"Do you mind—" My words fall when I turn fully and see the lunatic and cheating Barbie making out wildly behind me.

They break apart and Kit glares at me. "Well, if it isn't the judgmental, cheating, life ruiner, asshole himself."

Is that what Breslin told her? I shake my head. Of course, it is.

"Well, if it isn't the psycho who accosted me."

Behind me, I hear Landon praise my use of *accost* and Kit's stare focuses on him. "I thought you were better than this, Landon."

Landon looks sheepish and I shoot my gaze at Becca. "You know, those are some pretty heavy words for someone who doesn't even know the person closest to them." I glance at the ring on her finger and my nostrils flare. This bitch has some nerve and I can't wait to tear her world out from under her.

Becca pales and yanks on Kit's shoulder. "I'm not hungry anymore. Come on, let's go."

"Well, I'm hungry," Kit protests until we all look up and see Breslin walking through the cafeteria doors.

I swallow hard, because every time she walks in a room the entire world stands still for me.

I let my gaze roam over her freely. All the way from her gorgeous red hair that's piled high on top of her head in some kind of knot, the jeans that fit her curves in a way that has my own jeans growing snugger, down to the cute purple toes peeking out through her flip flops.

Every single inch of Breslin Rae is just as beautiful as I remember.

I know I told Landon earlier to give her everything I couldn't—but looking at her now makes me want to take those words right back.

It makes me want to start the war of all wars just to have her again.

She worries her plump bottom lip between her teeth, like this is the last place she wants to be right now.

Then before any of us can say a word—she's gone.

Just like a gust of wind on the hottest day of the year.

Funny thing is? I'd bet my life she's heading for the art studio, because that's the place she always goes whenever she's upset. Or happy for that matter.

It's the place she goes to get away from it all. It's also the place she goes to when she's thinking about her mom. It's her place where she lets all her emotions out.

I have to stuff down the instinct telling me to chase after her, because it's bad enough I ruined her Art class this semester simply by being there.

Becca yanks on Kit's arm again and she begrudgingly walks over to one of the tables with her and sits down. But not before raising her middle finger in my direction.

I raise mine right back at her in response, and she pulls Becca on her lap and they proceed to make out.

Beside me, Landon gives his head a shake. "What the hell is going on?"

"Becca and my brother Preston are together," I inform him and his eyes go wide.

"No. Becca is a lesbian." He flips a hand in their direction. "A very happily *engaged* lesbian by the looks of it."

"Well, then she's leading one hell of a double life. Because she's also a straight girl who just moved into an apartment with her college boyfriend." I pause. "In addition to being a lackey for her uncle Vincent Dragoni."

"No fucking way."

"Way," I say as I start loading my tray up with various food.

"Becca and Kit have been together even longer than Breslin and I have."

When I give him a look, he shrugs. "Sorry. Christ, this is insane." He drops his voice to a whisper. "Despite how she treated you, Kit's a good person. She doesn't deserve to be kept in the dark about this." He glances her way with pity in his eyes. "She's planning on marrying the girl for crying out loud."

We pay the cashier and I hold my hands up. "Look, the only person I care about in this scenario is my brother."

His gaze snaps back to me. "You have to tell her."

My jaw falls open. "Um...no. No, I don't—"

I'm cut off when the cafeteria doors swing open and in walks my younger brother. I guess when he meant *soon*, he meant now.

"Oh shit," Landon says beside me and I swallow hard. This is like watching a car crash happen right before your very eyes but being powerless to stop it.

Kit and Becca are still in a passionate lip-lock. Even after my brother, who looks equal parts confused and pissed stands in front of them and crosses his arms over his chest.

"Maybe we should have gotten popcorn for lunch," Landon says and I nudge him in the ribs.

"Becca," Preston grinds out, the bite in his tone severe enough that she gasps and her hands fly to her face.

"Who the hell are you?" Kit questions looking between them.

"I'm her boyfriend," Preston says and I can't help but wince. "You know, the guy she's living with."

"Fuck," Landon whispers. "This is so bad."

I place my tray to the side and nod in agreement.

Kit's hand goes to her heart and she laughs. "Wow, good one."

She grabs Becca's—who looks so pale she could pass for a vampire—hand and shoves it in his face. "Because last time I checked this is my soon to be wife."

Preston takes a step back and shakes his head. "Becca what the hell is going on? One threesome a few weeks ago and now you're full on lesbo?"

Kit stands up. "What?" The crack in her voice has my stomach dropping.

Becca seems to find her voice. "I—um."

"You're what?" Kit questions with tears in her eyes. "A liar and a cheater?"

Everyone's eyes are on them now and I'm torn between shouting at them all to mind their business, or walking over and ushering them to somewhere more private.

"I can't believe you're engaged to someone else," Preston says, the reality appearing to finally be hitting him.

"This isn't what you think, baby doll," Becca says, looking up at Preston and Kit braces herself against the table.

"Baby doll?" Kit squeaks, pointing to her chest. "That's me." The tears fall down her face like rain. "That's supposed to be *me*."

Landon slides his phone out of his pocket. "I'm texting Breslin."

"Good idea."

Hell, even I'm feeling bad for Kit now and he's my brother.

Preston's gaze locks with mine then and he gives me a nod, a nod that says—*I'll talk to you later.*

I give him a nod of my own and he holds his hands up in the air, looks at them, and says, "Fuck this. I'm out," before he turns on his heels.

"Preston, no," Becca screams, chasing after him, leaving Kit in the dust with tears rolling down her face.

Kit staggers, looking a second away from passing out and both me and Landon rush to her side, steadying her.

"Breathe, Kit. We've got you," Landon says and she sniffles, nearly collapsing right there on the floor.

She's so upset she doesn't even realize I'm holding up one side of her as we make our way out of the cafeteria and into the courtyard.

Where we find a panicked Breslin running toward us. "What happened?"

Kit cries harder and makes a beeline for Breslin who looks even more alarmed now. "Someone better start talking." Her eyes ping-pong between the both of us. "Now."

Landon takes a breath. "Cliff notes version is that Becca's been cheating on Kit."

Kit mumbles something between sobs and Breslin wraps her arms tighter around her. "That fucking bitch."

I take a step closer to her. "Tell me about it. I knew she was trouble the first time I saw her at a bar."

Breslin's eyes shoot daggers at me. "You *motherfucker*."

I blink. "What—"

"Jesus," Landon interjects. "She wasn't cheating on Kit with Asher." He swallows. "It was Asher's brother." His gaze slides toward me. "You are literally the worst at explaining things."

I open my mouth but Kit whispers, "Take me to the dorm, please," to Breslin before they start walking.

I automatically go to follow them but Landon stops me. "Class starts in 10 minutes." He pulls out his phone and types out a text. "But I told Breslin to text me if she needs anything."

Annoyance tightens my guts and I walk off. I used to be the person she went to if she ever needed anything.

CHAPTER 13

BRESLIN

"Oomph, sorry," I say, quickly apologizing for bumping into someone as I make my way through the courtyard. "I—" My words fall as I come face to face with gray-blue eyes and the deepest set of dimples I've ever seen.

Well, except for his brother that is.

"Preston?" I question, still in disbelief.

"Well, if it isn't the girl from the wrong side of the tracks," he replies, his tone clipped, angry even. Certainly not what I expected. Preston and I were never super close or anything, but we were always polite to one another.

He crosses his arms and looks down at me, like I'm the equivalent to a bug on his shoe. It's almost identical to the look his father used to pin me with and I feel myself shrink down. "What are you doing here, Preston?"

He side-steps me and I can't tell if it's because he's in a rush or doesn't want to talk to me.

"Sorry, no time for chit-chat—especially with someone like *you*." He sneers the last word and I balk at him.

"I beg your pardon?" I snap, pride swelling in my chest because I'm finally sticking up for myself when it comes to people like *him*.

He rubs his chin and sniffs. "Look, I have nothing to say to you."

I open my mouth to question him further, but he barks, "Stay the hell away from my brother, though. Lord knows you've hurt him enough, and the last thing he needs is you fucking up his life all over again when he's trying to put it back together."

With that, he storms off and I'm left wondering what in the world he's talking about.

"I loved her so much," Kit cries into my shirt and I rock her back and forth, my heart breaking for her.

I move her hair out of her face and cup her cheeks. "I know you did. She didn't deserve you, Kit."

That only makes her cry harder. "I knew she was bi and liked guys, but she assured me she had relationships with women and that she wanted something serious." She rubs her eyes. "Hell, she agreed to *marry* me, B. We started planning the date and every-thing." Her lower lip quivers as she looks at me. "I mean, why would she do that if she didn't really love me the way I love her?"

Because she's a gold-digging whore.

I don't realize I've said that out loud until Kit shakes her head. "Her family has money." She shrugs. "But who knows if she was lying to me about that, too."

I envelop her in another hug and she cries her heart out some more.

"You have class in 20 minutes, B," she whispers but I ignore her.

Class can wait, this is so much more important.

I wipe her damp face, but new tears fall, so I wrap her in my arms again. I'm pretty sure there's nothing on earth that sucks worse than consoling your best friend over a broken heart. I want to take all her pain on as my own.

Correction—I want that manipulative bitch *Becca* to take all her pain.

Rage trickles down my spine, plucking on my nerves and I stand up. Becca won't get away with cheating on my best friend.

Kit wipes her eyes with the back of her hand. "I'm glad you're going. I don't want you to miss your favorite class because of me and my shit."

I shake my head. "I'm not—" I stop and think better of it. "Actually, yes, I am going to Art class." I reach for a paint-stained sweatshirt. "But don't worry, because I'm coming back with ice cream and alcohol."

Kit sulks. "I'm pretty sure that's not going to help."

I plant a kiss on her forehead and reach for my purse. "Maybe not, but we can numb it away for a little while." I force her to look at me. "I love you, Kit. And it might not seem like it right now, but I swear you'll get through this." I give her hand a squeeze. "We'll get through this."

After I beat the living shit out of Becca that is.

She points to her bed. "I guess it goes without saying that I'm crashing here for a little while." She closes her eyes. "I can't go back to that apartment just yet."

"Kit." When she looks at me, I say, "This is your dorm too." I open the door. "I'll be back in a little while."

Provided they don't lock me up for homicide.

I feel like I have ice running through my veins as I walk around campus, looking for her.

According to Landon she hasn't shown up at Kit's apartment

and from what I remember when Kit rattled off her schedule a few days ago, Becca should be between classes now.

I take a left, deciding to check the courtyard once more. And that's where I find the blonde whore. Sitting on a bench, texting wildly on her phone.

"You bitch," I sneer. A few people's heads whip around, but I don't care.

When Becca finally looks up from her phone I snatch it from her hand and throw it. "How could you do that to her? How could you cheat on someone as amazing as Kit?"

She has the audacity to shrug. "Shit happens and better things come along." She gives me an evil, condescending smile. "But why don't you date her, given you're up her ass all the time."

My blood quickens and before I can talk myself out of it I snatch her hair with one hand and send a punch flying into her cheek with the other.

She tries to hit me back, but I don't give her a chance, I slug her again. I vaguely hear people shouting around me, but I ignore them.

A strong arm latches around my waist, but I disregard it and throw another punch. "Do you have any idea what it's like to be cheated on by the person you love?"

My vision is so blurry I'm not even sure if I'm hitting my target anymore.

Because suddenly, this isn't just about what Becca did to Kit. This is about those awful people that you fall in love with who end up breaking you in the end.

There's a sharp tug and then before I know what's happening, I'm being lifted high into the air and whisked away.

I'm crying so hard I can barely breathe let alone see straight, and those same strong arms cradle me.

When I finally manage to draw in a breath, a familiar masculine scent hits me like a brick to the head.

My stomach churns and I twist out of his arms. "Put me down, Asher."

When he does, I go marching back toward a blubbering Becca, ready to go another round.

"Stop, Breslin," Asher snaps, pulling me back.

I pay him no mind and charge forward, only to be picked up and tossed over his broad shoulder like a sack of potatoes.

"Stop it, asshole."

He ignores me and begins walking, opening doors and making a few turns that have my head spinning.

I bang on his back. "I hate you."

I'm aware that I sound like a five-year-old, but given he's no better due to his caveman antics, I don't care.

"Yeah, Breslin, I know you do." His shoulders slump and he finally stops walking. "You can't go after her."

I glance at the tiles on the floor. "I'm pretty sure that's none of your business. You gave up the right to have a say in my life and my choices three years ago."

His grasp around my thighs hardens and I curse myself for the way heat coils low in my belly. My mind hates his touch...but my body obviously didn't get the memo and still craves it.

"I'm here because Preston fucked up and got involved with the wrong people and I need to settle his debt," he says and I swear my heart stops.

I slap at his back, motioning for him to put me down again because the blood is rushing to my head and everything is zipping around me.

After he does and I gather my bearings, he continues, "And those wrong people? Are Becca's family."

I clutch my heart. I don't give a shit about me...but Kit. "Oh my God."

I start to walk away but Asher grabs my wrist, holding me in place. "I'm going to talk to him." He lets go of my wrist and places his hands on his hips. "My assistant coach is one of them and Becca's uncle...I can speak to him and make sure everything is squared away and that you and Kit are fine."

"I'm so confused," I whisper and he nods.

"I know, baby. But I'm gonna take care of it." My chest contracts and he puffs out a breath. "Breslin—"

When I hear the pinched tone of his voice, I hold up my hand, silencing him. "The second you say one word about our past this conversation is over."

His jaw flexes and I know he wants to argue but he gives me another nod. "I respect that."

A scoff escapes my lips and his eyes narrow. "Look if you're not ready to talk about our past I can deal, but it doesn't mean you can treat me like a fucking punching bag, either."

I draw myself tight and look at him. "Fine. Now finish what you were saying. Specifically, the part about Becca and your assistant coach."

I stand there shell-shocked for the next 15 minutes as he proceeds to tell me all about Preston's gambling problem, having to come here to play football against his will, and needing to win the championship or else.

A shudder runs through my limbs when I think about the —or else.

I rock back and forth on my heels, still stunned. "So that's why you quit Duke?"

Something passes in his gaze that I don't understand before he says, "Yeah."

"Shit, your father must be going out of his mind."

It's on the tip of my tongue to ask him why his father, who's loaded, doesn't just pay off Preston's debt, but he runs a hand down his jaw and says, "I wouldn't know. We're not exactly on speaking terms anymore."

Sadness wraps around me with those words. Despite his

protests that they didn't always get along, I know how much his relationship with his father meant to him.

"Was it because—" I struggle to find the words because they chip away at my heart like an ice pick.

His face goes slack. "Partly, yeah."

I tell myself not to give in, because each moment I spend with him that barrier between us begins to thaw and I can't have that.

Fear settles over me and I raise my guard, because I'm afraid of what happens if I don't. Besides, just because his father is a jerk, it doesn't excuse what he did to me.

It doesn't excuse what he's *still* doing to me.

Like his relationship with Landon.

"I love Landon," I tell him, praying to God he finally gets it. "He's good for me, Asher."

All I can hear is the thud of my heart against my ribs as he draws in a slow breath and gestures to the art studio. "Come on, we should get to class."

By the time we walk in, class is half over and students are working on their art projects in various corners of the room.

Asher grabs an easel, a set of paints, and a canvas and sets up shop in a far-off corner. I'm about to do the same but a touch to my elbow stops me and he motions for me to sit down.

The forceps around my heart constrict as I take a seat on the bench and stare at the blank canvas before me. I open my mouth to object but he shakes his head and leans down until his lips are hovering just above my ear. "I won't bother you, I promise." A tremble erupts and my chest caves in when he kisses my temple. "Paint, baby."

I draw in a shaky breath, pick up a brush...and I do.

CHAPTER 14

ASHER

I watch as she walks out of the classroom after class ends, taking my entire heart with her as she goes.

I decide to stay back and clean up after her. I figure, it's the least that I can do given she's basically the one doing the entire project herself.

When I cast a glance at the canvas, my breath catches. Breslin's talent for art has always been impeccable, but she's grown even more now.

But her talent isn't the only thing that leaves me in awe. Because she's managed to capture the essence of Landon while he's playing music perfectly. From the way his eyes close—to the way he touches those ivory keys with the kind of passion you can't fake.

I can't help but smile as I think about our project—various depictions of love—because there's no mistaking the love Landon has for music in this portrait.

"Hey," a familiar voice calls out. I look up as Landon strides in the studio. Thinking fast, I turn the easel with the painting on it. Breslin's always been weird about people seeing her art and I don't want to give her another reason to be mad at me.

I walk over to the sink and start cleaning her brushes. "Hey yourself." I turn on the faucet. "At the risk of sounding like a dick, why are you here right now?"

He gives me an adorable grin that nearly has my brain scrambling as he holds up a paper. A paper with a bright red A on it. "I stayed after class to help Mrs. Sterling grade the papers."

I almost start to smile, but then I remember. "You didn't have anything to do with it?"

He shakes his head. "Didn't need to. This was all you, Asher."

He puts my paper back in a folder and returns it to his bag. "I'm so proud of you."

Before I can say another word, he moves closer to me. Normally I can't resist the pull of him...but all I can hear are Breslin's words from earlier. "*He's good for me, Asher.*"

I back away, ignoring the way his lips thin and the look he shoots me.

"I thought you'd be happy."

I lift a shoulder in a shrug. "I am. Just have a lot of shit on my mind."

"Like?"

I let out a sigh and drop the brushes in the sink. "I don't know, Landon. Where would you like me to begin? How about needing to win the first game for starters? Hell, all of the games this season. Or what about my brother ignoring my texts now because he's probably out on a gambling bender and God only fucking knows what fun stuff it will add to this shit storm when he's done."

I rip some paper towels off the stand. "Or how about the fact that Breslin just beat up Becca in the courtyard and now she's probably on Dragoni's radar."

Landon's eyes become saucers. "What?"

I raise a hand. "Don't worry, I'm talking to Dragoni tomorrow."

He starts pacing. "What good is that going to do? He—"

"He still needs me if he wants to win all his bets this year."

Nerves rise in the pit of my stomach. "It just means the stakes are going to be that much higher for me."

Panic crosses over his face. "But what about your performance lately—"

I slam the wall with my palm. "I've got it under control."

His hand slides up my shoulder and he gives it a squeeze. "You're spinning out again, Asher."

"I know," I whisper and he takes a step closer, wrapping his arms around me.

"You're not alone in this."

I know his words are supposed to bring me some kind of comfort but they do the exact opposite. "That's what I'm afraid of. You, Breslin, and Preston getting hurt."

I can hear his sharp intake of breath before he says, "We'll get through it. You making yourself sick over it will only make it worse. There's no way you can win a single game, let alone all of them this season with this kind of pressure."

He's right. I can't.

"Make any headway on this apparent plan of yours that you were going on about before?" I ask, wanting to change the subject.

He drags a hand through his hair and his jaw tenses. "Haven't quite worked out all the details yet but if you swing by my apartment tomorrow night, we can talk about it."

"Yeah, okay." I start walking toward the door. "I'm going to go to the dorms."

When he starts following me, I look at him. "I take it you're coming?"

"Not exactly." He rubs the back of his neck. "I told Breslin I would stop by tonight and bring some clothes from Kit's apartment over to her." Something passes in his gaze. "But, maybe you should come, too."

I stare at him like he's crazy, because he most definitely is. "Breslin doesn't want anything to do with me. And Kit—"

"I know, but—" He pauses. "Breslin loves Kit and maybe if she sees that you give a shit, it will help."

"You do realize what you're suggesting, right?"

I have no clue why he's suddenly helping me out, but I'm in no position to refuse it.

He hikes his bag up his shoulder as we continue walking. "Yeah, Asher. I do."

CHAPTER 15
BRESLIN

K it fills her solo cup with more vodka and knocks it against mine. "To bitches who need stitches."

I raise an eyebrow because I'm not exactly sure why we're toasting to *that* of all things. But then again, we're both kind of buzzed right now. Besides, if it makes Kit feel better, I'm all for it.

After I click my cup against hers I take a sip. Given that it's Friday night, I suggested going to a party, but she wanted to stay here, which was perfectly fine with me.

There's a knock on the door and Kit raises her cup in the air and toasts to that as well.

"Do you get it?" she questions between large swallows. "Because Becca needs stitches."

I don't get it, and I'm pretty sure I already gave her a few, but I stay silent about that and go to the door instead.

I do a double-take when I see both Landon and Asher.

Landon, I expected because I asked him to come, but it goes without saying that I most certainly don't want *him* here.

Landon opens his mouth but he's cut off by Asher. "Hey, how's it going?"

Behind me, Kit sniffles. "Because she's a lying, cheating, whore."

Landon looks at her sympathetically, and I move to the side to allow him in, but block it when Asher takes a step. "I don't—"

Kit sits up straight on her bed and squints her eyes. "What is he doing here? He's the enemy," she says, taking the words right out of my mouth.

Landon looks like he's going to object but I look back at Asher. "I think that's your cue to leave."

"Damn right it is," Kit calls out from behind me.

Asher smirks, pulls something out of his pocket, and holds it up in the air. "I have weed."

"Oh, my God," I groan at the same time Kit yells, "On second thought, let the man stay!"

He winks at me. "You heard her."

I begrudgingly move to the side and he flashes his bright, white teeth in my direction. Fucking dimples and all.

Asshole Asher I can deal with. It's the charming Asher that's always an issue for me.

I open the window by my bed as Asher plops down in a chair by the desk and proceeds to roll a few joints.

He looks at Kit. "I'm guessing it's just going to be me and you partaking?"

Kit nods her head wildly. "More for us."

"I'll smoke," Landon says, shocking the hell out of all of us.

Asher makes a face, but I don't miss the hint of his smug smile. "Graduation parties aside, have you ever done it before, nerd?"

Landon shrugs and looks around the room. "Once. A long time ago."

Kit claps her hands and smiles wide. "Oh, this is going to be great."

Asher's eyes lock with mine and he licks the joint in a way that makes my thighs clench. "You want some?"

My jaw nearly hits the ground. "Absolutely not."

He peruses my entire body from head to toe from underneath that beanie hat of his and I feel my cheeks heat. "Didn't think so."

I don't know if I'm madder at the way he's calling me out for being a prude right now, or the fact that he just came in here like he owned the place and completely took charge of the entire room.

I fold my arms across my chest, hating that I'm suddenly feeling like an outsider in my own dorm.

He lights a joint, takes a puff, and passes it to Kit who happily tokes away.

He lights the next one and presses it between Landon's lips. "Take in as much as you can handle."

The end of the joint lights for a few moments before Landon brings his fist to his mouth and lets out a cough. "Damn, that's pretty strong."

"It's marvelous," Kit sighs, taking another puff off her joint.

Before I can stop myself, I find myself whispering, "I want some."

Kit bounces on the bed and Landon coughs again. "You sure?" He looks at Asher. "Don't let him pressure you."

"He's not." I walk over to where Asher is sitting and hold out my hand. "Give me."

Asher's thick arm stretches around my waist, pulling me closer and he bites his lip. "Not until you open your mouth for me."

I swallow thickly. The way he's looking at me right now has me feeling higher than a kite and I haven't even smoked anything yet.

I try to back away, but his hand finds my hip.

"Relax, I'm giving you a shotgun. All you have to do is suck it."

I don't miss the slight smirk on his face when he says that, and I watch in equal parts confusion and curiosity as he sticks the lit end in his mouth and places it between his teeth before motioning for me to lean in.

I lower my head, ghosting over his lips. The hand around my

hip tightens ever so slightly as I proceed to inhale and fill my lungs with as much as I can of it. It burns a little but not nearly as much as I thought it would.

When he takes the joint out of his mouth, I clear my throat. "Can I have another?" When his eyes go smoky I quickly say, "Not a shotgun."

He licks his lips and holds the joint out for me. "Go slow."

I inhale it, only this time, it burns way more than the first time and I start choking.

The hand on my hip finds the sliver of skin that's exposed on the small of my back and I gasp when his thumb grazes it, which only makes me cough again.

Out of the corner of my eye Landon comes into focus and I all but jump away from Asher. I'm not sure why I do, but I don't like this strange feeling coming over me. It's weird being close to Asher when Landon's in the same room. It just doesn't feel right...especially given that I have absolutely no desire to be with Asher ever again.

Landon's expression is stoic and unreadable as he presses a few buttons on his phone and *Sublime's -Smoke Two Joints* starts to play.

I quickly take a seat on the floor next to him and Kit laughs. "Damn, I haven't listened to this song since High School."

"It's a classic," Landon says with a smile. "But yeah, I used to listen to it and play it all the time back then."

"I hated High School," I grumble and hurt flashes in Asher's eyes before he looks at me and says, "I loved it."

My stomach knots and I force down painful memories.

"High school was hit or miss for me," Kit says woefully, tucking a hand behind her head. "Some days the teenage angst was unbearable." A slow grin spreads across her face. "But other days were awesome. Like the time I felt up Jackie Lawrence in my grandmother's pool house." Kit takes another puff. "Or rather, it *was* awesome...until my grandmother walked in right when I had her nipple in my mouth."

Landon spits out his drink and Asher laughs. "Talk about ruining the moment."

"Oh, Dude, you have no idea." She holds her hands out in front of her chest. "Girl had a rack for days and nipples like dinner plates. It was fucking heaven." Both guys nod in understanding and she cringes. "My grandmother is such a bitch. Can't wait until she kicks the bucket and I don't have to pretend to be straight anymore."

"Wait a minute," Landon says. "She doesn't know you're a lesbian?"

"Oh, she knows," I say, my irritation growing. "But Nanna Bishop is convinced that she can—" I hold up my fingers and make air quotes. "'Fix' Kit and won't pay for college or give her any of the family money unless Kit goes out on a date with a guy of her choosing once a month." I shake my head in disgust. "It's such bullshit."

"Damn," Asher says. "That sucks."

"Yeah," Kit whispers. "I mean, it's not like I do anything with them. Usually we just grab fast food and talk. Heck, I even took Becca with me on a few of them." She closes her eyes at the mention of Becca's name. "I was gonna give it all up for her."

When the guys give me a weird look I say, "It goes without saying that if Kit married a girl, she'd be cut off from her family's money."

Asher sits up in his seat. "Did Becca know that? Because that chick is a gold-digger if there ever was one."

Kit swings her legs over the bed. "I assumed she did, given she was cool with the dates I had to go on. But what makes you so sure she's a gold-digger?"

"My parents." When she gives him a look he adds, "It's no secret in my family that my mom married my dad for his money. I knew I'd never follow in the same footsteps because I'd marry for love, but I was always scared Preston would." He looks at Kit. "I know it hurts, but you're both better off without her. You dodged a bullet. Save your love for the person who deserves it."

Something in my chest shifts with his words. I never in a million years thought I'd be hearing the guy who broke *my* heart giving dating advice to my best friend. I look down and take a breath when Landon reaches for my hand, almost like he knows what I'm thinking.

Kit takes another sip of her drink. "It's gonna take a long time to get over her. I really thought she was the one." She puts her cup down. "Can't lie, though. I kind of want to kick her ass."

"You don't have to," Landon says, taking a sip of his drink. "Breslin already took care of that for you."

Kit's mouth drops open. "What? When?"

"When I left for Art class."

She picks up her glass again. "I can't believe you did that for me, *Sugar Rae*."

"Nah, it was more like Muhammad," Asher chimes in. "She had this shuffle thing going on with her feet."

"Well, she is kind of scrappy," Kit says before looking at me. "Good Lord, Breslin."

"What? She hurt you." I look down at my fingers which are entwined with Landon's. "Bitch deserved it."

Kit opens her mouth to say something but her phone goes off and her face pales. "Breslin how bad did you hurt her?"

What a weird question. "I don't know. I'm pretty sure she might have a broken nose."

Asher lifts a shoulder. "I broke it up before she could do too much damage."

Kit tosses her phone on the bed and clutches her pillow, tears streaming down her face again. "That's good." She looks at Asher. "Because she's pregnant."

I watch in disbelief as Landon—my sweet, adorable, *responsible* Landon wobbles in a drunken stupor before Asher and I haul him onto my bed.

Neither Asher nor I wanted to get carried away tonight given that I have a job interview at the coffeehouse I used to work at and Asher has practice in the morning. Which meant Landon took one for the team and went shot for shot with a now passed out Kit.

Asher reaches around in Landon's pockets and pulls out his meter and insulin. "Given all the alcohol he's consumed tonight, make sure you pay careful attention."

I snatch them out of his hand. "Yeah, I know. Not for nothing, but *I* dated him long before you were in the picture."

Landon reaches up, gripping both our hands. "Please no fighting." He kisses my hand and then Asher's. "I love you both so much."

Before any of us can say a word, he closes his eyes.

Asher grabs the back of his neck. "Looks like the weed made him a hippie."

I try to stop the smile from hitting my lips, but Asher notices. "Good to know I can still get one of those."

Put your guard up—I remind myself as I start tossing various bottles and garbage in a plastic bag.

When Asher starts to help, I stop him. "I've got this."

He throws a few cups in the trash. "Yeah, but you shouldn't walk outside to the dumpster by yourself." He looks out the window. "It's late, something bad could happen."

Like letting the guy who smashed my heart to smithereens inside of it again?

"Fine," I agree, moving toward the door.

He takes the garbage from me and I swear on all that is holy that I feel sparks fly like the Fourth of July when his hand brushes mine.

An awkward silence thickens the air as we make our way down the stairs and out to the dumpsters.

I stuff my hands in my sweatshirt, fighting a chill that I'm not sure is due to the weather or the fact that I'm standing next to Asher.

"Wasn't aware you turned into a pothead," I say suddenly, hating myself for being so concerned.

His teeth dig into his lower lip and he looks embarrassed. "I don't smoke all the time." He lifts one massive shoulder. "I've been having some issues with anxiety and it helps with that."

Something close to guilt for being so judgmental prickles my belly with those words and I inhale slowly.

I can feel his eyes on me right before he asks, "What made you choose Woodside?"

When I open my mouth he quickly says, "Aside from the obvious fact that I won't bring up. It's just...Falcon had an amazing Art program."

"Woodside has a really good Architecture program." I play with the strings on my sweatshirt. "Being an artist isn't exactly a stable career path, Asher."

No matter how much I may love it.

"You've gotten even better," he whispers and I glare at him. "You looked at my portrait."

"We're partners, Breslin."

There's a meaning behind those words that I don't want to touch, so I just nod softly, not wanting to ruin this unspoken agreement of ours not to argue momentarily. "Thanks."

He opens the top to the dumpster and tosses the garbage bag inside. "I think you'd be depriving the world of your talent if you didn't pursue it." He holds up his hands. "But that's just my two cents."

"What about football?"

When he raises an eyebrow in question I add, "Are you still headed for the NFL like you planned?"

He shakes his head. "No. That's not really in my future anymore now that I'm at Woodside." He closes his eyes briefly and my heart pangs.

"I'm sorry," I say, my chest aching for him because I know how much he wanted to play in the NFL. "You never know, though. They could still draft you."

He gives me a strange look and opens his mouth but then closes it and shrugs. "Maybe. But I'm not exactly a star on the field anymore."

"Why? I mean, football was your passion. What you lived and breathed for. What changed?"

He gives me a look that I feel all the way down to my marrow. "It's complicated, Breslin." He scrubs a hand down his face and sighs. "My team hates me. There was a guy named O'Connor, who's now expelled, but he caused some shit before he left. And now no one on the team listens to me or respects me. I know I'm partly at fault because I've been distracted lately, but they're no help. I make a play and they ignore me and do the opposite. Then they laugh behind my back because they know the coach comes down on me. Not to mention, we all know it's a bullshit team that's destined for failure anyway so no one bothers putting in the effort. Everyone's attitude sucks."

"Including yours," I mutter. "Try earning their respect by believing in them, Asher. You're the leader of the team, the one they turn to. Why should they believe in themselves let alone the team when you don't?" I glower at him. "Once you've earned their respect, give them a taste of what it's like to win out on that field and they'll start craving it. It's human nature."

His brows knit together. "You're right." He looks at me and I fight back a shiver because in typical Asher Holden fashion— he's looking at me like I'm all he can see.

"I needed to hear that. Thank you." he says as he holds open the door and I slip past him.

I stay silent as we walk up the stairs and back up to our dorms, fighting like hell to evade the pull of chemistry that surrounds us like a live wire. Because even though I have every reason to hate him...it's only grown stronger.

When my hand lands on the doorknob and I mumble a curt goodbye in his direction, he leans down and kisses my cheek.

I make the horrible mistake of turning my head, and that's when fire meets gasoline, the spark between us ignites...

And all hell breaks loose.

Blood rushes in my ears when his hands land on my waist and he spins me around, pressing me against the door.

"Breslin." The gravel and desperation in his voice is as thick as the emotion behind it.

I open my mouth and he takes the opportunity to press his lips to mine until we're breathing the same charged air that crackles between us.

Thump, Thump, thump goes my stupid heart and I have to grab on to him to stop myself from falling.

When his tongue darts out to lick mine and he groans, I become so lightheaded I have to close my eyes.

"Asher," I whisper against his lips, silently pleading with him not to do this, because I won't be able to resist him.

"Okay." He slowly backs away, his expression intent. "But I'm not going to stop trying, Breslin. No matter how much you hate me."

The organ in my chest kick starts and I despise that for one brief moment...I want him to make good on his promise. I want him to hold me and never let me go again.

But if he does that? There's only one way it will end.

In a catastrophe that can't ever be fixed.

I brace myself against the door and glare at him. "You know...it would be harder to hate you if you weren't here."

And then before he has a chance to stop me again, I throw open my door and run inside, safely locking it behind me.

A fter checking on Kit, I walk over to my bed that Landon's currently sleeping on and curl myself around him.

Despite the fact that he smells like a brewery and a Snoop Dogg concert, I breathe him in.

"You okay?" he whispers, his face twisted in concern. He turns to me and runs his hands through my hair as he waits for my answer.

"No." My voice cracks right before the tears give way.

He pulls me until I'm resting right over his heart. "I'm here. I'm right here, Breslin."

"I know you are." I kiss the spot above his heart and his arms tighten around me, steadying me, easing away the pain in a way that only he can.

By being the rock that he is. The rock he's always been but I was too blind to see.

"I love you, Landon," I whisper before I close my eyes.

And although it's not the first time I've said it...it's the first time I've truly felt it.

Something in my heart both cracks and mends with the realization.

The realization that you can love two people at the same time.

But you can only choose one to live for.

CHAPTER 16

LANDON

"My head," Kit whines from the other bed and I nod in agreement.

Breslin steps out of the bathroom and tosses a bottle of Tylenol to her. "Take some of these."

I catch sight of her and suck in a breath. She's always so damn beautiful, but the dress she has on fits her like a glove and her hair is done up in a way that exposes the long line of her neck, which has me longing to sweep my mouth across it.

"You look nice." I shake my head. "Actually, that's wrong. You look stunning."

She blushes and reaches for her purse. "Thanks. I have a job interview at the coffee shop today."

"The one we worked at before we left for Europe?" Kit asks in confusion.

Breslin nods, looking mildly annoyed. "Yup. When I spoke to Larry, he said my position was filled but that if I came in and interviewed again he'd see what he could do."

"That bastard," Kit grunts and Breslin rolls her eyes.

"I left for Europe with two days' notice, Kit. He has every right to not hire me back."

"Us," Kit says, determination in her eyes.

Breslin's eyes open wide. "Oh, no." When Kit frowns she groans, "Come on, Kit, you hated that job."

I stifle a laugh. God knows Kit isn't exactly employee of the year and usually was more of a hassle to work with than a blessing. I don't blame Breslin for trying to talk her out of it.

Kit stands up and opens a drawer. "Well, I need something to do now that I have all this free time."

Breslin shoves a t-shirt and jeans into her bag. "He's probably going to want me to start today."

"Us," Kit corrects.

Breslin rubs her temples. "I'm leaving in five minutes."

Kit runs into the bathroom like a bolt of lightning and we hear the faucet turn on a moment later.

I throw the covers off me, get up off the bed, and stretch. "Why don't you just tell her that you hate working with her?"

She looks down. "I would, but after what Becca did to her I don't have the heart to."

Yeah, I guess she has a point.

I walk over to her and grasp her jaw in my hand. "Kit aside, how are you feeling?" She tries to look away but I don't let her.

"Better," she finally says.

I drop a kiss to her forehead. "What time do you think you'll get off?"

My palms start to sweat and my heart rate speeds up. For a moment, I reconsider what I'm doing—but after last night...I know I can't.

This is the only way to fix everything. I know it. *I feel it.*

"Provided I manage to get my job back? Not too late. Around 8:00 or so." She looks at me skeptically. "Why?"

There's no going back now. "Come by my apartment later tonight." I inhale a breath. "So we can talk."

"Okay." Her voice shakes and I plant a kiss in the crook of her neck. "Trust me, it's—"

"Damn, Landon. I had no idea you had so many tattoos. That's some nice ink work," Kit says, giving me a once over.

"Thanks. I know a guy downtown. I can introduce you if you want. I actually plan on getting more work done soon."

Kit's eyes gleam but Breslin points to the door. "Come on, Kit. Before we spend all day at a tattoo parlor instead of being responsible adults." She looks at me. "Lock up before you leave?"

When I give her a nod, she smiles. "I'll see you later."

I return her smile and get dressed. I let out a laugh when I hear Kit talk about getting *'Becca is a stupid whore'* tattooed across her back and Breslin trying to talk her out of it before she closes the door behind her.

A few minutes later, I walk out and come face to face with a very worried looking Asher who's typing away furiously on his phone.

I walk over to him, thankful the hallways are empty and that no one saw me slip out of Breslin's dorm. "What's wrong?"

"Preston still hasn't called me back." He blows out a breath. "I figured he'd get back to me after practice, but no dice." He visibly swallows. "He's on a bender. I know he is."

"Not to come off like a jerk, but he's 19. He's not even old enough to gamble at most casinos. How bad of a bender can it be?"

"You'd be surprised," Asher mutters. "All he has to do is drop our father's name and people's eyes light up with dollar signs and they let him in."

"Shit."

He slides his phone back in his pocket. "I have to go look for him, before my father looks at his accounts and goes fucking ballistic." He starts to walk away but I grab his arm. "You don't have a car. Let me go with you."

"Don't you have better things to do with your time than help me fix my shit?"

I take a step forward and slip my hand around his neck, pulling him close, because just like Breslin needs to understand; so does he.

"How many times do I have to tell you that you're not alone, Asher? I'm here."

CHAPTER 17

ASHER

Landon shifts his car into drive and we peel out of the parking lot. "Where should we start?"

"I don't know," I tell him, my anxiety coming to a peak. "There are some big games happening tonight, but none this early. He has to be at a casino of some kind." I look out the window. "Problem is —I'm not really familiar with this area so I don't know any."

Landon types something into his GPS. "There's a 24-hour one a few towns over."

"Let's start there," I say and Landon reaches over the console for my hand.

I entangle our fingers together and fight thoughts of Breslin— because this was always our thing.

But she doesn't want me anymore. She won't even give me a chance to try and fix my mistakes.

My heart burns and I squeeze Landon's hand harder...because for the first time in a long time, I'm thinking that I might be worthy of happiness again, despite my monumental fuck-ups. *He* makes me believe that I am.

Landon's brown eyes find mine and he raises my hand to his lips. "We'll find him."

I muster a smile and the weight in my chest loosens. Because Landon Parker has a way of making everything better. Connecting with him has proven to be more than what I could have ever bargained for.

And more than what I deserve.

He's my second chance at something I never thought I would find again...if only the guilt surrounding my heart would let me take it.

Because she deserves him more than I ever will.

But there's not enough of him to go around...because good things like him are few and far between.

Which means there's only one solution at my disposal.

Bile rises in my throat because I don't want to give him up. I want to be selfish and keep him—just as much as I want my Breslin back.

"Did you get a chance to talk to Dragoni today?" Landon questions, interrupting my thoughts.

"Yeah," I say. "Turns out he doesn't really care about his niece getting into a fight. He's more concerned about the upcoming game."

Landon's other hand grips the steering wheel. "I guess that's a good thing."

"Sort of." I rub the knot forming in my neck. "But me bringing up Breslin made her a target, so there's that."

"Fuck," Landon mutters. "I hate this."

"Me too."

Rage simmers in my gut. I've never hated my brother and I still don't, but I'm so fucking mad at him I want to break something, preferably his face.

We pull up to the casino and I say a silent prayer that he's here, because as far as casinos go—this one is lacking. Which means there's a chance that Preston didn't go overboard and they'll be more likely to cooperate.

Preston's tried to explain his gambling issue in the past, but it's never really made any sense to me. The only thing I can compare it to is the high I get from winning a game.

That's the way Preston feels when he rolls the dice and wins. He said it's contagious. Like he's on top of the world and can do no wrong and every problem he has falls by the wayside when he's winning.

But when I find him slumped over a blackjack table with a large pile of chips in front of him, a stale beer in his hand, and a disgruntled dealer, I can't help but wonder how he doesn't see what a huge problem this is, because this isn't winning. Not even close.

I guess that's why they call it an addiction, though. Not all of them result in a needle sticking out of your arm in the back of an alley.

Sometimes it's the functioning and socially acceptable addictions like the one he has that are more dangerous. And sooner or later...it's all going to come to a head.

When I walk over to him with Landon in tow, he ignores me. Which only makes me angrier.

I haul his sorry ass up off the stool and slam him against the table. "I've been calling you since last night, asshole."

Security guards rush over to us but I pay them no mind.

"She's pregnant," Preston says, looking more frightened than I've ever seen him. "And it's mine."

My stomach drops to the floor, because that right there is what I've been secretly fearing ever since Kit dropped the bomb.

"Okay, one problem at a time." I look around. "First, how much of Dad's money did you blow in the last 24-hours?"

He snickers. "Come on now, brother. You already know the answer to that." He taps his temple. "You know I don't lose."

Just as I suspected. He counted cards and took them to the

cleaners. I breathe a sigh of relief because that makes this problem an easy one to handle.

"Did you swipe Dad's card here, though?"

"Yeah, I didn't have any money on me so I had to."

I look at Landon. "Don't let him out of your sight." When Landon gives me a questioning look I say, "I'm going to go talk to the owner."

I sweep the large pile of chips into a bag and look at the security guards. "I'm sure they'll have no problem getting their money back considering they let him in *illegally* in the first place."

One of the security guards shakes his head and leads me to an employee's only room.

Twenty minutes later, the charges on my father's card are reversed and I say another prayer that he doesn't look at his bank statements this month and rip into him.

I give Preston's arm a squeeze and we head out of the casino.

When Preston starts walking past the car, I grab his shirt. "Where do you think you're going?"

He shoves me. "You're not my keeper, Asher."

"No, but I am your brother. A brother who just saved your sorry ass...*again*."

"Yeah, well, I didn't fucking ask you to this time, now did I?" His voice cracks with emotion and he grips his hair. "Besides you can't save me from this mess." His eyes become glassy and he kicks a rock across the parking lot. "I'm not ready to have a fucking kid. I'm not even 20 yet."

I look at Landon and he tips his chin at me before he gets inside his car, giving us a few minutes alone to talk.

"I know." I take a step forward and wrap him up in a hug. He's scared out of his mind and I can't say that I blame him. Hell, I'm scared for him.

"We just moved in together and she hits me with this," he whispers. "Dad's gonna fucking kill me."

"You know I won't let that happen."

He shakes his head. "I told you, you can't save me from this." He all but chokes back a sob. "Becca's already talking about me going to the next doctor's appointment with her and getting married in the next few months."

Of course, she is. "Look, I'm not trying to lay into you right now, but why the hell didn't you use a rubber?"

His eyebrows pinch together. "I did. Every fucking time. I guess I fell into the two-percent." He laughs sardonically. "The one time the odds weren't in my favor."

"She could be lying." I stop and look him in the eyes. "Hell, she probably *is* lying, Preston. You've already caught her cheating on you."

"I know," he says. "But when I brought up doing a DNA test in the next few weeks, she legit flipped the hell out. She said she wasn't in her second trimester yet and that I was a horrible father for even suggesting such a thing because the test is dangerous to the baby." His eyes become glassy again. "I'm already royally fucking this whole fatherhood thing up."

Anger coils my insides and I find myself wishing Becca was a dude so I could beat the living snot out of her. I seriously regret stopping Breslin from kicking her ass now.

"Nah, man," I say. "Don't let her fuck up your head and guilt you. You have every right to a paternity test. Especially if she's demanding you marry her before the baby is born." I grip his collar, forcing him to look at me. "And if the baby is yours? You will make a good father, I know you will. And I'll be there for you every step of the way."

He throws his arms around me. "Thank you."

"You don't need to thank me. I'm your brother, asshole."

He pulls away and looks up at the sky. "I don't know how I'm gonna tell Dad about this. He was fine when I told him that we moved in together...but marriage and a baby? You know how he is.

He'll probably make me leave Yale and work for him as a punishment for fucking my life up."

I grimace, because I wouldn't put it past him. "I'll go with you, if you want." Irritation surges in my chest. "A word of advice, though? Wait a few months and get the paternity test done first. No use marrying the girl and riling Dad up if it's not even yours in the first place."

"What about Becca? She's relentless."

I want to tell him to leave the bitch and refuse to see or speak to her until the test results are in his hand, but if by some horrible chance the baby does turn out to be his? Becca seems like the type of person to use that against him. She'd tell their future kid all about how Daddy never wanted it, just to hurt Preston and cause his child to grow up hating him.

Therefore, the only thing I can do is give him the best brotherly advice I can think of.

"Go with her to her doctor's appointments," I tell him. "Make sure she eats and takes her vitamins. That's really all you can do until you know for sure. This way, you know you did everything that you could. Not for her...but for your child, and have no regrets."

"She's gonna want to start planning a wedding."

I shrug. "So, let her. No one says you have to be part of it."

He looks down at the ground. "How's that girl doing by the way?"

"Kit?"

His face turns serious. "Yeah, she looked pretty devastated."

"She is," I say, gesturing to the car. "But I think in time she'll be okay. It's just going to hurt for a long while. Just like you, she was hit with not one, but two bombs hours apart from each other."

"I had no idea Becca was seeing someone else, let alone a chick."

"Sometimes people do shitty things and keep things from people that they shouldn't, brother."

I slide into the passenger seat and reach for Landon's hand again.

"Speaking of which," Preston says. "I'm glad you two found each other, given Breslin goes to Woodside there's no doubt she's bound to hurt you again if you let her."

My hand tightens around Landon's and we ride in silence the rest of the way home.

CHAPTER 18

BRESLIN

I pull in the parking lot of the dorms after my shift ends and look over at Kit.

Aside from Larry hiring us both back at the coffee shop today, she hasn't really said much. Which considering the events of yesterday, is understandable.

"I'm canceling with Landon tonight," I tell her but she shakes her head.

"Don't, I'm fine."

When I give her a look, she sighs. "Okay, I'm not fine." She toys with a loose string on her jeans. "But I just want to be alone tonight. Maybe go for a drive and clear my head."

"Kit—"

"So, Landon's huh?" she questions and I know it's her attempt at changing the subject.

"Yeah. But only if you—"

She cuts me off. "I think you should go." She turns to face me. "But I have to ask—what the hell is going on with you two? Or should I say *three*?"

I smooth out my shirt and shift uncomfortably because I have no idea how to answer that. Actually, I do. "There's no three. Just two." I look away. "Just me and Landon," I clarify.

She gives me a pointed look. A pointed look that only a best friend who knows you're full of shit can give. "Could have fooled me last night. Because I would have sworn you and Asher were flirting...or something close to it."

"What are you talking about? I sat next to Landon the whole night." I wave a hand, hating the way my heart is suddenly pounding. "Besides you were drunk. What do you know?"

"Not too drunk to notice you left with him," she mutters under her breath.

I stay silent...because she's got my number.

She reaches for her purse, sadness crossing over her features again. "Remember all those times when I told you to get over Asher?"

I give her a soft nod and she opens the door. "Well, I get it now. There really are some things that you just never get over. I'm sorry I wasn't more understanding before."

With that, she slams my car door and gets into her own.

My heart pangs as I step out of the car, because this is not how I ever would have wanted Kit to understand what I was going through.

Hiking my bag up my shoulder I start walking toward the dorms. Only to pause when I catch sight of a sweaty, jogging Asher whizzing by.

A *shirtless* jogging Asher.

For a moment, I'm grateful he has a pair of headphones on and hasn't noticed me, because I'm certain I resemble a tomato.

I back up so I'm hidden behind a large bush, choosing to ignore how creepy that makes me.

His body...holy hell. His body is even better than what I remember it being in high school.

He's bulked up a little, filled out in places I wasn't aware a person could fill out.

Sweat trickles down his abs—the kind of abs that would put a fitness model to shame—and I follow the fluid as it slowly drizzles down, down, *down* to that mouthwatering and *very* indented 'V' of his lower abs— thanks to the sweatpants that are slung almost dangerously low on his hips.

I force my eyes back up to his face, because there's a war brewing in my own body and I'm afraid of the outcome.

However, looking at his face is just as devastating of a blow to my system.

Not only because he's sinfully good looking...but because those beautiful blue eyes of his...hold a sadness in them that didn't exist before.

And my chest shreds at the thought of what might have put it there.

"The last thing he needs is you fucking up his life all over again when he's trying to put it back together."

Preston's words from the other day nearly root me to the spot. I have no clue what he meant by that and I still don't, considering it was the other way around and Asher was the one who fucked up *my* life.

But there's only one way to find out.

I stare at Kit's laptop, debating if I should do this. Besides the fact that there's no guarantee searching his name will prove to be eventful in the first place, it's something I've intentionally avoided doing for years.

I check my watch, purposely stalling for time. Time that I have plenty of since I'm not due to meet Landon at his apartment for another 40 minutes.

Pulling up Google and typing his name in the search bar feels like the equivalent of Pandora's box and my hands shake.

How bad could it be?

My breath catches in my throat and I close my eyes and shake my head, certain what's right in front of me can't be real.

There are websites. All sorts of websites linked to videos.

Videos with names like: Hot football player gets sucked off by another guy.

And: Football prodigy Asher Holden is gay. Watch the video below.

There's a sharp ache in my heart and a whirlwind of emotions zipping through my head as I hover over the play button. Before I can talk myself out of it, I press play and...

My. Heart. Stops.

Because *Kyle* is the man pleasuring him...and pleasuring him he is because there's no mistaking the deep groan erupting from Asher—a groan I've only heard once in my life.

And there's certainly no mistaking the hand on Kyle's head holding him in place as he *swallows* him.

For a moment, I feel a bolt of sadness due to this being all over the internet...but then my eyes drift to the picture on the nightstand by his bed.

The picture of us. Smiling as we hold on to one another like we're the only two people who exist in the world.

Asher looks so happy and I look so...

Naïve...because I was hopelessly in love with the boy in the picture.

The video lasts all of five seconds before it loops to the beginning again and I click out of the browser, my stomach in knots and tears brimming my eyes.

I knew he cheated on me. He confirmed it that night. The night he took my innocence and turned me into what I am now. Jaded. Angry. *Ruined.*

But seeing the actual, undeniable proof? Nothing could have prepared me for that blow.

I slam the top to the laptop down and grab my keys and purse. I refuse to let him ruin any more good things in my life.

And Landon Parker...is the *best* thing. And if he's asked me to come over tonight because he's made his final choice?

I'm going to make damn sure it's me.

CHAPTER 19

LANDON

I'm not a cheater.

I'm not the kind of man who will keep stringing two people along.

I'm not the kind of person who adds to a problem. I prefer to be the solution. The one who fixes things.

I pause mid-song, my stomach rumbling with nerves. I wipe my sweaty hands on my jeans before I stroke the piano keys again.

I love them. This is the only way.

The only way I don't lose both of them.

Frustration and fear crawl up my spine and I slam down on the keys. *Because this may just very well be the way that I do lose them.*

And once it's out there...once I tell them what I want, or rather, what I think we should all do, there's no taking it back.

After I finish playing, I push away from the piano, preparing myself for what I have to do in the next few minutes.

And that's when gorgeous green eyes meet mine. "You finished the song?"

Breslin takes a step closer to me and I drink her in from head to toe, my heart beating a mile a minute, just like it always does whenever she enters a room. "When I left for Europe it was only half done but now—" She visibly gulps and I'd give all the pennies in the world for her thoughts right now...because the look on her face tells me she not only heard but understood every lyric of the song I wrote about her and Asher.

"What's it called?" Her voice is barely above a whisper.

"Complicated Hearts."

She expels a breath through those pouty lips of hers and right when she's about to say something...there's a knock on the door.

A wrinkle forms between her brows. "Were you expecting someone else tonight?"

There's a sharp tone to her voice that makes it less of a question and more of an accusation.

I grab her hand in mine. "I love you, Breslin. I swear to God I do. Please hear me out."

She wants to protest, I know she does. Breslin's as stubborn and head strong as the day is long. It's both frustrating and commendable.

When I drop her hand and start walking to the front door, her footsteps follow behind me.

I suck in a breath before I open the door with clammy hands and come face to face with Asher.

CHAPTER 20
BRESLIN

I cross my legs and pivot away from the jerk sitting next to me on the couch.

Landon paces the living room again, going on and on about how much he loves us both and how he's come to this big solution...but I barely hear a word of it because I'm still so riled up about watching that video earlier.

It physically hurts to be in the same room with him, but I refuse to let him see it.

Landon stops moving suddenly, facing us both head on. He looks so nervous right now...which is saying something considering he can sing and play music in a room packed full of people without so much as batting an eye.

He touches his pointer fingers to his lips, appearing to be choosing his next words very carefully.

His eyes find mine first. "The other day I had sex with you."

I blink. This conversation, or rather, this long-winded *confession* is getting stranger by the second. I thought he invited me here because he made a decision.

Instead he's spinning me round and round in circles.

He turns to Asher next. "And then I had sex with you."

I blink again, rapidly this time...and then an inferno slides up my esophagus as I take in his words.

Asher's eyes turn hard and he grips his knee, appearing to be just as angry as I am. "Is there a *point* to this shit, Landon?"

The low rumble in his voice reverberates through me and I hate it.

Landon's gaze turns inward. "Yeah. My point is that I don't want to keep having sex with the both of you unless you're aware of it."

My body goes rigid, automatically bracing itself for something my brain doesn't quite understand.

Landon's always been great at expressing himself. Clear cut and honest. It's a quality I appreciate.

But now?

Everything out of his mouth is muddled. Like he's trying to trek through quicksand without being sucked under.

"You're not making any sense, Landon," Asher says and despite myself, I nod.

"We can't go on not talking about it," Landon says, his voice filled with frustration. "Just like I can't keep sneaking around and sleeping with the both of you behind your backs."

There's something to be said for having an elephant in the room. The keeper of secrets that shouldn't come to the surface. I for one, rather like that damn elephant.

Of course, we all skirted around the issue looming between us like a big, fat, neon sign last night. But it was...I don't know...bearable?

However, right now? Not so much. I can feel my chest constricting with every beat of my heart as I wait for him to continue because the silence in the room is damn near deafening at this point.

Finally, Landon opens his mouth again. "I think we should all sleep together." He sucks in air and drops his head. "Be together."

He lifts his eyes until they're back on us. "The thought of you two together kills me. But the thought of not being with either of you kills me more. I know in my soul this is the right solution. This thing between us isn't going to go away...the only way to deal with it is to confront it and face it head on."

I don't know which plummets faster. My jaw or my heart. He can't actually be serious. "You can't—"

"It's not the worst idea," Asher whispers, his brows drawn together in deep concentration.

That inferno clawing its way up my esophagus erupts and I stand up.

I recall his words from last night, telling me he wouldn't stop trying and I lose it. There's no doubt in my mind that somehow *he's* the one responsible for the conversation taking place. Just like he's responsible for the weird as fuck situation we're in.

I run to the door, needing to escape, because although I love Landon; there's no way I can do what *Asher* wants.

My shattered pieces prevent me from being that strong.

Landon walks toward me, but I pause right before I step out and look at Asher. "You know, it wasn't enough that you lied to me and cheated on me. Now this?"

Asher's jaw tenses and he has the audacity to look offended. "You think this was all *my* idea? You think I intentionally planned to fall in love with your boyfriend after *you* broke his heart and left him?"

His words are the equivalent to a slap in the face. My stomach lurches and I swing open the door. I make a mad dash down the hallway...until a voice stops me.

"Wow, I'm impressed. Took you an entire five minutes to run this time, Breslin. That some kind of record for you?"

My breath seizes and my throat locks up. Just where does he get off?

Actually, I'm all too aware of where he *gets off* thanks to earlier.

I lift my chin and turn to face him.

And that's when Landon joins us out in the hallway.

Asher tilts his head in his direction. "Take it from me, man. The only way this conversation ends is with her leaving. She'll never accept you...she'll never accept *us*."

A combination of tension and anger rides down my neck and spreads throughout my limbs. Before I know what's happening— I'm charging toward him and jabbing a finger in his chest. "I didn't leave because I couldn't accept your sexuality. I left because I couldn't accept that you were a lying, cheating, asshole. Big difference."

I hardly recognize my own voice it's so sinister.

He steps in my direction and his intense gaze clashes with mine. I back up, my spine hitting the wall behind me. "If you would let me talk to you and explain—"

"There's nothing to explain," I cut in. I hate the way my voice cracks, but I refuse to back down. "Are you really going to stand there and tell me that Kyle didn't...that *you* didn't." I can't form the words, because my heart is breaking all over again. "Right on the bed that we used to lay in. Tell our secrets to one another in. Right next to our picture and—"

Landon comes toward me then, but I shake my head and look up at Asher. The dam I've tried so hard to contain finally breaks wide open. "Go on. Tell me it didn't happen. Tell me it was all just some nightmare. That you didn't take my virginity, tell me you were gay, *and* that you cheated on me with my enemy all in the span of a half-hour."

I move until I'm right in his face, giving him no choice but to hear everything I'm telling him. "Tell me you didn't smash my heart and my trust. Tell me you didn't break the girl who loved you so much that she worshiped whatever ground you walked on. The girl who believed in you. The girl who loved you more than she ever loved herself. The girl who gave you every ounce of that love...because it was the only thing of value that she ever had to offer another person."

I lean in, my eyes pinned to his. "Fucking tell me, Asher. I *dare* you."

A breath shudders out of him and he closes his eyes. "If I could go back in time, I would—"

Nausea barrels into me and I shove his chest. "But you can't. So don't."

He goes to cup my face but I swat him away as tears I don't recall shedding, fall down my face. "I won't go back there with you again. And if you ever fucking loved me...you wouldn't keep pulling me back there."

"Breslin—" He tries to touch me again but I turn away and look at Landon.

An ugly feeling churns my insides until it becomes a wave of anger and resolve. "One night."

Landon looks confused, which makes sense because I'm not even sure what it is that I'm saying or agreeing to.

All I know is that I want to get rid of this feeling I've been holding on to for the last three years. I want to conquer it.

But first— I want to hurt him and make him feel for one single night what's been simmering inside me for all these years.

And that thought...is what causes me to slip my t-shirt over my head and walk back inside.

CHAPTER 21
ASHER

I try to look at Landon but his gaze is focused on Breslin. It hasn't left her since the moment her shirt came off.

Not that I can blame him...I'm having a hard time concentrating myself.

If it weren't for the evil look directed at me as she presses a hand to Landon's chest and shoves him on the couch—I might have started counting my lucky stars.

But unfortunately for me? I know exactly what Breslin wants to do with this *one night*. She wants to rip my heart to pieces.

And after everything she said to me just moments before...I probably deserve it.

Her hands go to her jeans and she tugs them down her hips. I ignore the way my cock thickens as she stands there in nothing but her underwear now.

"We should have rules." I've never been one for rules before, but my heart is hanging by a thread here.

Breslin ignores me, and when she straddles Landon's lap, I toss a book across the room until it hits the nearest wall with a large thud.

I can't handle this shit. I can't watch him fuck her. And I most definitely can't watch her fuck him.

Finally, Landon turns his head to look at me. "He's right." His hands find Breslin's hips, halting her as she yanks down his zipper. "We need rules. This way we know not to cross any lines."

"But it's only for one night—" Breslin starts to say.

"Three," I interject. "There are three of us and each one of us deserve a *night*—" I intentionally emphasize that last word while glaring at her, because I know exactly what's going through her mind. I know her better than anyone. "To do everything that they want with the other two. No holds barred," I finish.

If Breslin wants to hate me and make me the bad guy...she's got one. And if she wants to start a war by fucking Landon in front of me right now? She better get that war paint of hers ready because I'm not going down without a fight.

One of those three nights are *mine*. And I will get everything I want out of it.

"Fine," she agrees.

She rubs her hand along Landon's groin and when she reaches inside his boxers, I clench my teeth so hard I swear a few crack.

She looks up at me and winks. "I'm calling dibs on tonight, obviously." She tugs Landon's ear with her teeth and smirks, as if to say, '*but I won't be needing you.*'

"One more rule," I grind out and Landon tilts his head to look at me.

"What?"

"We all get off before the night is over. No one gets left out."

The color drains from Breslin's face but Landon nods. "Yeah, agreed."

I give Breslin a smirk of my own. That's right, baby. Better prepare yourself.

She licks his bottom lip in response and my nostrils flare.

"Since we're adding rules to this," Landon says, gasping for air between kisses. "I have one." He moves away from her lips and points to his bed. "I want you *both* in my bed at the end of each night. No exceptions or excuses."

I nod and so does she. This is without a doubt the strangest conversation I've ever been a part of. But then again, there's no way for it to be anything but awkward—considering the fucked-up circumstances surrounding us.

Circumstances...like the way Breslin pulls Landon's cock out right before she kisses him with so much passion, a sharp pain infiltrates my chest.

She whispers something into his ear then, something I can't hear because I'm not part of what's going on.

Because Breslin wants to punish me.

And I have no choice but to take it.

He leans his forehead against hers and cups her cheek. "I'm here," he whispers right before he tips her chin and kisses her tenderly.

Blood rushes in my ears and red-hot anger pulses through my bones when she pulls her panties to the side, bares that sweet, little pussy of hers, and slowly sinks down on his dick.

The look she shoots me when he's filled her up to the hilt is so full of venom I rear back. Pure agony crushes my insides into nothing but powder as she begins to ride him right there on the couch.

"Fuck." Landon's gravelly voice pierces right through me. I feel so sick to my stomach, I damn near keel over and puke.

This isn't just payback...this is a hanging. A slaughtering.

A fucking assassination.

She's breaking me. He's breaking me. *They're breaking me.*

She speeds up her pace, like she's trying to fuck both me and the past out of her system. I turn to leave, because I can't take another second of it, but her eyes hold mine at that moment and I see the pain flash through all the wrath in them.

This is torture. The same kind of torture she's experienced for the last three years.

Because I lied to her. Because I did this to her. I did this to *us*.

And that right there is what causes me to stay.

When Landon yanks down her bra with a growl before he sucks her nipple into his mouth and groans her name around the soft pink flesh, my jaw tics.

It nearly snaps in half when she closes her eyes, tosses her head back, and starts bouncing up and down his dick with such fervor, my own balls ache.

"Jesus fucking Christ, Breslin," Landon roars with a giant shudder and for the first time in my life, I wish he wasn't so responsive and vocal in the sack.

He lets out a slew of curses as she rides him to the finish line—but it's the orgasm coursing through her that steals my breath.

I know those moans and gasps falling from those gorgeous lips of hers...because they once belonged to me and me only.

She once belonged to me and me only.

But the fact that she's sighing *Landon's* name as she climaxes and falls against him...tells me she'll never be only mine again.

Neither will he.

The three of us are tied together in a way that all of us hate...but none of us can evade.

When they disentangle themselves, I have one of two choices. One—I could leave with both my dick and tail tucked between my legs.

Or two—I can man the fuck up and show Breslin who I really am.

Because the fact of the matter is...I've got nothing left to lose anymore.

But maybe...just maybe, I'll have something to gain after all the painful dust settles around us.

I walk over to where they are, intentionally disturbing their little post-coital cuddle and grab Landon's jaw until his head falls backward and he's looking at me.

"It's my turn," I say, before I press my lips to his.

Breslin Rae wanted to start a war—well, she's fucking got one.

Only this is a war that I have every intention of winning.

CHAPTER 22

BRESLIN

W hen one starts a war...they should be prepared for the counterattack.

But nothing could have ever prepared me for the brick that forms in my chest when Asher kisses Landon.

Or the lead that fills my stomach when Landon gets off the couch and follows him.

While I have no choice but to situate myself...and watch.

When they finally dislodge themselves, Landon looks back at me.

I wipe away the tears streaming down my cheeks, hating that I'm so emotional, but I can't help myself. This is the very definition of heartache.

Landon looks between the both of us before his gaze settles on Asher. "I can't do this while she's in tears."

My heart squeezes in my chest and pain ripples through me, despite the fact that I was the one who cast the first stone and set this train wreck of a night in motion.

But it's the sorrow and pity in Asher's eyes when he looks my way that sends another flood of resolve through my system.

I don't need or want his pity. I'm stronger than the girl I was. I can handle his retaliation.

I take a heavy breath and let it out slowly. And then I look at them and say the words that will change everything between us forever. "Wrap your lips around his cock and show us both how much you want him."

Because I need to see it with my own eyes.

I need to see the nightmare that infiltrates my brain every night before I go to sleep in the flesh.

I need the green-eyed monster under my bed to be dragged out in the open.

I want to see what Asher needs that I couldn't give him. Why I wasn't good enough for him.

Why he didn't love me the way I loved him.

I need to see all of him. The real him.

And I need to see what makes it impossible for Landon to choose me and only me now.

Landon hesitates, the concern in his eyes is poignant and palpable, but I silently urge him on. And then I steel every muscle in my body as he turns his back to me and gets down on his knees before Asher.

My chest heaves and my insides twist excruciatingly as I watch him undo Asher's pants, take out his cock, and gently stroke him.

My heart slams against my chest and another tear falls down my cheek...it mirrors the one that slips out the corner of Asher's eye.

My insides begin to tremble and Asher's body begins to shake. Emotions are swirling in the air like tangible particles around us.

"I don't think," he starts to say, looking at me and my tears fall faster, because it hurts so fucking much.

But it needs to happen.

I want to tell them to continue, but I'm unable to form words due to the boulder lodging in my throat.

Asher looks down and Landon squeezes his hand. There's this moment between them that takes my breath. A moment without words, but one that's so palpable the tiny hairs on my body stand on end.

Slowly Asher's tremors subside and he brushes Landon's cheek. Then he closes his eyes and Landon's head begins to move.

It's so tender between them, the ache in my chest dissipates and my tears vanish as I continue watching them together.

An electric buzz goes through me and my mouth opens with a gasp of surprise when Asher's hand goes to the back of Landon's head and he lets out a soft groan. Landon's movements speed up in response and my breath catches for an entirely different reason then.

One —I'm no longer watching my ex-boyfriend's hook up. I'm watching two men who care and love one another in an intimate moment. And two—is something I didn't anticipate feeling. *Arousal.* The kind that gives me goosebumps. Because even I can't deny there's something so erotic and raw about what's happening.

I find myself even more grateful for Landon at that moment.

Because he's the only one who could do this. Make the worst...better. By giving us each what we needed to get through it.

He gave me my vengeance during my moment, let me use him and fuck him the way I needed to. And right now, he's giving Asher what he needs.

Understanding in a way I'll never quite be able to, because only Landon can.

Asher's chest rises and falls, his breathing is choppy and uneven as he grips Landon's hair tighter and he starts to spasm.

A quiver of desire starts low in my belly as I watch his Adam's apple bob and hear the husky sigh escaping from him as he comes undone inside Landon's mouth.

When his head falls back against the wall and his gaze slides to me, I hold my breath.

In spite of the fact that I have every right to hate him...I can't bring myself to look away. He commands every morsel of my attention.

But for once, it has nothing to do with the fact that physically speaking, he's the most gorgeous thing on this planet.

It's because for a single moment, I don't see the cheater and the liar.

I see *him*.

The boy I gave my heart to so long ago. The one who never gave it back.

I blink back another round of tears and the smokescreen lifts—allowing me to see the man that he is now in all his complicated glory.

The man that I'm no longer supposed to love...but the one I *always* will.

The organ inside my chest pulverizes with shame and I hate myself for letting him penetrate me again. I'm supposed to be stronger than this. I *want* to be stronger than this, but Asher Holden breaks through my defenses each and every time.

When Landon stands up and walks to the bathroom, I all but run after him—because Asher's eyes still haven't left mine. Only now he's looking at me like the cat that ate the canary.

"You're looking a little flushed there, Breslin," he says, as he makes his way over to where I'm seated on the coffee table.

"What—"

My words fall and my abs pull tight when he kneels down in front of me. Before I can ask him what he thinks he's doing, he runs one long finger along the seam of my panties, stopping to circle the large damp spot that's formed. "Liked what you saw, huh?"

The taunting bite to his tone has my eyes narrowing. "No," I fib, refusing to let him know just how much I enjoyed it. I didn't agree to this because I was horny and wanted to get off. I agreed to this to not only prove to myself that I could, but because I thought seeing them together would somehow fix my issues.

He drops his head to lick a path up my inner thigh. "Your lies taste delicious," he whispers, burying his nose in my panties and inhaling me.

I clutch the coffee table I'm sitting on as another wave of lust plows into me.

Then silently cursing myself, I steel my gaze before I push his head away and close my legs.

He stands up and bites his lip, not looking at all offended, only more determined. "That's okay...because the only thing you'll be riding tomorrow night is my face."

With that, he shoots me another smug and cocky smile before he slides into Landon's bed.

I look at the bathroom door and give him a smile of my own. "I might be riding your face tomorrow, but I'll be pretending you're someone else."

His dimples deepen and he grabs his thick dick through his boxers like the crude bastard he is. "Baby, by the time I'm done with you, you'll be down on your knees begging me for it." He looks at Landon when he walks out of the bathroom and winks. "Just ask him."

Landon looks between us, confusion marring his handsome face as he gets into bed. "What did I miss?"

"Nothing," Asher says as he leans over to flip off the light on the nightstand. "Because I haven't started yet."

On shaky legs, I walk over to Landon's bed. But even in the darkness, I can feel Asher's eyes pinned on me like I'm his prey.

My thoughts flit back to earlier as I lie between them, unable to sleep. *When one starts a war...they should be prepared for the counterattack.*

CHAPTER 23
BRESLIN

I go to open the fridge, but I can't, thanks to a massive, tall jerk in my way. "Move."

Asher opens the door instead and pulls out a jar of mayonnaise. "I'm not done."

I glare at him. "I don't even know why you're bothering in the first place." I point to the plate sitting on the counter. "I've got it covered."

He snorts. "Turkey is a better choice for people with diabetes than peanut butter is."

Slipping my arm past him, I snatch the milk from the fridge and walk back over to the counter. "Wrong. Peanut butter helps control blood sugar." I pull down a glass from the cabinet. "Turkey is just...turkey."

"You know, I don't remember you being this argumentative and stubborn when we were together."

I toss the knife in the sink. This way, I'm not tempted to use it on him. "Funny, I don't remember you being this much of an asshole." I pause. "Oh...wait. Actually, I do."

I go back to making Landon's sandwich but take a heavy breath when I feel his presence behind me.

Before I can protest, he opens the cabinet above my head to take down his own glass. "For your information, turkey is protein."

"So is peanut butter."

"I think it's safe to say I know a hell of a lot more about sports and nutrition than you do."

My cheeks heat and embarrassment creeps up my spine with those words. I find myself wishing I wasn't standing here in nothing but one of Landon's t-shirts, putting my imperfections on display for him to make fun of. "God, be a dick, why don't you."

He slams the glass down on the countertop. "Breslin, that wasn't a dig." He dips his head until his lips are hovering above my ear. "Not that kind of dig, anyway."

I gasp when he presses his hips against my ass and I feel every inch of him. "Trust me, I love your body. Always have." He sucks my earlobe between his teeth and I have to clutch the counter to stop myself from falling. "And I can't wait to see every inch of it again tonight."

I ignore the impact those words have on the heartbroken Breslin who used to cry herself to sleep thinking he didn't want her because she wasn't attractive enough for him.

I pick up his glass and face him. "Don't you have someplace to be?"

He leans in, invading every inch of my personal space. "As a matter of fact—"

"Hey."

The glass in my hand falls at the sound of Landon's deep voice.

Asher catches the glass less than a second before it hits the floor. "Hey, make any progress in the studio this morning?"

Landon lifts a shoulder in a shrug. "Some. I'm gonna head back, though. I just stepped out to grab something to eat because I felt a little off."

I pick up my plate at the same time Asher picks up his. "I made you lunch." I say at the same time Asher does.

I give him a dirty look and he gives me one right back.

Landon looks between us, a grin tugging at the corners of his mouth.

I take a step forward and hold my plate out to him. When Asher does the same, it's all I can do not to stomp on his foot. "Which one do you want?"

Landon's lips twitch and I fight the urge to do a happy dance when he picks up my sandwich.

I'm about to give Asher a shit-eating grin but then Landon picks up Asher's sandwich and lays it on top of the one I made.

He takes a huge bite and swallows. "So good."

Whatever tension in the room breaks up with those words and Asher and I both make a face. There's no way in the world that tastes good.

Asher swipes his gym bag off the floor and looks at Landon. "Coach called an emergency practice, so I have to head out."

Before any of us can say a word, he strides across the room to Landon and kisses him full on the mouth. I stare at them as they kiss, feeling equal parts jealous and fascinated with their interaction.

"Create something amazing today," Asher says against his lips and Landon smiles. "I'll see what I can do. Have fun at practice."

Asher turns to face me then. The heat blazing in those blue orbs of is enough to make my temperature skyrocket and I shift uncomfortably. "See you later, Breslin." I don't miss the challenge in his voice.

I can feel Landon's eyes on me after the door closes and guilt snags me. There's no way he missed the way Asher looked at me or my response to it. Something about this scenario just feels so...tricky and complex.

I can't meet his eyes. "I should get ready for my shift at the coffee shop."

I start to walk away but his hands find my hips, and the next thing I know I'm being picked up and placed on the counter.

He steps between my thighs and kisses my temple. "What's going on up here?" he murmurs into my hair and tingles race up and down my spine.

I want to lie and tell him I'm fine, but I can't. So, I tell him the truth. "I don't know."

He closes his eyes and inhales. "Are you—" He swallows thickly, looking so insecure and worried that my own chest constricts. "Are you disgusted by me...by what I did last night?"

My heart sinks because that isn't at all true, and the fact that Landon thinks that is like a kick to the stomach.

I grab his face, and when his eyes come to rest on mine I tell him, "No. What you did last night wasn't disgusting." I pull him closer. Our weird situation aside, he needs to understand one very important thing. "And don't you ever let anyone tell you differently."

His body goes slack and he wraps his arms around me, like all the pressure he was holding onto has now evaporated.

"I'm scared," I admit. "I'm scared of what's going to happen." *What's already happening.* I'm scared of all the things I don't understand—like how much I hate Asher for what he did, but crave him at the same time. Or how jealous I get when they're together, but how utterly captivated and turned on I am by it.

His fingers curve around my neck and he waits for me to look up at him. "I know you and Asher have some kind of...whatever is going on between you two right now. But you never have to do something that you don't want. I promised you I would keep you safe and I meant it, Breslin."

"I know. I just think—" I stall, because I don't know how to explain something to him that I don't even understand myself. I glance at the clock and curse, thankful for the distraction. "I think I'm going to be late for my shift."

He moves away and I jump off the counter, but not before he captures my lips. I hold myself steady against him as he flicks his tongue along mine in the softest and sweetest caress there is, like I'm fragile and delicate. *Like I'm valuable.*

"I'll see you later," he says, tucking a strand of hair behind my ear. Unlike Asher's goodbye that was laced with a challenge, Landon's is filled with uncertainty, like he doesn't think I'll be back tonight.

But I will...because I need this.

I walk into his living room/bedroom and quickly begin getting dressed before I hustle toward the front door. "You will see me later," I promise right before I close the door and my cell phone rings.

Irritation and nerves fill me when I see my father's name flash across the screen. I haven't talked to him since right before I left for Europe...which means he's only calling about one thing.

I bring the phone up to my ear as I walk down the stairs and head out to my car. "Hey, Dad."

"I'm late on the electric again," he slurs.

The fact that he didn't even bother to say hello to me has me grinding my molars. "But you were sent money last month, remember?"

I leave the implication hanging in the air—because we both know the only way he would have went through the money that quickly is if he spent it all on alcohol and drugs.

There's a long pause on the other line before he says, "Guess that college living of yours makes you all high and mighty now, huh? Thinking you can talk to me any old way."

Here we go. "Dad—"

"This is the thanks I get for taking care of your stupid, sorry ass when she didn't want you. Being questioned by my daughter who thinks her shit don't stink. Well, guess what? You ain't shit. You never will be."

His words sting. Even though I've heard them so many times over the years I lost count, it always stings.

But he's right in a way. He might not have taken care of me the way other parents take care of their children...but he didn't give me up, either. He was there...he didn't abandon me.

"Maybe if I had given you up my life would be better," he adds, digging the knife deeper. "Maybe I'd be happy without you just like she is."

"I'm sorry," I whisper, hating the way my voice is starting to shake, but I can't help it. His words hurt so fucking much.

In the back of my mind, I know there's a million things wrong with his statement. Even though I've never had a healthy family dynamic, I know his words are abusive and not the loving words a father should tell their child. But he's *my* father. For better or worse...he's the only family I have. He stayed when she didn't.

"I just started my old job back up again. If you can give me a little bit of time I can send you a check."

"Whatever," he barrels out before he hangs up the phone.

With a heavy heart, I slide into the driver's seat and peel out of the parking lot...silently praying for the day when I'll be strong enough to kick him out of my life. The day I won't crave love so bad that I'll accept his version of it. The only version I think I deserve.

CHAPTER 24
ASHER

I finish suiting up and close my locker. I've never dreaded being out on the field so much in my life. The first game is in a few days and we aren't even close to being ready. In fact, I'm pretty sure we only manage to get worse after every practice.

A few guys talk amongst themselves, but for the most part; everyone stays silent. There's no camaraderie between us. No sense of family, unlike every other team I've been a part of.

No wonder we play like shit.

Breslin's words hit me like a brick to the chest...because she's right. I need to find a way to forge us together somehow. As the quarterback, it's my job. Problem is, I have no idea what the first step would be. From my observations, it's not even like the other guys talk and hang out.

I walk over to the group of guys making small talk, figuring it's best to start there. The center, a guy named Glen Morris—who I'm supposed to be the closest to, but I've avoided because he was one of O'Conner's buddies, shoots me a dirty look.

The guys around him—a few wide-receivers and linebackers —

eyebrows shoot up in surprise, unsure of why I'm trying to talk to them.

Out of the corner of my eye, I see Coach Crane studying the exchange.

"Hey," I start, trying to remain casual. "So, I was thinking, we should all hang out after practice today. You know, get to know one another."

Morris laughs. "Are you asking us out on a date or something?"

A few guys in the locker room snicker but I lift my chin and look around at my teammates. "As a matter of fact, I am." I pull out my credit card, the one I told myself I'd only use for emergencies this year and hold it up. "Beers and burgers are on me after practice today." I look at Morris. "Don't worry, Morris. Homosexuality isn't contagious—but winning is."

I see a hint of a smile on Coach Crane's face and I continue, "And I don't know about you all, but I'm sick of this shit. I've only been a Wolverine for a few weeks, but man, it reeks of loser."

A few of the guys nod their heads in agreement and I take a deep breath. "I think it's time to prove everyone wrong about us. But it will require us all to pull our own weight and trust one another."

I start walking toward the locker room door. "Anyone interested in being a champion and kicking ass this season, meet me at Fatty's after practice. I'll be at the winner's table."

With that, I walk out of the locker room with my head held high. And for the first time in a long time, I feel excited to be back on the field.

CHAPTER 25

LANDON

"Morris is still kind of an asshole, but I think we understand each other now," Asher says, his eyes practically gleaming as he goes on and on about having dinner with his teammates.

I can't help but smile as I sit across my kitchen table from him. I don't think I've ever seen him so happy. It's damn near contagious.

When he comes up for air, he looks at the clock. "What time will she be here?"

And just like that, my good mood is gone. Not because of Breslin's arrival, but because of what I know will be happening.

I told myself I'd be fine with it, but I don't know how I'm going to handle sitting there and watching him fuck Breslin tonight.

The thought is enough to churn my stomach. But this is what I wanted. This is what I asked for.

I just hate being second best.

Asher reaches across the table for my hand then but the sound of the front door opening has us both pausing.

"Shit, I'm sorry," Breslin says. "I keep forgetting to give you your key back."

I stand up and walk over to her. "I don't want it back."

I make a mental note to make a key for Asher as I bend down to give her a kiss.

I pause mid-dip when I notice how puffy her eyes are, like she's been crying for most of the day. A surge of anger goes through me and I want to beat the shit out of whoever's responsible for this.

Breslin doesn't cry often, I've only seen her do it twice and both times were enough to make me never want to see it again. "What happened?"

When she waves my concern away, I cup her face in my hands, coaxing her to tell me the truth. We've finally come to the point where there are no pretenses between us and I don't want to go back to the way we once were.

I can feel Asher's presence behind me, but my eyes stay focused on her. "I um—" She looks down. "I talked to my dad before work today and it wasn't the best conversation we've had."

I wrap her in my arms and out of the corner of my eye I see Asher fold his arms across his chest, looking as mad as I feel.

When Breslin finally opened up to me about her past, I told myself I wouldn't judge her...but I hate that she still talks to that asshole.

And while I would never control her...I do want to keep her safe.

I may not be the kind of guy who puffs my chest out and bangs on it like Asher looks like he's about to do right now...but it doesn't mean I love her any less. It doesn't mean that my need to protect her is any less profound.

I look at Asher and he nods in agreement. Breslin might be angry with us for what we're going to do behind her back, but it needs to happen. I don't want him talking to her anymore and I most certainly don't want him making her cry. It's clear Breslin's not at the point where she can do it...which means it's up to me, or rather us, to block the fucker's number so he won't be able to hurt her anymore. And if the bastard shows up in person to harass her?

He's sure as fuck going to wish he hadn't.

She buries her face against my chest and I breathe her in and kiss her forehead.

She looks up at me and starts to smile, but then tenses in my arms when she catches sight of Asher.

The energy between them is like a live wire and whenever they're in the same room together it's...*intense*.

And even though they might not admit it—well, I'm sure Asher will have no problem admitting it—but I think they're very aware of the pull they have toward one another. The problem is Breslin, stubborn girl that she is, won't acknowledge it because of the way he hurt her. She doesn't want to give him his power back. And as much as I love Asher, I can understand where she's coming from. I just hate the wedge between them because it's preventing them both from healing. And yet, I can't help but feel a bit petrified of what will happen to *me* when they finally do.

They stare at one another for a beat and that damn elephant joins the party again, silently mocking us because it knows what's supposed to happen.

I tug Breslin tighter against me, feeling the weird combination of both possessive and resentful.

Possessive because I want her. Resentful because I know she's going to have him tonight...and I want him just as much.

This is what I wanted—I remind myself.

"I'm ready whenever you are," he tells her, dragging his gaze from her eyes to her feet and back up again.

She pushes away from me. "I think I need a drink."

My eyes ping between them as I follow them into the kitchen, unsure of what to do or what my role is. Do I intervene? Do I talk to them? Sit on the couch with my dick in my hand and use my tears as lube while they have at it in front of me?

What the hell are the rules when the two people you love the most, who happen to be exes...fuck again—because *you're* the one who told them to.

I look at Asher, but he's too focused on Breslin's ass when she bends over and fishes a bottle of wine out of the fridge.

And suddenly, I don't know how he's not rocking my jaw with his fist for last night, because it's what I want to do to him.

She pours her wine into a glass and looks at him. "Where do you want to do it?"

Her tone is all business, her expression giving nothing away. Almost like she's preparing to face a firing squad instead of having sex.

Asher reaches inside his pocket for something and walks over to her.

And that's when the seesaw my heart is on goes the other way and I ball my fists, silently willing him not to forget about me while he's planning to do God only knows what to her tonight.

Christ, this bitter pill is a hard one to swallow. But then again, being second place in the hearts of those you love always is.

When he pulls out a blindfold we both give him a strange look.

He stands behind Breslin and she stiffens. "Why a blindfold?"

He positions it over her eyes and ties it. "You told me you'd be picturing someone else, remember?"

She crinkles her nose. "Oh, I remember."

His mouth grazes the long line of her neck. "Good, because you're not allowed to take it off for the rest of the night. Even if you beg."

She snorts. "Trust me, I won't be begging."

His eyes go to me and my pulse speeds up. "We'll see about that."

She lets him take her hand and he leads her into the bedroom. My stomach turns sour as I make my way over to the couch that's at the end of the bed.

Right before I reach it, I'm lugged back. "Not so fast."

I shake my head, confused as all hell. "What—"

I can't finish that sentence because his lips are on mine. I kiss him back, taking his bottom lip and sucking on it. His response is to snatch my shirt over my head but I freeze when I notice Breslin standing there.

She can't see us, but her flushed cheeks and the way she's biting her lip tells me she knows what's happening.

It also tells me she might even be turned on by it.

I turn to Asher. "I thought tonight was about you two?"

His nostrils flare. "No. Tonight is about what *I* want." His hand hovers over my package. "And if you think that doesn't include you —" He grabs my dick through my jeans and I groan. "You're very mistaken."

His lips find my Adam's apple. "I told you that night that I was fighting for the both of you...didn't I?"

I nod, desire ripping through me. I go to kiss him again, but he backs up. "Go sit on the end of the bed for me, nerd."

His eyes shift to Breslin as I make my way over to the bed. He stalks toward her like a predator—and fuck me if I can tear my eyes away.

I've always been drawn to them both from the very first second I laid my eyes on them; and right now is no different.

It's probably because the creative artist in me has always enjoyed looking at beautiful things.

And the two of them? Are fucking mesmerizing.

She pushes her shoulders back when he slowly unbuttons her shirt, and I take in her lacy white bra.

When he gets down on his knees and pulls down her zipper next, it nearly echoes in the quiet room. I don't know whether I should be thanking him for unwrapping the gift that is a naked Breslin...or decking him for touching her body. It seems to fluctuate and change on a dime.

He slides her pants down those curvy hips of hers, revealing a matching lacy white thong that makes my cock stir.

Good God, she looks so innocent right now, standing there in her blindfold and little white panties.

The angel on my shoulder's blood stirs at all the ways he's planning to corrupt and defile her.

But the devil on my shoulder? He can't wait for it. In fact, he wants to join and burn in the flames between them.

He throws her discarded pants across the room and there's a gasp of surprise from her when he presses his mouth to the lace of her panties—right before he proceeds to take them off with his teeth, baring her smooth pussy to the both of us.

Her chest heaves and she draws in a ragged breath when he undoes her bra and those full tits of hers fall into his hands.

"Goddamn, I missed these," Asher says before he sucks her nipple into his mouth.

The joke Asher once made about me being a voyeur might not be so far from the truth anymore, because what should make me seethe with jealousy; is making me harder than a rock. Want and need tangle in my chest. The ache to touch both her and him is so strong I have to slip my hand inside my jeans and stroke my cock.

As if sensing what I'm doing, Asher turns and grins, his eyes hooded. A moment later, he grabs Breslin and walks her until she's right in front of me.

"Sit on Landon's lap for me, baby," he whispers and I see goosebumps break out across her delicate skin.

"Landon?" she questions, reaching behind her.

I gently pull her down on my lap. "I'm right here, Bre."

Her entire body relaxes and when she tilts her face in my direction, I lick her lower lip.

"Hold her legs open for me," Asher says as he kisses his way down her stomach and she shivers.

I place my hands on her inner thighs, parting them, and she grinds into my pelvis, sending all my blood rushing south.

When Asher lowers his head and his tongue darts out to lick the length of her slit, my cock twitches so hard against my zipper it's painful.

Breslin squirms in my arms and digs her nails into my leg as he tastes her.

I trail my knuckles over her belly. "Does it feel good?"

She's about to answer, but then Asher sucks her clit into his mouth and she moans.

"Answer the question, Breslin," Asher taunts as he separates her with his thumbs, exposing her silky pussy before he begins lapping at her.

Her face scrunches in turmoil, like she doesn't know how she should answer, but then whatever Asher does causes her to scream and she bucks her hips into his mouth and then my dick.

When I groan at both the visual before me and Breslin's motions, Asher gives me a knowing smirk. "You want some of this?"

Before I can answer, he spears Breslin's pussy with his tongue again.

She curses and arches her back, lifting her tits high. I pinch one of her nipples as I watch his jaw work, licking her in long, deep strokes. She tries to fight it, headstrong girl that she is—but a moment later she's shaking and riding Asher's face as she comes apart in my arms.

My heart is racing and lust is pumping through my veins like heroin to an addict. "Give me a taste."

"Fuck," Breslin whispers and her cheeks turn pink.

Asher raises his head, his chin damp with her juices, and opens his mouth, showing me the white creamy substance on his tongue.

"Jesus—" I start to say, but my sentence is cut off when he crushes his mouth to mine.

I suck her cum off his tongue and it's like being struck by lightning twice in a row because this is *everything* I want. The both of them here with me.

Breslin whimpers and gyrates on my lap, but when she tries to pull her blindfold off, Asher stops her...by grabbing the back of our heads and fusing all our mouths together.

We're all lips and tongues colliding, and it's honest to God the hottest kiss I've ever had in my life, especially with Breslin's taste being passed between us.

"God," Breslin whispers, driving her tongue into my mouth and then into Asher's.

"That was just foreplay, baby," Asher rasps, going for my jeans. Holding on to Breslin, I raise my hips so he can slip both them and my boxers off. Asher nudges me so I'm lying down on the bed with Breslin on top of me, her back to my chest. When my cock slaps against Breslin's pussy, I bite back another groan.

What I thought was going to be one of the worst nights of my life is turning out to be one of the best. There's no jealousy anymore, there's only this. Only us. Because it's the only thing that feels right.

Asher wraps his hand around my base and gives me a long jerk that ends with him thumbing the precum around my head as he goes back to feasting between Breslin's thighs.

"Look at this pretty pussy. So pouty and wet for me," he rasps before he sucks one of her pussy lips into his mouth and she mewls. He's starving for her and I can't blame him. I'm well acquainted with that holy grail of hers and the power it has over me.

His grip on my dick tightens and I swear I see stars when he pulls his mouth away from her and stretches his lips around me. My hand finds the back of his head, urging him to take me deeper. When he finally does, a jolt of yearning runs through me.

A moment later he releases me, but only so he can slip my length between Breslin's pussy.

"Holy hell," Breslin cries out, her slick, wet skin coating me as my cock slides between her lips.

I look down at Asher and our eyes connect. Heat surges to my groin—I've never seen him more turned on before and I know I've never been so turned on before. This is without a doubt the best of both worlds. A world that only gets better when his mouth goes to work on pleasuring us both at the same time, licking and sucking us like he'll never be able to stop.

He drags his gaze over me and I can feel the heat rolling off his body. That's the only warning I get before he slips a lubed-up fingertip in my ass, softly teasing that spot that drives me out of my mind.

Fuck me, I can't take it. It feels too good. I snatch the bedsheets in my hands and roar both their names into the ceiling.

"You ready for me to fuck you now?" Asher questions.

I thought the question was directed at Breslin, but I soon find out otherwise when he slowly enters me.

Breslin squeals when he yanks her savagely, pulling her hips up so he can continue eating the hell out of her as he fucks me.

I never thought I'd allow, let alone like the feeling of another guy fucking me, but I love the way it makes Asher go wild and I crave being able to do that to him.

His first thrust feels so good, I can barely breathe. The only thing I can do is pump my own cock in my hand to relieve the ache as he fucks me harder.

"That's it, let me watch you jerk it," Asher grunts as Breslin tightens her legs around him, muffling his groans.

A curse escapes me when he lowers Breslin back down and raises her legs, pinning her flush against me again. Lust surges through my system hard and hot when I feel her wetness collecting on my lower stomach.

"Please let me take the blindfold off," she pleads, her body shaking.

"Not until you admit it," Asher rasps.

"Admit what?"

He slams into me harder, his balls slapping against me. "That you like seeing the two of us together. That you like me licking this sweet pussy of yours while I fuck him right in front of you. Admit that this right here is everything you want."

"Fuck you," she whispers.

He punches the bed. "Admit it, Breslin."

She shakes her head and he slides out of me, only to pump back into me again. "Say it and I'll let you watch me fuck him."

She whimpers but refuses to answer, although her body and her moans betray her. This is nothing more than a battle of wills right now, and I know them well enough to know that neither of them are going to back down until the other one does.

I look at Asher, I'm so close to coming, so fucking close. I know he is too by the way his movements pick up speed and he pants my name. I can practically feel his balls clench a moment later when he thrusts a final time and comes inside me.

I jerk my cock so hard my wrist hurts, and right when I'm about to join him, he pulls out and lines Breslin's ass up with my dick.

There's a dare in his eyes now, and I angle my cock so my tip nudges her puckered hole, causing Breslin to gasp and push up on her heels. He shoots me a sly smile and I look down the length of her body as he flicks her clit, then shoves two fingers inside her.

Air leaves my lungs in a rush and my balls draw tight, there's no way I can hold back any longer, so I don't. I shudder and spasm as I let go, half of it ends up streaming in long, thick ropes inside Breslin's ass cheeks, the other half ends up all over my hand and my dick.

I'm fighting to catch my breath, but then Breslin shouts, "Fine, I admit it," into the air as she orgasms.

In a flash, he flips Breslin over on the bed beside me, snatches her blindfold off, and licks my come out of her ass, his eyes locked with mine the entire time.

"Oh, my fucking, God!" Breslin shouts. The muscles in his back flex as he continues licking her, and even though I just got off; my dick twitches. I've never seen anything hotter in my entire life.

And just when I think it can't get any better, he moves and settles between my legs where he proceeds to suck the come off my finger before he ventures to my balls, causing me to groan his name.

Breslin's eyes are wide as saucers as she watches Asher clean off my dick with his mouth. She doesn't look bothered by seeing us, though, it's the exact opposite.

Asher releases me with a plop and stands up—and then, like the smug bastard he is, shoots a dimpled smirk at the both of us before he walks to the bathroom. That tight, bare ass of his taunting us just like he did moments before.

I look over at Breslin...and I know she feels it too.

Things just got even more complicated between the three of us...because Asher Holden's just managed to fuck us up all over again.

No holds barred.

CHAPTER 26

BRESLIN

I raise a brow at the note Asher drops on my desk. We're currently sitting in our Intro to Ethics class and it's all I can do not to transport back to the events of last night as Mrs. Rogers goes on and on about *Hedonism* and *The Experience Machine*.

Just when I'm about to open the note, her stare snags on Asher. "If you had a chance to go inside a machine and have all your hopes and dreams come true and experience nothing but pleasure and live your most satisfying life, would you?"

I turn to look at him but then she proposes the same question to me.

It's on the tip of my tongue to point out that she's asking a girl who grew up in a trailer park with an addict as a father and was lucky if she managed to get one decent meal per day, but instead I look her right in the eyes and say, "No," at the same time Asher says, "Yes, in a heartbeat."

Her eyes crinkle at the corners as she surveys us. "You both understand this pleasure would be simulated and you wouldn't actually be interacting with anyone?"

"But according to this machine I wouldn't know that," Asher counters. "Sometimes ignorance can be bliss."

I take a breath past the lump forming in my throat. "Or painful. Sometimes ignorance can be painful."

I see Landon sit up straight in his seat and Mrs. Rogers studies us both intently.

"Ignorance isn't painful, Breslin," Asher whispers. "It's the experience and awareness that's painful."

I have absolutely no argument for that, because he's right.

Mrs. Rogers goes back to her lecture and Asher points to the note on my desk.

Against my better judgment I open it:

You're still thinking about last night, aren't you?
Check the appropriate box:
☐ *Fuck yes.*
☐ *Hell yes.*
☐ *I'm going to need a repeat performance to make up my mind.*

I roll my eyes and give my head a shake.

A smirk spreads across his face right before he passes me another note:

I think I understand that line in the song Glycerine now. You know, the one about having a beautiful taste. Because you're gorgeous, Breslin. Every single part. Every. Single. Drop.

My chest and cheeks break out into a flush and my mouth goes dry. I take out my pen and scribble my own note back to him:

Wow, someone is laying it on thick.

He grins as he writes back a reply and tosses it back to me:

A thickness you're well aware of. ;)

I can't help but laugh as I write my response, but as soon as I do my heart twists because these are the moments I miss him so much it hurts:

God, you're cheesy.

He laughs into his hand, those beautiful dimples on display as he writes on the paper and gives it back to me:

I totally am. But cheesy or not, it's true. Now answer my first note. I'm dying over here, baby.

I open his first note again and hover my pen around the boxes. I time it perfectly so by the time I pick one, the class has ended and students are filing out. I stand up and stick the note in my bag. "Sorry, I have to meet Kit for lunch."

With that, I turn, but not before Asher sticks another note in my hand.

I wait until he and Landon leave the classroom to open it.

I wish I could have given you the experience machine, Breslin. I wish I could have given you everything you ever wanted.

I close my eyes and exhale as I walk over to the trash can and throw away the paper.

Me too, Asher.

Kit releases a sigh and turns back to face me. "They're still staring at you."

I stab at a piece of lettuce with my fork. "I know."

Even from across the cafeteria I can feel both Landon's and

Asher's eyes on me as they eat their lunch.

She takes a sip of her soda. "Okay, that's it. The suspense is killing me. What is going on? You haven't slept at the dorm the past two nights, and no offense, but you look exhausted."

"I'm not exactly sure," I tell her. "But I don't want to talk about it right now."

She opens her mouth to speak but then clamps it shut, her eyes widening as they shoot across the cafeteria.

I pivot in my seat to see what's caught her attention, and that's when I see Preston Holden walk in. I assume that he's come here for Asher, but when all he does is give him a nod as he passes his table and heads in our direction, I'm all sorts of confused.

My eyes fall on Asher and he shrugs, looking just as perplexed as I am.

Preston sits down in front of us but his eyes are stuck on Kit. I have no clue why he's here right now, but when I make to stand to give them some privacy, Kit squeezes my hand under the table and I sit right back down.

Preston's hand grips the back of his neck and he pulls something out of his pocket. He then slides it across the table to her and I realize it's the same jewelry box that Becca's engagement ring was in.

"Give this to someone who deserves it next time," Preston says and something passes in their gaze.

When he stands up, her expression turns even dourer. "How's the baby?"

He looks around the room and lets out a sigh. "Baby's good. We had our first sonogram today."

Kit draws in a ragged breath and nods.

"I'm sorry," Preston says solemnly in her direction before he exits. And that's when Kit loses her composure completely and has a full-on breakdown right there at the table.

I stand up and wrap her in my arms, shooting dirty looks to all the people staring at us as I usher her into the nearest bathroom.

I'm mad at Preston for showing up today and upsetting her like this, but I'm so crazy angry at Becca for being such a dirty, rotten whore and hurting my best friend that I'm seeing red all over again.

"I'm so sorry, honey," I whisper as she sobs in my arms. "I wish I could take it all away."

"Me too," she chokes out as her hand tightens around the jewelry box. "This was my mom's."

My heart hits the floor and I can't help but shed a few tears along with her now. Kit's parents died in a plane crash when she was only eight. And unlike my parents, hers were amazing and they were all super close. The fact that she proposed with her mom's engagement ring proves how serious she was about Becca.

Dammit that fucking bitch didn't deserve her.

After a few minutes, she walks over to the sink and washes her face. "I have to get to class."

I pull my bottom lip between my teeth, because I can't help but wonder, as crazy as the thought may be. "Is there something going on between you and Preston?"

Her eyebrows shoot up. "What? No. What the hell is the matter with you?" She points to herself. "Strictly pussy over here." She snatches some paper towels from the dispenser and grits her teeth. "I can't believe you'd even think such a thing. Let's put it this way—if an asteroid hit the earth, leaving only me and him to repopulate the planet or face my untimely demise via being eaten and probed by aliens...I'd gladly skip toward the aliens and thank them."

I guess that settles that then. "Look, I'm sorry—"

She glares at me, her pretty face taking on a maroon color as she stomps away. "I don't want to talk about it right now."

Before I can say another word, she bolts out the bathroom door.

CHAPTER 27

ASHER

S he twists away. "No, you can't look at it, Asher."
Everyone else has left the art studio, but Breslin wanted to stay after to work on our, should I say, *her* project. Which of course, means I wanted to stay behind with her.

I try and look over her shoulder again but she swivels on her stool and turns the easel. "I'm not done, yet."

"Just a little peek."

She grumbles something under her breath and holds the paintbrush in her hand. A moment later, her eyes zero in on the canvas—and off she goes in her little world.

I swear on everything that I could watch her paint all day and night. The way the tip of her tongue darts out of her mouth as she concentrates with such precision. The way those green eyes of hers damn near sparkle every time her paintbrush touches the canvas.

She illuminates when she creates. She and Landon both do.

Some time later she looks at the clock on the wall and jumps up. "Crap. I wanted to check on Kit before tonight." I don't miss the pink hue her cheeks take on after she says the word *tonight*.

I stand up and start cleaning up her art supplies. "Go, baby. I've got this."

Her teeth dig into her bottom lip. "Are you sure? I mean I can—"

"Go check on your friend," I insist, and because I can't help myself I let my gaze roam down her body. "I'll see you later."

Nerves and heat splash across her face briefly before she heads for the door, only to pause and look back at me. "Promise you won't look?"

I shoot her a smile. "No."

She mumbles a curse as she closes the door behind her and my smile gets bigger. Ever since last night things between us have been...oddly better. Things between *all* of us have been better and I can't wait to have a repeat performance again tonight.

My entire body stills as I remember—*it's Landon's night.*

I tried getting him to spill what was on his agenda during lunch today but he wouldn't. He just smiled and hummed to himself as he went back to studying.

I take a deep breath. Since the ball is in Landon's court, the last thing he would do is hurt us. That's not my boyfriend's style.

I pause again as a million questions plow into my brain. Is Landon my boyfriend? Am I his? Is Breslin his girlfriend? Is she mine?

I know what I want. But unfortunately, those are questions I can't answer without all parties involved.

Sighing, I steal a glance at Breslin's latest portrait.

My heart wells up with pride and amazement. She painted me on the field, football in hand, capturing my expression right before I throw it. I know this because I always look up to the sky, close my eyes for a split second, and take a deep breath. It's kind of a spiritual moment for me...one I didn't think anyone ever noticed because it happens so fast.

But Breslin noticed.

I make quick work of gathering up the supplies she used and head over to the sink, my head still spinning.

I'm washing my third brush when the hairs on the back of my neck stand up and an eerie feeling washes over me.

Setting the brushes aside, I chance a glance at the door, only to find it ajar—which is funny because I could have sworn Breslin closed it on her way out.

She did close it on her way out.

I grab my gym bag and jet out of the art room. I'm not a pussy, it's just that ever since that fucking video surfaced, went viral, and people did nothing but point, laugh, and stare at me for months on end—I hate the feeling of being watched. And if I'm not careful to get out of an uncomfortable situation entirely, I chance being hit with a full-blown anxiety attack, which of course, only makes my nerves worse—because God only knows the shit people will talk about the 6'4" football player that's crumpled in a ball on the floor fighting to breathe.

The night air greets me as I step out of the building and walk across the courtyard, the eerie feeling of being watched only seems to get worse with every step I take.

Despite the few people hanging out in the courtyard, I start counting my steps, estimating how many I have left before I reach the dorm building across campus.

My little trick isn't working though because my heart only seems to pound harder.

When a hand clasps my shoulder, I lose it completely and shove them away. "Get the fuck off me!"

"Whoa," Landon says, taking a step back, concern marring his face. "What's going on?"

I look around, the few people around us seem to be going about their business, oblivious to my freak out. "Were you just in the art room by any chance?"

He shakes his head and points in the direction of the library.

"No. I just got out of a tutoring session." He takes a step closer. "What happened?"

"I got a weird feeling as I was cleaning up and kind of freaked out." I hike my bag up my shoulder and start walking. "Didn't mean to snap at you."

He starts walking alongside me. "No apology necessary. You got spooked, it happens to the best of us." He reaches for my hand. "I'll walk you back to the dorms."

I pull away from his touch, since we're not out of people's eyesight. "Dude, what are you doing? We're still in public?"

He looks around. "Forgot we're still on school property. Thanks for looking out."

"Right," I say, hoping it covers my fumble, because Landon getting in trouble wasn't on my mind when I pulled away.

Landon stops walking abruptly. "If we weren't on school property would you have pulled away like you did?"

One of the things I love most about Landon is how direct he is. I don't feel like I need a manual to decode anything with him because he just tells you how he's feeling and exactly what he's thinking. But right now? Yeah, right now I kind of hate it.

I go to answer him, but my moment of hesitation causes his jaw to tic. "I knew it."

I scrub a hand down my face. "Knew what?"

"Me being a TA aside, you're never going to hold my hand or kiss me in public, are you?"

"I've never been one for PDA," I start to tell him and his nostrils flare.

"Bullshit."

He's got me. "Okay, fine. I'm just not really comfortable with affection in public." I close my eyes. "Or rather, I'm comfortable with it, but there are tons of people who aren't and I—"

"Would you kiss Breslin in public?"

My eyes pop open with his question. I don't want to lie to him. "Yes."

He looks down at his feet. "She means more to you than I do."

"What?" I take a step closer to him. "Landon, you know how I feel about the two of you."

He looks up at me. "Then I deserve the same." He starts to walk away. "But hey—I guess it's good to know where the guy that I love stands before I spill the beans about my sexuality to my parents."

I press a hand to his chest, halting him. "You're coming out to your parents?"

He nods. "Within the next few weeks, yeah. I came to the decision the other day when Breslin told me not to let anyone ever make me feel disgusted or ashamed about myself. I don't want to keep my feelings for you or Breslin a secret anymore. If it wasn't for me being a TA, I'd shout it from the rooftops." He laughs. "But thanks for letting me know that I'll always be *your* dirty little secret."

My heart cracks and pangs with his statement, for two reasons. One—I can't deny the jealousy I feel over the fact that Breslin said that to him...yet she walked out on me. And two—Landon's not my dirty little secret and I don't want to ever make him feel like that. So, he's right, he deserves the same kind of respect that Breslin does in that regard.

I throw my bag on the ground and push him against the wall of the building. It's nearly pitch black where we are and no one is around us, which is good because we are on school property.

He gives me a look, but I slam my lips against his. "After we graduate, I'm going to kiss you just like this in public," I say before I take his mouth again.

"Promise?" he questions, gripping my shirt.

I work my way down his jaw and then back up until I'm hovering right over his ear. "I swear it."

He smiles and I give him another kiss before I pick my bag up. "Now walk me back to my dorm so I can grab a change of clothes before we head over to your apartment for the night."

When he starts walking beside me, I shoot him a look. "What exactly are we doing tonight by the way?"

A cocky grin spreads across his face. "You'll just have to find out."

My body jolts at the thought of all the wicked and sexy things Landon has planned for us.

"And that's the story of how my Great Grandmother and Great Grandfather met during World War I," Landon finishes, twirling both mine and Asher's fingers with his as we lie on either side of him in his bed.

"Fascinating," Asher says and I tamp down the impulse to giggle.

Landon wanted to spend his night in his bed asking questions and getting to know us even more. Personally, I think it's kind of romantic, but the look on Asher's face when he found out how we were spending our night was hysterical.

"Give me one of your favorite days," Landon says. "But it can't have anything to do with any of us."

He's been adding that disclaimer at the end of all his questions.

Asher shrugs. "Easy. The day I threw my first touchdown." He tucks one hand behind his head and looks up to the ceiling. "Never knew I had it in me. It was fucking awesome."

Landon looks at me. "What about you, Bre?"

My stomach turns because there's no way I can tell this story without disclosing the bad parts of it, and I don't want their pity.

He sweeps a hand down my cheek. "Please?"

I clear my throat, steeling myself. "Okay, fine. One weekend when I was in the first grade my father left me in the trailer longer than usual. So long that when I left to go to school on Monday morning, he still wasn't back."

I stall for a moment, my composure shaky. "I don't think I'd ever been so hungry in my life before. I had pretty much eaten what I could of the moldy loaf of bread he left me that Friday night, but it wasn't enough; and there's only so much water you can drink to fill your belly before you cramp up."

Landon's eyes soften and Asher's jaw tics, but I continue, "Anyway, I left for school. I was so dizzy and sick, but I knew better than to go to the school nurse for fear that she would take me out of my father's trailer and stick me in the dreaded foster care system. I kept telling myself to hold on until lunchtime because I knew I'd get a sandwich thanks to the lunch assistance program."

I can feel both their gazes on me and I look down at my hands. "I will never forget the moment the teacher came around with paper and little paint sets and told us to paint whatever we wanted, and that she would hang the best ones up around the classroom later that day." I push my hair out of my face and smile. "I painted my heart out, drew every beautiful thing I could think of and when I ran out of paper, the teacher gave me more. I'd never felt happier than at that moment. Creating...like I was in my own little world. A world where I wasn't hungry, my mom wasn't gone, and my father wasn't an addict who didn't care about me. I created my own perfect universe that day and it was *everything*." I laugh. "In fact, I was so distracted the teacher had to pull me away and remind me it was lunchtime."

I finally cut my eyes to them. "But the best part was that the teacher chose my painting to be hung up that day and even gave me a little award for it." I tap my chest. "Me. The girl who was never good at anything was finally recognized for something."

I leave out the part about walking into the classroom the next day just as Kyle Sinclair ripped down my painting from the wall and told me how ugly it was.

Landon tugs me closer to him and plants a kiss on my cheek. "I'm so sorry—"

"No," I tell him. "Don't be, because I'm not. I had my moment and no one can ever take that away from me."

There's an awkward silence in the air before Landon asks, "Most recent disappointment?" He pauses. "Again, it can't have anything to do with us."

"Not being able to watch the super bowl in person this year," Asher answers quickly.

When we turn to look at him he adds, "I know it sounds superficial, but it was something me and my dad always did every year without fail. It just sucks that I'm going to miss it this year."

Landon gives his arm a squeeze and looks at me. "What about you?"

"Europe," I blurt out without thinking and Landon winces.

"Let me finish," I say. "There was this little village we went to visit one day while I was abroad. And although it was beautiful, there wasn't anything particularly distinctive about it. Apart from one thing."

"What?" Asher questions.

"A man with a tent."

When Landon raises an eyebrow, I say, "He had the most amazing tent. When you went inside there were all these twinkling lights with different hues and soft music playing in the background. It was almost like a fancy wedding, but even prettier. He had even set sleeping bags on the floor for people to lay on for however long they wanted to. Didn't even charge anything for the experience, either. He just did it for people to enjoy." I close my eyes. "It was so serene and breathtaking."

Landon slides a finger up my arm. "How long did you stay in there?"

"I didn't. I had to get going to make it to the next tour stop, but I told myself I'd go back later that night." I sigh. "But I didn't. I ended up falling asleep early in the hotel and the next day we had to leave."

"That sucks," Asher whispers and I nod. "It does. But, what can you do, you know?" I drape myself across Landon and rest my cheek on his chest. "What about you?"

"Well, now that graduation is looming ahead of us, I'd say it's not standing up to my parents and choosing music from the beginning." He shrugs. "I just wanted to make them happy. I know they had really big expectations of me after Levi's death. Of course, they never told me that, but it's how they made me feel. Kind of like they stuck me on a pedestal and I was expected to fulfill everything he wouldn't be able to. Like all their hopes and dreams were pinned on me because I was up to bat now...because their first choice and first child couldn't." He casts his gaze downward. "And now I sound like an asshole who didn't love his brother."

Asher grips his shoulder and I meet his steady gaze for several beats. "No, you don't." I trace his cheek. "I'm sorry you were made to feel like that. No one should have to live in anyone's shadow."

His eyes dip to my mouth and I tilt my head and kiss him. The kiss starts off light and sweet at first, but with a flick of his hot tongue it becomes needy and urgent. The energy in the room shifts entirely when he pulls away and grabs Asher's head next, kissing him with just as much passion.

Tingles zip up and down my spine and I push forward and join them, lightly running my tongue along the seam of both their mouths.

Landon brushes his knuckles down the side of my neck and Asher curls his hands around my hips, and the next thing I know, I'm straddling Landon's thighs.

Asher moves behind me and motions for me to raise my arms. When he takes off my shirt, his fingertips brush over my ribs, sending sparks along my nerve endings. I grind against Landon and he pulls us into a sitting position, planting slow, sensual kisses down my jaw. When I mewl, he lowers his mouth to my collarbone and gently sucks the skin there.

I arch my back and press against Asher whose fingers wander down my stomach until he reaches the button on my jeans and pops it open.

I feel like I'm spinning out of control, there's so many sensations crashing into me at once and I can't wrap my head around what's happening right now, but I don't want it to stop.

My heart skips into overdrive when I feel the hard muscles of Asher's bare skin against my back. I take off Landon's shirt next and I openly ogle his chest and tattoos.

Their bodies are so different. One lean and toned, the other cut and muscular, but both are so gorgeous in their own ways. It's a struggle to keep my breathing in check.

When I feel Landon's cock harden against my thigh, I run my hand along his length. And then before I can put too much thought into it, I shift until I'm hovering over his lap.

I toy with his zipper that's bulging with his erection and give him a coy smile. "What do you want me to do about this?"

He bites his lip and looks at Asher. "What do you think she should do about this?"

The heat in both his stare and his words has my blood turning to lava.

A pair of rough and calloused hands tugs me against a hard body and the muscles in my belly contract when Asher undoes my bra and cups my breasts.

He lowers his lips to my temple right before he whispers, "Suck him for me, baby."

I push down Landon's jeans and boxers in one long movement and his cock springs out, slapping against his stomach.

Landon holds that long dick of his out to me. "You want this in your mouth?"

My cheeks flame. "I do," I say as I dip my head.

A sharp tug on my hair stops me the second I part my lips.

"Tease him," Asher rasps, wrapping my hair around his hand.

Landon looks at Asher and a slow smirk spreads across his face.

My tongue darts out and I swipe the precum forming on the head of his cock. When he grunts, I open my mouth wider, slowly sucking his crown, flicking the sensitive slit.

Landon's abdomen flexes and he hisses. "Take me deeper."

I ease my mouth down his length but Asher pulls on my hair, stopping me when I'm mid-way.

"Fuck," Landon groans and I lap at the vein throbbing against my tongue.

Asher eases his grip and I take Landon as far as I can, until Asher tugs on my hair again, gliding me up Landon's shaft.

"Why don't you get down here and join her?" Landon growls and my stomach somersaults.

Nerves catch in my throat when Asher sidles beside me, but it's overpowered by the hunger in Landon's gaze as he stares down at us.

When I stretch my mouth over Landon's head and Asher licks his base, our tongues touch.

Landon jerks his hips up. "Fucking hell."

With a smirk, Asher moves to his balls and I deepen my strokes around his shaft.

Landon goes crazy, his body spasming and contracting. "If you two don't stop I'm gonna come."

Asher circles one of his balls and I speed up my pace.

Landon cups my cheek, halting my movements. "I want to fuck you at the same time he does," he groans, his dick pulsating in my mouth. "I want to come in that tight little pussy of yours while he fucks you from behind."

Holy Shit.

Landon is no stranger to dirty talk, none of us are, but he's never been quite so candid before. It's hot as hell.

I release him and Asher slides my jeans and panties down before he rummages around for something in the dresser drawer. I'm confused briefly because I'm on the pill and we've all had the talk about being tested, but he pulls out a bottle of lube. "Ever had anal before?"

I glance at Landon and his eyes blaze.

"I have," I tell Asher, recalling my very first time, which just so happened to be the first time me and Landon ever had sex.

I ended up watching one of his shows at the Black Spoon and of course at the request of the crowd he played *Glycerine.* I loved everything about that night up until that moment. I was so upset and needed a distraction from my thoughts—so right after his show, I trapped him in an abandoned staircase as he was leaving and all but begged him to take my ass right there and then.

And he did.

It was an unforgettable night. And the smile currently plastered on Landon's face tells me he remembers every bit of it just as much as I do.

I return Landon's smile and then before I know what hits me, I'm slammed against the bed.

Asher works his way down my torso, nipping and licking at my skin, his forearms caging my body.

When his lips travel to my pelvic bone and he sweeps his hot mouth across it, I open my legs and look back at Landon who's stroking his cock, his gaze pinned on us.

And that's when Asher tongues my clit before pulling the sensitive flesh into his mouth and suckling it. I propel into his jaw and grab a handful of his hair, my legs shaking around his head.

"Yes," he groans into my wetness. "That's what I want, baby."

When he lifts his head and presses a finger to my mouth, I instinctively lick it. A moment later, everything around me spins when his face settles between my thighs again and he inserts the same finger into my narrow hole while he laps at my slickness, preparing me for what's to come.

I buck, arch, and clench around his finger and his tongue, so lost in pleasure as I orgasm, I have no time to second guess anything.

Until he props himself on his elbows and I feel the tip of his cock at my entrance, causing painful memories to slam into me.

The last time Asher was inside me, he broke me.

I tilt my head and look over at Landon, because I need him right now in order to get through this. I need him to be that shield for me and protect me from myself. *Protect me from Asher.*

I press a palm to Asher's chest and when he draws back, I crawl across the bed to Landon—whose arms are open, waiting for me.

I don't waste another second being in them. I wrap my legs around his waist and his arms snake around my lower back as he holds me steady.

No words are exchanged, but his eyes tell me everything that I need. They tell me he's right here with me and I'm safe, that he'll keep holding onto me for as long as I need him to.

I sink down, letting him fill both me and the hollow ache in my chest.

When Asher maps gentle kisses up and down my spine, I close my eyes and bury my face in Landon's neck.

"Do you still want this?" Asher whispers and I nod my head, because I do.

More than that...I *need* this. It's why I agreed to this.

It hurts to breathe and my muscles lock up when he starts to enter me. I dig my nails into Landon's shoulders and nuzzle the crook of his neck but Asher tugs my head back, forcing me to look up at him as he pushes forward.

Emotion clogs my throat and he swipes away the tear that rolls down my face with his thumb as he drives himself to the hilt.

The heavy air around us stills as they wait for me to get used to them. Physically, my body feels pushed to the sexual brink, stretched and fuller than I ever thought possible. Mentally, my mind feels uncongested and clear for the first time in a long time. I've already made it through the hard part, the only thing left to do is let go.

Slowly, I start to move, gliding myself along Landon's cock, finding the perfect rhythm. On the way down Asher grabs my hips and thrusts, controlling the sequence as he wraps his legs around Landon, connecting all of us as we maneuver together fluidly, almost like we orchestrated this.

Landon closes his eyes, both our names a whisper on his lips. He looks so far gone and swept away by lust, I can't help but lean over and taste the smile on his face. Brushing my mouth across his neck next, I lick the goosebumps on his skin as Asher kisses between my shoulder blades and runs his hand up Landon's thigh.

The air around us is charged and intoxicating, the scent of sex and pheromones from our sweat-soaked bodies surrounds us like a fog as our finish line approaches.

Landon pulses inside me and I feel Asher's cock jerk. Grabbing the headboard for leverage, I pick up my pace, losing myself in the sensation.

Asher's teeth dig into my back and he groans as he reaches between us to stroke my clit.

I slide up Landon's length, clinging to his shoulders and rocking my hips as his hand joins Asher's—causing torturous pressure to build until I'm writhing and gasping, sucking in air faster than my lungs can take in, begging them for the release that I so desperately need.

"Let go, baby," Asher whispers as Landon plants the softest of kisses along my breasts before he takes turns sucking my nipples into his mouth.

My head swirls as the pressure releases and I clench around Landon, my body vibrating with a bolt of intense pleasure I never knew it was capable of feeling. Groaning, they both shudder as they fall apart with me.

We stay silent in the aftermath—all of us touching and holding each other as we fall into bed, afraid to break the connection that tethers us to one another.

It should be awkward and strange.

It should be wrong and immoral.

There are a million things it should be.

But right now? None of that matters, because there's only one thing that I feel.

And that's exactly what scares the hell out of me. Because I know all too well what's waiting on the other side of the divide.

And the fact that I want nothing more than to stay here with them...is exactly why I have to leave.

There's no way this could ever work out. Not just because of me and Asher's history—but this dynamic is just asking for a broken heart. Nothing healthy can ever come out of this fucked up and unusual situation. And I need the healthy. I've had so much toxic poison in my life I can barely gather the strength that it takes to keep waking up every morning.

Being careful not to wake them, I gather my clothes off the floor and get dressed as quickly as I can.

I take one last glance at them and my eyes land on the clock on the nightstand. A clock that reads 12:00 a.m.

Which means it's no longer day three...and whatever was happening between us has officially come to an end.

CHAPTER 29
LANDON

Losing someone you love the first time around is hard. But losing them the second time around?

Is a torment I wouldn't wish on my worst enemy. Which currently just so happens to be the guy sitting across from me.

The guy with the deep blue eyes and dimples who looks even worse than I do.

Ever since Breslin left my bed two nights ago and refused to speak to either of us, Asher and I have been dancing this fucked up tango with one another. Waltzing around the fact that we know the ugly truth. We didn't just lose Breslin, we lost each other. Because there's no us without her...not anymore. Not when we know how right the three of us are together. There's no way our relationship will survive the impact of not having her.

Leaning back in my chair, I remove my glasses and scrub a hand down my face. The last 48 hours have been spent in complete disarray and I hate it.

I can't help but let my eyes drift across the cafeteria to where she's eating lunch with Kit. She looks miserable, which equally makes my heart hurt and pisses me off because there's no reason for it.

I'm not flippant enough that I can't understand her concerns about our arrangement. Hell, I have them myself, but not enough to deter me from it.

I toss my books in my bag and stand up. "I'm going over there."

Asher stands up so fast the force sends his chair sailing back. "Me too."

Without another word we walk over to where she's sitting, only for her to whisper something to Kit before she gets up and all but runs out of the cafeteria.

The fact that she won't even acknowledge us causes my jaw to harden.

Asher and I exchange a glance and I plop down next to Kit.

She shakes her head. "Nope." Her eyes dart between me and Asher who takes a seat across from us and folds his arms over his chest. "I'm not—"

Asher slams his hand on the table. "For fuck's sake, Kit. Give us something."

She ignores him and goes back to eating her burger. Anger swells hot in my chest and I push her tray away, sending it flying across the table.

Her lips pull tight. "Christ, is this a shakedown?"

Asher leans in, getting close to her face and snarls, "It could be."

She wipes her mouth with a napkin. "Listen, Batman and Robin, I don't know anything." She chews on her bottom lip. "Not anything that you guys don't already know anyway."

Asher quirks a brow at her. "What the hell does that mean?"

"It means," she says, glaring at us. "That you both are fucking morons if you can't understand why she's upset and doesn't want to talk to you anymore."

Asher and I exchange another glance. "I don't quite follow."

"She's confused, hurt, and scared and you two bozos are the reason for it." She rolls her eyes. "Good grief, did you really think sex or whatever the heck happened between you all was going to fix the issues?" She points a finger at Asher. "*You* pop up out of fucking nowhere after breaking her heart into a thousand pieces *dating* the guy she was trying to move on with." Her eyes flit to mine. "And *you* acted like her damn knight in shining armor for months on end, only for her to return from Europe and find you dating her douchebag ex. I mean, come on. Telemundo doesn't have shit on you people."

My heart knocks against my chest. "I didn't expect—" I look at Asher. "I didn't expect to fall for someone else. And not for nothing, but she broke up with *me*—"

"I know," Kit says, standing up. "I'm not saying Breslin didn't make mistakes. But the thing is, she's aware of her mistakes. All she does is think about her mistakes and blame herself for everything internally. The girl has the confidence of a fruit fly." She stares at Asher for several beats. "All she does is wonder what she must have done wrong to deserve to end up so broken and why she's never good enough for those she loves."

I look down, it's like she put her fist through my heart with those words.

Asher's jaw works. "If she would let me explain—"

She pops a hand on her hip. "Why should she?" A scoff pushes through her lips. "The fact of the matter is, if you wanted her, you would have found a way to talk to her over the last three years. If you were really sorry about what you did, you would have found a way to tell her."

He lets out a frustrated sigh. "She moved away and shut down all her social media sites. She didn't want to be found. Not to mention the fact that I couldn't—"

"Anyway," Kit says, cutting him off. "My advice to you both is to stop trying. Not because Breslin isn't worth it but because you've already blown your shot."

"I love her," I whisper and she frowns.

"It doesn't mean shit if she doesn't feel like you do. It doesn't mean anything if she won't accept it." Her expression softens and she looks up to the ceiling. "Look, maybe I'm wrong. Maybe I'm just being a bitch because of my own shit that I'm dealing with, but either way, you can't force her to talk to either of you until she's ready." She gathers her books off the table. "You know the old adage, *'If you love something, set it free'.*"

"What if she doesn't come back?" Asher questions, the pain in his voice damn near penetrating through my skin.

She cuts her eyes to the door and exhales. "You find a way to go on and get over her."

When she walks away Asher squeezes his eyes shut and whispers, "I couldn't get over her the first time around."

I run a hand through my hair, my chest caving in. "We give her a little more time." I meet his stare for a few solid beats. "She'll come around, I know she will."

"How are you so sure?" he questions when I start to walk away.

I look over my shoulder at him. "Because I'm not out of hope yet. And Breslin Rae has a way of making even the toughest cynic a believer again."

Because she saved me the first time. She saved me when I didn't think there was anything left to salvage.

CHAPTER 30
BRESLIN

I *shouldn't be doing this.*

I take a nervous step up the bleachers, my heart hammering in my chest the entire time.

I didn't plan on coming tonight but as the seconds on the clock ticked by, I couldn't stay away.

Tucking a strand of hair behind my ear, I step up the next bleacher. "Hey," a familiar deep voice calls out and I freeze.

Warm brown eyes encased by black-rimmed glasses meet mine and I swallow hard. We haven't spoken in days, but I guess it's no surprise to see him here.

"Wanna sit?" Landon offers, pointing beside him. I look around, wincing at the turnout. The away team's bleachers are packed with people, but hardly anyone is here for the Wolverines.

My insides constrict in protest but I take a seat next to him anyway.

When my eyes land on a number 3 stretched across a broad and muscular back covered by a gray jersey, I hold my breath and my pulse thrums wildly. We're sitting too high up, making it impossible for him to see us, but he turns toward the bleachers anyhow, helmet in his hand. The look on his face gives nothing away. One would never know just how much is riding on him winning.

The game begins and I'm so nervous for him I nearly puke. I need him to win this game. No matter how much I may hate him, if something ever happened to him...I'll cease to exist. The universe will have to take me too because my soul won't survive it.

I grip the aluminum so hard my knuckles turn white. I try to suck in air, but it's impossible, panic has my body frozen with fear. My pulse kicks up another notch then and everything swirls around me in one big blur.

A warm hand slides over mine, unclenching my hand and squeezing my fingertips.

"Hey," Landon whispers. "You got an A on your Ethics test."

I sit there baffled and my jaw hangs open. I have no idea why he's talking about the stupid Ethics test we had yesterday when so much is hanging in the balance. I take a deep breath, intending to tell him off and that's when I realize.

I can breathe again. His statement was nothing more than a distraction so I wouldn't pass out.

He cups my cheek. "Keep breathing for me, sweetheart."

I nod and suck in more air, focusing on the hint of amber in his eyes. When the away audience erupts in loud cheers, I flinch because I know they scored.

No. They can't win.

Tentacles wrap around my lungs, suffocating me. I can't bring myself to look at the field again, not without losing my shit entirely. "Tell me something," I say to Landon. "Tell me anything. I need you to keep talking to me."

His other hand comes around to cup both my cheeks, preventing me from turning my head. "Do you remember the day we met?"

My mind floats back to that day and I smile at the memory. "I was locked out of the apartment with all my stuff because Kit forgot to leave me a key and went off with Becca somewhere."

He laughs. "You looked so upset sitting against the front door with your head in your hands, cursing at your cell phone."

"I was so mad at Kit for not leaving me a key. We had to move out of the dorms that day and I had nowhere to go. And neither her or the landlord would answer their phones." I lick my lips. "But then I saw you leaning against your own door studying me. You were so kind and sweet, offering to let me hang out in your apartment until things got sorted."

He squeezes his eyes shut. "I was in a really bad place back then."

His words take me by surprise. "You were?"

When he opens his eyes, they're full of sorrow. "It was the anniversary of Levi's death." His gaze slides away. "Plenty of anniversaries had passed, but that one was the hardest on me. Or rather, the few months leading up to it were the hardest if I'm being completely honest. I was in a depression so dark, I didn't think I'd ever be able to crawl my way out of it. I stopped socializing with what little friends I had. I stopped taking care of myself and my diabetes. I stopped playing music. I stopped living."

But you played me music that day.

"I know," he whispers, and I don't realize I've said those words out loud. "I did." He inhales and pulls me closer. "I remember lying in bed the night before I met you, praying for a purpose. Praying for someone to love me. Praying for someone to fix me because I didn't think I could go on much longer. I was tired of feeling like people's leftovers. Tired of life in general."

He recoils. "I was making plans to end it soon, because I couldn't take the pain. I couldn't take how hollow and alone I felt."

My eyes well with tears and my throat closes up on me again. "Landon."

His thumb strokes my cheekbone. "And then I met you. And

you were adorable, sexy, and stubborn. So full of fire and ice. So different than anyone I'd ever met before. I hung on to every word you said as we talked. I was completely transfixed by you. I still am."

I draw in a shaky breath and his hand comes to rest on my knee. "And when you told me you loved music, I pulled out my guitar and played for you. It was the first time I played in months." He smiles and rubs his neck, looking embarrassed. "I even called my boss that night and begged for him to squeeze me in at the Black Spoon and give me my old job back."

His fingertips draw little circles on my inner thigh that have me trembling. "You told me you were already working at the Black Spoon."

"I did. I had quit two months before. But I wanted to impress you so I told you that I still worked there. I wanted you to see me play. I wanted you to fall for me the way I was already falling for you."

I reach up and touch the stubble on his jaw. "I did. God, you were amazing. I remember crushing on you so hard that night."

"I remember you breathing life back into me, Breslin."

My heartbeat accelerates as he lowers his head and his lips find the base of my throat. "You saved me that summer," he murmurs into my pulse. "I'm sorry I ended up returning the favor with someone else. I'm sorry I wasn't able to do for you what you did for me."

He draws in a deep breath. "And I'm sorry I waited so long to tell you."

"Why are you telling me now?" I whisper, my voice quivering.

He holds my gaze, tugging me so close that his lips are almost touching mine. "Because the broken recognize the broken, sweetheart. Because I want you to believe that good things can happen when you're at your lowest. Because I want you to put your trust in someone again. But mostly? I want to be the person to fix what everyone else broke in you." He cups the back of my neck, the pads of his fingers trailing over my vertebra. "I can't speak for him so I won't, but I know that I would rather die than ever hurt you again."

His words resonate through my bones and a shiver courses through me.

When a tear slips from my eye, he catches it with his thumb. "But the only way this could ever work now is with all three of us. I know you and Asher have a long road ahead of you and you may never be able to heal those old wounds. But deep down inside, I think you want this, or you wouldn't have agreed to it in the first place. So, please give it a real chance before you give up, because you and I both know you have nothing left to lose at this point."

I open my mouth to speak but it's cut off when the away audience cheers again. Those damn tentacles around my lungs tighten once more when I check the scoreboard.

Woodside Wolverines—0: Canyon View Cardinals—10

Landon's wrong. I do have something to lose. We both do.

"Fuck," Landon mutters when he looks at the scoreboard. "I didn't realize they were that far ahead." His face pales, the reality appearing to be dawning on him. "Shit, they're going to lose."

I check my watch and stand up. Half time is in five minutes. "No, they're not."

His eyebrows crash together. "Where are you going?"

I start walking down the bleachers. I have no idea if this stupid plan of mine will work but it's better than sitting here doing nothing. "What does Asher want?"

He starts walking beside me. "Uh, right now? I'd say to win the game."

When I give him a look, his face goes slack. "Oh."

We walk off the field and he grabs my elbow. "Not to be crass, but you can't just barge into the locker room during half time and start blowing him, Bre."

Ignoring his concern, I make a right turn and see both the locker room and a storage closet.

I point to the storage closet. "I'll be in there. You wait out here and grab him right before he walks in."

He puts his hands on his hips, looking at me like I've lost my mind. "Bre, I'm not trying to be a buzzkill here but half time is when the coach talks to his players and—"

I close my eyes, hating the memories that are ripping through me. "Whenever he was having a bad game in high school he'd sneak out of the locker room and we'd find a way to make out during half time. All I need is five minutes. I know what I'm doing, Landon."

"Okay." He wrests his gaze away from me. "Go in the closet and I'll tell him to meet you there."

I start to walk away, but not before I reach for his hand. I can't believe I'm agreeing to this, but I know if I don't, I'll regret it forever. Landon was right before, I have nothing left to lose because you can't fall once you've already reached the bottom. And even though a broken heart can't break twice...just maybe it can heal. "Promise you won't hurt me?"

His hands find my waist and he steers me to him. "Never."

The serious expression on his face and the vehemence in his tone tells me he means it. "Promise not to bring up mine and Asher's past when we're together?"

He tucks two fingers under my chin. "If that's still your deal breaker then I won't. I'll do whatever it takes to keep my promises and not hurt either of you."

I nod, and then I close the distance between us and kiss him. "I have no idea what I'm agreeing to," I whisper against his lips.

His fingertips dance up and down my spine. "I don't think any of us do. But we'll figure everything out together. One day at a time."

"This is so fucked up."

A grin tugs at his mouth. "Isn't college all about the experience?"

A laugh breaks out of me and it feels so foreign because I can't remember the last time I laughed. But, God it feels good.

He presses a kiss to my forehead. "Fall and I'll catch you. Even if he can't, I always will."

The sound of heavy footsteps and male voices fill the air and I give him one last kiss before I walk into the storage closet.

"What the hell, Landon?" Asher roars. "I'm in the middle of a fucking game here."

Landon shoves him inside the closet and closes the door, leaving only the two of us.

The dim light above us flickers, barely illuminating the small space. His large frame is little more than a shadow in front of me. A shadow that haunts me whenever I close my eyes.

Memories slice through me and I rub the spot above my heart, hoping it will take the ache away.

God, I miss him so much.

My heart slams in my chest as I walk to him, reminding me that a broken heart can still beat through all the pain pumping through it.

"Hi," I whisper into the darkness.

"Breslin?" he questions, his voice gruff.

When he turns around he's right in front of me. "What—"

I don't give him a chance to finish, I jump into his arms, wrapping my body around him. His scent is heady and intoxicating, like testosterone and clean sweat and I can't help but breathe him in.

His large hands slide up and down my body, grazing over my rib cage and slithering down my back. His touch is so familiar it's like his hands have never left. Almost like three years and a broken heart didn't happen.

And right now? It didn't. Because I need to revisit our past to ensure he has a future.

"Breslin," he repeats, coating my name in such despair and desire my legs that are wrapped around him weaken.

When he licks his lips, my tongue comes out for a taste and he groans. "I don't understand what—"

"Do you want me?"

His response is automatic. "I never stopped wanting you."

My senses all stand at attention as he pulls me closer. His breathing becomes shallow and his heart thumps against my chest like a jackhammer.

I grab his face, melt into him a little more. "I need you to win for me."

His shoulders slump. "I—"

I sweep my mouth over his. I intended to give him a peck, a tease at what's to come, but electricity charges through us and he grabs the back of my neck and presses me against the wall, his hard body sinking into me. His kiss is equal parts rough and needy, demanding that I submit and give in.

And I do. Because there is no other choice right now. He gives me no other choice. *He never did.* I was his the very second he wanted me to be.

His tongue thrusts against mine and I drink him in, letting him poison me, letting him take down all my defenses that I worked so hard to build up.

My hands tangle and twist in his hair, gripping the short strands, and his mouth drops to my neck, licking a path from the tops of my breasts to the hollow of my throat and back up to my lips as he starts unbuttoning my shirt. His rough fingertips smooth over every inch of skin that he uncovers, marking me, claiming me as his once more.

I become lightheaded and my heart plummets as I orbit around him again, drowning in his universe. A universe that I'm so accustomed to, it's like coming back home.

A deep growl rips out of his chest. "I miss you so fucking much."

Ice injects into my veins, coursing through my bloodstream, causing reality to crash all around me. I wasn't supposed to let myself fall. I was only supposed to tempt and goad him. Give him just enough to make him want to win. I have to get control of this situation before everything goes up in smoke.

I sink my teeth into his lower lip until I taste the hint of copper and he finally pulls back. "If you want to fuck me you have to win."

Confusion spreads across his face. "What?"

"You heard me." I look at the door. "We can continue where we left things the other night. But only if you get your ass out on that field and play the shit out of the game."

"Why? I mean, *why* are you doing this? Why are you helping me?"

"Landon can't lose you," I tell him, locking my heart back up and tossing away the key. "And I love him enough that I'll do anything for him. Including share him with you."

It's not a lie. I do love Landon.

His rugged jaw tics and his face turns red with anger. "That's what this was about? He *asked* you to—"

My stomach free falls, afraid I've ruined my own plan by pushing him away too fast. "No. This wasn't his idea." I sigh in defeat. "I don't want you to lose." My hand curves around his face and I look up at him, hoping he can sense the words I won't ever bring myself to say again.

I love you big. I've never stopped loving you.

His body stiffens. The heat in the glare he shoots me is almost tangible. "Don't move from this spot." He lets go of me and I slip down his body. "When I get back you better be ready."

He starts to walk away but I halt him. "Ready for what?"

His smile would almost be evil if it wasn't so beautiful. "To continue this war that you keep insisting on, because I'm going to fuck you senseless after I win this game."

When the latch on the door clicks and Landon appears, he looks at him. "Keep her nice and wet for me."

My body buzzes as he closes the door and Landon walks inside. Asher's right, I shouldn't keep this little war going on between us but I can't help it. It's how I protect myself. *It's how I allow myself to have him.* Making him the devil prevents me from seeing the angel he once was.

Landon runs a hand over his head, looking all sorts of puzzled. "What—"

I don't give him a chance to finish that statement because I sink down to my knees, pull down his zipper, and give him a coy smile. "You heard him."

CHAPTER 31

ASHER

Hands pat my back and excited voices congratulate me as I step out of the quickest shower I've ever taken, throw on a pair of sweatpants, and high tail it the fuck out of there.

Adrenaline beats through me like a drum the closer I get to the storage closet. My body humming in need, want, and anger.

Because no one can wind me up or push my buttons like she can.

Irritation surges through me with every step I take. *I won the game because of her.*

I've never hidden the truth about the power she holds over me, but I can't say that I like the idea of her wielding it whenever and however she wants. Even if it did save my ass today.

I grind my molars and my heart pounds like it's trying to break free from my chest. Because that's not the real reason I'm mad. Not even close.

I'm mad because I thought we had a moment back there, a real moment where we connected like we used to, because for a single solitary second...she was mine again.

I thought I got my Breslin back.

But no. Because she wants to continue playing the part of the princess stuck in her ivory tower while I continue to be the big bad wolf to Landon's white fucking knight.

My dick gives a jolt and I can't help but smile with my next thought. Because unfortunately for her, she just provoked the wolf...and he's fucking famished. Breslin offered herself up as a prize and I'm here to fucking collect.

I throw open the door of the storage room and my craving becomes damn near insatiable due to the position I find them in.

Landon's jeans are around his ankles and Breslin's half-naked, her arm snaked around his neck and his hand inside her leggings. Through the thin material I can see his fingers working her over.

The moans coming from those full lips of hers tell me she's close.

Breslin starts rocking into his hand, her breaths coming in uneven bursts as she starts to spasm. Landon's eyes are closed so he can't see me, but Breslin can. Because she's looking me right in the eyes the entire time, her mouth curving into a smile as he gets her off. A smile I can't decipher—because I'm not sure if it's because she knows that I won, or because of what I'm watching. Knowing her, probably a little bit of both.

Landon pulls his hand out of her pants and sucks his fingers, licking the remnants of her orgasm from them.

And that's when he opens his eyes, sees me, and his face lights up. "You won." He rushes over to me and I don't hesitate to grab his face and kiss him, tasting her on his tongue.

"What was the score?" he asks when I release him, but I don't respond.

I'm not interested in talking about the game, there's one thing and one thing only that I'm after right now.

I stalk toward her and she raises her chin like she's preparing for a battle, but I don't miss the hint of urgency in her eyes.

Even though she'll tell anyone who asks just how much she hates me, I know the truth. Breslin needs me to scratch this itch just as much as I do. No matter how different we are now and no matter what happens with us, the flame between us won't ever die out. She knows it as much as I do. It's part of what fuels her hate for me.

The air in the room stilts as arousal hits me full force and I latch onto her hips, my thumbs skimming the skin above her leggings.

She licks her lips nervously and when my hands come around to grab that plump ass of hers, she swallows and averts her gaze to Landon.

I clasp her jaw, forcing her to look at me. As much as I want Landon, this doesn't have shit to do with him right now.

This is about *us*.

I give her a smirk, making sure I flash her some teeth and dimples, and then I throw her up against the wall so hard the shelves around us shake.

She wraps her legs around me and claws at my back, her nails sending shivers up and down my spine. I can feel how soaked she is through my sweatpants. "Looks like he got you all hot and bothered for me, huh, baby?"

Her eyes drift to Landon again, but my grip on her jaw hardens. "*Don't* look at him."

The sharp tone of my voice has her eyes snapping back to me. She wants to protest, but I push my hand inside her pants, move her panties to the side, and plunge a finger inside her. "Such a naughty girl, letting Landon finger fuck you and get you off before I do."

I pull down her bra and pinch her nipple between my fingers. When she arches into me, my lips find the juncture of her neck and shoulder and I run my mouth over those freckles I love so much. "You taste so fucking sweet."

Behind me, I hear Landon make a husky noise in the back of his throat and my cock twitches. "Did you take care of him earlier?"

She nods and I lick the shell of her ear. "You suck him off? Take that thick cock of his into your pretty little mouth?"

Her heart is pounding against my chest, her eyes becoming dilated. When she doesn't answer, I add another finger and curl them deep inside her pussy. "If you don't tell me what you did to him, Breslin, then I'll make you show me."

She clenches around my fingers and throws her head back. She's dripping all over my hand and I know she's about to come, but I'm not about to grant her that privilege just yet.

I remove my fingers and call Landon over to me. "Open."

He doesn't waste a second, he sucks my fingers into his mouth and laps at them insatiably. I look down at where he's touching himself, watching the tendons in his wrist flex with every slow stroke, making my dick jerk.

I put Breslin down and place her hand over my package. "Take my cock out."

There's a sharp intake of breath as her shaky fingers dip into the elastic of my sweatpants. But then she shoots me a sly smile and turns those fierce green eyes on me. "Make me."

In an instant, I grab her ponytail and pull her to the floor.

My abs contract and my blood pressure rises when she yanks my pants down and my cock springs out, heavy and thick.

Her eyes zero in on the drop of liquid on my tip and I hold it out to her like an offering. "Open your mouth."

The second her lips part, I drag the head of my cock across her tongue, groaning when the liquid hits it and she moans. When the tip of her tongue stabs the small hole for another taste, I swear to fuck my balls lift. A shudder quickly follows when she closes her mouth around me and sucks me in one long motion, almost from root to tip.

I have to brace one hand on a shelf nearby when she repeats the movement, my dick hitting her tonsils this time.

Jesus, she's good at that.

Tightening my grip on her hair, I pull her back. There's no way I'm going to last and I'll be damned if I'm about to come in her mouth like a two-pump chump right now.

Easing her back up off the floor, I pull her in for a kiss. Something I know she didn't expect by the way she hesitates.

And she's right to hesitate...because before she can catch her next breath I tug her leggings down and pick her up.

Hands cupping her hips, I shove her against the wall. Then I maneuver her legs until her thighs are pressed firmly against her stomach and pin her in the position. A position that exposes her slick, pink flesh and causes her to blush when I slide my hands up her legs, drop down, and inhale her arousal.

My balls throb as I take in her glistening pussy that's so fucking swollen and pouty for me. Breslin can deny how she feels about me all she wants, but her body doesn't lie. I lean in for a taste, planting wet, sloppy kisses all over her slit and her clit.

Little breathy moans escape her as she digs her nails into my head, urging me on. A rush of lust plows into me when she shudders against my mouth. I flatten my tongue, taking her in long laps that end with a flick against her clit and her juices drenching my chin.

"Oh, God," she screams. "Oh, my fucking God, I'm coming."

Goddamn right you are. She comes so hard she clamps my tongue for dear life, her tight walls caging me in as her thick cream seeps into my mouth.

My dick fucking sizzles as I swallow every bit of her climax and she rocks her hips back and forth. My name shreds out of her when I nibble her sensitive bud and when I take it between my teeth, she cries out in a combination of pleasure and agony. I can practically taste her hate for me spewing from her.

Hate me all you want, baby. But you can't deny that you're mine.

I stand up as her tremors subside and she fights to catch her breath. When she makes the mistake of looking over my shoulder at Landon—I slam into her so fast I swear her teeth chatter. Her eyes cut to mine, so full of every single emotion a person could ever feel. I have to take a breath past the ache that's crushing my heart as I drive into her, because I remember what it felt like to be this deep inside her the first time.

When I pull back and thrust into her again, she latches onto my dick, molding herself around me. Christ, she's so fucking tight. So fucking perfect. So fucking *mine.*

Her eyes become glassy and her chest heaves. She looks at Landon again, but I don't stop her. Because I know she needs him.

She needs him in all the ways she doesn't need me.

Because I'm the asshole. The bad guy. The one who broke her.

And this is our unspoken deal now. *The only way I get to keep her.* It's both a fucked up gift and a curse. But I'll take it. I'll take every scrap she's willing to give me.

I fuck her hard and fast, grabbing her hips and gliding her up and down my shaft. My dick swells as she grips me harder and when I look down and see Landon on the floor beside us with his mouth open, inching towards us, I almost spill my fucking load right then.

I grab his neck and bring him closer to where we're connected. When I pull out slightly, his eyes blaze with heat that has my balls tingling.

I lift my gaze to Breslin and we both pause, staring at each other, wondering what his next move will be.

And that's when Landon—motherfucking sexual chameleon that he is—moves forward and wraps his lips around the base of my cock, licking and sucking me so goddamn good after every swift and deep thrust.

Breslin pounds the wall with her fist and starts going crazy, cursing and mewling both mine and Landon's name as he begins lapping at us both while I fuck her, his mouth going from her pussy to my balls now.

"Holy hell," she says and I drive into her again, then pull out slightly so Landon can continue his fucking torture and lick Breslin's cream from my dick.

I pick up my pace and Landon does something with his fucking mouth that makes us both groan. "You like this, don't you, baby? Like him cleaning you off my dick while I fuck you."

Her eyes roll back and she grips my shoulders, looking so far gone in pleasure I wish I could take a snapshot of her in this moment. "Yes. Fuck, yes," she rasps. Her head hits the wall and she twitches and clasps her pussy around my length, coming so hard I can only fall against her as she milks me to my own orgasm.

I slip out and watch as Landon spreads her, eagerly licking me out of her as she convulses with the aftershock.

Every part of me vibrates with my need for her and I bury my face in her neck, inhaling deeply. "I love—"

"Landon," she whispers before shoving me away.

When Landon stands up, she leaps into his arms, discarding me completely. Putting me back in my place, cutting me back down to size.

It's then that I realize that while I may have won the battle this round, I lost the war.

I'll always lose the war when it comes to her.

Because I'll always love her...even when she hates me. Even when I'm watching her fall in love with him.

Landon reaches for my hand but I pull away. I start to walk out but he grabs my shoulder and gives it a squeeze. When I look at him, my throat closes in on me. Because I see nothing but love and desperation in his eyes...for the both of us.

He runs his hand along my jaw, his eyes pleading, telling me not to give up.

Because that's who Landon is. He's the glue that holds us together when we fall apart. He's the one that puts us back together again.

When I lean into his touch and give him a nod, he throws one of his arms around me and the other one around her. "Come on, let's go home."

CHAPTER 32

BRESLIN

"Well, according to *Cosmo* you are 100% addicted to sex."

"What?" I ask above the din of the cafeteria. A cafeteria that's unusually crowded the day before Thanksgiving Recess begins. But then again, most of us are just getting out of exams and starving.

Kit holds up her phone. "100 out of 100. You, my floozy friend, are an addict." She nudges my ribs and waggles her eyebrows. "Which would totally explain the last few months, huh?"

When she starts singing *Addicted to Love-* by Robert Palmer with a singing voice that could wake the dead, I roll my eyes. "Since when do you read *Cosmo* anyway?"

She gestures to the very long line ahead of us. "I'm hungry and bored." She cups a hand over her mouth. "Especially since people are taking for-freaking-ever to get their food."

I start to laugh, but when I look across the cafeteria it comes to a rapid halt. I feel like someone just stuck me in a *DeLorean*.

Because there's Asher Holden— smiling, laughing, and lighting up an entire room with his presence while the people surrounding him treat him like goddamn royalty.

I'm not being petty. Far from it, actually. Truth be told, I couldn't be happier that he's put Woodside back on the map and he's on a winning streak of epic proportions. With only two more games left in the season—one of them being the championship—he's damn near invincible and he's basically become a celebrity around here.

I just...I hate this feeling in my chest. I hate how familiar it all is.

Well, with one very big exception. My eyes fall on Landon. My adorable, sweet Landon who's sitting in a corner of the cafeteria by himself with a laptop in front of him and a pair of headphones on.

The past few months have been...interesting to say the least.

Kit snaps her fingers in front on my face. "Hello, earth to B."

I look back at her. "Sorry. What's up?"

"I asked if you were sure that you didn't want to go to Nanna Bishop's with me for Thanksgiving dinner."

"Positive," I tell her. I hate that bigoted woman with the fire of a thousand suns and I won't be able to spend five minutes in a room with her let alone an entire meal. "Plus, I'm kind of cooking dinner for Landon and Asher since Landon's now decided that he doesn't want to go to his parents' house anymore."

I'd ask Kit to join us for dinner but I already know she'll decline because she doesn't want to upset her grandmother.

She looks across the cafeteria at him. "Still hasn't told them yet, huh?"

I shake my head. "Nope, but he will whenever he's ready. He said he didn't want to do it over the holidays." I take a breath. "Also, he's planning on going to England and touring with one of his favorite indie rock bands over the Christmas break and wants to be in the right headspace."

The line moves up and we each pick up a tray. "Man, that's so awesome. Maybe they'll ask him to be a permanent member."

"They might, but Landon said he doesn't—" My words fall

when I see some brunette sidle up to Asher and stroke his arm. I can't hear what Asher says to her but she tosses her head back and giggles, her exposed cleavage practically jiggling with the movement.

I swallow hard. The girl is gorgeous. Like model gorgeous. Tall and slim with shiny dark hair and tits that are as perfect as the rest of her.

And although I've never spoken to the girl, I already hate her.

I hate her because she's everything I'm not.

My hands tighten around the tray I'm holding. The dynamic between the three of us is...weird. I mean, yeah, we have sex—*great* sex—but it's sort of an unspoken rule that I keep Asher at an arm's length and we both just focus on Landon.

Kit follows my gaze and frowns. "Look, if you want Megan Fox's doppelganger to stop flirting with your boyfriend then go over there and put a stop to it."

I turn back around, grab a plate, and start loading it up with food. "He's not my boyfriend."

Kit makes a face. "Okay, officially color me confused. Last time I checked you told me that Landon was your boyfriend and that—"

"Yes," I say, harsher than I intended. "Landon *is* my boyfriend. Asher is most definitely not."

Nor will he ever be again.

"But—" Kit starts.

I turn to face her...but instead come face to face with Asher.

"Excuse me," he says to Kit. When he reaches over her for a plate and utensils, I don't miss the way his jaw tics.

I pull on my bottom lip. "Hey—"

"Yooo, Asher," some guy ahead of us calls out. From the looks of it he's another football player. "Saved you a spot in line, man."

Without so much as a look in my direction he walks over to his teammate.

Kit taps her chin. "You were saying?"

I drop my tray. "I'm not hungry anymore."

"**W**hat the fuck? What is *that*?" Asher questions when he walks into Landon's kitchen, looking horrified.

"That," I answer as I take the pan out of the oven. "Is Thanksgiving dinner."

Asher drops his workout bag on a kitchen chair and gives me a look. "Why would you do that? For fuck's sake they're just babies, Breslin. They didn't even get a chance to become full on turkeys yet." His eyes widen. "You monster."

"They aren't turkey babies, you moron. They're Cornish hens. Supermarket ran out of turkey."

Landon strides into the kitchen and does a double-take when he looks in the pan. "What—"

"Dude, I know," Asher says, frowning. "She even stuffed the little guys. Saddest thing I've ever seen."

I wipe my hands on my apron. "If you don't like it, you don't have to eat it." I stir the mashed potatoes. "I spent all day preparing this."

Landon kisses my forehead. "It looks great."

"Traitor," Asher mumbles when he walks over to him and gives him the same greeting.

I grab three plates and start filling them with food and Landon grabs his laptop.

"It's Thanksgiving," I remind him when he sits down. "Think you can put that away while we eat?"

I'm not trying to sound like a mother hen, but it's the first Thanksgiving that I've prepared and it means something to me.

My stomach sinks as I look at the food and I silently debate making a fourth plate. My father lives a little over three hours away by car. I could take a plate to him and see how he's doing.

Given I haven't heard from him in months and whenever I call him I can't seem to get through, I'm really worried about him. I mean, I know he's still alive...the checks he keeps cashing tells me so.

Which I know in the back of my mind can only mean *one* thing.

My own father *blocked* me.

On some level, I should be relieved considering our relationship, but I'm not. Truth is, it makes my heart ache. Losing one parent is hard enough, but losing both of them?

"I'm just checking the airline for available flights to England," Landon says, interrupting my thoughts.

"I thought you already booked your flight to England?"

"Yeah," Asher chimes in. "Didn't you book it last month when you officially agreed to go on tour with them?"

Landon looks sheepish. "I did. But they asked me to come two weeks early. You know, hang out with them on the tour for a little bit so I know what to expect."

"That's the entire winter break you'll be gone," I whisper and he looks down.

"I can tell them no," he starts to say but I shake my head.

"Don't you dare," I tell him. "I know how excited you are about it. When do you have to leave?"

He presses a few more keys. "There's a cheap flight a few days before Christmas actually."

Asher sighs and takes a sip of his water. "Don't go snogging or chatting up any blokes, got it?"

"Or shagging any girls," I cut in and he looks between us.

"You're kidding me, right? Why in the world would I ever—"

"Didn't stop you the last time," I blurt out and both him and Asher turn to look at me.

I want to take back what I said but it's the truth. The fact of the matter is—Landon's technicality aside; because I broke up with him before I left for Europe—I'm the only one in the room who hasn't ever cheated.

He stands up and walks over to me, framing my face in his hands. "I wouldn't do that to you. There's no other girl in the world who could ever compare to you."

I force a smile and nod. We don't exactly have a great track record when it comes to one of us leaving the country, but I believe him when he says he'll stay faithful.

Out of the corner of my eye, I see Asher scanning us intently. I don't know what to make of the expression on his face. It's somewhere between sadness and exasperation.

I bring the plates over to the table. "We should eat."

Asher rubs the back of his neck, appearing uneasy. Right when Landon closes the top to his laptop, Asher looks at him. "Mrs. Rogers grade that last test yet?"

Landon scrunches his face. "I think so. Haven't had a chance to read her email yet, but she'll be posting the grades the day after tomorrow. Why?"

Asher pales. "It wasn't exactly my favorite test."

I can see the panic on Landon's face and my stomach flips. Asher's been doing great in all his classes, English included, but he's really struggling when it comes to Ethics.

I fight the urge to laugh. It would be almost ironic and comical if it wasn't so serious.

Landon flips the top open on his laptop. "We studied for that test for hours."

Asher digs into his mashed potatoes. "I'm sure it's not that bad. I'm still maintaining a C+ like I'm supposed to."

Landon closes his eyes and curses. "You were maintaining a C+." He turns his laptop and my hand flies over my mouth when I see the big, fat F next to his name.

"Shit," I mumble at the same time Landon says, "Fuck, Asher."

Asher throws his hands up in the air. "Don't look at me like that." He stands up. "What the hell do you guys want from me? I'm doing the best I can here." He starts ticking things off with his fingers. "I've won every single game so far. I'm up at the butt crack of dawn for every single practice. I'm busting my ass in all my other classes. I work like a slave for Coach Crane, picking up people's garbage all the time. Not to mention, I still find time for this relation—whatever the fuck this is."

Landon drags a hand down his face. "You're gonna need to put in the effort if you—"

"No, don't even!" Asher shouts loud enough that the windows rattle. "You know how hard I already work. You know the sacrifices I make."

"We *all* work our asses off," I cut in. "You think I want to work doubles at a coffee shop and study my ass off so I can keep my scholarship? You think Landon wants to tutor idiots who don't pay attention to him all day in addition to attending classes for not one but *two* majors? Of course, not. But we do anyway. Welcome to the world of being a responsible adult, Asher. Not all of us were born with a silver spoon and a rich Daddy. Some of us have to make sacrifices for the things we want."

He stabs the table with his pointer finger. "I didn't choose to make *these* sacrifices, Breslin."

I fold my arms across my chest. "Well, maybe the person you should be yelling at is your asshole brother instead of my boyfriend."

He pounds the kitchen table with his fist. "Christ, you're a real piece of work."

"What the hell is that supposed to mean?"

"It means—" he starts to say before Landon stands up.

"Enough!" he shouts, glaring at us both. "Breslin, cut him some slack. The amount of pressure Asher is under is...enormous."

I play with my stuffing. Landon has a point. Being threatened by a bookie who has ties to the mob because your brother has a gambling problem isn't exactly a walk in the park.

"I'm sorry," I mumble in Asher's direction.

Landon puts his hands on his hips and blows out a breath. "I hate to say it, Asher but you're gonna have to really try and make this a priority. The Dean isn't going to give a shit about how many touchdowns you score, and considering you got a D on the Ethics test before this one, you have no choice but to get an A on your final." He looks back at his laptop. "Hopefully she doesn't bench you for next week's game. I'm gonna see if I can talk to her first thing on Monday. Tell her you weren't feeling well when you took the test. The fact that you're doing so well in your other classes will help me plead my case."

Asher nods. "Sounds like a plan." He rubs his hands together. "I can hunker down, we can put in some more hours studying before the final—"

"I can't," Landon whispers, rubbing his temples.

Asher slumps down in his chair. "What do you mean?"

"It means," Landon says slowly. "That I can work in some extra time to help you with the next test, but my schedule for finals is all booked up." He pulls a piece of paper out of his bag. "I literally have no time. Look how many students I'm scheduled to tutor during finals week."

I suck in a breath when I notice all the time slots blocked off for the middle of December. "You'll hardly be sleeping."

Landon nods. "It's insane. I'm not looking forward to it." He sits back in his chair. "Not to mention I have a show at the Black Spoon the night before finals. And I have to spend whatever free time I have, which is pretty much none, making sure I know every single note and chord to every single song for *The Resistance* before I go on tour with them."

My heart pulls, I've never seen Landon look so stressed.

"I can see if I can get a copy of the final..." Landon starts to say but Asher grabs his hand. "No. I appreciate the gesture, but I told you back then that I never wanted you to do that for me. It's okay. I've got this. I—"

"I can help," I blurt out before I can stop myself. When they both look at me I add, "I'm getting an A in our Ethics class. And I'll be studying for the Ethics final myself anyway so it's really not a big deal."

"You're gonna tutor me for the final?" Asher questions, raising a brow.

"Do you have a better option in mind?"

He leans back in his chair. "Nope."

A bolt of annoyance hits me when I see the hint of a smile on his face. "What's your problem?"

He points to his chest. "Who me? No, I'm not the one with the problem here." He flits his gaze down my body and back up again. "But you might have one."

I balk at him. "Why?"

I want to reach over and wipe the sly smirk that spreads across his face. Especially after he looks me in the eye and utters, "Because I've been known to make my tutors fall in love with me."

When you've spent the better part of the last two months sleeping in a bed with not one but *two* men almost every night...it's weird to wake up all alone.

Since classes are still out for the holiday I'm stumped as to where they both could be. I check my phone to see if Landon left me a text message and when I don't see any, I decide to stretch my limbs and get up out of bed.

I'm making my way across the small apartment to the kitchen when I hear it. The sound of something buzzing.

It sounds like it's coming from Landon's studio, which means he must have the door open.

When I walk down the short hallway and enter the room...

I scream. Or rather, it's more of an, "Eeekkk!"

My hand flies over my mouth as I take in the small pile of brown hair on the floor. The short, slightly wavy, beautiful strands once belonging to Landon.

A Landon who apparently now has...a freaking Mohawk.

They both look at me then. Both meaning Asher—destroyer of not only relationships, but hair. "Chill, Breslin," he says, the buzz from the clippers in his hand going silent. "You almost made me fuck it up."

Landon pivots on the piano bench he's sitting on. "I take it you don't like it?"

I fidget as I take in his new haircut. Both sides of his head are completely shaven, almost down to the scalp, leaving only the trail of short, spiky hair right down the center.

Asher rests the clippers on the bench before he reaches for a towel and wipes Landon's neck and shoulders. It's only then that I realize they're both shirtless and my heart does a little skip of appreciation.

He grabs his neck until Landon's head falls back and he looks up at him. "I think you look fucking hot," Asher murmurs before he kisses him.

I clear my throat. "It's not that I don't like it. It's just...you know...sudden." The truth is I've always hated change and I've never adapted well to it. And not for nothing, but they could have given me a heads up. "What made you want to get a Mohawk?"

"Technically it's more of a Fohawk," Asher says. "His sides aren't completely shaven and his hair is short."

"Right," I whisper, unable to take my eyes off of Landon's hair.

"Told you she would freak," Asher says and I glare at him.

"I'm not freaking." I cross my arms and look at Landon. "I'm just caught a little off guard. How would you react if I decided to shave half my head one morning? Or change my hair color?"

Both Asher and Landon wince. "Fuck that noise," Asher says. "Natural redheads are hard to come by. You're practically extinct." A slow smirk touches his lips. "You might have bare floors, but I for one really dig the fact that your carpet would match the drapes." He winks. "If you catch my drift."

I roll my eyes because leave it up to Asher to make me feel like some kind of poodle at a dog show. "Wow, talking about hair and interior decorating in the same breath. How equally chauvinistic and stereotypical of you."

He places a hand over his chest. "You wound me." He grabs his dick through his basketball shorts. "But don't worry, baby. I'll let you get down on your knees so you can suck your apology out of me."

I take a step forward. "That won't be happening, you fucking—"

"Enough," Landon says, standing up. "Christ, I feel like I'm a goddamn referee instead of a boyfriend half the time."

"Just half the time?" Asher scoffs, eyes on me.

"What is that supposed to mean?"

He shoots me a smile. "It means your little damsel in distress bullshit is getting old." He mock gasps. "Oh, wait. I better shut my mouth before you go running to Landon to kiss your boo-boo."

I take a breath and let his harsh words roll off my back, but not before I say, "I run to Landon because he makes me feel good. Something you never do."

He flicks a piece of hair off him. "I'm pretty damn sure I make you feel good when my mouth is between your legs."

I crinkle my nose. "Yeah, well, you know what they say. Everyone has a purpose."

We stand there glaring at one another for the better part of a minute, the anger between us rising like a tidal wave.

"If you two don't mind, I have to get some work done," Landon says, shaking his head.

My heart pulls because he wasn't wrong before. He really does play the part of referee when it comes to me and Asher.

I look at him, intending to apologize and I swear I do a double-take. I've always been attracted to Landon, but somehow it's kicked up a notch. His new haircut combined with his tattoos have him looking 100% sexy rocker. The freaking women—and men—in the U.K. are going to be tossing their panties at him...or should I say *knickers*, while he's over there.

I lick my suddenly dry lips and Landon's eyes track the movement. "You okay?"

I back up and heat rises to my cheeks. "Yeah. I'm f-fine." *Jesus, did I actually just stutter?* I take another step back, suddenly very aware that all I have on is a t-shirt and underwear. While these two insanely attractive men are staring at me like I'm their breakfast.

"Dude, she's totally turned on," Asher says. "Look at her nipples. Those suckers could cut glass right now."

I narrow my eyes, intending to tell him off for talking about me like I'm not even here but then my insides swoop when Landon grins and takes a stride in my direction, backing me into a wall. "Is that so?"

"I um. I think maybe I really like your haircut after all," I whisper.

He looks down at my tits and my nipples get even harder.

A rush of air escapes me when he grabs a fistful of my shirt. And then before I can say another word he lifts it up, exposing my boobs. In my peripheral vision, I see Asher adjust his erection as Landon lowers his mouth and circles one of my nipples with his tongue.

"Take off your panties," he says between my breasts, his voice rough and tight. "Show me how wet you are for me."

Good lord, there isn't enough air to suck in with that statement.

My fingers find my hips and slowly I peel them down my legs and step out of them, kicking them to the side.

Landon's eyes darken when he picks them up and my entire body shakes when he brings the crotch up to his mouth and licks.

Behind Landon, Asher's nostrils flare and he squeezes his dick through his basketball shorts while muttering a curse.

When Landon swipes his tongue across the fabric a second time and groans, my legs turn to mush.

His gaze dips to where I'm clenching my thighs. "Open your—"

A loud, almost obnoxious knock on the door stops him mid-sentence.

I open my mouth to ask if he was expecting any visitors but then his phone rings and the color drains from his face. "It's my mom."

"Talk about ruining the mood," Asher says.

Landon turns and looks between the both of us. "I should probably let her in." He cringes. "Considering she has a key and all."

He starts walking. "Would you two mind hanging out in here? Just until I tell her about the both of you."

Without waiting for a response, he walks out.

When I start to pick up my t-shirt and underwear, Asher smirks. "Don't get dressed on my account."

I quickly put my clothes back on. "You're such a—"

"Oh, my goodness, Landon. What happened to your hair?" a woman's voice shrieks, effectively cutting me off.

"Guess his mom doesn't dig it, either." He starts to walk toward the door but I grab his elbow. "What are you doing? He told us to wait in here."

"I'm walking out to the hall so I can hear them better."

I pinch the bridge of my nose. "That's called eavesdropping."

He shrugs. "So? Trust me, Landon's no stranger to popping in on people during a private moment. Besides, what if he needs one of us to be there for him when he tells her, but we won't be able to hear him because we're stuck in here." He points a finger at me. "And you can't tell me you're not curious to hear what he says about us in the first place."

I pull on my bottom lip. He has a point. Not about being curious, but about not being able to hear him in case he needs us.

At least that's what I tell myself as I follow Asher out to the hallway and prop myself against the wall, with him on the other side of me.

"You said you were sick yesterday," his mom starts. "So, I brought you some soup."

"Thanks," Landon says. "I'm feeling better now."

I hear the sound of a kitchen stool scraping across the floor. "So, what's with the hair? It doesn't exactly scream professional. Thankfully it will grow out before you graduate."

There's a long sigh from Landon. "I wanted something different." He pauses. "I also thought it would be kind of cool since I'm going on tour with a band over the Christmas break. I'll be traveling to England so it's—"

"I'm sorry, what?" his mom yells. "Exactly when were you planning on telling me?"

Landon starts to speak but then he's cut off again. "You can't go all the way to England, Landon. You're sick, something could happen to you."

"I have diabetes, Ma. Not cancer," Landon counters.

"No," his mom says sternly. "I'm sorry, but absolutely not. You're canceling your trip."

Landon laughs. "I'm 21. And I've been much better about taking care of myself lately."

Silence stretches between them for what feels like hours before she says, "I'll talk to your father about it. Maybe one of us can go with you since we'll be on Christmas break, too."

Geez. Landon wasn't kidding about his mother being overprotective.

"I've already paid for the flight and signed a contract. I'm not canceling and I don't need a chaperone. I've been living on my own for almost four years and I'm still alive. I can handle going to the U.K. by myself."

"Landon—"

"How's the rug rat doing?"

"Lainey is fine, she's doing much better in her Math class now. She said the notes you emailed her have really helped."

"Good, I'm glad."

Beside me, Asher smiles, then Landon's mom speaks again. "So, I spoke with my boss the other day. He's agreed to set you up with an interview after you graduate and all but guaranteed me a job for you. It's obviously close to home and you'll save on rent by moving back in—"

"Mom," Landon whispers. "I appreciate it, I really do, but I already told you that I wasn't sure what I wanted to do after I graduate."

"Working at my school district and moving back home were the terms when your father and I paid for your tuition and agreed you could attend Woodside University," she says sharply and both me and Asher frown.

"Things change." He sighs. "I'm not trying to upset you, but you know how much I love music—"

"It's a hobby, Landon, not a suitable career path. We've talked about this."

Anger flickers in my chest. For some people that might be true, but not for Landon. He bleeds music from his very soul. The world would be a cold and dark place if he ever stopped creating or playing.

He was meant to play and create music, not the other way around.

"What is going on with you?" His mother says suddenly. "You seem so different now."

I hear the sound of the microwave turning on. "You mean happy. I think the word you're looking for is happy. Because I am happy now. Really freaking happy."

Warmth coats my heart with those words and I grin.

"Well, that's good to hear." Before Landon can follow up she quickly says, "I take it you're still seeing that girl. The architecture major. Brenda, right?"

Asher shakes his head and I roll my eyes.

"Breslin," Landon corrects and pride surges in my chest. "Her name is Breslin and yes I am. She's amazing." I can practically feel my heart stop with his next pause. "She's not the only one I'm seeing, though."

His mom clears her throat. "Well, you know what I think about that. But as long as you're safe I suppose there's no harm in not settling down with a girl right now—"

"His name is Asher," Landon whispers and beside me Asher's body goes rigid.

"Who is Asher?" his mom questions, sounding confused.

He blows out a breath. "My boyfriend. His name his Asher. That's the other person I'm seeing. I have a boyfriend and a girlfriend."

My heart folds in on itself. Talk about ripping the band-aid right off and putting yourself out there. But that's who Landon is, fearless and brave.

His mother laughs. "You're joking, right? You've always liked girls."

I wince, my mind flashing back to prom night. When I look over at Asher he closes his eyes.

"I know, and you're right—I did and I do still like girls," Landon answers. "But when Asher and I met we had a connection that I couldn't turn away from. He's really great and I can't wait for you to meet—"

"You're not a homosexual, Landon," his mother yells, sounding irate. "This is just a stupid college phase."

"This isn't a phase," Landon argues. "And you're right, I'm not a homosexual. I'm bisexual, technically. But none of the labels even matter because I love both of them."

Someone slams something on the kitchen counter. "I knew sending you away to college was a bad idea. Your father said you needed to spread your wings, but I knew something horrible was going to happen—"

"Me being happy and in love with two people is something horrible?" Landon questions and a loud sob breaks out from her.

"Oh, my God," his mother croaks out. "I can't believe this is happening." She sucks in air. "Do you know you can catch AIDS from being gay! This supposed boyfriend of yours is going to give you AIDS and I will end up losing you just like I lost Levi."

Beside me, Asher flinches and rage flares deep in my belly. While I can sympathize with her losing her son, it's not okay to lash out at Landon like this. Her son is bisexual, and most important-ly...he's happy. Something that should make her feel good as a parent, but instead she's acting like he just confessed to murder.

My blood whooshes in my ears and I start to shake. I might not be bisexual myself, but I've faced people like this woman my whole life. The world is *full* of people who think like her. People who judge those who are different and don't fit into a nice little box and it makes me sick.

I'm ready to walk out there and let this lady have a piece of my mind, but Asher clamps a hand on my shoulder and shakes his head.

"He's got this," he mouths.

"You can catch AIDS regardless of who you have sex with if you're not careful—" Landon starts to say before she cuts him off.

"And the girl. I mean, what self-respecting woman actually gets involved with two men!" My stomach sinks as she continues. "Just what kind of girl encourages this type of behavior or relationship? A disgraceful girl... that's who. Not the kind of girl you marry or have children with." Asher's jaw flexes and he balls his fists. When he makes to go out there next, I halt him by reaching for his hand.

"My God, this whole entire thing is disgusting and sick," his mother cries out. "It's clear these two have corrupted you somehow."

She lets out another sob. "You've always been sensitive and people have always taken advantage of you." A stool scrapes across the kitchen floor again. "But this isn't normal," she says. "Nothing about what you're telling me right now is normal. Healthy people don't lead lives like this. You need help." There's rummaging of some kind. "My friend knows a shrink and—"

I don't hear the rest of her statement because my heart falls to the floor with those words and tears spring to my eyes. Not just because her statement is cruel...but because it's dripping in honesty.

Landon's mom is right, nothing about our situation is normal and there are days where I can barely wrap my head around it. It's probably why we never talk about it—because it hurts too much to scrutinize the life that we're living, and we already know what society would say about our little arrangement as well as about us individually.

This whole thing started out as a solution to a problem. A way to deal with the anger and get over what happened. And while that didn't happen...something else did.

Because as complicated as this situation may be...there's something real and raw about it. When I have a bad day, I come here and talk about it. When I'm feeling insecure about something, both of them somehow know without me having to say a word.

When I need fire and passion. Someone to go toe to toe with until I've gotten every ounce of whatever I'm feeling out of my system for the day—there's Asher. Challenging me. Provoking me. Being the constant mirror that shows me how much I've overcome all while shaking me up and tearing me apart at the same time. He's the reminder to never be that girl I once was. The reminder that I need to be stronger than her.

And when I need someone to soothe the ache and lick my wounds, both the past and present ones —Landon's always there. Grounding me. Showing me it's okay to be vulnerable and let someone in again. Making me believe that good people really do exist all while loving me with everything he has. The kind of love I'm not so sure that I deserve most of the time. But still, he gives it to me in spades.

One sets my soul on fire and rocks me to my core, breaking me into a thousand tiny pieces over and over. The other is the balm that heals me and puts me back together again.

I close my eyes and sink against the wall, fighting back tears.

I loathe one and love the other...but I'm unable to let either of them go. I'm too far gone to stop what's already been started.

"I know you're worried and confused," Landon says above his mother's loud sobs. "I get it, this is a lot to take in. But I don't need a shrink. Please just listen—"

"Pack up your stuff. I'm taking you home," his mother says and I squeeze Asher's hand tighter. "This place...these *horrible* people have ruined you."

"Jesus, I'm not ruined, Ma. Take a breath, tone down the damn dramatics, and listen to what I'm saying," Landon barks, his tone laced with irritation. "I'm happy and I'm not going back home. And I'd really appreciate it if you would stop speaking badly about the people I love. You don't even know them."

"The people you love?" she scoffs. "Do you even hear yourself right now? This isn't right, Landon. This isn't the life we had planned for you—"

"I'm not him!" The sonorous timbre of his voice vibrates off the walls and I jump. "You can't resurrect Levi by controlling every aspect of *my* life. It won't bring him back."

"You're right," his mother says softly, her voice cracking. "And I know you're not him, because Levi *never* would have disappointed me like this."

Before I can stop him, Asher lets go of my hand and charges out there. I'm right on his heels.

His mother's jaw falls open and she gapes at us. All I can think is that it's rather ironic that Landon inherited his kind and beautiful brown eyes from her, because right now hers are filled with nothing but malice for the two of us.

Asher crosses his arms over his chest. "Get the hell out." His voice is so dark and gritty I fight back a shiver.

She jabs a finger at the both of us, looking appalled. "Excuse me?"

I mirror Asher's stance, not even caring that the only thing I'm wearing currently is one of Landon's t-shirts. "You heard him."

I look at Landon, gauging his reaction. My heart cracks when I see his glassy eyes and distraught expression. I run over to where he's standing and throw my arms around him.

Her head swivels to Landon. "If you choose this lifestyle." The finger that she's pointing at him shakes. "You can kiss your tuition and the job I just got you good-bye." She takes a step toward the door. "If you do this, you will have no one. Do you hear me?"

Landon stays silent...but I don't. "That's not true, because he has me." My eyes find Asher's. "He has *us*."

When Asher walks over to the door and opens it, she grimaces. "Don't even think about contacting your sister until you've come to your senses. You know how much she looks up to you and I don't want you contaminating her with this filth."

When Landon closes his eyes and winces, Asher bangs on the frame of the door. "Out!"

The second Asher closes the door behind her, Landon

collapses in my arms, his entire body defeated. I hold him tighter than I've ever held anyone in my life. I whisper how much I love him and how brave he is for doing what he did and having the courage to not only tell her, but stand up to her when she didn't accept him. I tell him he's the greatest human being that I've ever known.

He lifts his head when Asher walks over and I release him.

Asher blows out a breath. "Maybe I shouldn't have thrown her out. It's just...hurtful things were being said and I couldn't stand by and—"

"Thank you," Landon whispers, looking at both of us.

He starts to turn around but Asher touches his shoulder. "I'm sorry." His voice almost cracks on the word and tears sting my eyes.

Landon's eyebrows draw together. "For what?"

"For being the reason that she—"

In a flash, Landon wraps him in a hug. "Don't you ever apologize for that. Meeting you was one of the best things that ever happened to me." He looks at me. "The both of you." He squeezes his eyes shut. "She'll come around someday." His mouth tightens. "Or at least I hope she does."

When he takes a step back, he rubs his face. "I'm gonna go in the studio for a little bit."

Before either of us can say a word, he walks down the hallway and shuts the door behind him.

"He told me his mother was overprotective but—" Asher's voice trails off.

"I know," I say. "I feel horrible about what happened to her son but the way she treats Landon is—"

A loud boom coming from the studio causes me to stop mid-sentence. Asher and I look at one another and then we both run down the hallway and charge through the studio door.

Only to find Landon slamming his piano with a hammer, the beautiful wood splitting and pieces of ivory keys flying across the room with each swing he takes. He's shaking and there are tears in his eyes and my heart shreds with every chunk of the piano that breaks.

"Landon, stop!" I go to intervene, but Asher pushes me to the side and catches him in his arms mid-swing, holding him against him.

"Don't let her do this," Asher says, pressing Landon's back to his chest. "I know it hurts, I get it, but do not let her make you feel like there's something wrong with you." The hammer Landon's holding drops and Asher kisses his cheek. "Because there's nothing wrong with you. And you're not a disappointment, Landon. Far from it, man. You're all the things I'm not. All the things I wish I could be."

Landon's chest rises and falls and when Asher gestures for me to walk over, I do. "You have people who love you, Landon," I whisper. "For being exactly who *you* are."

He inhales slowly, going slack in Asher's arms.

When Asher releases him, he makes his way out of the studio and we follow. We can clean up the mess later, right now this is more important.

Landon sits on the end of the bed with his head in his hands, looking so dejected I want nothing more than to track down his mother and make her feel exactly how she made him feel.

But I can't...because that won't do any good at this point. The damage is already done.

The only thing I can do now, is show him that he is loved.

Asher and I walk over to him—and then we proceed to spend the entire night making love to Landon, separately and together.

"Hey," Landon whispers, turning on his side to face me in bed.

"Hey," I whisper back.

The sound of Asher snoring softly on the other side of me makes us both laugh.

One of Landon's shoulders rise with a half-shrug. "Well, at least one of us can sleep." His face screws up. "Did I scare you when I went off earlier?"

"A little," I tell him honestly. "But I get it. You were hurting."

He slides a finger up my arm, leaving goosebumps on my skin. "I kind of feel like a wuss for losing it and crying in front of you."

I graze my thumb along the stubble on his cheek. "I don't think you're a wuss at all. One of the things I love about you is that you're not like all the other guys out there. You wear your heart on your sleeve and you're not afraid to say what you're feeling. There's something admirable about that."

He starts to smile, but then his mouth draws tight. "Are you going home for Christmas break?"

I shake my head. "No. I mean, I thought about it, but given my father blocked me there's really nothing to go home to."

Who am I kidding? There never was.

I tuck my hands under my chin. "Kit asked if I wanted to go to the Caribbean with her and Nanna Bishop but I declined." I sag back against my pillow. "The University closes the dorms for winter break but I filled out a slip to stay since I'm not planning on changing dorms. Plus, they're holding classes over winter recess for the local students so the cafeteria and stuff will still be open. It won't be that bad."

"You could come with me to England," he suggests.

"Can't. I'm scheduled for doubles at the coffee shop over the break and Larry will fire me for good if I screw him over by going on vacation again. Besides, you'll be off being a rock God. I'll only be a distraction."

His mouth curves into a grin and he lifts the sheet, exposing my breasts. "I'll say."

I slap his shoulder playfully. "Asshole."

"Thought that was your nickname for Asher?" he questions as I tuck the sheet around me again. Before I can offer a rebuttal, he bites his lip. "I think he's staying on campus, too."

I sigh heavily, annoyance plowing into me. "Yeah, I figured as much."

He adjusts his position on the bed. "It can't go on like this forever, Bre. You guys are going to end up killing each other one day."

I narrow my eyes at him. "I'm not talking about this."

We're both silent for a long beat, and then he says, "What if things between you two didn't happen exactly the way you thought they did?"

My heart bashes inside my chest and I look him in the eyes. "What do you mean?"

His forehead wrinkles and he opens his mouth, but then closes it before he whispers, "Nothing."

I exhale slowly and turn so I'm lying on my back. "Wouldn't matter anyway," I decide. "There's nothing you could say that would make me forgive him for what he did, and lord knows there's no way to take back the years of pain he caused."

Or the pain he's still causing me. Because every time I look at him it still hurts.

CHAPTER 33

ASHER

Sweat drips down my face and my fucking heart pounds so hard against my goddamn chest it burns.

We're so close to winning this damn game I could piss myself. Morris shoots me a look and I give him a pound and clap my teammates on the back before we walk out on the field.

When we line up, one of my old teammates from Duke snarls at me and I blow him a kiss.

"For Christ's sake stop blowing kisses to Duke and focus, Holden," Coach Crane grinds out through the microphone in my helmet. "We're so close I can taste it. We're already in the lead. You've got this, son. I know you do."

When he calls the play, my stomach cramps up. I hate to go against him, but given I've played for Duke for three years I have an advantage that he doesn't realize. Both Duke's defense and offense is practically un-fucking touchable and I swear to God they're all half psychic. If it was any other football team we were up against, his play would be golden.

But it's not. Which means I have no choice but to take matters into my own hands and do something risky.

But then again, I'm all about the element of surprise.

I puff out my chest and roll my shoulders back. I want all the attention on me right now.

I get into position and I can't help but smirk. Better get some condoms out, Duke boys. *Because I'm about to fuck you. Hard.*

The second the ball is in my hands it's on. I can't intentionally fumble so my only choice is to be slick like mother fucking butter and pass it to a wide receiver on the low in stealth mode, hoping like hell Duke doesn't realize what I've done until it's too late.

Unfortunately, it seems the odds aren't in my favor today because the only person I can pass it to is Mr. Butterfingers himself —otherwise known as Rodriguez.

My heart jams in my throat because I can't stop this play now that I've made my mind up to trick the defense, my only option is to run like my ass is on fire and make them think for another half-second that I haven't handed it off yet. In other words, I have to make them think that I'm tricking them all while I'm actually tricking them by doing something else entirely. Trick plays are dodgy, but at this point it's either go big or go the hell home. And I'd prefer to be going home a winner.

Christ, Rodriguez better not fuck this shit up.

I pass it to him quicker than lightning and then I swerve to the right and run faster, throwing them all off. I can't look at Rodriguez, but I know it's a success when people start cheering like crazy.

But unfortunately for me...that's the only thing I hear before a massive force plows into me, the world turns upside down, and everything goes black.

CHAPTER 34

LANDON

I make my way up the nearly packed bleachers, being careful not to drop the three hot chocolates I'm balancing.

Breslin and Kit are huddled together under a blanket but they make grabby hands when they see what I'm carrying.

"It's so freaking cold and windy," Kit says, her teeth chattering.

"That's December on the East Coast for you," Breslin says, fixing the hat on her head. "Can't wait until this game is over."

Kit removes one of her gloves and eagerly takes the styrofoam cup I hand her. "I don't even understand how they're playing without coats right now."

"Adrenaline and the good ol' love of football, baby," Breslin quips, taking her cup from me. "Thank you."

I bend down to give her a kiss, but think better of it since we're on school property. According to the Dean my parents paid for this semester in full already; and given it's almost over it's non-refundable. So, there's that.

We're almost at the end of the fourth quarter now and the Woodside Wolverines and Duke's Heart Devils are practically neck and neck in the playoff game, fighting to make it to the championship. Which is all kinds of crazy considering it was Asher's old school and team.

Setting down my cup, I rub my hands together to warm them. I'm so fucking proud of him I could burst.

Are you proud that you lied to Breslin?—my mind taunts.

Guilt is a funny, fickle thing and not something I'm used to feeling on account that I generally try not to do harm to others. I keep telling myself that I was only doing what Asher asked and not telling Breslin the truth, but deep down I know it's more than that. I had an opening that probably would have fixed everything between them...and I didn't take it.

"Hey, you," Breslin whispers, snuggling against me. Her eyes are bright and the tip of her nose is red and she looks so fucking adorable I want to kiss her more than I want my next breath.

"Hey, sweetheart." I kiss the top of her head and she snuggles closer.

"So, are you going to the after-party? I know it's not really your thing but Asher said that he would go, and his teammates are going. Also, Kit's going, too, so I figured it might be fun for all of us to go." She blows on her hot chocolate. "Geez, that was a lot of *goings*."

I take a sip of my drink. "I'm not really supposed to fraternize with students but I guess I can make an exception."

She gives me a coy smile and my eyes catch on some freakishly tall man in an expensive suit making his way up the bleachers. "Holy shit, I think a scout is here."

"What? Really?" She follows my gaze and blanches. "That's not a scout."

"How do you know?"

"Because that's Asher's dad."

Sure enough, I watch the large man take a seat next to Preston who's sitting a good ten rows down from us.

"Shit."

"Yeah, you can say that again," she says. "Can't say I'm

surprised, though. Asher's dad is obsessed with football and now that Asher's found a way to make it on his own and he's brought Woodside this far, he probably wants a piece of the action."

"Douche-canoe," Kit mutters and we both nod.

When Woodside's defense takes out one of Duke's wide receivers seconds before they can score, Breslin jumps up so quick her hot chocolate falls. "That's right!" she screams and a few people around us give her fist bumps.

I can't help but grin. My girl can deny it all she wants but she loves football.

Just like she loves him.

Kit nudges her ribs. "Guess all those years spent dating the quarterback rubbed off on you, huh?"

Breslin flips her the bird and sits back down. "Sorry. It's just...Woodside is in the lead right now and they're so close to making it to the championship it's not even funny."

"I know," I say, sitting up straight when I hear the two-minute warning.

My heart beats erratically in my chest even though it's Woodside's ball and they're already in the lead.

Breslin reaches for my hand and gives it a squeeze. "He can do it. I know he can."

I nod because she's right. Asher Holden is an unstoppable force and watching him out on that field is like watching a rock concert.

Heavy, intense, and addicting. My dick almost gets hard from the anticipation and adrenaline alone.

I can't help but steal a glance down below to where Asher's dad is sitting. I can't see his face but his elbows are resting on his knees and he's bent over, gripping his hands. He looks to be about as nervous as we are. I can only assume that he's eager for Asher to win, too. *Fucker.*

I take a breath when my guy walks out, practically preening like a fucking peacock as he gets into position. Even from all the way up here his energy is infectious, almost like I can feel him coursing through me as he commands the field.

When the center snaps the ball to Asher, he starts running the field faster than a speeding bullet, gaining momentum with each second. Duke is right on his heels, though and my stomach knots. He better pass that fucking ball soon or...

Holy. Fuckballs.

Out of nowhere number 34 races for the end zone with the ball.

How the hell did he pull that off? Doesn't matter, I'm so happy I could cry.

That is until two things happen.

One—Breslin screams.

And two—I watch as number 3 gets slammed by not one, but two players. By this point they have to know he doesn't have the ball, but it doesn't matter. They ram into him so fucking hard from *both* sides, he flips and his helmet comes off before he hits the ground and goes limp.

My heart stops beating and Breslin jumps up when the medics rush the field.

"He's not moving," Breslin yells, her voice cracking. "Oh my God, he's not moving!" Before I can say a word or stop her, she starts running down the bleachers. Preston's already ahead of her and I start running too. Until I trip over something and stumble. When I realize that the something I tripped over was a large foot, I peer up at them.

I don't know what pisses me off more. The fact that this good for nothing asshole tripped me while I was running, or the fact that he's calm as a cucumber. Actually worse than that. This mother-fucker looks damn near pleased that his son is lying on a stretcher, injured. Or worse.

My stomach reels with that thought and I stand up and glare at him. "You're a piece of shit." White hot rage boils my blood and before my brain can catch up with my body, I clear my throat and hock a loogie that lands right in his face.

And then I run, because this guy can and probably *will* pummel me to death.

I'm panting by the time I make it to the locker room, but the sight of Breslin leaning against the wall at the far end of the hallway damn near brings me to my knees.

She's shaking like a leaf when I walk over to her. "Preston's in there but they won't let me in because I'm not family," she croaks. "They won't even tell me anything."

My heart plummets and I envelop her in my arms. "He's gonna be okay," I say, praying like hell that I'm not wrong.

"What if he's not?" She clutches her chest, her breathing becoming erratic.

When she starts to slip out of my arms, I tighten my grip.

She shivers against me and starts wheezing, but I force her to look at me. "Breathe, Breslin. I need you to breathe for me, sweetheart. Asher is going to be fine."

She shakes her head, the color draining from her face. The tremors racking her body are getting even worse and I'm at a loss what to do. The only thing I can do, I quickly decide, is cradle her to my chest and whisper soothing words to her over and over until her breathing starts to regulate again.

When I hear the sound of the locker room opening, I turn my head, expecting to see either Preston or Coach Crane.

My breath freezes in my chest and I silently thank whatever God or higher power may exist when Asher walks out.

I let go of Breslin and run over to him. I don't think, I just wrap my arms around him. "You scared the shit out of me."

When I look him over, his hand touches my cheek. "I'm okay. Knocked the wind out of me and gave me one fuck of a concussion, though." He rubs his head. "Preston's bringing the car around since

Coach says I have to go to the hospital to get thoroughly checked out. You wanna come?"

I bridge the distance between us. "Of course."

When he kisses me, I sink into both him and his lips. "Fuck, I'm so happy you're okay."

His thumb slides along my jaw. "Me too."

He smiles when he pulls back. "I guess Breslin is still—" His words drift off when he shoots his gaze down the hall to where Breslin is leaning against the wall. Her eyes are red and puffy and she's still shaking.

When they look at one another the connection between them is enough to nearly knock me on my ass.

He sucks in a breath. "Breslin—"

He doesn't get a chance to finish that statement because Breslin runs to him.

When he catches her, she buries her face into his neck and wraps her legs around his waist.

And then there's nothing but sobbing as she melts into him.

One of his hands smooths her hair and the other rubs her back. "I'm okay, baby. I'm okay."

"I thought—" Another sob escapes her, cutting off her words and he crushes her against him.

She sniffles and he runs his nose along her cheek, kissing her tears. "Breslin, baby," he whispers. "Baby, I'm okay."

He closes his eyes and inhales her, rubbing slow circles up and down her spine. And that's how they stay for the better part of five minutes. Eyes closed, bodies wrapped around one another, heartbeat to heartbeat, with Breslin's soft sobs filling the hallway as he holds her like she's the only thing that exists.

"Preston, I'm fine. You can go home to Becca," Asher says, sitting up in his hospital bed.

"They're still waiting for the test results," Preston argues.

Asher rolls his eyes. "You heard the doctor say himself that it wasn't anything serious."

Preston shifts his feet and then looks at me. "Call me if anything changes."

I hold up three fingers. "Scout's honor."

He gives his brother a quick hug and I check my phone again.

Breslin: Did you get all the results yet?
Landon: Nope, not yet. The Doctor doesn't think it's anything serious, though. But you should come here anyway. I know Asher would like it if you did.

Dots appear on the screen and then disappear.

With a sigh, I slide my phone back into my pocket. After they had that moment out in the hallway, Breslin made up some excuse as to why she had to leave. I tried to get her to talk to me, but she wouldn't. Breslin's not great at dealing with or processing her emotions, and combined with her anger at Asher, I guess it's really no surprise she bailed once she found out he was okay.

The only surprise was Asher's response to it. He wasn't at all upset by the fact that she ran off. My guess is because he knows without a shadow of a doubt now just how much Breslin still loves him...because there was no faking the way she came undone before. I don't think I've ever seen her or anyone else so upset in my life.

I lift my gaze and look at Asher. "That was Breslin, she wanted to make sure you were okay. Said she can't wait until you come home."

It's not a lie—I tell myself. Breslin is really worried about him.

A sly grin spreads across Asher's face and he moves to the edge of the bed. "You know, if it's a concussion like the medics said, I won't be able to sleep. So, it goes without saying that I'm gonna need some help staying awake."

I look up to the ceiling and fight back laughter. Only Asher would be thinking about getting off while he's in the hospital. "I'm sure we'll be able to think of something, Casanova."

Those dimples peek and he summons me over to him. The second I'm in his vicinity he pulls me closer and I fold like a cheap lawn chair and kiss him. Focusing on Breslin falling apart kept me from the reality of the situation earlier, but I can't help but flashback to what happened on the field and the hit he took.

"Are you shaking?" he murmurs against my lips. "When was the last time you ate?"

"I want to kill them," I say, edging back, my heart beating wildly. "I was scared shitless the second I watched it all happen, but now? I just want to beat the living shit out of them. If something ever fucking happened to you—" I swallow hard because I refuse to finish that sentence. "I might not be as big, bad, or as tough as you are, but trust me when I say that I can—"

He reaches for my hand. "I get it and I would do the same for you, but I'm okay, Landon. It was just a game."

My mind rears back to his father's face and the slick expression he had while his son was lying in the middle of the field not moving and I clench a fist. I have no idea if Preston ever got around to telling him he was at the game due to all the commotion.

"Your father was there today," I inform him, because he needs to know.

He looks down. "I know. He called Preston this morning and asked him to go to dinner but he slipped up and told him he had plans to watch one of my games and couldn't. Preston said he showed up during the fourth quarter."

"He did." I grip my neck. "Look, we've always been honest with one another, right?"

He gives me a questioning look. "Yeah, why? What's up?"

I stuff my hands in my pockets. "Your father tripped me when I was running down the bleachers after you were hurt. Now, I'm not one to start shit, but the look in his eyes...it was like—"

"Like he was happy that I failed?" Asher supplies.

I hold his gaze. "Yeah, exactly like that. I mean, what kind of person—"

"The kind of person that beats the shit out of his son for years in order to groom him to be everything he's not. My father hates failure. And in his eyes, that's what I am now."

"You're not a failure. Look how far you've brought the Wolverines this season."

"Doesn't matter. He only sees what he wants to see." He runs a hand over his head. "Sick thing is, I'm sort of happy he cared enough to show up in the first place." He shrugs. "He's a horrible person and yet I still value his approval and want his love. What kind of person does that make me?"

I skim his cheek with my finger. "Human."

I grimace when the thought hits me. "I'm almost positive they knew you didn't have the ball when they slammed into you."

"What?"

"You said it was just a game, but what if it wasn't? What if they did that on purpose and he had something to do with it? I watched the whole thing happen, Asher. Everyone was running toward number 34 then, and yet those two still attacked you."

His eyes flicker with suspicion for a moment but then he says, "Look, Landon—"

Annoyance flares in my gut and I press on. "Isn't the rest of the season over for them now? Think about it, what did they really have to lose."

"Nothing, but—"

"Your father owns a successful football team, Asher. It wouldn't be that far of a stretch to think—"

His jaw hardens. "My father is a lot of things, Landon. Most of them bad, but he wouldn't do that to me. He's still my *father*."

"Right," I scoff. "Because beating the shit out of your kid for years and—"

"You don't know what the hell you're talking about!" he growls, his face red with anger. "He wouldn't fucking do that to me."

My stomach knots and I realize that I have one of two choices here. One— I could continue arguing with him and potentially ruin our relationship. Or two—I could drop it and let him continue to believe what he wants. It's not like I have any proof anyway, just a gut instinct.

"Okay, I'll drop it," I tell him as the doctor walks in.

"Test results are all normal, but you do have a concussion," the doctor starts to rattle off and Asher nods, his focus completely on him now.

When Breslin walks in a moment later, my heart skips a beat and then squeezes when her eyes land on Asher and he looks back at her.

I guess that's the thing about delusions, though.

They're not always a bad thing. Sometimes delusions protect you from the cold, hard truth.

Because once you crack open that shell and expose it...there's no going back.

CHAPTER 35

LANDON

"You're expelling me?" I have to take a seat because the room is suddenly spinning.

I had a bad feeling when Dean Crane called me into her office, but I shrugged it off. I figured it was because finals are in five days followed by winter break and she wanted to talk to me about the upcoming spring semester.

She crosses her legs and purses her lips. "We have a strict no fraternizing policy between TAs and students, Landon. You know this."

"I'm sorry," I start, sitting up in my seat. "I didn't expect to—" I almost say Asher's name but stop myself in the nick of time, the worst thing I could do is incriminate myself.

"Become involved with a student by the name of Breslin Rae?"

When I don't answer her, she says, "You're the TA in Mrs. Rogers' Ethics class and she reported that you two were very close during last week's game." She opens a file on her desk. "Apparently she's quite the football fan."

Shit. "We started dating over the summer when she rented the apartment next to me. Her schedule was switched at the start of the semester and Mrs. Rogers' class was the only available class for her to take."

"Well then, you should have informed Mrs. Rogers about the nature of your relationship."

"You're right," I agree. "But we had broken up when she went to Europe to study abroad. But we've grown close again over the last few weeks—" I look at her, because even though I should cover my own ass, I don't want to lie. "Look, I won't blow smoke up your ass. I fucked up. I should have told Mrs. Rogers and you about it. I've had a lot on my plate with my parents and—"

Her eyes grow soft. "I know you have. And I'm not expelling you." She folds her arms across her chest. "I told Mrs. Rogers that unless she witnessed something more between you two and she could give me indisputable proof that it was impacting Breslin's Ethics grade, that there was no rule against a TA and a student sitting next to one another during a school football game."

Thank you," I whisper. "I'm sorry—"

"I actually called this meeting for another reason," she says, cutting me off. "You have a grant to cover you for your music classes next semester but—"

"I need to find a way to pay my tuition for my education classes in order to graduate."

She nods. "The deadline to apply for grants and student loans for the spring semester passed last month."

My stomach rolls and I clutch the chair. I have some money saved and I know I could probably work out a payment plan with the school, but still...

"Landon, look at me." When I do, she says, "You and I both know that while you're an amazing tutor and would make a great teacher, it's not where your heart is."

My first instinct is to object, but I can't. "It's not," I admit, feeling like a weight has been lifted off my shoulders.

"Can I give you some advice?"

When I nod, she says, "Don't spend your energy and your life doing what makes other people happy. It's *your* life, Landon...yours and yours alone. Live for you and pursue what you're passionate about, because life is too goddamn short. It's clear that music is your passion, not education. Chase it, follow it, and don't ever stop."

The tiny hairs on my arms stand on end as I get up off the chair. "So, you're not expelling me, you're—"

"Being a good educator and encouraging you to follow your dreams...because it seems like no one ever has before." She looks down at her file and I can't help but notice a check inside. "So, here's what's going to happen. You're going to finish up your classes this semester. You can still keep your job at the student center and tutor if you want. And considering you only need two more classes to fulfill your credits for your education degree next semester, I'll be signing off on a very special and very private grant—provided you agree to attend all your music classes and graduate."

I stand up on legs that feel like rubber and shake her hand. "Of course. Thank you, Dean Crane."

She signs a piece of paper and closes the file. "I'll see you in January, Landon."

I pause right before I walk out. "I'm probably pressing my luck here, but I'm not going to be able to attend the first two days of classes. You see, I've agreed to go on tour with an indie rock band and—"

She pushes her glasses up her nose and sighs. "As long as you contact your professors and complete any makeup assignments it shouldn't be a problem."

My heart explodes and I swear I'm a second away from telling this woman I love her. Instead I just give her a big smile, tell her thanks again, and walk out, feeling happier than I've ever felt in my whole damn life. For the first time in what feels like forever, things are looking up and there are no dark clouds hanging over my head.

"Let me get this straight," Breslin says, sticking another ornament on our poor excuse for a tree. "Dean Crane is basically paying for your education classes next semester but only if you fulfill the rest of your music requirements for graduation?"

"Yup," I say, taking a sip of eggnog, still in disbelief.

"That's awesome," Asher says between large bites of food and Breslin nods in agreement.

Given none of us have time next week and I'll be in England for Christmas, we decided to celebrate the holiday tonight.

Breslin's still glowing from the easel and shit-load of art supplies that were waiting by the tree for her—supplies that *Asher* insisted on chipping in for. And Asher's still on cloud nine and keeps staring at his super bowl tickets in awe—tickets that *Breslin* insisted on chipping in for as well.

But of course, in their typical weird as fuck fashion—neither of them thanked one another or even acknowledged it after I informed them that it wasn't all me and that they each helped pay for the other's gifts.

Breslin's back to keeping Asher at arm's length— even though she's still agreeing to tutor him for the Ethics final. And Asher is back to being his charming self and insulting and arguing with Breslin whenever he gets the chance.

And me? I'm considering hiring a damn bodyguard for them so they don't murder each other while I'm gone.

"Should we show him?" Breslin asks...to the pitiful Christmas tree.

"I thought we agreed to wait until later?" Asher mumbles into his plate. I don't miss the bite in his tone, and judging by the way Breslin looks like she wants to rip his jugular out with her teeth and use it as one of the Christmas ornaments, she doesn't either.

"Show me what, guys?" I pipe up because this shit is bound to turn into an argument if I don't.

Breslin walks over to her purse and pulls out a card. "Asher and I got you something."

They both look like they're holding their breath as I open it. And when I see what they did...what they got me—I'm the one who's breathless.

There's a picture of a black baby grand piano. Somehow, it's even more beautiful than the one I had and saved my ass off for in high school. My parents were pissed I spent all my savings on it, but I made sure it was non-refundable and there was no way they could take it back.

"You got me a piano," I whisper in awe, looking between the both of them.

"We did some research and we were able to track down one that was exactly like the one you had," Breslin says.

"Unfortunately," Asher adds, lifting his fork. "They can't deliver it until after Christmas, but we'll both be here and set it up for you while you're gone."

My mouth drops open. "This must have cost a fortune."

Breslin reaches for a brownie on Asher's plate. "It wasn't so bad with the two of us splitting it."

Asher snatches it from her right before she takes a bite and shoves it into his mouth instead. "We both had some money saved up. Plus, it's a second-hand," he says through a mouthful of brownie.

Breslin reaches for another brownie but Asher yanks it away from her. "Say the magic word."

She squints her eyes. "I made the brownies, you douche-baguette. You've eaten almost all of them."

Asher says something in response but I don't hear a word of it because I'm still too floored by what they did for me.

CHAPTER 36
ASHER

L ittle white flakes whiz in front of my eyes and my heart stops beating for several agonizing seconds when the ball leaves my hands and goes straight into Rodriguez's.

It's the last play of the championship game and everything is hanging in the balance. It all comes down to this moment, right here. Right fucking now.

My ears ring and my lungs burn—everything seems to happen in slow motion as I watch Rodriguez run his ass off to the end zone.

My body breaks out in chills when the crowd cheers and it isn't until hands slap my back and someone grabs my cheeks that I come to.

"We fucking did it!" Morris yells in my face as the snowflakes become bigger and the wind whips around us.

I should go and find Preston, but when I look around at all my teammates, I can't stop the rush of exhilaration that shoots up my spine.

We won. And fuck, it feels so damn good.

My eyes connect with Rodriguez's and I rush over to him— he starts to smile and say something that sounds like a thank you, but I pick that son-of-a-bitch up and shake the shit out of him. I owe this butterfinger, motherfucker my life right now. The entire team erupts in another round of cheers and that's when my gaze sweeps over to Coach Crane. There's no mistaking the pride in his eyes as he watches us. This man deserves every bit of recognition for being the great coach that he is.

I put Rodriguez down and I point at my Coach. Less than a moment later we all rush forward in one giant wave and dump an entire jug of Gatorade on his head. Then we lift him in the air and chant his name as the crowd goes wild.

This is one of the best nights of my life and when I finally do spot Preston in the stands, he smiles from ear to ear and gives me the finger. I return his gesture with a grin, and then my eyes fall on Breslin and Landon. They're both screaming and hugging one another, but when they see me, they start running down the bleachers.

The energy in the air is infectious right now. Hell, even Coach Crane's wife—the Dean herself—comes down to celebrate with tears in her eyes.

I grit my teeth when Dragoni's hand latches onto my shoulder and I glare at him. He narrows his eyes in response but I stick out my hand, because a deal is a fucking deal and I made good on it. "We square?"

He spits his toothpick on the ground and reluctantly takes my hand. "Square." I start to let go, but he pulls me in and says, "Word of advice? Keep an eye on that brother of yours, because word on the street is that he's starting to piss off a lot of people with his little problem."

My insides twist. "Will do."

I search the crowd for Preston again but all I catch is his back as he heads for an exit. Out of the corner of my eye, I spot a tall figure in the stands and a rush of air passes my lips when I realize it's my father.

We stare at one another in the middle of the commotion for a moment until I raise my hand and wave. I shouldn't want him to be proud of me, just like I shouldn't care that he came to watch me play, but I can't help it. His response is to give me a curt nod and then walk away.

I guess some things will never change. But I refuse to let him ruin my good mood and the win that I worked my ass off for.

"Hey," Landon says and I turn to face him and Breslin.

Their teeth are chattering and their noses are red but you'd never know it from the smiles on their faces.

"Come on," I tell them. "Let's go celebrate."

CHAPTER 37

ASHER

"Are you even paying attention?" Breslin asks, clapping her hands in front of my face.

I look down at the stacks of index cards on the living room floor of Landon's apartment.

Tomorrow is the Ethics final—because evidently Mrs. Rogers is the antichrist and scheduled it for Sunday even though our classes were on Mondays and Wednesdays.

I look at the luggage that's piled up on the other side of the living room and grimace. Landon's at the Black Spoon performing, but he's leaving for England early in the morning. Which means he won't be here when we take our final.

"Of course I am," I say when she gets up off the floor.

My eyes zero in on Breslin's ass when she walks to the kitchen for a bottle of water and I bite my knuckle. I am most *definitely* paying attention.

She walks back over and sits down Indian style on the floor. Then she takes her hair down from its messy bun and runs her fingers through it. "What is the principle of utility?"

I catch a whiff of some vanilla-strawberry mix that I know is from the shampoo she uses and I can't help but lean in. Those green eyes of hers go big when I run the tip of my nose along her throat and inhale her.

She shoves me away. "Uh-huh, I knew you weren't paying attention. You need to focus, Asher. If you don't cut the shit I'm studying on my own."

How the hell am I supposed to focus when she's sitting across from me looking good enough to eat?

"Landon was a nicer tutor," I mumble under my breath.

She levels me with a stare. "Yeah well, Landon has the patience of a saint. I, however, don't have that luxury because I'm studying for my final here, too."

I pick up an index card. "What is the principle of utility?"

She makes a face and lets out a groan that goes straight to my cock. "You can't ask me the same question that I just asked you."

I grin. "Sure I can. Unless, of course, you can't answer because you don't know."

I can see the challenge in her eyes now and my pulse speeds up. As much as I love spending time with her, I equally enjoy getting a rise out of her. And deep down inside, I think she enjoys it too.

She straightens her spine and clears her throat. The move pushes those tits of hers out and my mouth waters. "That an action or behavior is morally correct or obligatory if and only if the action maximizes pleasure for the greatest number as a net result." She crinkles her nose and shoots me a snide smile. "Utility is a teleological principle."

Goddamn, she's fucking gorgeous. I want to devour every last inch of her before the night is over.

I press my pen to the sheet of paper that Breslin insisted we use to keep track of how many questions we got right during our study session. "You know, I was going to say the *exact* same thing." I put a checkmark next to her name and then mine. "Would you look at that? We're really on a roll tonight, baby."

She arches an eyebrow. "God, you are such a bullshit artist."

I start to smile, until her expression turns serious. "Asher, if you don't put in the effort and pay attention you're not going to—"

"Football season is over," I bark before I can stop myself. "It doesn't really matter if I pass or fail this stupid shit anymore."

"Wow." Her tongue finds her cheek and she cocks her head to the side. "I knew you were going to say that."

"What is that supposed to mean?"

"It means," she answers, scooping up some index cards. "That old habits die hard."

When she makes to stand and leave, I reach for her hand and yank her back down to the floor. "Why is me passing this ridiculous final important to you?"

"Because it's not important to you." She pulls her bottom lip between her teeth. "You and Landon are the most talented people I've ever met in my life. But unlike him, you've always had everything handed to you."

"That's not—" When she gives me a look I grind out, "Okay, that's sort of true."

As much as I hate to admit it, she's right. Other than the last few months at Woodside, I've never had to work for a damn thing in my life.

When she leaps up, grabs my face, and forces me to look at her, my heart tumbles over itself. "Just try, Asher. Prove to yourself that you can do it, because I know you can."

The unwavering belief that Breslin apparently still has in me is enough to move mountains and part seas.

"Okay," I say because when she looks at me like that, like she *used* to look at me, I'll do anything she wants.

She quickly releases her grip and my body aches at the loss. Breslin never touches me anymore, not unless we're having sex with Landon, and to be perfectly honest? I fucking hate it. It's just another reminder of the brutal fact that the two of us aren't together and we'll never be.

My chest tightens. It's just another reminder that she's *his*.

But she was *mine* first.

When she goes back to her spot on the floor, I hold her gaze because something she said before doesn't sit well with me. "You know you're talented too, right?"

She opens her mouth to protest, just like she always does whenever I praise her art, but I cut her off before she gets the chance. "We got an A in art because of you."

It's true. Mrs. Kennedy practically had a heart attack right there on the spot when Breslin showed her our final project. Every single painting Breslin did was gorgeous and they all packed so much emotion it's all everyone in the classroom could talk about.

She shuffles the stack of index cards and looks down. "I'm not talented like you and Landon are."

"Bullshit," I say and she holds up a hand.

"Look, people are going to be lining up by the millions to see Landon perform one day, and you're going to have football stadiums packed while you throw endless touchdowns." She chews on her thumbnail. "But me? I mean, what exactly am I gonna do? Open an art gallery or something?" She clutches her chest and laughs. "Who would even buy my sorry-ass paintings anyway?"

I look her right in the eyes. "Me."

I'd gladly buy anything and everything Breslin paints in her life.

I'd do anything to put that beautiful smile on her face. I'd do *anything* to make her happy again.

"I appreciate it, but it's not gonna happen. Architecture is my best bet. It's the practical choice."

She means *easy*. It's the easy choice. I'll let this slide for now, though, because if I keep pushing the issue, she'll just get up and leave. And I need her to stay. Besides those few times in Art class, this is the only moment alone that we've had together in over three years. Therefore, I intend to make the most of it.

"I usually study better if there's a reward."

She rolls her eyes and looks down at the index card. "You're not a child."

"Breslin." The tilt of my voice must give me away because she looks up at me.

"Okay, fine," she concedes. "What do you want?"

You.

She catches herself and a blush creeps up her cheeks. "I'm not having sex with you." Her eyes turn hard. "I have a boyfriend."

"Who happens to also be *my* boyfriend," I remind her.

She looks down her nose at me. "Just because he allows you to have sex with me it doesn't mean he'll be cool with us having sex without him present. In fact, that's one of the rules we have and why we all agreed to this arrangement in the first place."

I ignore that last part because I'm too focused on the first part of her statement. "Because he *allows* me to have sex with you? Christ, what century are we in?"

"You know what I mean," she whispers.

I cross my arms over my chest. "No, I fucking don't."

She looks away and huffs out a breath. "You know how weird our situation is, Asher." She closes her eyes. "We're in love with and dating the same person. And when you love someone, you do things that you know will make them happy."

And here I was under the impression that while Breslin might not want to be in a relationship with me again, she most definitely was sleeping with me because *she* wanted to.

My heart squeezes and then free falls with the reality that she just dealt me. And suddenly, I need to remind her what we had.

"If I get the next question right, then you have to kiss me."

Her head whips around. "What?"

I give her a lazy shrug. "You heard me. Unless, of course, you're afraid."

"I'm not afraid of anything." I don't miss the hint of nervousness in her voice now. "But I'm not kissing you. And the fact that you would even want me to when we're both dating Landon is—"

"Fucking hell, Breslin. I'm *inside* you at least once a goddamn week, pounding you out like a fucking ketchup bottle while he stuffs his dick in your mouth. You think Landon would give a shit about a kiss?"

Her eyes widen, and then her mouth opens, slams shut, and finally; opens again. "Five questions."

"Three," I argue and her nostrils flare.

"Fine. But you have to get them all right. No exceptions."

"Bring it on, baby." I tap my skull. "I'm a lot smarter than you think I am."

She practically gulps as she starts going through the index cards. "My choice of questions."

I smirk and her eyes fall to my dimples. "Of course."

She holds a card in front of her face. "What is Ethnocentrism? Also, give me an example."

It's an easy question but I wrack my brain, because Breslin's not going to accept some half-assed answer. Slowly, something jiggles inside my neurons. I remember that class lesson vividly, now. Breslin was wearing a low-cut pink sweater that gave me a hard on. She hates wearing pink and she once said redheads couldn't pull it off, but she couldn't have been more wrong, because she looked gorgeous that day.

"It's a judgmental view that interprets all of reality through the eyes of one's culture. Basically, it's a form of bias. And I guess an example would technically be *Hitler,* given the bastard felt he was superior and everyone else was inferior."

She blinks. "Correct."

I lean in closer. "Give me another one."

With shaky hands, she picks up the next card. "How does one account for the difference between women as compared to men?" Her gaze sharpens. "If there is such a thing."

I almost want to smile because I remember that day in class clearly as well. Not only because it wasn't that long ago, but because Mrs. Rogers was out that day and Landon had to teach the class—and the lesson that day was feminism. He looked so fucking hot up there with his Mohawk and tie, the serious expression plastered on his face as he spoke with such conviction made me harder than a rock. The sex between us all after class was hot as fuck, too.

"Of course, there's a difference, Breslin," I start, and that earns me the middle finger from her. "Women by nature are nurturers. Therefore, they think differently because of their assigned social role." Breslin looks down, but I continue, "And since women are society's child-bearers, women's nature as mothers makes them natural caregivers. They want to protect and love their young. It's practically instinctual."

"Right," she whispers and I tuck a finger under her chin. When she looks at me and I see the pain flickering in her eyes, I feel like the biggest asshole in the world. "Shit, I'm sorry. I didn't—"

"I know." She inhales a breath and releases it. "Not your fault I'm so sensitive about that."

I cup her cheek and she leans into my touch. "I wish you would have asked me what the similarities between women and men are because I would have answered that women can be just as big of an asshole as men. The bitch didn't deserve you, Breslin. And I hope that poor excuse for a woman wakes up every day of her life feeling the regret and impact of losing you."

Because I sure as fuck do.

She gives me a small smile that wraps around my heart and I edge forward, both hands cupping her soft cheeks now. When her tongue darts out to lick that lower lip my dick grows hard against my thigh. Fuck the consequences, I'm so desperate for her I could explode.

Her breath hitches and I drop my forehead against hers. The air between us is thick with so much tension that it would only take one small move, the tiniest action, to ignite the spark between us into a full-on inferno. Because once she gives me an inch, I won't stop there. I want it all. I want everything that was mine.

"Give me another one."

She doesn't pick up an index card this time. "Definition of ethics."

Holy fuck. That question is so easy it won't even be on the final. "A philosophy which studies the nature of moral rightness," I say, ghosting her lips, my craving for her cracking the surface, threatening to consume me entirely. "Principles that govern a person's behavior—"

I don't get a chance to finish because her mouth is on mine and I fucking detonate. I nibble on her lip until she parts her mouth and then I glide my tongue against hers, tasting every inch of her. This kiss is so different from the ones we share when Landon's around.

Because this kiss is all us. *Only us.*

She tastes just the way I remember. Like sunshine and sunrise...like fucking air. Like everything I've always wanted and nothing that I will ever deserve. She tastes like my past and my future. Like regret and remorse and second chances.

She tastes like the one who got away and then found her way back to me again, right where she belongs.

She breaks the kiss first, but when I pull her back to my mouth she drags her fingers through my hair and moans. But it's not enough, it will never be enough. I need every single morsel of her.

I tug her hair until her head falls back, exposing her throat. Slowly, I lick my way down until I meet the sensitive dip where her pulse is pounding wildly and suck it. Then I move her t-shirt over the curve of her shoulder and plant kisses over my favorite freckles there.

"Asher." The sound of my name on her lips has me prickling with an insatiable kind of need. I want to hear her say it over and over again while I'm balls deep inside her. But when I look at her, there's uncertainty and panic in her eyes and it fucking kills me.

I find her sweet mouth again and give her gentle kisses until she grips my shirt and her teeth graze my lip, begging me for more.

And I give it to her. I kiss her with everything I've got, everything I feel for her.

She leans back and gasps for air, her mouth swollen. When she props herself on her elbows, I settle between her legs and push her until she's flat on her back, caging her in with my forearms. A moment later I'm grinding my dick against her, letting her know just how much I want her and what she does to me.

I stroke the skin above the band of her jeans and she breaks out in goosebumps. When I feel her start to tremble, I work my way down her body, kissing and licking every inch on my journey.

"Asher," she rasps when I bury my head between her breasts, my breath and tongue leaving damp patches on the fabric.

I push her t-shirt up, taking in her black lacy bra. When I see her taut nipples peeking through, I yank it down until her tits pop out. Before she can protest, I pluck one of her nipples into my mouth and lave it with my tongue. "I fucking love your tits," I groan before I pull the puckered pink flesh into my mouth again and suck.

Her hips shoot up and she whimpers when I move to her other nipple and give it the same attention.

"We can't," she pants out. Her words are the equivalent of being dunked in a vat of ice water and I sink my teeth into her skin until she yelps.

"We can't do this," she repeats, trying to shove me away.

I pin her arms down and look at her. "Give me one good reason why."

"Because of Landon." Her eyes darken and pain flashes in them. "Because I'm not *you*."

Her words sting far more than I thought they would and I release my grip on her. I try to get a hold of my emotions, but fail. This girl will forever have my heart and mind in a vise, and I'll forever be paying the price for my mistakes.

"And who am I, Breslin?" My voice comes out desperate and tattered. I need her to realize that I'm not the sum of my mistakes or the bad events that tore us apart. I need her to see that I'm still the boy who loved her...and the man who always will.

She reaches down and skims my lips, the contact sending bolts of hunger through me like a warm knife through butter.

"You're my undoing." I kiss the pad of her thumb and she closes her eyes. "My beautiful poison."

And she's my antidote. She turns the static down in my head when the world becomes too loud.

Some days she's my calm when everything around me is chaos. And others? She *is* my chaos.

She's the flip of my switch and the match to my gasoline. My fire and brimstone and my beautiful angel.

She's my Breslin. I was done for the day she turned those beautiful green eyes my way and let me love her.

When I flick open the button of her jeans and tug her zipper down, she starts shaking. "We shouldn't. Landon—"

I silence her by biting the denim between her legs, making sure she feels the sharp sting. She arches her back and groans in response and I take the opportunity to push her jeans down further.

I run my lips over the little turquoise heart that's smack dab in the middle of her white panties and all my blood rushes south.

She's so wet I can see the outline of her pretty pussy through them and I can't help but lean in for a taste.

"Oh, God," she breathes and her hand goes to my head, urging me on.

I look up at her and suck in a breath. Her hair is wild, her eyes are hooded, and her body is flushed as she writhes against my face.

Not even hell could be hotter than Breslin Rae right now. I've corrupted my little ivory princess and brought her over to the dark side with me. A place where her white knight *Landon* can't save her, and I'm loving every second of it.

I slide a finger over her pussy, the fabric of her panties sticks to her wetness as I tease her and I can't help but grin when I move them to the side, baring her glistening lips to me.

And that's when I hear the click of the door. In a flash, Breslin yanks her jeans up and fixes her shirt. But it's too late...he saw us.

To say Landon is surprised at what he walks in on would be the understatement of the century. His jaw flexes and his eyes narrow, and combined with his haircut, black tank top, and tattoos, he looks every bit the part of the angry and brooding rocker right now.

Except his anger isn't for show, because the vehemence simmering in his icy brown eyes tells me he's fucking pissed. Which of course, only makes me even more enraged. Because he has absolutely no reason to be mad or upset. Breslin isn't his.

Breslin springs up and rushes over to where he's standing. Then she folds her hands around his neck and kisses him.

"We were waiting for you to get home," she whispers against his lips and my heart spasms.

Like hell we were. It's quite obvious that what I was about to be partaking in was a dinner for one, not two. Besides, Landon's far from stupid, he knows what he walked in on. And yet, she's trying to justify it. Or worse, deny it.

Question is *why*? What happened between us wasn't wrong

and she shouldn't be feeling guilty about it. Landon wanted all of us to be together—and here we fucking are. *Together*.

He drops his guitar case. "That so?"

Breslin doesn't answer him, instead she pulls him in for another kiss and pushes him toward the couch. When he falls against it, she straddles him. "I want you so much," she says between long kisses that leave him breathless.

It's one hell of a distraction because he doesn't even spare me a glance. He's so wrapped up in her, she's the only thing he can see.

I know the feeling well.

When she takes off his shirt, he starts to speak, but she clamps her hands over his face and kisses him again and again, silencing him with her mouth and body. "Fuck, I'm so wet for you. I couldn't wait for you to get home."

His eyes go hazy and my heart beats painfully against my chest as she sinks down to her knees before him.

I always knew there was a thin line between love and hate...but there's one hell of a line between lovers and enemies too. Because that's exactly what Landon is now—or rather, what he's always been.

She looks so innocent and full of adoration, so willing to please him, it makes me sick. But then again...I was there when she handed him her heart. I watched her fall in love with him over these last few months and there wasn't a damn thing I could do to stop it.

She licks her lips and runs her hand over his hard on through his jeans. "Tell me what you want, Landon."

Christ, it's like I'm not even in the room.

Landon tucks a strand of hair behind her ear. "I want your lips around my cock."

The sight of her lowering her head combined with her soft slurps as she takes him into her mouth feels like a thousand knives stabbing me at once.

He winds her hair around his fist and jerks his hips up, matching her movements. And that's when he looks in my direction. "Feels so fucking good, *baby*." Wrath douses his statement and there's an obscure and dark note to his voice that's unmistakable.

My insides roll and I seethe right down to the bone. The pendulum that my feelings for Landon swing from snaps in half and I walk over to them. I know he's pissed, but I'm not going to stand by and watch him try to take her from me again. The moment Breslin and I shared before tells me that while he may have her heart...I have her fucking soul. It's time I remind the both of them of that.

I push the coffee table out of my way and kneel down behind Breslin. "You look so pretty with your lips wrapped around him."

Breslin halts her movements at the sound of my voice, but I shove her jeans and panties down in one fell swoop and smack her bare ass. "Almost as pretty as you look when I'm fucking you and making you come." I kiss along her earlobe, tilting her head so she can look at me. "You want me to fuck you and make you come right now, don't you?"

She closes her eyes, her bottom lip quivering. She's caught in a catch 22...because there's no way she can deny how much she wants me. Not even when she's with him.

They both stay silent as I raise Breslin's arms so I can take off her shirt. I don't miss the way she shakes when I undo her bra and cup her tits in my hands, planting a hot line of kisses over her skin while I look right at him.

With a look that could melt a glacier, he pulls Breslin and leads her back to his cock so she can continue pleasuring him.

I grind my teeth, this is the ultimate game of tug of war if there ever was one.

His head lolls back and his lip curls as she resumes her sucking. He opens his mouth to say something, but I nudge Breslin's legs apart, spread her pussy, and thrust inside her...causing her to moan around his dick. She's so wet the sounds of me fucking her fill the room. Soft and slippery sounds that harden all the angles of Landon's face.

I pick up my pace, taking her in long and deep strokes. I pull back slightly and when I notice Breslin's arousal coating my cock, I whisper, "You're soaking my dick and dripping all over my sac, baby." I thrust into her again. "Is this what you were hoping I'd do to you before Landon came home tonight? That I'd take you just like this while he was gone?"

Breslin freezes and before I know what's happening, Landon's hand is wrapped around my throat. I've never seen this side of him before, but I guess everyone has their breaking point.

My response is to grin and raise my chin. "Do it, I fucking dare you."

I shouldn't be goading him considering the predicament we're in, but this shit has been marinating between us for a while now. It's time we bring it out into the open. I'm tired of feeling like I need to ask *his* permission to fuck her or look at her. I'm tired of her looking at him like he strung up the goddamn moon and handed her all the stars in the universe. In other words, the way she used to look at me.

Breslin bolts up, but Landon latches onto her arm with his other hand.

"Let him keep fucking you, Bre." His voice is sharp and he's practically vibrating with anger now. "I mean, that's what you were gonna do before I walked in, right? You were gonna let him fuck you while I was gone, weren't you?"

"No—" she protests, but he puts a finger over her lips, silencing her.

His gaze ping pongs between the both of us. "Since I'm here now, you might as well continue." The anger in his eyes is replaced by pain, and despite the hand around my throat, the fury in my chest, and the fact that he's the one acting like an asshole in this situation, my heart pulls for him.

"Landon—" she starts to say, but I've had about enough of this shit. He brought it upon himself. I'm about to reap this fucked up web he sowed for us.

I drive into her hard, my balls slapping against her. "You wanted this," I remind him, working my dick slowly, drawing out each thrust until her pussy clamps around me, begging me for more. The hand around my throat begins to constrict and I slam into Breslin violently. I'm so mad at the both of them I can't even see straight. "Hell, you fucking *asked* us for this, Landon."

His hand goes slack and he sits stoic and silent, but there's a storm brewing on his face and I relish in it.

I grab Breslin's hips and she drops her forehead against Landon's chest. Her face is a mixture of euphoria and utter heartbreak as she comes apart. A moment later she squeezes my dick so hard, I groan her name, shooting my load inside her as she convulses.

When my eyes connect with Landon's again I sneer, "But then again, our situation only works for you when you can delude yourself, huh?"

I open Breslin's pussy and my dick jolts when I see my come dripping out of her as I pull out. Eyes on him again, I snort. "This way, you're safe and protected in your little bubble of bliss and you don't have to deal with the fact that you'll always be second best."

My words are cruel and at the heart of it, I don't mean them, but I'm so fucking angry all I can see is red.

That is until a sharp punch to my face has me seeing spots and I rear back, blood spewing from my nose.

Breslin turns around and her hands fly to her mouth. "What the fuck, Landon!"

She goes to kneel down beside me, but I stand up at the same time Landon lurches up from the couch, tucking his dick back in his pants. That's all he has time to do, though, because I throw a punch and he tumbles back.

Less than a second later he comes toward me, but I'm already prepared for him. Breslin's screaming her head off, shouting at us to stop, but I send my fist flying into his face again.

Landon's stronger than I give him credit for, or maybe it's the indignation coursing through him because he yanks me by my collar and head butts me. Given it wasn't that long ago that I suffered a severe concussion, pain radiates throughout my skull and I close my eyes and shove him the hell away. Only I don't connect with the hard planes and muscle of his body. I connect with Breslin's soft curves right before she slams against the floor and my heart jumps to my throat.

"Fuck," Landon says before he takes a step forward and points to the front door. "Get the fuck out."

I ignore him and look at Breslin who's huddled up on the floor, drawing her knees to her chest. "I'm sorry, I didn't mean—"

"I know you didn't," she whispers, her voice cracking. "But I think you need to leave."

CHAPTER 38

LANDON

When you come face to face with your fear—you have one of two choices. You can either face it...or fight it.

I did both.

Tonight was the culmination of everything I'd secretly been dreading and I snapped. Asher was right...I was enjoying my bubble of bliss. And every time they argued, it was my protection. The fucked up foundation of our relationship. I should have known that sooner or later it was bound to crack and fall apart.

Not only do I hate the connection they have, I was so afraid of them shutting me out and leaving me once they reconnected, once Breslin had forgiven him—that I pretty much took it upon myself tonight to make sure it's what they would do. Talk about a self-fulfilling prophecy.

I thought us all being together was the solution to our issues, but it was just a band aid. Asher—Mr. Pillar of fucking truth bombs tonight— was right again. Our relationship was something that only worked when it was convenient for me and when Breslin had her guard up. Because once the tables turned? I couldn't fucking deal. The thought of them loving one another destroys me.

I sink down to the floor beside Breslin. "Are you okay?"

It's a shitty way to start but it's all I've got. The fact that she won't even look at me right now has my stomach sinking to what feels like the pits of hell.

"I'm fine." Her eyes turn somber and regretful. "Are you?"

"No," I say, dropping my forehead to hers. "Seeing you with him and him with you, the way you were tonight...killed me. It fucking tore my heart out."

Finally, she looks up at me. "I didn't mean to hurt you." Her brows draw together. "You've seen us together before, though and—"

I glare at her. "Not like that. Tonight was different." *Significant.* "It happened behind my back."

She rises to her knees. "You're right and I'm sorry." She pulls me in, staring at me with sad eyes. "I'm so sorry, Landon."

The twinge in my heart tells me she means it, but that's not the cause of this feeling in my chest.

The silence stretches between us and I swallow hard, fearing the answer to my next question because it's the hardest one I'll ever have to ask. "Do you love me?"

She blinks back tears. "The fact that you even have to ask me that—"

"Please, just tell me the truth."

Those green eyes pierce me. "Yes. I know I didn't treat you right in the past—and that was *my* fuck up. That's all on me. But I fell in love with you, Landon." Her hand brushes my jaw and the contact shivers over my skin. "I love you."

I was wrong before, because this is the hardest question I'll ever have to ask. Because I already know the answer. "Do you love him?"

Something flickers in those eyes of hers, but it's gone just as quickly as it came. "What you walked in on was a mistake," she starts, getting up off the floor. "I wasn't thinking and I—"

"You don't have to defend what happened. Just answer the question, Bre."

She gathers her purse and index cards off the floor, but the tears threatening to spill down her face are my answer. "I'll be at the 24-hour coffee shop down the street. I have a final to study for."

My throat closes in on me, this isn't how I want to leave things between us before I leave the country in a few hours.

It feels like she's reaching inside my chest and pulling my heart out with every step she takes toward the door. I know without a shadow of a doubt that I won't just carry a torch for this girl...I'll keep burning right down to the bone for her. Over and over again.

"Do you have any idea just how much I love you?" I call out and she stops in her tracks.

She turns and we stare at one another for a beat, emotions filling the space between us.

Then, to my utter surprise, she walks over and throws her arms around me, kissing me with so much passion I feel dizzy and nearly rock back on my feet. "I do, and I swear I never meant to hurt you." Her hand goes to the back of my neck, her eyes squeezing shut. "You're going to be amazing in England."

Dread coils my insides because something about this moment feels so familiar I nearly choke on it. "Why does it sound like you're breaking up with me?"

There's a long pause that stops my heart. "I'm not." Her voice is pained. "I just...I think I need some space. I need to sort my head out after what happened tonight, you know?" She presses a hand to my chest. "But I'm not ending things." Her fingers slide over my heart, tracing patterns over it. "I don't want to lose you."

All I can hear is the organ that belongs to her thudding rapidly under her palm. "I don't want to lose you either."

She leans up on her tiptoes and kisses me again. "I'm not going anywhere." She hikes her purse up her shoulder and gives me a small smile. "Well, except to the coffee shop to study. Call me when you land."

I nod and she starts heading for the door. "This is going to sound strange coming from me and all...but I think you should go talk to him."

Her request throws me. "Because I punched him?"

She pauses right before she walks out. "No, because you love him too."

CHAPTER 39

ASHER

The world tilts on its axis and I have to brace my arm against the wall to stop from falling down the stairs. Buying a few rounds at a bar seemed like the right thing to do earlier, but now that everything is starting to whirl, I'm not so sure.

I take another step; my dorm is only a few feet away. I can make it.

I close my eyes and another round of the evil spins hits me. When I exit the staircase, I see some hot guy with a Mohawk and glasses sitting outside my door. Or rather, sleeping outside my door.

In other words, the guy responsible for my current state of alcohol abuse. "Gah da fuck away," I tell him, my voice sounding all kinds of slurred.

His eyes pop open and he jumps up, but when he reaches for my arm, I push him. "I hate you." My words are mean and sour and my heart protests the second they leave my mouth, but I don't take them back.

Concern pulls on his features. "You're drunk."

I get right in his face and poke him in the chest. "And you're an asshole."

His hand touches my cheek. "We both are."

I try digging in my pockets for my keys but come up empty.

"Here, let me," he says and the second his hands are on my body my pulse speeds up. A moment later he pulls them out of my back pocket and the door opens.

"You can stay on the other side," I tell him as I stride in.

He follows me anyway, closing the door behind him. "You have a final in—" He looks at his watch. "Five hours and 45 minutes."

I shrug, or at least I think I do. "So?"

I go to sit on my bed but my aim is a little off and I hit the floor with a thud instead. "Fuck."

"How many drinks did you have?"

I sharpen my gaze, making sure there's one of him and not two. "I wasn't keeping a tally."

He sits next to me on the floor with his head in his hands. "Everything is so fucked up right now. I don't know how to fix this, Asher."

I snort, pain gripping my chest. "You can start by sucking my dick, asshole."

He mumbles something I can't decipher under his breath and before I know what's happening, he's in front of me, reaching for my belt buckle and tugging down my zipper.

I wasn't actually serious, it was just a dig to piss him off, but my balls give a little tingle anyway. *Fucking traitors.*

I should stop him, but lust and rage are dueling it out with one another, pinging around the walls of my skull. The second his warm mouth is on me my head rolls back.

I'm soft—whiskey dick is a bitch—but he sucks me in long and languid pulls, swirling his tongue around my head before swallowing me deeper.

When he looks up at me, my eyes narrow. "Can you taste her on my cock?" His teeth graze my shaft and I hiss as I begin to thicken in his mouth. But when my gaze snags on him again, I falter. There's so much anguish in his eyes, my chest stings. He's not doing this because he wants to, he's doing this because he wants to fix what happened, because that's who Landon is.

He takes me deeper, but I grip his hair and pull him back up to face me. I need to know what's going through his head. How and why things happened the way they did tonight. How I can resent someone so much for loving the same girl that I do...and yet I know in my heart of hearts that I love him too.

"How did we get here?" I ask and he closes his eyes.

"I wish I knew. All I know for sure is that I'm the odd man out in all this."

I grip his jaw. "I don't know why you think that." My heart feels unsteady and I have to force in a breath. "Because she loves you."

He looks down. "You said it yourself, I'm second best. You and Breslin have a history and a connection that I can never compete with."

His eyes snap to my face and there's no mistaking the affliction burning in them. "And once she forgives you, that's it. You two will move on without me." He frowns. "I'm not just in love with one person...I'm in love with *two* people who will never be able to love me the way I love them."

I tip his chin up. "That's not true." My hand slides to his neck and I pull him closer. "Trust me, I know just how much she loves you, because I watch her give you everything that she used to give me."

He searches my face, his frown deepening. "She won't admit it but she still loves you too, Asher."

"No, she hates that she used to love me, big difference. And I know now that we'll never get back what we had. She'll never forgive me for the way that I hurt her." Something in my chest dislodges. "God, I miss her so fucking much."

I miss her laughter and her smiles. The way I used to hold her in my arms before she fell asleep. Or how whenever something good happened to me she was the *first* person I wanted to tell. I miss holding her hand and kissing her. I miss her filling the void and fixing all my fucked up pieces in that way that only she can.

But she has all of that with *him* now.

When he pulls me into his arms, I collapse, the feeling in my chest is almost paralyzing. "And why shouldn't she be with you. You're the good guy. The perfect one. The one that she deserves and the right choice for her." I snort. "Hell, you're so perfect you made me fall for you."

"I'm not perfect, Asher." His lips hover over my ear and his breathing becomes strained, almost like it hurts him to say his next statement.

"If I was perfect, I wouldn't have done what I did earlier." His breath stutters in his chest. "If I was perfect, I would have told her the truth about what happened. The truth about that asshole Kyle and the blackmail." His face contorts in pain. "I had the open-ing...but I couldn't do it. I wanted to keep her mine a little longer. I was so afraid that once she realized the truth...there would be no room left in her heart for me. She wouldn't need me to fix her anymore because she wouldn't be broken." He bows his head. "And it goes without saying that you wouldn't need me, either and I'd lose the both of you."

He looks up to the ceiling. "Fuck, I am a horrible person. I spewed so much shit about us all being able to get through things together and this relationship being the best thing for all of us. But in the end, I was the one who folded and fucked up when things got hard. I was the one who couldn't handle it when things didn't go my way."

"Well, in your defense, it's not exactly easy or conventional. I don't see how it ever could be considering everything that's happened between us."

He sits back against the bed frame. "You're right. I just don't know how to fix this now. I don't know what the fuck happens from this point on." His eyes turn hard. "I don't know how to stop hating you."

A frustrated breath escapes me. "I don't either."

"I suppose I could start by saying that I'm sorry for punching you." He winces. "And choking you."

I look over at him and grin. "I'd say I'm sorry for fucking her when you were wound up, but we'd both know that would be a lie."

His eyes flash. "Asshole."

"You know what they say...it takes one to know one."

His eyebrows pinch together. "Can I ask you something really freaking weird?"

"As long as you don't punch me again when I answer honestly."

"You said before that Breslin was in love with me, but where do you stand?" He looks down at the ground. "I know it's strange for me to ask considering we attacked each other earlier. It's just, with everything so fucked up between all of us right now, I figure I have nothing left to lose since you don't have to lie about your feelings for me anymore."

My heart twists with those words and I shift on the floor so I'm facing him. "I never lied about my feelings for you. They just fluctuate between wanting to fuck you and wanting to kill you. Because I hate watching you live the life that I was supposed to have with her, if that makes any sense."

He nods. "I can understand that."

"If I was a better man, I'd walk away from you both and let you be happy together. But I'm a selfish bastard, Landon." My insides dip as I continue. "So even if I can't have her, it doesn't mean that I don't still want or need you."

I inhale and try to stop my head from spinning because I've never been good at explaining myself and I don't want to fuck it up. I've never had feelings for another guy like I do with him.

"The truth is, meeting you changed my life in all the best and worst ways. And even if all my wishes came true and Breslin ended up forgiving me and we got our happily ever after...I'd still want you by my side. Because my life wouldn't be the same without you now that you're in it." I rub my chest. "I guess what I'm trying to say is—you have a piece of this." I look at him. "You're my best friend. And my worst enemy, depending on the day and all."

I tap my chest. "But you're in here—even if you don't want to be — your spot is permanent." I look around the room. "I suck at explaining things and it's probably not the most—"

The second his lips are on mine, the world spins for a different reason entirely and all the anger and pain I felt evaporates with each soft stroke of his tongue.

"I guess I'm not that bad at explaining things after all," I say into his mouth.

He shakes his head. "You flipped my life upside down and you changed everything I thought I knew about myself. You also piss me off and I'm so envious of you that I can't see straight sometimes, but I love you, Asher. Even when it feels like hate and bitterness...there's still love."

He starts to speak again, but I crush my mouth against his.

Since the second our lives intertwined, he's been my anchor that saves me when I'm drowning and sinking further into the depths. He knows me better than anyone else, because he's the only one who knows what it feels like to be me. But most of all? He gives me chances when I don't deserve them. He makes me believe things can be different. He gives me hope when I have none.

"Your mouth tastes like a distillery," he says and we both laugh, until I realize.

"Don't you have a flight to catch? What time do you have to be at the airport?"

He checks his watch. "In a few hours." He draws out a sigh. "I should be more concerned about you not being able to make it to your final in time."

He reaches over and sets the alarm on my clock. Then he pats his thigh. "Come on, you lush, you can still catch some sleep before your final."

My eyes close the second my head hits his lap. "You're just gonna watch me while I sleep?"

He grabs the sheet off the bed and drapes it over me. "Until I have to go to the airport." He pauses. "I'd go to the coffee shop to say goodbye to Breslin but..." his voice trails off.

"What's she doing at a coffee shop right now?"

"She said she's studying." His voice softens. "She also said she needed to take some time out and think about things. And as much as it hurts...I think maybe she's right. This whole thing spiraled out of control tonight."

"It did."

I feel his sharp intake of breath. "Maybe it's a good thing I'm leaving in a few hours. Maybe a break is what we all need so we can sort out our shit."

"What if we can't sort out our shit?"

He runs his fingers over my scalp, lulling me to sleep. "We just need to have faith. Because in the end, things have a way of working out exactly the way they were meant to."

That's the last thing I hear him say before I drift off.

CHAPTER 40

ASHER

The pounding in my head intensifies the second I open my door. Taking a step forward, I pull out my sunglasses and stick them on.

The final from hell is in a half-hour and I figure I should try and get some studying done at the library.

I head for the staircase and I can't help but smile as I recall Landon whispering study points from our Ethics class in my ear during the wee hours of the morning while I was trying to sleep. Evidently, he thought hypnosis was worth a shot.

I take another step but halt in my tracks when I see Breslin taking the steps two at a time, looking like a hot mess. A gorgeous hot mess, but a mess nonetheless. The bird's nest on top of her head held together with pencils and highlighters and the bags under her eyes tell me she had a worse night than I did.

Shit, I forgot all about her anxiety issues before big tests. It doesn't matter that the girl has an A in the class, which means she can fail the final and still pass the class—she was still up studying all night anyway.

"The final is soon," she says when she sees me standing at the top of the staircase, her voice coming out in one big rush. "We need to be there 15 minutes before it begins." She pauses and blinks rapidly, and that's when I notice the jitters coursing through her. Damn, she's wired right now.

I eye the steaming cup of coffee in her hand. "How many of those have you had so far?"

She starts moving again, attempting to take the stairs three at a time now. "Who me? What—"

And down she goes...only I don't have time to catch her before she falls. Or before the piping hot coffee spills all over her shirt. Jesus.

I rush down the stairs and pick her up. "Are you okay?"

"Ouch, no. Shit, that really hurts," she whispers and even through her white t-shirt I see her chest turn red.

I surge up the staircase and damn near break my dorm room door down.

I sit her on top of the tiny sink in my bathroom and turn on the faucet. Then I peel her shirt off and press the cool towel to the red spot on her chest. It's not nearly as bad as I thought and I breathe a sigh of relief.

"Thank you," she whispers and I rummage around the small bathroom.

I hold the first-aid ointment up when I find it. "I don't think you'll scar or anything, but you should put this on anyway." She takes it from me and I scratch the back of my neck. "It helped when I had a spider bite."

She understandably looks confused and I'm pretty sure my ears turn red. "Spider bite?" she questions, rubbing the ointment on herself.

I shuffle my feet. "Long story short, a spider bit my testicle a few months ago. Landon actually helped—"

She holds up a hand. "Yeah, I'm pretty sure I don't need to hear the rest of that story."

She gives me back the tube. "Thanks." When I take it from her, she worries her bottom lip with her teeth. "Did he come by to see you...after?"

I nod. "He did."

I don't know what to make of the expression on her face. "I should probably get changed before the final."

She starts to jump off the sink, but I reach for her arm, my heart pounding in my chest. "Do you want to maybe grab a bite to eat after the final? You know, this way we can talk about things."

She blinks and her mouth opens. "I...um. I can't, Asher. I have to work."

"What about tomorrow then?"

She hops off the sink and grabs her shirt. "Sorry, but I can't." She halts right before she walks out. "I don't think it's a good idea for us to hang out without Landon."

My heart twists. "Look, I know what happened last night was—"

"A mistake," she whispers. "What happened between us last night was a really big mistake."

She might as well slap me across the face. "No, it wasn't."

She turns around slowly, clutching the door frame. "You know what the worst part about last night was—other than hurting the man that I love?" She continues without waiting for a response. "I recognized that look in Landon's eyes. That look of utter heartache and betrayal. Because I still feel it whenever I think about you and Kyle together. And last night was like salt being poured over a wound that won't ever heal."

I stand there breathless, my chest caving in with the words that I so desperately want to tell her. My heart is wound tightly in one big throb of pain and fear, but I know I need to tell her now while I still have the nerve. "Bre—"

Her nails dig into the door frame, almost like she's trying her hardest to keep it together. "I don't ever want to hurt Landon again.

I don't ever want to inflict that kind of pain on another person. I don't ever want to be you." A breath shutters out of her and she looks me right in the eyes. "I choose him, Asher. If you want to know who it is that I choose...the answer will always be him. As far as I'm concerned, you're just the baggage that I have to deal with if I want him."

I take a step back, her statement ripping through me and slicing through my skin like dull glass.

She starts to leave but I take a step in her direction. "Breslin, there's something—"

"No, there isn't. There's *nothing*." She couldn't hide the pain in her voice if she tried. "Our past is over and it can't ever be fixed. It's time we both accept it and move on. It's time we let each other go."

CHAPTER 41
ASHER

When your coach calls you into his office two days before classes are scheduled to start again, you know something serious is going on.

I know it can't be about the results from the Ethics final, because somehow by the grace of God I ended up getting an A-minus.

I try to calm my nerves as I make my way across campus to his office, fighting the urge to look at my phone the entire time.

I've talked to Landon a whopping two times since he's been in England. But the pictures on his Instagram and Twitter tell me he's having one hell of a time there and people are loving him.

Seemingly overnight, my nerd turned into a rock star. And while I'm happy for him...it does nothing to alleviate the ache in my chest from missing him.

The *both* of them. Because it goes without saying that I haven't talked to Breslin since our last conversation.

I've seen her, though. Sometimes it's while I'm out jogging and she's getting home late from work. Sometimes it's passing her in the dorm hallways.

Sometimes it's in my dreams.

But she's there. She's always there.

I knock on Coach Crane's office door and he calls me right in.

I stand there shell-shocked for a moment because—*holy shit*— there are tears in the man's eyes. Just what in the actual fuck is going on?

"Are you okay, Coach?"

He props his elbows on his desk, looking lost in deep thought. "There are only four acceptable reasons for a grown man to cry," he starts. "When someone you love dies. The day the love of your life walks down the aisle. The first time you hold your child." He looks at me. "And when a coach finds out the NFL is interested in one of the best players he's ever had the honor of coaching."

I blink and step back, because there's no way I'm hearing him correctly. "What?"

"I didn't tell you because I didn't want to get either of our hopes up, but I submitted some tapes of you a couple of months ago and there was a scout at the last game." He wipes the sweat from his brow. "And they're interested. It hasn't been made official yet, but I heard from a very reliable source—one that I can't tell you about on account that I'm not supposed to be talking to them—but the Saints are looking at you for their first draft pick. Of course, you have to make it through the drafting process, but since it's at the end of April we have time to prepare and train and I have no doubts that you'll be picked." He smiles. "They want you, Holden. Real fucking bad."

Everything in the room turns to one big whirl, but one small thought prevents me from enjoying this moment. "Are they aware of who my father is? That he owns—" I swallow because my next thought is even worse. "Do they know about the video?"

He stands up and nods. "They do and they don't give a shit. Their current QB is getting long in the tooth and his body's breaking down. They need fresh blood to revive the team and you're just what they're looking for. They don't care what you do inside your bedroom or who your daddy is, Asher. All they care about is the way you play out on that field for them."

Everything stops—my brain, my heart and my breath—as I take in what he's telling me. I've wanted to be in the NFL since the day a football was put in my hand. It's what I've worked all my life for, and when I thought it was ripped from me for good because of getting kicked out of Duke and the video, I was crushed. And although I loved being able to play football again at Woodside— dangerous threats aside— I've basically spent the last few months grieving what was taken away from me.

I try to speak, but fail. This moment is too much for me to process. Something my coach seems to understand because he walks over and puts his hand on my shoulder. "I know it's over- whelming right now, but you deserve this, Holden. Be ready to start training again in the next 72 hours."

"Thank you," I manage to choke out, even though I'm not sure how I'll ever be able to thank this man for everything he's done for me.

He walks back over to his desk and his lips twitch. "Hope you like gumbo."

I leave his office feeling like I'm actually floating on cloud nine. I start to take out my phone but slide it back in my pocket. Then, before my brain can catch up with my head, I'm running as fast as I can toward the one person that I need to tell first.

I t takes me just over forty minutes to make it to Breslin's job on foot , and when I walk through the doors, she's so busy with a customer's order, she doesn't even notice me.

I wait in line behind some guy who's eyeing her up and down

while her back is turned. I have to suppress the urge to tell him off, but it's not like I can blame the guy for looking.

When she turns around and hands the guy his drink, her eyes snag on me and she blanches. That is until the guy standing in front of me clears his throat and drawls, "So, is today the day you finally cave and give me your number, Red?"

Breslin smiles politely, something I give her credit for. "I'm sorry, but I can't."

"Why—" he starts to inquire but I step up to the counter, irritation surging in my chest.

"Because she has a boyfriend."

The guy looks between us and when I cross my arms and I stare him down, he's the one who turns pale. "Shit, dude, I'm sorry. I didn't mean to hit on your girlfriend right in front of you."

"I'm not his girlfriend," Breslin mutters under her breath.

The guy grins from ear to ear then, his attention back on her. "So, does that mean I can get your number?"

Man, this guy has a set on him.

Breslin starts to shake her head but I tap him on the shoulder. "If you don't stop hitting on my boyfriend's girlfriend and learn to take no for an answer, I'm going to shove my fist down your throat."

His eyebrows shoot up and he looks between us again. "I'm so confused."

"It's complicated," Breslin says. "But he's right, I do have a boyfriend."

The guy backs away and shakes his head before walking out the door.

Breslin looks up at me. "Thank you. That asshat is relentless. I've declined his offers countless times, but it's like he has amnesia whenever he walks through the door."

My heart does a double-take. It's the first words she's spoken to me since that day in the bathroom. "Yeah, he seemed pretty annoying."

She pushes her hair out of her face. "What can I get you?" She eyes me skeptically. "I don't think I've ever seen you drink coffee before."

"I'll take whatever is easiest. And you're right, I'm not here for coffee."

Her shoulders rise on a deep inhale. "Oh."

Before she can say anything else, I tell her, "I had a meeting with Coach Crane today."

She reaches for a pot of coffee and grabs a to-go paper cup. "I thought football season was over?"

"It is." I wait for her to look up again. When she does, I say, "New Orleans wants me."

I can see the confusion spread across her face before she gasps and drops the coffee cup on the floor. "The Saints? The NFL Saints?"

I nod, hearing her say it makes it all real. "Coach heard through the grapevine that they want me for their first pick in the draft. I won't find out for sure until April but he says it's pretty much a sure thing."

Her hands fly to her face. "Oh, my God."

She gives me the biggest, most gorgeous smile and I swear my knees get weak.

I'm caught off guard when she shoves a bunch of muffins in my hand suddenly. "What's with the muffins?"

She looks down and laughs. "I don't know, I feel like this moment calls for something more than just regular ol' congratulations. So, it was either muffins or cookies, and the baker brought these fresh today and they're so good. Oh, and everything is on the house by the way. I mean, obviously." She finally stops for air and I can't help but grin at her. "I'm really happy for you, Asher. This is really, really, really great."

"Really?" I tease.

She laughs again before her expression turns serious. "Have you told Landon yet?"

I reach for the new cup of coffee she hands me. "You were the first person I told actually." I look down. "I've only spoken to Landon twice in the last three weeks." I snort. "I'm still waiting for him to return my last ten phone calls."

She reaches for the mop and starts cleaning the floor. "Yeah, same here."

"From what I can see on his Twitter and Instagram, though, he seems to be having a lot of fun."

She walks back over to the counter. "Yeah, I've noticed." She smooths her hands over her apron. "He seems to really love it over there."

There's a heavy silence and then she whispers, "I miss him."

I lean against the counter and pull out my phone. "Me too." I bring the phone up to my ear. "But if he actually picks up this time, I'll tell him to call you."

Her face lights up. "Thank you."

I make a thumbs down sign when it goes straight to voicemail. "Hey, rock star, call me back when you get this. I have some really exciting news to tell you."

I hang up and sigh. "At this rate I'll be telling him face to face since he comes back in a few days." An idea hits me and I look at her. "Can we hang out and celebrate later?" I reach for her hand...only for her to pull it back like I singed her.

"No, I'm sorry but I meant what I said the last time we spoke, Asher. Maybe I didn't say it very nicely, but the message is still the same." She takes a step back. "Congrats on the news, though. Despite what happened between us, I want nothing but the best for you."

It's such a diplomatic response it takes everything in me not to throw my coffee and muffins against the wall and kiss her like there's no tomorrow. If she really wanted the best for me she'd be in my arms.

Instead, I take my coffee and muffins and walk out like the heartbroken and lovesick bastard that I am, the reality of her words finally sinking in.

Our past is over and it can't ever be fixed. It's time we both accept it and move on.

The sound of my phone ringing wakes me out of my restless sleep and I mutter a curse.

Until I realize, there's a good chance it might be Landon on account that it's the afternoon in England.

My stomach drops when I see it's a number that I don't know but I pick up anyway. "Hello?"

"Is this Asher Holden?" some woman's voice greets me on the other line.

I sit up and swing my legs over the bed. "Who wants to know?"

"I'm calling from Truesdale General Hospital. Your father has been involved in a bad automobile accident and we're unable to reach his wife, but your name is listed as his emergency contact. We need you to come down here as soon as you can—"

I don't hear the rest of her statement because the phone slips from my hand and it becomes impossible to breathe.

CHAPTER 42

LANDON

I jump when I open my eyes and come face to face with Callum, the bassist for *The Resistance*. "Bloody hell," he says. "You were completely arseholed last night, mate."

"Surprised he woke up alive," Jude, the singer, comments from across the large hotel suite.

At least I made it to a bed this time. The other morning I woke up in the bathtub, an experience I wouldn't recommend to anyone. My back still hurts.

I look around and sigh. It turns out that *The Resistance* has absolutely *none* when it comes to partying hard after our shows. No matter how big or small the performance or venue, there's always a party in a hotel suite.

Every single part of my body aches when I sit up and swing my legs over the large bed. Maybe I did overdo it last night. Or rather, these last few weeks if I'm being completely honest. I can practically feel my liver begging me to take it easy.

My heart stops when someone rolls over beside me and I turn my head to find some sleeping, scantily clad blonde who I don't recall ever meeting. "Please, tell me that I didn't."

Jude and Callum shake their heads. "You didn't, mate. We wouldn't let you cock up and stray on your boyfriend and girlfriend."

Relief fills my chest and I thank them. For a bunch of partying rock stars, they really are stand-up guys. I'm gonna miss the camaraderie we've built when I leave in a few days.

Callum takes a sip of what looks to be beer and grins. "She was my guest." Jude shrugs. "And then mine."

I rub the knot that's starting to form in my neck. Unlike me, they seem to have the art of sharing down to a science.

We all watch as Freddie, the drummer, stumbles into the room a moment later.

He scratches his stomach and his eyes zero in on me. "You gave everyone quite a show when you went full monty last night," he informs me.

"While singing *God Save the Queen*," Jude adds.

"Fuck my life," I mutter and they all laugh.

"That rang a few times last night," Freddie says, pointing to my cell phone on the nightstand.

When I look, I see that I have one text message from Breslin and three missed calls from Asher. Along with a voice mail.

"Are you going to ring them back today?" Callum asks.

I walk over to the fridge and grab a bottle of water. "I don't know." I unscrew the top and take a sip. "Considering we only have one more show before I go back, I probably should."

"You can't avoid them forever," he says. "You need to either learn to deal with it, or let them go."

I rub my eyes and stifle a yawn. Callum's right, I need to find a way to deal with what happened, because partying and getting drunk for three weeks straight did nothing to help clear my mind. Whenever I close my eyes, I still see them together. Which is all kinds of messed up because technically they have a right to do whatever they want with one another, whether or not I'm around.

I squeeze the bottle in my hand and throw it across the room. This whole thing would be easier to deal with if it was just about sex...but it's so much more than that. It's about their connection and how it threatens my individual relationships with them. I just don't know how to accept it.

When I approached them about a relationship, it wasn't contingent on them only dating me. It was for all of us to be together. And in the end, it was my fault that everything got messed up between us because I didn't think about the overall outcome of our situation, which is just plain stupid on my part because it was fucking inevitable that this would happen.

And yet, I didn't think about—correction, I didn't *want* to think about—what would happen when their old feelings for one another resurfaced. Or rather, when Breslin's old feelings resurfaced because Asher's were always there. He made that perfectly clear from day one.

The worst thing in this shitstorm is that I know Breslin in particular feels guilty. Which at first, I wanted her to, because her guilt assured me that she still loved me in some fucked up way. But now? It only serves to prove what an asshole I've been. She doesn't deserve to feel bad about what happened, and neither of them deserve to be ignored.

I need to get my shit together before I go back to the states if I have any hope of this working out, because I want it to work out with us. I love them both so much I'd do anything in the world for them. They're my family. They're who I want by my side, no matter what.

And even though I have no idea where the chips will fall when I get back, I do know that pulling my head out of my ass is the first step in the right direction.

I check my text message from Breslin first and my heart pangs when I see the picture of the piano Breslin and Asher got me with a caption that reads: 'I miss you so much.'

I go to respond, but then I decide to walk into the bathroom, take a piss, and listen to my voicemail. "Hey, rock star, call me back when you get this. I have some really exciting news to tell you."

The sound of his voice flows through me. He sounds so happy I can't help but smile.

Until I check the clock and grimace, because it's the afternoon here, which means it's morning over there, and Asher's probably sleeping in since the first day of classes are tomorrow.

I hold the phone up to my ear and take my chances anyway.

"Hey, you," I start when I hear him pick up. "Sorry I didn't call you back sooner. I've been kind of a giant douche lately and I'm sorry. What's the big news?"

All I can hear is heavy, frightened breathing on the other line and my heart falls to the floor. "Asher?"

"Landon." His voice comes out strained and dread washes over me.

"What's the matter? Talk to me." When his breathing becomes even more panicked, I say, "I'm right here. But I need you to tell me what's going on so I can help you, okay?"

"My dad," he chokes out. "He's been in a bad accident." I close my eyes as he continues. "I tried calling my mom but the maid said she's on a cruise and Preston isn't answering his phone. It's really bad and they need me to go there and make—" His breathing goes shaky again. "Decisions about..." his voice trails off. "I don't have anyone I can...I don't think I can do this."

Oh, fuck. This is bad. Even though I hate Asher's dad for what he did to him, I know that Asher still cares about him and there's no way I'm letting him go through this alone. "I'm catching the next available flight."

CHAPTER 43

BRESLIN

I'm in love with Asher Holden.

I squeeze my eyes shut and shove my pillow over my head, attempting to drown out that thought.

For the last 3 weeks, 29 hours, and 4 minutes it's been the first thought I have when I wake up and my last thought before I close my eyes, replacing my old thoughts of how much he hurt me and how I need to move on.

I figured that demanding he stay away from me was the solution, considering I do love Landon and I'd rather cut off both my arms than ever hurt him again. But no. It's only made everything worse.

When he came into the coffee shop yesterday I damn near keeled over. And when he told me about being drafted, it took everything in me not to wrap my arms around him and hold on to him for dear life.

I look at the ceiling and fill my lungs with air, hoping the movement will smack some desperately needed sense into me.

When that doesn't work, I force myself to remind my heart and brain why falling in love with Asher again is literally the worst thing I could do.

The guy has already hurt me worse than any other human on the planet ever has. Not to mention, admitting my feelings for him and pursuing them would hurt Landon, and I know that hurt is the kind that never heals.

But he was yours first—my stupid brain insists.

You never fell out of love with him—my stupid heart reminds me and I place my hand on top of it.

Thump, thump, thump.

The heart is a dangerous thing, because the organ never lies. No matter how many deceptions you try to feed it...it always knows what and who it beats for.

And while Landon has part of my heart—it's Asher who holds it firmly in his grip...and he's never letting go.

I sit up in bed and rub my temples. I have no idea what I'm supposed to do when Landon gets back. How the hell is our relationship supposed to work when the thought of Asher being in the same room makes me sick because I want him so much?

Rising from the bed, I walk into the bathroom and look at my reflection. And then, I force myself to repeat the same mantra that I have for the last three weeks. "Asher Holden destroyed you, Breslin. He cheated on you with the enemy."

I turn the faucet on and splash cool water on my face, and finally, I repeat the last part of my mantra while looking myself in the eyes. "You will hurt Landon. The *other* guy you love."

When my heart starts to protest again, I slam my chest with my fist in time to my next thoughts. Hoping I can beat all the love I have for Asher out of my heart.

Kyle Sinclair. Prom night. He wrecked you.

After another minute or so, I walk out of the bathroom. My loathing for Asher flows through me once more like a protective shield and I cling to it like a lifeline, because that's exactly what it is right now. Without it—I shudder and stop that thought before it can take root— because I won't let myself think about what would happen without it.

I need the pain of what he did to continue being the barrier that exists between us.

Pushing those thoughts aside, I start getting ready for my shift at the coffee house. I startle when my phone rings, until I hear Landon's ringtone and make a mad dash for it.

I've only spoken to him twice since he's been gone. And while it's probably my fault because I said I wanted space before he left, it still hurts that he's been so distant.

Can you really blame him?

Guilt plucks on my heartstrings as I bring the phone to my ear. "Hey—"

"Breslin, I need you to listen to me," Landon says and my heart jumps to my throat.

"What's going on? Are you okay?"

"I'm fine." There's a long pause before he says, "But Asher's dad is in the hospital. It's bad, Bre. Real bad."

My hand cups my mouth. It goes without saying that I don't particularly like the man, but Asher must be freaking out right now. "That's horrible."

"I know," he says. "I'm trying to get on the next available plane back but there aren't any for a few hours. And even then, it's still over an eight-hour flight." He exhales sharply. "I need you to go with him to the hospital."

I stand up and begin pacing. I'm pretty sure I'm the last person that should be there considering our last conversation. Heck, I'd probably slam the door in my face if I were him. Not to mention the fun fact that his family hates me.

"Landon, I don't think—"

"I know you and him have issues," he shouts. "I get it, Bre. I know there's a lot of shit that we all have to work out. But right now, he has no one. His mother is on some cruise, Preston isn't picking up his phone, and I can't be there until tomorrow. Please, Breslin, put all the bullshit aside because he needs one of us."

"Okay," I whisper. I snatch my keys off the dresser before I can talk myself out of it. "I'm going over to his dorm room now. I'll text you when we get there."

"Thank you," he says, relief filling his voice. "I love you."

I open my door and lock it behind me. "I love you, too."

With shaky hands, I hang up and knock on Asher's door. When he doesn't open it after my second knock, I yell, "It's Breslin. Open the door for me, Asher."

A moment later it swings open and he stands there, his expression completely shut down.

That is until I launch myself at him and he hauls me into his arms.

I wrap my limbs around him and he holds me so tight it hurts to breathe.

"I don't know what to do," he says, burying his face into my neck. "I don't know what I'm supposed to do."

I run my fingers over his head, attempting to soothe him. "First, you're going to take a deep breath." I ease back and look at him, cupping his face in my hands. "And then we're gonna drive to the hospital together, okay? No matter what happens, you will get through this and I'll be right by your side."

When I motion for him to put me down, I reach for his hand, holding it firmly in mine as we walk out the door.

CHAPTER 44

BRESLIN

The steady hum of the machines connected to Asher's father is unbearably loud in the quiet hospital room.

Asher hasn't said a word since we've been here. Not even when Preston walked in, took one look at his father, and walked right back out.

The staff want him to make a decision, but I told them to give him some space. It's not every day that a 21-year-old college student is forced to choose between the life or death of their parent.

Or in this case...vegetative state and death.

It turns out that Mr. Holden's car hit a patch of black ice and his brand-new *Mercedes* wrapped around a tree at a hefty 65 miles per hour. Technically he should have been killed on impact, but the first responders found a pulse and brought him here.

The police have been by and they told us they were going to do a full investigation, but as of now, they're chalking it up to the bad weather and bad luck.

I hear Asher's sharp intake of breath and I get up from my chair and rush over to him, wrapping my arms around his waist, my chest pressing against his back. For the better part of three hours he's just been standing over him, unable to speak.

One of his hands squeeze mine and my heart thumps against him so hard I wince as I mold around him like a second skin.

"He used to be my hero," he whispers and I press my cheek to his back, letting him know that I'm here and I'm listening. "But right now, I don't feel a damn thing. I keep waiting for it to hit me, keep waiting for the tears and the realization to come, but there's just nothing. Almost like I'm numb."

His statement throws me, but I don't want to judge him so I silently urge him to continue talking now that he finally is.

"I should feel something, though, right? Because what kind of person doesn't feel anything when their own father is on his deathbed?"

I kiss his shoulder blade, trying to think of the right words to say to comfort him, but I come up empty.

The only thing I can tell him is the truth. "Sometimes feeling nothing is feeling something." I press another kiss to his back. "Sometimes going numb is the only way to protect yourself from the things that hurt."

He's silent for another moment, and then he whispers, "He used to beat me."

I go stiff against him. "What?" A surge of guilt plows through me and I feel equal parts heartbroken and betrayed at his confession. "Why didn't you ever tell me?"

"I couldn't." He turns around to face me then, his expression somber. "Besides, what would you have done? Beat him up for me? Report him to the cops who would have laughed at you after he paid them off?"

I narrow my eyes, feeling mildly annoyed with his statement. "I don't know exactly what I would have done, but I would have done something, Asher."

His thumb strokes my cheekbone and my gaze zeros in on the

scar above his eyebrow. Intuition hits me like a brick to the gut. "He did that, didn't he?"

Asher always told me that he didn't know how he ended up with the scar, but something about that never sat right with me. I guess I know why now.

He nods. "He rammed my face into the corner of a coffee table when I was nine. Preston ended up saving my ass, or it would have been worse."

I ball my fists and my eyes drift over to where his father is lying peacefully in his hospital bed. My stomach turns with the need to unplug every wire attached to the various machines that are keeping the asshole alive right now.

He hurt my Asher. The boy who held my heart in the palm of his hand.

The man who still does.

I don't even realize I've taken a step toward him until Asher clamps both of his hands on my upper arms, holding me in place. "Can you give me a moment alone with him? Maybe go out to the waiting room and check on Preston for me?"

My gut is telling me no, given what he's just told me, but the look in his eyes tells me he needs this. Leaning up on my tiptoes, I brush my lips over his scar. "I'm so sorry, Asher."

Our eyes connect and it takes everything in me not to kiss him. I feel the barrier covering my heart start to chip, because all I want to do right now is hold him in my arms and take every ounce of his pain away.

He ruffles my hair and presses a kiss to my forehead. "Thank you for being with me today."

I give his hand a squeeze. "If you need me you know where I'll be."

I slide my phone out of my pocket when I step out of the room and check my messages. I sent a text to Landon ten minutes ago updating him on Asher, but he hasn't responded yet.

Pressing send on my cell, I return Kit's phone call. "I know, worst best friend ever," I start, as I walk down the hall. "I'm sorry I wasn't able to get you from the airport."

I can almost see her rolling her eyes on the other line. "Are you kidding me? Don't even worry about it. I took a cab back to the dorms." She sighs. "How is he?"

"He's holding himself together as best he can. The hospital wants him to make a decision but he's not in the headspace to do it. I think he's hoping his mom comes home from her cruise soon and that she'll take it off his hands."

"Can't say I blame him."

I make a sharp left and continue down another short hallway toward the private waiting room. "Yeah, me either. Listen, I don't know when we'll be back at Woodside. I'm assuming late tonight or early tomorrow, though. It all depends on what Asher wants to do." I stuff my hand in the pocket of my jeans. "I was supposed to pick up the early morning shift at the coffee house tomorrow before classes start but—"

"I'll cover it," Kit cuts in. "My classes don't begin until the afternoon anyway."

"Are you sure?"

"B, I've got you. But, if you want to make it up to me, meet me in the cafeteria before classes start, this way we can grab a late lunch and catch up. It feels like forever since we last talked."

She's right, it really does. "It's a date," I say before I hang up.

Putting my phone back in my pocket, I enter the small waiting room that the staff at the hospital closed off for us due to Mr. Holden's *celebrity* status—and that's where I find Preston sitting in a chair with his head in his hands.

I slowly approach him, feeling like I'm walking on eggshells.

It's a little unnerving to be stuck in a room with someone who pretty much hates your guts, but you're not exactly sure of the reasons for it. I mean, I guess from his perspective, I broke up with his brother and hurt him so he's just being protective over his sibling.

Even still, the amount of sheer disdain in his eyes when he lifts his head and sees me is...perplexing. But then again, who knows what Asher told him about me after our breakup.

Whatever it was, though, I'm not about to dispute it here of all places.

Preston and Asher look so much alike they could almost pass for twins. The only exceptions between them are that Preston's build is slimmer, his hair is a few shades darker, and his eyes are a dark gray-blue instead of the piercing blue like Asher's are, giving him a harsher appearance than his older brother. Something that's even more apparent when his jaw hardens and his eyes become tiny slits.

I can practically feel the hate he has for me seeping off him.

I backtrack, a hair away from running out the door. Instead, I decide to be the bigger person. "I'm thinking about going down to the cafeteria. Is there anything I can get you? Coffee, water, maybe a sandwich? You've been here for a while so you must be hungry."

His expression turns to ice. "Why the fuck are you even here right now? Haven't you done enough to him already?"

I can't help but wince at his hostility. "Look," I say slowly. "I know you have your feelings regarding our breakup and all—"

"Breakup?" he scoffs, cutting me off. "More like set up."

To say I'm beyond confused would be an understatement. "I have no idea what you're talking about."

"Save it," he spits, rising from his chair. "You might have my brother fooled with those rose-colored glasses of his, but I know the truth about what a lying, manipulative, spiteful little bitch you really are. And if you don't get the fuck out of my sight, I will blow your shit up and tell him everything."

I rear back as though I've been slapped. "Whoa. First off, you're not making any sense. Secondly, you're completely out of line."

"Am I?" he questions, taking a step closer. "Or are you just covering up for your dear old dead-beat dad?"

I shake my head, because the words coming out of his mouth legitimately don't make sense to me. Even more so after that last remark. "What does my father have to do with anything?"

He laughs, but there's not a drop of humor. "Wow, you're good. Real good. You've got that whole, wide-eyed innocent act down to a science. Your daddy teach you that?" He smirks, his finger skimming my cheek. "Or maybe it was your slut of a mother. This way, you could learn the proper way to rope a rich boy in. You know, before she left your sorry asses and moved on to greener pastures."

Before I can stop myself, my hand connects with his face. "I was never with your brother for his money. I love him. I have always loved him." I go to slap him again but he catches my wrist. "And don't you dare ever talk about my mother, you son of a bitch."

He moves in, getting uncomfortably close to my face. "Get the fuck out of here, before I tell my brother the truth about you."

I edge forward so that we're nose to nose. "Mind informing me what that truth might be first?"

Something flashes in his eyes for a moment, before they turn hard again. "Okay, that's the way you want to play it?" He takes a step back, running his hand over his jaw. "How about the fact that your father was the co-conspirator with Kyle behind that fucking video?"

I gape at him. "You mean the sex tape that went viral?" I gasp when I realize. "Kyle set that up?"

My stomach churns with my next sentence. "And what do you mean when you say that my father had something to do with it?"

His nostrils flare. "You know, my patience with you is spreading real thin."

"Jesus, I don't know what the hell you're talking about, Preston!" I shout, my voice cracking. "All I know, is that whatever you think about me is wrong. I would never set up your brother.

Not even after he broke my heart would I ever do something like that to him." I meet his gaze. "And if you knew the video was a set up why wouldn't you tell him?"

He looks baffled, his anger long gone now. "Why would I tell him when he already knows Kyle set him up and blackmailed him?"

"Blackmail?" I croak out. "I don't—"

His eyes go big. "Fuck, you really have no idea, do you?"

"No," I whisper, my chest caving in. "The only thing I know is that your brother broke up with me after he told me he was gay and that he cheated on me with Kyle of all people." Even in this moment the memory twists my insides, but I press on. "Preston, please—I know you hate me but I'm begging you to tell me everything." I take a breath, my head whirling. "I don't understand why your brother never told me but—" I clutch my stomach, nearly keeling over with shame and guilt. Because Asher *did* try to tell me.

A few times.

"Oh, God." I look up at him through tear-soaked lashes. "You're right. I am a spiteful bitch."

Surprisingly, Preston leads me to a chair to sit down. "Shit, Breslin. I honestly thought you *knew*."

I give my head a shake. "I didn't...I don't."

"My brother didn't cheat on you," he says as he begins pacing. "Not exactly, anyway." He pauses to look at me. "You know how Kyle used to sleep over our house a lot after football practice?"

When I give him a nod, he says, "Well, one night while Asher was sleeping, Kyle decided to blackmail him...his props were his mouth and a video camera. The results of that blackmail were twisted and altered."

I lean forward, resting my elbows on my knees. "Why would he blackmail Asher in the first place? Kyle was a jerk to me, but they were friends, teammates. Plus, Kyle's family is well off, I don't understand the motive."

"This is where things get complicated." He looks at the ceiling. "I don't know every little detail, that's something you'll have to talk to Asher about, after he reams my head in for telling you this shit. But, the gist of it is that Kyle's dad threatened not to give him his inheritance if he didn't make it onto a college sport's team."

He shrugs. "Kyle sucks at sports, the only reason he was put on a team was because my father talked to the coach and pled his case. Anyway, for some fucked up reason, Kyle decided that blackmailing my brother was the bright way of going about it. Asher had offers coming out of his ass, everyone wanted him. Guess he figured Asher would make it happen." He flinches. "He also might have taken a nude photo of you in the school locker room as extra leverage."

Horror creeps up my spine. "What? How is that even possible?" My hands find my face, when I realize that it was actually quite possible. "I thought it was Marcy Bush and her cronies who hid my clothes after my shower that day."

He looks down at the ground. "Sorry, Breslin. I thought maybe you or your dad added that to the mix to throw Asher off the trail from suspecting you were behind it."

"I don't know anything about the trail, Preston." I grind my teeth. "And I'm not behind anything."

"I know that now." He rubs his head. "Needless to say, everything got all fucked up and it quickly became obvious to Asher that Kyle was obsessed with him in addition to being an asshole. I don't know the ins and outs of it, but I guess some lines in Asher's head became blurred the further Kyle pushed him."

He plops down on the chair across from me. "Asher struggled with his feelings, but he didn't talk about it with anyone. The only choice he felt he had was to accept Kyle's blackmail and give him what he wanted. He couldn't go to my dad because he'd get the shit beaten out of him, and depending on his mood when he told him, he might have even tossed him on the street. He couldn't come to me because I was even younger than he was and there was nothing I could do. And he couldn't go to you because he was afraid he'd lose you once he told you the feelings he was having."

It feels like my lungs are being wrung out and I can't breathe. "I didn't know. When he told me, he didn't—"

I didn't give him a chance to tell me. I was already gone. I'd already abandoned him.

"He couldn't, because Kyle said that if he told anyone he'd go viral with the video and your nude picture. Kyle wanted you gone, that was one of the stipulations. And after you were gone, he basically forced Asher into a relationship with him at Duke. Which, of course, only made Kyle even more obsessed with him. He's got major problems. Dude is fucking sick in the head, Breslin."

Yeah, he most definitely is.

"What made Kyle release the video?" I sit up in my seat. "Don't get me wrong, there are more crucial things that I need to know about, but I'm just trying to connect the dots here."

He expels a breath and lifts a shoulder in a shrug. "I don't know to be honest. Asher said it was because Kyle walked in on him sleeping with someone else and went postal. And given that he's fucking crazy, I guess it makes sense. Although, it's also strange because if money was really his main motive, why would he choose to release the video a year before Asher would undoubtedly be drafted to the NFL."

He leans forward, his expression pinched. "Which brings me to how I found out about your dad being the one who helped Kyle."

I can't help myself, my immediate response is to defend my father. "Listen, Preston. My father is an addict and a drunk who on his best days can't even manage to tie his shoes. I highly doubt he was part of Kyle's blackmail. He's not smart enough to do something like that."

"But he is greedy enough." He stands up again. "Or at least that's what he was hollering about in his drunken state at the bar that night. Cursing up a storm about how some faggot stopped paying him his money and that he was going to get even."

It's my turn to stand up. "He could have been talking about anyone."

He rests his hands on his hips. "You know, I thought that too. I mean, addicts aren't exactly reliable." He cocks his head to the side. "Unless you give them what they want so they spill."

I match his stance. "You just said it yourself, addicts are unreliable. He could have been baiting you." I cross my arms over my chest, ignoring the crater of suspicion gnawing at me. "But tell me what happened at the bar. Also, how were you allowed at a bar anyway? You're only 19."

He makes a face. "I'll be 20 in a few weeks. Besides, I've had a fake ID since I was 16. Not to mention, everyone knows who my father is." He looks embarrassed. "I was at that piece of shit bar after I lost my first bet with a bookie. You know, Dragoni's family."

"Yeah, kind of hard to forget that shitstorm you put your brother through."

His jaw locks. "You wanna hear the truth or not?"

When I gesture for him to continue, he says, "I was throwing a few back when I saw the owners tossing your father out of the bar for not paying his tab."

"Sounds about right," I mutter.

"Curiosity got the best of me because he kept shouting that it wasn't his fault that his business partner wasn't paying him anymore." He laughs. "It probably makes me a shitty person, but I found it funny as hell because not only is your father the epitome of a loser, but who in their right mind would ever do business with him." He shrugs. "I wanted to find out, so I walked outside. He thought I was Asher at first and told me to tell my boyfriend to pay up, or else. That's how I knew something wasn't quite right. Asher and I had lost touch while he was at Duke, I really had no idea what was going on in his life back then."

A look of regret sweeps over his face. "When I offered your dad a few hundred bucks, he spilled the beans about Kyle approaching him a few years back and how there was a lot of money to be made for setting Asher up. He said he agreed without any hesitation."

My mouth falls agape. "No, he wouldn't—"

"Kyle told Asher that he had an accomplice," he says, cutting me off. "Someone who would go public with the tape if Asher hurt Kyle or spoke. All your father had to do was give it to the right person. Doesn't take much brains to do that."

He looks away. "I tried to warn Asher after that conversation at the bar, but I was too late. A few hours later the video was in circulation and there was nothing I could do but be there for him. I didn't tell him about talking with your father or about my suspicion that you had something to do with it because I wanted him far away from you. I was trying to protect him like he'd always done for me. I was afraid that once I brought you or your father up, it would sever whatever string he was barely hanging on to and you'd sink your claws into him again while he was at his lowest—and God only knows what else you people would do to him then."

He lifts a shoulder. "That and I was afraid he wouldn't believe me in the first place and hate me for accusing you." Slowly, his eyes find mine again. "I know you want to defend your dad, Breslin. Believe me, I get it. I know all about what it's like to have an asshole for a father and still crave his love. But you wanted to know the truth...and that's it."

My heart thunders against my ribs and bile works up my throat. I don't know which slams into me first—overwhelming sadness or betrayal. Turning on my heels, I start walking toward the exit and down the hall. I'm in such a daze I barely register all the commotion going on.

That is until I come face to face with the last person I ever expected to see again.

CHAPTER 45

ASHER

Pulling a chair to the far-off corner, I stare out the window of the dimly lit hospital room, willing myself to feel something, *anything* for the man who raised me.

The man I used to worship.

But there's nothing, not even anger or resentment for all the years of abuse. No love for the man who made me what I am today.

The moment I walked in and found out how severe his injuries were, the big ball of anxiety that I had, turned into...relief.

Shit, guess I do feel something after all.

My chest spasms and I force in a breath. I have no idea how to choose between life and death for a man who I both loved and hated.

My gold-digger of a mom would have been the far better option, which is probably why he didn't put her in charge of this decision, because we already know what she would choose.

Question is—what's stopping me from choosing the same thing?

I sink down in my seat and run a hand over my head. I'm mulling over the idea of telling the doctor to pull the plug when out of the corner of my eye I notice a shadowy figure enter the room.

Assuming it's one of the nurses, I stand.

The tiny hairs on the back of my neck stand on end when I realize who the figure belongs to.

I haven't seen him in months. Not since the day he ruined my life. "What the fuck are you doing here?"

He takes a step forward, and I almost cringe as I take in his appearance. Not only is he even skinnier than I remember, making his hollow cheeks more prominent, but he has a crazed look in his dark eyes—that despite all the fucked up shit I know he's capable of, wasn't there before.

Saying he looks a mess and out of sorts would be a compliment right now, because he looks nothing short of positively deranged.

He smiles at me, which only makes him look creepier. "It was on the news." He takes another step closer to me, his smile widening. "I knew I'd find you here."

I suddenly regret not seeking legal counsel and filing for that restraining order now. I figured I'd seen the last of him after he fucked up my life, since there wasn't anything else he could do to me that hadn't already been done. There was nothing left for him to blackmail me with, I'd already lost everything.

I feel my shoulders relax with that thought, because he has no leverage over me anymore. Which means, I'm no longer scared.

"I'm going to give you exactly one minute to get the fuck out of here before I call security."

He ignores me and takes a step closer to my father's bed. The thread that my composure is barely hanging on to is plucked like a string on a guitar, and I'm a mere second away from snapping.

"He looks so peaceful," Kyle whispers, his attention on my father. When he brushes his hand over his cheek, I fist his shirt and tug him back. "Get the hell away—"

My words fall from my lips when he pulls a gun out of his pocket. "I need to say goodbye to him."

My stomach knots up and I raise my hands, a combination of

fear and confusion billowing through me.

Gun in hand, he gestures to the chair. "Sit down and let me tell you a little story."

When I open my mouth to object, his lip curls and he points the gun back to me. "I love you, Asher. But if you don't do as I ask, there will be repercussions. Understand?"

Nodding my agreement, I walk over to the chair and sit.

He purses his lips. "Throw your cell phone on the bed. I don't want any distractions."

I quickly do what he asks, silently praying for someone to walk in. That is until that crazed look in his eyes becomes even more intense. On second thought, it's better that no one else is subjected to this.

His gaze drifts to my father again. "When I was 16, I fell in love." He toys with the gun in his hand and I have to keep my breathing in check. "He was handsome, powerful, and I honestly thought he loved me too."

I always knew Kyle was delusional but this is a whole new brand of crazy. "My father's not gay," I blurt out and his eyes narrow before he cackles.

"Funny, he used to say the same thing." Sadness crosses over his features. "He also told me I was special, and he promised me that one day when the time was right; we'd run away together. Just the two of us."

I sit there frozen, stunned at what I'm hearing. My father disowned me when he found out about the video and said he refused to acknowledge a faggot as a son. Those were his exact words. I remember them because they're practically seared into my skin, branding me.

Kyle's eyes brim with tears and he starts circling the bed.

I almost feel bad for him. *Almost*. But considering all the shit he did to me, and the gun currently pointed at me, I just can't.

But I need to know the truth, although some things are starting to make sense. "That's why you slept over my house all the time, wasn't it?"

He nods. "It was easier for us to find time together that way, under the guise of a friendship with his son. This way no one would suspect a thing."

"I had no idea."

"You were never supposed to. No one was. You see, your bitch of a mother refused to sign the prenup without an infidelity clause. She said she didn't want to be embarrassed and broke in the event that he ever cheated and left her for another woman." His laugh is sinister. "Little did she know, huh?"

He runs a hand over my father's leg. "Anyhow, that combined with the public possibly finding out about us terrified your father." His brows pinch together. "But he promised me that when I turned 18, we would be free. It would have been sooner, but he figured the only thing worse than the public finding out he was gay, was that he was involved with an underage teenager." He crinkles his nose. "The wealthy must keep up appearances."

His grip on my father's leg tightens. "Two years. I waited for him for two years. I mean, we had all these plans together, you know?" The hand pointing the gun at me shakes. "Do you know what that bastard did to me a mere two weeks before my 18th birthday?"

I shake my head, even though I'm pretty sure I know where this is going.

"He dumped me. Said I was a little phase that he needed to get out of his system and that what we had wasn't real. Said that he loved his wife and family and that I was nothing more than an experiment. Something to use when he wanted his dick sucked and his wife couldn't be bothered."

My stomach turns to lead. "Jesus."

"As if that wasn't bad enough, he threatened me. Said if I ever told another soul about what we did he would destroy me. Tell everyone that I was an obsessed teenager with mental issues who was making up lies. I wasn't even 18 yet, and he was a 45-year-old man with more money, power, and influence than I could ever dream of. He had the means to wreck me."

Everything becomes crystal clear. "So you blackmailed me as payback."

He raises a finger. "Hush. You're spoiling all the good parts, handsome." He waves his gun around. "Anyway, I thought to myself—Self, how can you make this man who broke your heart pay for what he did to you?"

He taps his head. "Ahhh, his strapping son. The prodigy. The proverbial apple of his eye. Using you would be the perfect way to get under his skin. Worming my way into your life even more would drive him positively insane."

His smile is so evil, a chill skitters up my spine. "You see, I didn't just want to get back at him...I wanted to drive him mad. Mentally fuck with him like he did to me. Put him in a position where *he* couldn't say anything and reverse the roles."

His hand clenches into a fist. "I wanted to watch the turmoil in his eyes when he went to visit you during your first semester at college and saw me, living with you. I wanted it to haunt him and eat at him. And when the moment was just right, the stars were aligned, and he begged me for mercy...I wanted to stomp on him like a bug by showing him a video featuring his ex-lover and son. The ultimate fuck you for what he did to me. Of course, I'm not that stupid. I wouldn't do something like that to a rich man and not get any money out of it. I planned on giving him a choice. Pay up, or the world would see my mouth wrapped around his son's dick."

He sucks his teeth at my father. "At least, that's the way it was supposed to be." He turns back to me. "Until...the ball started rolling." He bites his lip and peruses my body from head to toe while I fight back nausea. "And I found out that you and Daddy Holden were so much more alike than I ever would have thought."

His eyes soften and he walks over to me before running his finger over my lip. If it wasn't for the gun pointing at my head, I'd rock his jaw right about now.

"You became so much more than a revenge plan for me, Asher." He trails a finger down my stomach and I swallow the disgust lodging in my throat. "You put me back together and unbroke my heart. You were the salve to the gaping wound in my chest caused by him. And soon, my plan became altered, because I just wanted to spend my life loving you and worshiping you like you deserved."

His forehead creases. "But I fucked up because I had already gotten someone else involved in my original plan. And once they found out that I didn't want to extort your father anymore...they weren't very happy about it."

I open my mouth to ask who this person is but he pinches the bridge of his nose and sighs. "The only thing I could do was give him money from my inheritance every month to ward him off. A lot of fucking money. This way, they wouldn't release the video." He pauses and I can practically see the infatuation he has with me blazing in his eyes. "I didn't want to hurt the guy I fell in love with. I just wanted him to love me back."

He presses a finger to his lips. "Only one major problem stood in the way of that. A certain redhead trailer park bitch." He studies his nails. "Good thing we got rid of her before we started college, huh?"

His statement causes a volatile reaction in me and I bare my teeth at him. "Only because you gave me no choice."

He waves a hand dismissively. "Nonsense, I believe I gave you two choices. Tell your little girlfriend the truth, or I would *show* the world the truth. You chose the road you went down, Asher. Not me." He smirks. "But enough about her, I want to talk about us again."

"There is no us," I grit through my teeth. "There never will be."

The gun slams into the side of my head so hard I see stars. "Fuck."

"See what you made me do?" The gun pointed back at my face starts to shake. "You made me hurt you."

He sweeps some of the blood from my cut onto his finger and brings it to his lips. "Now, where was I? Ah, yes. Those three years we spent together were the best years of my life. You were so—"

"Blackmailed," I cut in, because despite his past with my father, he needs to get the truth through his skull that we were never together. "Everything I ever did was out of fear and blackmail, not because I wanted to."

His face twists. "What we had was real. I know it and you know it."

"No."

"You're only saying that because of her," he sneers. "Because she's back in your life, fucking your head up again."

I can feel the color drain from my face, because the worst thing to do to someone with a gun in his hand is make the person you love their new target. "I don't know what you're talking about. I haven't spoken to Breslin since—"

"Don't lie to me. I know what you've been up to, Asher." He backs away, walking to the opposite side of my father's hospital bed. "Do you have any idea what it was like seeing you run back to her again? After everything I did for you."

I know I shouldn't be arguing with a mental case but I can't help myself. "Everything you did for me? You mean ruining my life?"

"I didn't leak the video!" he shouts. "It was Breslin's father. He was my partner. I tried to pay him off every month and hold up my end of the agreement, but I fell behind when my inheritance money ran out."

I take a breath and let it out slow. I should probably be surprised at the news, but I'm not. Breslin's dad is an asshole and he'd do anything for the money to support his addiction. Including hurting the boy his daughter loved, and breaking her heart in the process.

"I told him to give me some more time, but he was too impatient, so he leaked it."

"If that's the case, why didn't you tell me. You knew I had access to money. You knew I would have found a way to pay—"

"Would you? Or would you have tracked Breslin down and told her the truth about the blackmail? In other words, undoing all the years I had put into you when you were *so* close to submitting and finally loving me."

Christ, I regret not telling Breslin everything that night even more now. None of this bullshit would have happened. Or maybe it would have, but things would have been so different.

Would they?—my mind taunts. *She still would have left you and the video still would have gone viral.* Only difference is that Kyle wouldn't have had my balls in a vise for three years. Fucking nutcase.

He sniffs. "We were so close, Asher. By that third year together, I could physically feel your love for me, and I couldn't take that chance. The chance that you would end up together again and ruin what we had."

All I can think is that I'm watching a madman unravel as he pounds on his chest. "Because anytime you think about that cunt your head gets all fucked up." His jaw hardens. "But I guess the joke was on me, because look who you crawled back to after the shit hit the fan."

I shake my head and get up off the chair, because even if he kills me, it's better than not standing up to him anymore. I've had enough. I'm done with being the pawn to an obsessed psychopath.

"Look, Kyle, I'm sorry for what my father did to you. And I guess in your own twisted way you tried to make it right. But it still doesn't excuse what—"

"I tried to get help," he whispers, tears streaming down his face. "Remember that day in the parking lot, right before prom? You told me I needed help. Do you remember that, Asher?"

"Yes," I answer, and for a split second I truly pity him. I take another step toward him and he thrusts the gun at me. "I need you to listen. I'm not done with my story yet."

I pause mid-step. "Okay, I'm listening."

Maybe if he gets it all out he'll just hand over the gun and walk away.

Right, Asher. Because when the mentally unhinged hold others at gunpoint, it always ends well.

"After the video went viral and you told me you never wanted to see me again and I had lost you, I found a therapist. I thought maybe if I spent a few months getting help and came back to you, we could start again, you know? That maybe you would see that I'm not some crazy person who's obsessed with you but that I really do love you."

I stay silent, because my only response to that is something he's not going to want to hear.

On second thought, maybe I can manipulate him into giving me the gun and get security to lock him up where he belongs. I just have to play my cards right.

"I'm proud of you," I tell him and he looks surprised.

"You are?"

I nod and will my body to keep calm. "You were really brave to do that. Must have taken a lot of courage."

"It did." He licks his lips. "There were so many pills, though. Lots and lots of medications."

I bet. "Are you on any of them now? Do you have them with you?"

He shakes his head. "I stopped taking them that *night*." He spits the last word like it leaves a bad taste in his mouth.

"I'm probably going to regret this, but what night?"

"The night that I went to see you at your new college and found you in the art room with her."

Shit. Guess that explains why I felt like someone was watching me.

I take another step forward, because as much as I'd love to draw this shit out, Breslin might walk through that door at any time and there's no telling what he would do to her. "I know what you think, but we're not together, Kyle. We just happen to attend the same college now." I figure it's best to tell him what he wants to hear at this point. Whatever will make him hand over that gun.

He eyes me skeptically. "Yeah right."

"It's true. She moved on from me and has a boyfriend," I say, ignoring the way my chest burns. "She's in love with someone else. A guy named Landon. He's a musician." My heart squeezes in protest, but I continue. "They're really happy together." I take another step. "She doesn't want me anymore. She loves Landon now, not me."

His face twists. "Hurts doesn't it?"

"Like hell." I close the distance between us. "But maybe we can heal each other this time around." He starts to jerk away but I sweep my palm over his cheek. "But in order to do that, you're going to need to put down the gun. Can you do that for me?"

"How do I know you're not just telling me what I want to hear? How do I know that you're not really with her?"

"Because of this." My stomach lurches as I crush my mouth to his and it's all I can do not to throw up.

"Give me the gun, Kyle," I whisper against his lips. "Please, give me the gun so we can walk out of here together."

"Promise?"

"Yes."

"Okay," he starts to say, until a nurse enters the room, sees the gun in his hand, and screams for security.

Kyle shoves me away and points his gun at her. Less than a

second later my ears ring and my heart's in my throat when the nurse collapses and Kyle barrels down the hall.

I start to run, but slip on the pool of blood on the floor.

Righting myself, I chase after him, but unfortunately he has a head start due to my fall. I can hear security behind me and I'm relieved, until Kyle makes a sharp left and I see Breslin walk out of the waiting room.

No.

Adrenaline surges through my bloodstream and I run faster than I ever have in my entire life.

"What the fuck are you doing here?" Kyle shouts, but that's all he has time to say because I tackle him so hard his head slams against the tiles and the gun slips from his hands just as Preston comes flying out of the room. Relief fills my chest when he makes the quick decision to grab it.

"You lied to me about her," Kyle barks as security forms a tight circle around us. "You tricked me."

After they handcuff him, I stand up and glare at him. "Sucks when people do that, doesn't it?"

I expect him to tell me off before they take him away, but to my absolute horror, a large smile stretches across his face and he looks at Breslin who looks like she's seen a ghost. "Just wait, you fucking cunt." He fights against the security guards as they haul him away. "I love you, Asher. I won't let her take you away from me again."

The venom in his eyes has me lurching toward him, but Breslin runs over to me. "Asher, stop. You're bleeding."

I look down at my shirt that's now stained with the nurses' blood. "It's not mine."

She wraps her arms around me. "Oh, thank God. What the fuck is going on?"

I don't even know where to begin. Right as I start to tell her what happened, a hand clamps down on my shoulder. "You're gonna need to come with us and answer some questions," a police officer says.

The officers let me go after 45 minutes, appearing satisfied with my answers.

When I walk back out to the waiting room in search of Breslin, she's nowhere to be found. "Have you seen her?" I ask Preston, who's sitting slumped in a chair.

He looks guilty, something I only know because I've seen that expression on his face plenty of times when we were kids. "She told me she was going to the bathroom." He checks his watch and stands. "About 20 minutes ago."

Annoyance flares in my gut. "You didn't think to check on her?"

I move toward the bathrooms but his next statement has me coming to a halt.

"I told her about Kyle blackmailing you, but in my defense, I thought she already knew." When I turn around he winces. "I also thought she had something to do with it up until an hour ago."

"What? Breslin would never—"

"Yeah, I know that now. I just figured with her piece of shit father behind it that maybe—"

"How do you know about that?"

The guilty expression on his face deepens. "To make a long story short, I ended up running into him at a bar a few hours before the video went viral. I gave him all the money I had on me in order to get him to spill the truth. Once he did, I tried to talk him out of releasing the video, but it obviously didn't work. Old drunk had a bridge to burn."

He runs a hand down his face. "I tried to warn you that night but you didn't pick up your phone. And I didn't tell you it was Breslin's dad behind it because the last time we talked about Breslin was before you left for college and you lost your shit. I didn't want you contacting her. I was trying to protect you and did what I thought was right. Turns out I was wrong."

"Yeah, no shit." I notice Breslin's coat on an empty chair and intuition hits me like a motherfucker. I know exactly where she went.

I gesture for him to follow me as I head for the exit. "I need a lift."

"Where are we going?" he questions when we reach the parking lot.

I open his car door and get inside. "Seeing as Breslin knows that Kyle blackmailed me and that her dad leaked the tape, there's only one place she could be."

The snowy wind whips around as we pull up to the trailer park and I hover my palms over one of the vents, soaking up the warmth.

I haven't said a word to him on the short drive because I'm still pissed about him not telling me that Breslin's father played a part in this.

I go to grasp the door handle but pause and glance over at him. "Sure you're not keeping anything else from me?"

He grips the steering wheel. "Nope. Sorry to disappoint, big brother but I've been preoccupied with my own shit lately."

"Right," I seethe, recalling the last few months. "Guess that means I better get my shovel ready so I can clean it all up for you again."

He slams his foot on the brake so hard the car slides as we come to a stop in front of the trailer. "What the hell is that supposed to mean?"

It takes everything in me not to bitch slap him. "You know, you could have at least said thank you to me for winning the championship."

He snorts. "I should have said thank you? Funny, because last time I checked, me losing that bet and getting involved with Dragoni is what's making *your* NFL dream come true."

I fix him with a glare. I can't believe he doesn't see what a problem he has. "You really don't get it, do you? What if I lost? What if things didn't turn out for the best? What then?"

"I don't know." His shoulders rise on a deep inhale. "I would have figured out another way to settle the score. I always do."

Dragoni's words to me after the championship game sear through my skull. "How? By placing another bet? One that you might lose. Christ, when does the bullshit stop? Where do you draw the line, Preston? When someone you love gets hurt, or when they've taken your life?"

I swing open the car door. "You're going to be a dad soon, brother. It's time to grow the hell up before you end up fucking an innocent life up right along with yours."

Preston's expression falls and he closes his eyes. "No, I'm not." When I open my mouth to ask him what he means, he says, "There's a reason I didn't answer my phone when you called me about dad earlier today. I was getting the results back from the paternity test."

I exhale sharply. "You dodged a bullet."

He looks down. "I wanted the baby to be mine."

"Prest—"

"Part of me regrets having the test done now, but I couldn't take it, Asher. I needed to know." His eyes become glassy. "I started talking to the baby every night when Becca went to sleep. Telling it stories. Promising him or her that I was going to be a better father than mine ever was."

Shit. I reach over and give his shoulder a squeeze. "You will. When the time is right."

He leans his head against the headrest. "I thought that time was going to be now." He looks out the window. "Maybe I just wanted something to give me the push I needed to clean my life up and get my act together."

"Well, you know what they say. Admitting you have a problem is the first step." I give him a pointed look. "You'll get through this."

I get out of the car just as a sharp gust of frozen wind blows. "Looks like the weather is getting worse."

"I know. I was thinking about heading to Woodside tonight, but I think I'll wait for tomorrow."

I laugh. "I can't wait to see the look on Becca's face when she sees her shit all over campus."

He balks at me. "What the hell is wrong with you? I might be an asshole, but I'm not tossing a pregnant chick out on the street in the middle of winter. No matter how much I can't stand her."

I raise an eyebrow. "Then why are you going to Woodside tomorrow?"

A long pause stretches between us before he whispers, "To see Kit." There's a hint of sadness in his eyes. "I'm not the only one Becca hurt and Kit has a right to know that the baby isn't mine."

I wrap my jacket tighter around me and think about his statement for a moment. I suppose in some way it makes sense. At the very least, it's the decent thing to do.

I give him a smile and tap the hood of his car. "Drive safe, little brother."

He salutes me. "Call me if you need me. I'll answer."

I turn my attention to the trailer as he drives off and when I hear a loud crash, my blood becomes lava and I run.

CHAPTER 46

BRESLIN

My nostrils fill with the unpleasant odor of what I know is a filthy and unkempt trailer and I hold my breath, knowing the worst is yet to come.

Hands shaking with both rage and sadness, I muster up some tenacity and push open the front door. The fact that it's almost midnight and he didn't even bother to lock it speaks volumes.

When I finally step a foot inside, I see it's even worse than I thought it would be. Empty beer cans and liquor bottles litter the already dirty floor and when I swivel my gaze around, I see a few broken crack pipes and used needles covering various tables and chairs.

If hopelessness and despair were tangible manifestations. It would be *this*.

The thought is almost enough to make me forget why I came here. Almost.

"Virginia," my father's slurred voice bellows from the back of the trailer. "Get your ass over here. I'll pay Johnny what I owe him tomorrow. Unless you want half of this here eight-ball."

Wow, he must have a fondness for her. Lord knows he never

shares his stash. Something I know from all the countless times I've had to clean his cuts and scrapes after his drug buddies beat the shit out of him for *hogging the party* as they called it.

My stomach rolls as I start walking toward the bedroom. I wish I could say it's the first and only time that my father's mistaken me for one of his hookers, but it's not.

Deciding it's better not to walk in given he's waiting for his whore, I still myself. "It's Breslin."

There's nothing but silence for the better part of a minute and then, "Breslin?"

"Yeah, Breslin. You know, your daughter," I say through clenched teeth.

A sigh of frustration passes my lips and I suddenly regret coming here. I mean, what was the point?

The point is to stand up to him—I remind myself. Confront him and move on with your life.

"Quit your hollering," he grumbles, staggering out of the bedroom. "I know who you are." His bloodshot eyes narrow. "Someone who can't bother to pick up the phone for her father anymore."

"Me? You were the one who blocked my number."

He barges past me, heading for the kitchen. "I did not." He opens the fridge and grabs a beer. "Tried calling you a few times when I was late on the bills."

All I can do is stare at him. It's like watching a car crash happen right before your very eyes...only I've watched this same car crash so many times I've practically become desensitized to it.

And for the first time in my life, I don't want to be the good Samaritan who tries to help him. I want to walk on by without a second thought.

God, I used to feel so bad for this man. My heart hurt for him because I knew how much he missed my mother after she left us.

But now I'm realizing that heartbreak and bitterness can only excuse so much bad behavior.

As much as I hate to admit it, I know Preston was right about my father leaking Asher's video, and holy hell that hurts, because why in the world would he ever do something like that?

Not to Asher...but to *me*? His own daughter.

My body shakes with nerves but I steel myself. I need to hear him admit it or I'm afraid I'll keep making excuses for him instead of doing what I came here to do.

"Dad?" My voice cracks because it's the last time I'll ever utter that name again, and after this conversation; I'll have lost both my parents.

Who am I kidding? I've had a ghost for a father for as long as I can remember. I'm just finally acknowledging it.

He pauses mid-sip. "What?"

I draw in the biggest breath that I can...and then I rip the bandage off. "Did you or did you not help Kyle Sinclair set up Asher Holden?"

For a fraction of a second, I see surprise flash in his eyes, but then he just shrugs. *Shrugs* like it was no big deal that he wrecked Asher's life and mine. "Yeah, but I done fucked that up. Should have brought the dang video to that big wig father of his like we were supposed to. Would have gotten more money from him instead of that loony Kyle."

I don't even know where to begin with that statement because all I can feel is my blood boiling like a volcano.

I take a step toward him, limbs trembling because I need someplace to put all this new-found rage that I have for him. "How could you do that to me?"

He leans against the counter, scowling. "Stop being so dramatic. I was doing you a favor." His scowl grows. "Turns out an even bigger one than I thought on account of him turning out to be a fag and all. Least you can do is say thank you."

"You want a thank you for ruining my life?" I slam my hand on the countertop, the anger simmering beneath the surface bubbling. "You know how much I loved him. You know how much it destroyed me when we broke up. How could you stand by for years and watch me spend every ounce of energy hating someone who didn't deserve it?" I swallow the lump forming in my throat when it hits me. For over three years I've been encapsulated in acrimony because I couldn't let go of all the pain and bitterness. "How could you let me become you?"

His expression is so malevolent I rear back in surprise. This is the most emotion this man has ever shown me.

"Like I said, I was doing you a favor. That boy was gonna leave your ass the second they put a diploma in his hand and he found out there were better things out there than you. Just like your mama left us."

I can't help myself, the words are already rising up my throat in one big swell of indignation. "My mother didn't leave us...she left *you*."

The blow from his hand across my cheek has me stumbling back. "Don't you ever say that again," he grunts, right before he deals his next blow. The sting from that slap is even sharper this time around, but I stand tall and look him right in the eyes. I've never felt so resolved about anything in my life and I'm done being his punching bag. I'm done with him blaming me for why she left when the real reason is looking right at me.

"She gave me her paint set," I say, jabbing myself in the chest. "She left me a note telling me to always chase my dreams. She cared about me. She didn't love you anymore."

His mouth drops open but I'm not done yet. Not even close. "And why should she, huh?" I look around the trailer. "You're a pathetic waste of a human being. You were a shitty husband, a horrible provider, and the world's worst father."

I get close to his face, the stench of alcohol and rotting teeth permeating my nostrils. "You didn't deserve her love and you sure as hell don't deserve mine anymore. As far as I'm concerned you're dead to me."

It all happens so quickly I don't even have time to process it. In one fell swoop, my back is smashed against the dirty counter, sending a slew of empty beer bottles crashing to the floor.

"You fucking bitch," he sneers, squeezing my throat so hard white spots form in front of my eyes. I try and push him off me but I can't, his grip is too strong and I'm becoming lightheaded.

Oh, God. This is it. I'm gonna die right here in this godforsaken trailer by the hands of a man who never once loved me.

I scratch and claw at his fingers, desperate for oxygen but that only makes him tighten his hold. "I kept you when she didn't want you. I—"

He doesn't get to finish that statement because Asher yanks him off me. I briefly wonder what the hell he's doing here but I'm too busy taking air into my lungs and watching him beat the living shit out of my father.

My father tries to shove him off, but it's no use, Asher's not letting up. He rams his fists into his face, throwing so many punches that if I blink I'll miss a few.

Finally, he pauses, but only so he can sneer, "I swear to fuck I'm gonna kill you, you worthless piece of shit," before he punches him so hard my father spits out what's left of his teeth.

I've never in my entire life seen him or anyone else so angry. But as indebted as I am to him for coming to my rescue, I can't let Asher kill him. My father's taken enough from him already, I won't let him ruin his future.

"Asher, stop," I yell, when I see the blood pouring down my father's face and hear him start to gurgle.

Asher doesn't hear me, though. Or if he does, he doesn't care because he keeps at it, making my father his personal piñata.

I have no choice but to grab one of his arms and scream his name at the top of my lungs. "Asher, it's over. It's done."

He shakes his head, his breathing erratic, his knuckles oozing. The look in his eyes is so disturbing and maniacal it sends a shiver up my spine.

"Asher, please."

We stare at one another for several heart stopping beats and I silently plead with him, until, at last; he stands up—but not before giving the man who's curled up in a fetal position on the floor one last glance. "You ever contact her again...I *will* finish what I started."

With that, he takes my hand and leads me out the front door.

For the first time in my life...I don't look back.

CHAPTER 47

ASHER

"Fuck," I mutter, shoving my hand into the snow that's piled up outside. Somewhere between the fourth or fifth punch, I split my knuckles open on that shithead's skull.

"Are you okay?" Breslin questions, her lower lip trembling. "That's your throwing hand."

I maneuver my fingers around. "At worst it's a sprain."

"Maybe we should go back to the hospital and make sure," she says but I shake my head.

"No. The NFL looks into your medical records. Last thing I need is them seeing this shit. I'll be fine."

It's only then that I notice the thick red mark around her neck, complete with finger indentations marring her delicate skin. It takes everything in me not to turn right back around again. Never in my life have I wanted to murder someone with my bare hands and drain the life out of them like I did now.

If it wasn't for the chattering of Breslin's teeth and the way she's shivering, I'd be tempted to run right back and kick his face in.

Instead, I take my jacket off and hand it to her. "You left yours at the hospital. Take mine."

She starts to decline but I'm not backing down. "You're shivering, Breslin. Take the fucking jacket."

Reluctantly she slips it around her shoulders. When she pulls her keys out and heads for the car, I take them from her and slide into the driver's seat. "You're not driving in the middle of a blizzard."

I expect her to argue with me but she stays silent as she gets into the passenger seat.

I start driving down the snow-covered road. "At this rate, it's going to take us twelve hours to drive back to Woodside instead of three." When I make a left turn and the tires skid I say, "There's a hotel up the road. We can head back in the morning after the roads are plowed."

I brace myself, preparing for the argument that I know is coming but she doesn't say a word so I take that as her agreement.

I lean against the headboard when I hear the water from Breslin's shower turn off.

She still hasn't said one word to me since we've been here, but I kind of expected it. Breslin's the ultimate paradox, because while she can argue until she's blue in the face and stand up for her convictions, she's never been good at processing her emotions in the aftermath of any kind of turmoil, and deep down inside; she hates confrontation.

Her go-to is to shut down until she's ready to speak again. It's something I absolutely hate, and yet something I can't help but understand.

When she walks out a moment later clad in nothing but a little white towel, I inhale deeply and force both my dick and heart not to react. Which is basically like telling the sun not to shine.

In other words...im-fucking-possible.

COMPLICATED HEARTS   367

Her gaze lands on my bare chest and boxers briefly before venturing up to find my eyes. "Sorry, I...um. I don't have a change of clothes." She stares down at the floor. "Obviously."

I gesture to the nightstand where two brand new t-shirts are folded, one for her and one for me, courtesy of the guest shop downstairs.

"Thank you," she whispers, making no move to pick hers up.

Instead, she walks over to the large window and draws back the curtain, staring at the snow that's falling.

"Looks like it's getting better out there—"

"Why didn't you tell me?"

My heart spasms in my chest with her question. I knew it was going to come to this sooner or later, but no matter how much I tried to prepare myself for it, I'm not. Not even a little.

I've spent years thinking about what I would say to Breslin if I ever got the chance, but nothing ever seemed right.

There's nothing I could say that would pardon me.

She turns to face me and the hurt in her eyes is enough to make me want to keel over. "We always told each other everything."

"I did try to tell you."

She keeps her eyes trained on mine, like she's seeing through my soul in the way that only she can.

Like she knows all the things that I don't want her to.

"For months he blackmailed you and you never said a word to me. For months you held my hand, kissed me, and told me you loved me while looking into my eyes...but you never once told me what he was doing to you."

A line forms between her brows. "When you finally did tell me what was going on, it was a twisted version of the truth. Almost like you wanted me to leave you, like you purposely pushed me away." A tear falls from the corner of her eye. "You told me about your sexuality, but you never told me about Kyle threatening you. You never told me the real truth that could have saved us. Because you didn't want to save us...did you?"

And there it is in all its ugly glory. The thing I never wanted her to know.

I didn't tell her the truth because I was scared or because I couldn't find the right words.

I didn't tell her, because for one single, solitary moment in my life...I wasn't selfish.

I wanted Breslin to leave and never look back. Because I loved her enough to let her go.

I just didn't realize the giant hole in my heart that her absence would cause when she did. And by the time I chased after her...it was already too late. She was gone.

"You deserved better than me," I start to say and she grimaces.

"That's a cop out."

"It's not," I say sharply. "You deserved better than some sexually confused teenager who had no idea what the fuck was going on in his head or his dick."

I stand up. "The way I saw it back then, I was going to hurt you sooner or later. Either that, or I was going to resent you for something you couldn't possibly understand." I lift a shoulder. "In the end, it was easier to go along with Kyle's blackmail because it was the punishment I thought I deserved for ruining us and having feelings that I shouldn't be having."

Her face falls flat. "No one deserves to be punished for their sexuality. It's not your fa—" She catches herself mid-sentence and gives her head a shake. "What I mean is, you shouldn't be ashamed of being bisexual."

I hook my finger under her chin, forcing her to look at me. "That's what you think now, but what about then?"

She wretches out of my grip. "I left you because you said you cheated on me with Kyle, not because—"

"Bullshit." I don't mean to be so harsh but I can't help it, this shit has built up for years between us and it's finally coming to a head. "Would you really have been able to accept the fact that I had the urge to sleep with guys back then? Would you have been okay with it?"

Her mouth falls open and I know I've got her. "I don't know, maybe not. I'd like to think in time that I would have. Obviously I accept it now." She presses her lips into a line and swallows. "But you didn't give me a chance to accept anything back then, Asher."

Before I can tell her that she's right, she jabs a finger in my chest. "Instead, you took me to prom, took my virginity, and then told me you were gay and that you cheated on me with Kyle." Another tear falls. "You broke me into a thousand different pieces and demolished me. Do you have any idea how much I loved you? Any fucking idea how much?"

I grab her by her shoulders, need, lust, and despair are pummeling into me like a category five hurricane. "I do, because multiply what you feel for me times infinity and it wouldn't even come close to how much I love you."

There is nothing in the world that I wouldn't do or give up for her. Hell, if she asked me to physically rip out my beating heart and offer it to her on a silver platter so she could feed it to vultures, I would.

I'd do anything to make this right again, but the only thing I can do right now is tell her everything I feel for her—and hope she can find it in her heart to forgive me for being the monumental asshole that I am.

She turns her head away in disgust and my body knots up at the loss of our connection, it's like she's filleting me open, leaving me vulnerable and exposed.

"That can't possibly be true," she says. "Because if you loved me you would have chosen me. You would have chosen the truth."

"I did what I thought was best, Breslin. I—"

I wish I could take it back.

Her eyes squeeze shut. "God, I hated you so much. I spent years despising you for what you did and—"

"I deserved your hate. It's what I wanted you to feel when you left."

I don't want her blaming herself for any of this or apologizing to me when it was my fault.

She opens her eyes. "I thought about you all the time. I used to wonder what I did, why I wasn't enough for you. And then when I thought about all the reasons *why* I wasn't—I used to cry myself to sleep wishing that I was smarter, more interesting, skinnier, prettier, and that my family life wasn't so fucked up. Hell, I even wished that I was a different gender. I wanted nothing more than to be what you needed me to be because I loved you so much. More than anything or anyone."

Her confession stabs through my heart. I go to grab her again but she spins around, her soft sobs fogging up the window.

"Breslin—"

"No. I don't want your pity."

I take a step closer, pinning her between my body and the window, making sure she can't go anywhere because she needs to hear this. "Good, because you don't have it."

I sweep her damp hair to the side and trace my lips along her earlobe. "I fucked up, I know that now. I messed things up with us so badly that I don't deserve your forgiveness, no matter how much I want it. But baby, you need to know that despite my mistakes...there is nothing wrong with you."

I run my lips over my favorite freckles lining her shoulder. "From the second we collided in that hallway, I wanted you, I needed you, I craved you." I press a kiss to her skin and she shivers. "The moment you opened your mouth, I knew I was going to fall head over heels in love with you and I was right."

I inhale her sweet scent like she's my drug. "You have my heart, Breslin. I might have let you go, but I made damn sure you took that with you when you left, because it doesn't belong to anyone else but you. Every single part of it is yours."

Including the part that belongs to someone else now.

When she doesn't say a word, I sink my teeth into her skin, branding her flesh before soothing the spot over with my tongue. "I'm sorry I hurt you, so fucking sorry. It's a mistake I'll always regret. But I'm not sorry about us crossing paths again, or for making you mine back then."

Or making her mine now. Because she is mine. She knows it as much as I do. She can't escape what we have any more than I can.

No matter what happens between us, we'll always find our way back to one another. Regardless of who gets in the way.

And even though freeing both her and Landon so they can lead a happy life together is the right and noble thing to do in this situation...I won't.

The fact of the matter is, I'd rather bleed my heart out on this shitty hotel carpet than ever live without her.

We're all trapped together, entwined in a way that no one else can ever understand. One is under my skin, the other is in my bones.

Question is—what is she going to do about it now that the truth —all of it—is out there? Leaving no ifs, ands, or buts between us anymore.

Because the way I see it, she only has one of two choices. Either she chooses me...or she chooses both of us. Either way, I'm *never* letting her go again. I barely survived it the first time around.

Her palms flatten against the window. "I don't regret you either."

Her voice is so faint that for a second, I think I imagined it.

My heart thuds against my ribs when she turns back around and faces me. Those green eyes are filled with so much sadness, but I see the love shining through.

"I'm so sorry, baby," I say, cradling her face in my hands.

Another tear slips down her cheek and I catch it on my thumb. "Me too."

We stand there staring at one another. The air between us is too thick with friction, making it hard to breathe.

"I love you," I tell her, because it's the only thing that makes sense in this moment. The only thing I feel. "I love—"

Soft lips crash into mine and my heart tumbles over itself.

A groan tears out of me and I can't keep my hands off her now that her lips are on my skin, exactly where they should be. I want every part of her body, every square inch of her heart and soul.

I find the knot on her towel and toss the damn thing across the room, I don't want any barriers between us. I just want to devour and consume her until the day I take my last breath.

When I venture down, I can feel her heartbeat in her throat. I gently suckle the spot until her head lolls to the side and she cries out my name.

I ease back, watching her chest heave up and down with scattered breaths, uncertainty splashed across her face.

"Breslin, if you don't want this, you better tell me now because I won't be able to stop. I'm not that fucking strong." I give her a smirk. "Or honorable."

A flush of heat comes over my body and settles in my dick when her fingers find the waistband of my boxers and she tugs them down, freeing my aching erection. Christ, I'm so hard for her I'm liable to come at any second.

I reach for her hand and thrust into it, because I need her to know how much I want her. I don't want there to be any room for doubt inside her head. "See what you do to me?"

She licks her lips and swirls her thumb around the fluid weeping from my tip. I have to fight back a smile when it jerks and her cheeks flush. Fuck, she really has no idea what kind of impact she has on me. The way she makes my heart beat faster and slower at the same time. The way I yearn for her.

My gaze drops to her tight nipples that are longing to be sucked. I lift one into my mouth and then take turns laving and pinching them until she fastens her grip and strokes me in one long glide, making my knees buckle.

When she starts to sink to the ground, my balls seize up so fast I have to pull away before I jet all over her fingers.

"Baby," my voice comes out strangled and choppy. "If you do that, this is gonna end real fast."

I can practically see the memory from years ago slash across her face and I silently curse myself. The last thing I want is to remind her of our past right now.

I motion to my erection that's throbbing and leaking. "I'm trying to hold on for as long as I can here, Breslin. But you're not making it easy." I grab her hips and turn her toward the bed. "Have mercy on me."

When she lands on the mattress with a soft plop, I slowly work my way down her body, taking my time, exploring every inch of her skin with my mouth.

"Asher."

There's an impatient and pleading tone to her voice and I graze my teeth along her hip bones, causing her hips to buck off the bed. "Not yet." I pry her thighs apart, baring her soft pink flesh to me. "I need to eat you first."

With that, I bury my head between her legs, tasting her in one elongated swipe. *Fuck, that's good.* And just like a fiend, I'm back for more—dipping my tongue inside her, flicking that sweet spot that drives her crazy, and giving her pretty clit messy kisses as she rides my face and yanks my hair.

She trembles as she stares down at me. "Please, Asher."

I take her clit between my teeth and she mewls, gripping the bed sheets. "Inside me," she begs, her voice cracking with emotion. "*Inside* me."

My heart beats like a drum as I crawl up her body and settle between her thighs, dragging my dick along her slit.

My throat works on a swallow and I bite back a groan. I'm a razor's edge away from being inside her and I'm losing every scrap of control.

Her eyes drop to my mouth that's damp with her juices. "Kiss me," I taunt her, and when I stick out my tongue, she massages it with hers.

"See how good you taste?" I murmur and she repeats the movement, this time ending it with a little suck that goes straight to my groin before licking my chin.

She wraps her arms around my neck and hooks her legs around my waist, pushing the tip of my cock inside her. The swollen head beats against her warm slick flesh and my body thrums.

"Now, Asher," she rasps and I drive the rest of the way inside her in one fluid motion. She clings to my shoulders and I slam back and rock into her again, pleasure spiking and coiling my insides.

I want to close my eyes and get lost in the moment, but there's no way I can take my eyes off of her. She's so beautiful she shines and I wouldn't miss this for anything.

I kiss the tear that falls down her cheek and my lungs freeze when she looks at me and says the words I've been dying to hear again. "I love you."

I lean my forehead against hers. "I love you bigger."

Tension in my limbs tightens and I reach between us and take her clit between my fingers, hoping like hell she follows me because I can't hold back.

I pump inside her one last time and she clenches around me, holding on to me with everything she has as she lets go. I come so hard my body shudders with the force and I collapse on top of her, burying my face into the crook of her neck. "I promise next time I'll last longer."

A laugh escapes her and it's music to my ears. I can't help but lift my head and look at her again.

Her eyes are wide and her heart is galloping underneath me, and for a moment, I fear she'll say it was a mistake.

But when she smiles and it reaches her eyes, I know she feels it too.

What we just had...was the way it was always supposed to be between us.

And maybe, just maybe, somewhere between all the chaos and heartache, we were gifted our second chance.

T he sound of my cell phone ringing wakes me out of a dead sleep and I curse.

At first, I think it might be the hospital, but when I see Landon's name flash across the screen I jump up out of bed. I stop to look back at Breslin who's still sleeping soundly before I make my way to the bathroom and bring the phone to my ear.

"Hey," he greets on the other line.

The sound of his voice burns a trail over my heart. *Fuck, I miss him.* "Hey, rock star," I say and he laughs, which only fuels the ache in my chest.

"Yeah, I don't know about all that." He clears his throat. "Sorry for waking you but I wanted to tell you that I'm stuck on a three-hour layover. However, I should be at the hospital by early after-noon the latest."

Shit. My heart pounds in my ears as I lower the lid to the toilet and sit. "Wow," I say slowly, trying to find my vocal chords that are currently wound up like a ball of yarn. "Breslin told me you weren't able to catch a flight."

"I know, I wasn't. I decided to go to the airport and wait it out, thankfully at the last minute, one opened up. I texted Breslin back a little while ago to tell her but she didn't answer." He inhales a breath. "I know we haven't talked much over the last month and that's my fault, but I'm on my way. I'll be there, Asher."

I lean down, resting my elbows on my knees, my heart spasming. I shouldn't even be surprised by this because that's who my boyfriend is.

Compassionate, caring...a good human being.

My polar opposite in almost every way.

I open my mouth to tell him—because I do have every intention of telling him—what happened, but then I clamp my mouth shut.

I'm not informing him about the events that transpired over the last few hours when he's between flights. It will drive him sick with worry...and rage. Not to mention, this is a conversation that needs to be had in person, not over the phone.

I scrub a hand down my face. "Look, uh. I can't wait to see you, but you don't have to come to the hospital."

I hear him mutter a curse on the other line before he says, "I'm sorry, Asher. I wish I could have gotten there sooner—"

"No," I interject, realizing how he interpreted my statement. "He's not dead." I release a breath I wasn't aware I was holding. "Don't get me wrong, he's not exactly alive, but I can't bring myself to tell them to pull the plug. Preston can't do it, either. We decided it's best to let our mom make the decision when she gets home from her cruise." I tap my fingers on the porcelain of the sink, trying to make sense of my conflicting feelings. "It just doesn't feel right, you know? Kind of like I'm playing God or some shit."

"Yeah," he says softly. "I get it."

"Anyway, there's no point for me to be there round the clock given the grim outcome. Plus, the first day of classes are tomorrow and I feel like if I miss it because of him, it's just another thing that I let him have control over."

"Totally understandable."

Guilt settles in my chest with my next statement. "We would

have been back tonight but there was a snowstorm. We decided to ride it out and wait until the roads were plowed before driving back to Woodside."

I leave the implication of us being at a hotel together hanging in the air.

There's a long pause before he says, "Right. Smart thinking."

"Yeah."

"She sleeping?"

I don't know what to make of his tone now. It's not irritated or bitter...it's barren and devoid of any emotion which is so rare for him.

"I can wake her up if you want."

"No, it's fine. Let her rest. In fact, you should probably get some sleep, too. I'll see you both tomorrow when you get back." His voice drops to a whisper. "I love you."

"I—" The line goes dead.

CHAPTER 48

BRESLIN

The light from the bathroom stretches across the carpet briefly before I hear Asher's footsteps pad over to the bed.

A moment later, the sheets rustle and then his big body is behind me, caging me in with the heat of his buttery skin.

Instinctually I burrow closer to him, seeking his warmth, basking in his touch.

"I didn't mean to wake you," he whispers, running a finger up my bare back, leaving goosebumps in his wake. "Landon called—"

I don't hear the rest of his statement because my heart skitters and then restricts at the sound of his name.

Landon. The other man I love.

The one who I'm undoubtedly hurting by being in this bed.

It doesn't matter that what happened between me and Asher doesn't feel wrong, and that technically speaking, it's not fair for Landon to be upset about it.

Landon drew the line in the sand and we hopped right over it tonight without a second thought.

I know because the look in his eyes when I last saw him still haunts me. Just like the distraught expression on his face when he asked me if I loved Asher does.

I don't know how I can ever explain this to him—because I have to— without losing him.

I can't lose him.

"Baby?" Asher questions, turning my chin to look at him. "What's going on?"

I don't answer him. Instead, I find his mouth and the sinking feeling in my chest quickly turns to rapid flutters when he parts my thighs and settles on top of me.

The first thrust is so good, I claw my nails down his back, desperately seeking more. More of this escape, more of him. More of us.

I reach up and touch his face, wanting to memorize this moment forever because it's going to rip my heart and soul out when I can't have it anymore.

His brows furrow, his sweat soaked body and delicious thrusts coming to a halt. "Don't, Breslin." He encloses my face with his palms. "Don't check out on me. Don't end this."

It feels like my heart is being pulled in two different directions and I'll never be whole again—because I need them both; in equal measures, for entirely different reasons.

Those blue eyes, so full of longing and intensity imprison me and I can't help myself. I fold, I bend, and I break. "I'm not." I run my hand down his jaw. "I'm right here."

I raise my hips and cling to him for dear life and when he stammers out a breath and drives into me...

I immerse myself in his universe and let myself fall for him once more.

I know what the future holds for me tomorrow—but right now?

I want my supernova to keep burning me until I'm nothing but ash.

T he sun shines brightly as we continue traveling down the highway. We ended up getting a later start than we antici-pated this morning, but as long as we don't hit any traffic we should end up making it back in time for our afternoon classes.

Asher brings my hand to his mouth and kisses my knuckles, his eyes trained on the road ahead as he drives. "It's gonna be okay."

I pull my hand back. I don't know how he can be so calm and optimistic about this when I'm close to puking with every mile that brings me closer to Landon.

I'm absolutely terrified about how he's going to react when he finds out. My stomach jolts and I bring my knees up to my chest, trying to shove down the thoughts bouncing around in my head and my heart.

I love him. I don't want to lose him.

Asher may be my universe, but Landon's my home.

He gives me the kind of security and love that no one else can...and if I was forced to choose.

No.

I glance at the clock on the dashboard and when I see that despite the lack of traffic we're still running behind, I decide to call Kit and tell her that I won't be able to meet her for lunch after all.

I frown when it goes to voicemail. Since I hate leaving those, I text her instead.

Breslin: Hey, looks like we're getting back later than I thought. Want to meet up for dinner after classes?

I shrug off my concern when she doesn't respond. She did just finish working a shift at the coffee shop this morning, thanks to me. She's probably resting before her class starts.

I wipe my now sweaty palms on my jeans and tell myself to calm down.

Asher quirks a brow at me. "You okay?"

"I'm nervous."

He starts to open his mouth but then the sound of his phone ringing snags his attention. Before I can tell him that he shouldn't be talking on the phone and driving at the same time, he brings it to his ear.

"Speaking," his gruff voice answers.

When his face falls and he pales, the tiny hairs on my arms stand up.

I assume it's the hospital calling about his father, until he says, "Thank you, Officer. I'll call you if I hear anything."

"What's going on?" I ask the second he hangs up.

I have no idea what to make of the expression on his face right now and it's scaring the shit out of me.

"That was the Truesdale Police Department." Both of his hands grip the steering wheel. "It turns out that last night on the way to the precinct, a police car hit a patch of ice and ended up in a ditch."

"That's terrible, but why—"

"Kyle was in that car." My stomach clenches and his eyes cut to mine. "But when they found the vehicle, both officers were dead and there was no sign of him."

"Oh my God." I bring my hands to my face as the full impact of what he's saying hits me. "It happened last night? That means he could be anywhere right now. Why did it take them so long to find the car?"

"According to the officer on the phone, the precinct was swamped because of the storm and no one realized that those two officers didn't return until the shift was close to ending. They didn't find the car in the ditch until sunrise." He rubs his jaw. "They figured they would find Kyle's body around the area because they didn't think he'd survive out there in the storm, but now since they can't locate him and he was close to a highway, they're starting to suspect that maybe someone gave him a ride."

He looks at me again. "They've issued a nationwide APB for Kyle as a precaution and the officer wants me to call him in the event that he tries to contact me." He sighs. "The only thing I can do right now is wait and hope they find him."

The idea of waiting around like sitting ducks makes my stomach bottom out. "I think we should go to the police station."

"We can if you want, but I don't think there's a reason to right now. For all we know Kyle's dead and they just haven't found him yet. Probably buried under the snow somewhere."

His tone along with his words might be placid, but the look on his face tells me a different story.

I start to argue again but my phone lights up with a text message. Panic wraps around my lungs when I see that it's from the college.

Emergency Alert: *Active shooter on campus. Get to a safe area and take precaution until further notice. Avoid the Dining Hall and any areas in the vicinity. If off campus, remain off campus. Woodside University is on immediate lockdown.*

CHAPTER 49
LANDON

I knock on Breslin's door for the fifth time and step back with a sigh. Right when I'm about to turn around, it swings open and I come face to face with a very tired and annoyed looking Kit.

She shoves her sleep mask up and squints her eyes at me. "You know, there are these nifty things called phones. You press a few buttons and it allows you to speak to someone without having to wake a poor innocent person up with your relentless knocking. You should try it sometime." She steps aside and motions for me to come in. "She's not back yet."

"I left my cell phone on the plane," I tell her, stepping inside.

She takes her phone off the nightstand and hands it to me. "Knock yourself out."

Apprehension surges through me and I stare down at it. Ever since my conversation with Asher last night, this knot of doom has been sitting smack dab in the middle of my chest and I hate it.

"Ugh," Kit says, stomping around the room. "Okay, let's go."

I lift a brow. "Go where?"

She throws a sweatshirt over her head. "The cafeteria." She reaches for her jacket and knapsack. "Breslin's still not home and you obviously need someone to lay your shit on before you talk to her. Plus, I'm grumpy when I'm hungry so you're buying me lunch."

"I'm fine." She gives me a look and I falter. "Okay, I'm not fine. I'm jealous and I don't know how to make it go away."

She points to the front door and I follow her. "You're not jealous, Landon. That would imply that you're envious of what someone else has. But you already have what Asher has." She pauses. "And what Breslin has." We start walking down the hallway. "What you are, my friend, is threatened."

I think about her statement for a moment. "Fair enough. I keep trying to get over it, but whenever I picture them together without me I'm—"

"Hurt?"

I shake my head because that's only a small part of it. "Afraid. They have a connection and a past that I can never compete with."

"Then why are you? Trying to compete with it that is."

I'm not entirely sure that I understand her question. "Because I love them and I don't want to lose them."

"Look, I don't know shit about being in a polyamorous relationship, and Lord knows the thought of one penis let alone two seriously skeeves me out, but I have fallen in love more than once in my life."

"Okay," I drawl, not understanding at all where she's going with this.

She stops mid-stride. "Did you fall in love with Breslin for the same reasons that you fell in love with Asher?"

I run a hand over my jaw. "No. Different reasons entirely. Same feeling, but the two aren't mutually exclusive because they aren't the same person. I'm attracted to and value different aspects of them individually." I hike my guitar case up my shoulder. "Breslin because she's feisty and stubborn, and yet underneath that hard exterior she's sensitive and warm." I tap my chest. "We run on the same wavelength and I can be myself around her, no pretenses. She gets me and accepts me for who I am. And even when she frustrates me, I'm somehow at peace when I'm with her."

She takes a seat on a bench in the courtyard. "And Asher?"

"Asher is a wild card. On the surface he's unpredictable, reckless, and self-centered. And yet, there's a genuine depth to him once he lets you in." I rock back on my heels. "He challenges me and even though we're opposites, we somehow fit when we're together. He's my best friend and rival all in one. We're turbulent and complicated, but that's part of the draw."

She purses her lips and studies my face, almost like my response has her perplexed. "I don't understand why you're threatened by what they have when it sounds like you have something pretty amazing with them too."

I open my mouth but she holds up a finger and says, "Their connection and past doesn't negate the connection they have with you, because if it did, no one would be fighting to make this relationship work. One or all of you would have given up by now."

She stands up. "I get that you're insecure and afraid that they're going to run off into the sunset without you, but look at the big picture here. If they didn't want you or love you, they would have dumped you to be with one another. You give them something that the other can't. And before you get upset, that doesn't mean you're lacking, it simply means that you're important, Landon. You matter to them. For the same reasons they matter to you." She pats my shoulder. "You're not spare parts. Quite the opposite actually, you're the part that makes them complete. And I bet if you communicated and told them your concerns, they would reassure you of that in a way that I can't."

My mind flits back to the conversations that I had with them individually after everything went down before I left for England.

Kit has a point. A big one.

I take a breath, feeling better than I have in a while. All I want to do is see them both so we can figure out how to make it work. Because I want it to. I need it to.

I don't want to give up on them. On *us*. I'm in this for the long haul.

I gesture to the dining hall and begin walking. "Come on, Kit. You've earned that lunch. I'll buy you two of anything you want."

She rubs her stomach as we walk through the doors. "Good, because I am starving." She makes a face. "I had to do five whole hours of coffee slave labor by myself this morning."

I laugh as we look for an empty table in the moderately packed room. "Otherwise known as work?"

We spot a table all the way in the back and head for it. We exchange a look when we notice some guy wearing a black jacket hunched over at the very end, his back to the wall. Given that his hood is on and he's face down, resting his forehead on his arms, I assume he's sleeping. How someone can manage to do that in a noisy room full of people is beyond me.

"Hey," Kit says in his direction. "Mind if we join you?"

When there's no response, she shrugs and sits.

I grab the seat across from her, placing my guitar case down next to me. "Ready to go up and get food?"

She opens her arms wide. "And give up this prime seating? Uh, no. I'll take the grilled chicken and avocado club, though." She gives me a shit-eating grin. "Two of them, and a *Dr. Pepper*."

"Got it." I give her a warning look as I stand up. "Watch the guitar."

She starts to wave me off, but then she turns whiter than a sheet of paper and yanks me back to my seat. "Don't go."

"What?" I turn my head. "Why—" My words fall when I see Preston Holden walk in. I'm not really sure why he's here right now, but it's clear Kit wants no part of it by the way she's looking at the exit.

She's out of luck, though because Preston's standing in front of us a moment later. "Hey, can we talk?"

Out of the corner of my eye, I see the guy at the end of the table shift.

"Sorry, can't," Kit says. "My class starts in a few."

When Preston starts to object she adds, "Breslin will be walking through those doors any minute now and I haven't seen my bestie in almost a month." She reaches for her knapsack. "Bros over hoes and all that." She gives him a look that makes it clear she's referring to *him* being the hoe.

She motions for me to get up. I look down, unsure of what to do next. There's no way I'm choosing sides between my boyfriend's brother and my girlfriend's best friend. That's just asking for trouble.

I stand up. "Listen, guys I don't—"

I'm cut off when Preston blanches and says, "You're supposed to be in jail." At the same time Kit yells, "What the fuck? Stop it," as the guy in the black jacket stands and tugs her to him.

And then before any of us can comprehend what's happening, he's pulling two guns out of his jacket.

He points one at Kit's head and the other he uses to open fire in the dining hall.

Everyone starts screaming and running for the exits. Except for me and Preston because the guy in the black jacket sneers, "Run and I'll kill her."

"Kyle, don't do this, man—" Preston starts to say but then the guy *does* do it.

He does the worst thing I've ever seen when he points his gun at the rush of students who are all fighting to get out of the cafeteria alive.

The hairs on the back of my neck lift and my stomach drops when two people fall to the floor and everyone's screams become even louder as they all shove each other through the double doors.

When the last of the students have exited, he points one of the guns at me. "You—get the bag from under the table and pull out all the bungee cords. Then, I want you to secure the doors shut with them. I'll be watching you so make sure you make it nice and tight. Got it?"

When I nod, he digs the gun into Kit's temple. "If you run out those doors, I will kill her and then him. Their lives are literally in your hands right now, four eyes. Understand?"

My hands shake as I pull out a black bag with the word *Police* on it. A moment later, I locate the bungee cords and my eyes connect with Kit's.

"Please don't," she chokes out and my heart clenches.

"I'm not gonna run," I assure her. "I promise."

Sorrow slams into me when I pass the two students' bodies on the floor. The sorrow spreads through the center of my chest and coils when I recognize one of them. Her name was Kelly and I tutored her in Physics during the start of our junior year. She had a dog named Rooster and her favorite color was purple, something I only know because all of her binders and notebooks were purple and she wore the color for good luck on test days.

And now she's dead.

"No one move until those doors are secured," the guy with the gun barks. "Then we can get this party started." He looks at Preston and his eyes narrow. "Maybe I'll take another bite of a juicy apple off the Holden family tree and make it a real party."

Preston glowers, Kit gasps, and I almost drop the bungee cords I'm tying around the door because I realize exactly who *Kyle* is now. The sick bastard who tormented Breslin and blackmailed Asher for all those years.

I try and control my breathing but it's near impossible, because I know without a shadow of a doubt that I'm not going to make it out of this cafeteria alive.

I finish securing the doors just as the elevator on the opposite side of the room chimes. There's a photography classroom along with a dark room and studying lounge above us and my heart jumps to my throat because whoever is on that elevator has no idea what's awaiting them down here.

The horror on Eddie's—an exceptionally talented photography student—face when the doors open and he sees a man pointing a gun at him is nothing short of a nightmare.

A nightmare that only gets worse when Kyle pulls the trigger and fires two bullets, causing his large body to drop between the doors of the elevator.

The smell of gunpowder and the sounds of poor Eddie gasping for what I know are his last breaths has my blood whooshing in my ears as I stagger over to them.

"Now that *that's* all taken care of," Kyle says as he walks around the room, dragging a sobbing Kit with him.

Suddenly, he stops and focuses on me. My body locks up and I brace myself for the impact.

He sucks his teeth, looking me up and down. "You know, I'm not sure what to do with you." He gestures to Kit and Preston with the gun in his right hand. "The bestie and the brother are valuable assets in my revenge plan. But you? You serve no purpose, which means you're dead weight in this scenario. Pun intended."

To say I'm confused would be an understatement, and I know Kit and Preston are too. Clearly, he has no idea about my relationship with Asher or Breslin—something that might work to my benefit if I play my cards right.

Cards that turn right around to bite me in the ass because he says, "Which means you have to go."

"Wait," Preston and Kit yell as the gun in his right hand shifts to me.

"What do you want, Kyle? Tell us and we'll do it," Preston says.

"Unless you kill him," Kit adds jutting her chin at me. Our eyes connect at that moment and I've never been more grateful to someone in my life.

I can see Kyle mulling it over in his head before shrugging. "We're all gonna die today anyway. What's a few more minutes."

Preston visibly swallows. "What exactly do you want before that happens?"

A smile stretches across Kyle's face. "Call your brother and tell him about the little predicament you're in. Make sure you put him on speaker phone so I can hear the agony in his voice as he pleads for your life."

"Okay," Preston says, inhaling deeply. "I can do that, no problem. But first, can I ask you for a favor?"

Both me and Kit exchange a glance, because who in their right mind has the balls to ask a person holding people at gunpoint for a favor?

The look on Kyle's face tells me he's thinking the same thing. "What?"

Preston gestures to Kit. "Let me trade places with her."

I have absolutely no idea what to make of the look passed between Preston and Kit then. Or the reason behind Preston's request.

Kyle scratches his head with one of the guns. "Look, I'm not interested in whatever star-crossed lovers shit you two have—"

"We're not lovers," Kit interjects. "I don't swing that way."

That response has Kyle rolling his eyes. "Christ almighty, I don't think you people understand the meaning of the words not interested or *dead*." He sighs. "Fine, but no funny business. Make it snappy."

"I owed you one," Preston mumbles to her as they exchange places.

Gun to Preston's head now, Kyle walks them backward, stopping when he reaches a wall near the elevator. "Call Asher."

Preston pulls out his phone and a moment later, Asher's deep voice fills the room through the speakerphone, causing a cavernous hole in my stomach.

"I was just about to call you," Asher says. "Don't go to Woodside today, there's a shooter on campus and the police called—"

Kyle hits Preston with the gun, urging him to start talking. "Yeah, I know. Because Kyle Sinclair is currently holding me at gunpoint in the cafeteria." He looks at Kit. "Kit's here too and—" He looks at me and I silently plead with him not to tell Asher that I'm here.

I know Preston's a gambler and from what Asher told me, he's intelligent. Since I can't outright tell him about the plan I'm currently working out in my mind, I hold his gaze and roll the sleeve of my shirt up, hoping he's both smart and perceptive enough to understand the meaning behind it.

I have an Ace up my sleeve.

It was a long shot, but I can practically see the wheels turning in Preston's head. "Yeah, that's pretty much the situation right now, brother."

I can hear Asher's heavy and panicked breathing on the other line before he says, "Kyle, I know you're listening right now. Tell me what you want and I'll make it happen. I'm driving to the campus, I'll be there in less than five minutes. Let Preston and Kit go, they don't deserve this."

There's muffled crying over the speaker then and my heart folds in on itself because I know it's Breslin. "Please, Kyle don't do this. Take me instead."

Rage splashes across Kyle's face and he scowls. "Tell that stupid bitch to shut the fuck up before I make her friend's murder long and painful instead of quick and painless."

Beside me, Kit goes rigid.

Asher mumbles something to Breslin on the other line and a moment later she's quiet. "You don't have to kill anyone. We can work this out, I know we can. Talk to me about what's going on and tell me what you want. I'm listening."

Kyle laughs maniacally. "You know, I thought killing Breslin would be enough. This way, I could make you both suffer for what you've done. Her for being a dumb trailer whore that took you from me, and you for still being obsessed with a dumb trailer whore when you know how much I love you." His forehead creases. "I hid out in the cafeteria today hoping I'd spot her, because we all know that was Breslin's favorite place to hang out in high school and it was only a matter of time before she'd show up."

He chuckles to himself and I have to stuff my hands in my pockets so I don't walk over and wrap them around his neck. "But then an opportunity presented itself and I thought to myself—Self, there's a better way to make them both pay. I can kill the two people they love the most. This way, you'll both have to live the rest of your lives with the agony of losing someone you love. Then maybe you'll know how I felt, because you'll feel that ache every moment of every day."

"Kyle," Asher says calmly. "That doesn't have to happen. I know you're hurting and I know you're upset. I get it. But it doesn't have to be like this, you can still have what you want. I'm standing in the parking lot of my dorm right now. Come and get me. I'm yours."

I watch with bated breath as a flash of hope lights up Kyle's face before his eyes turn wide with panic. "Too late for that now. Do you hear that?" The sound of sirens in the distance are becoming louder and acid rises in my stomach.

Those sirens are both a blessing and a curse.

"You had your chance, Asher," he continues. "I loved you so much but you blew it. Now it's game over. The only way any of us are coming out is in a body bag."

Both Asher and Breslin start begging for Preston and Kit's lives then, which only causes Kyle to grin sadistically before he begins shouting at them with so much vigor the veins in his neck bulge and the barrel of the gun pointed at Preston tilts up to the ceiling, instead of directly at his head.

I'd breathe a sigh of relief, but the other gun, although wavering slightly, is still pointing at me and Kit.

Jesus. I look over at Kit who's shaking and then at Preston whose shoulders are slumped in defeat.

There has to be some way to stop him. Or, at the very least, save *them*.

My finger brushes over the insulin syringe in my pocket. Turns out there's a better plan than the one I was conjuring up. That plan consisted of telling Kyle all about my relationship with Asher at the last moment in hopes that he would become so enraged he'd attack me, this way Preston and Kit could make an escape.

That plan was too risky, not to say that this one isn't, but at least this one involves a weapon, albeit a shitty one.

I lock eyes with Preston again...and then I turn my head to the left...zeroing in on the elevator that's a few feet away. The one currently being held open by poor Eddie's limp body.

The elevator is their best bet because there's no way they'll be able to untie those bungees on the door in time, no matter how preoccupied Kyle will be.

Preston raises an eyebrow in question but when I look back at Kit who's so distraught she's not paying attention, and then to him again before my stare falls on the phone in his hand that Kyle's still shouting into—I think he gets what I'm insinuating, because his eyes open wide and he starts to shake his head.

I narrow my gaze in response, because this isn't up for negotiation. This is the only chance they have.

Preston takes a deep breath and I unscrew the cap to the syringe inside my pocket and get ready.

There's a million in one chance that this will go off without a hitch and won't end with all of us dead. But the thing is, our fates have already been sealed, because according to Kyle, we're all going to die soon anyway.

And at this point, I'm pragmatic enough to realize that a mentally ill person who's at the end of their rope—one who's so blinded by hate, jealousy, and torment—isn't going to spare our lives when he doesn't even value his own anymore.

Kyle's still yelling incoherent things and I know I better make this quick, because pretty soon this conversation is going to be over for good and we'll have lost our one and only chance to fight.

Preston gives me one final look...and then he drops the phone and it goes silent.

"Pick that up," Kyle barks, his focus now on the ground, which means he doesn't realize his crucial mistake until it's too late.

The second Preston starts to sink down, I pull out my needle and charge at him full force, stabbing him in the eye.

He howls in surprise and pain and the gun in his left hand drops when he instinctively tries to pull the needle out of his eye...just like I was hoping he would do.

I reach for the gun on the ground and point it at him at the same time he fires a shot in the direction of the elevator that Preston's dragging Kit into.

"Landon," Kit cries out as Preston shoves Eddie's body to the side and the doors close.

Kyle staggers back, gun on me now. "Landon?" he questions. "You—"

He doesn't have a chance to finish that statement because I pull the trigger as many times as I possibly can.

Evidently, luck is on my side after all, because it's the entire magazine. All seven bullets.

The sound is so deafening and the feeling of killing someone is so chilling I become dizzy as I watch his body slump down the wall.

I go to run out the door, but a deep burning sensation pumps through my chest, like hot metal searing through my skin. It's so intense, I collapse on the floor.

It's only then that I realize Kyle shot me.

Fear ripples through me as blood starts soaking my clothes. I try to put pressure on the wound, try to prevent the blood from pouring out but it's near impossible. It's gushing out of me quicker than I can stop it. Like a hole that I can't seem to plug no matter how hard I try.

The sirens which were once becoming louder seem so faint now...until it's eerily silent.

My eyelids feel heavy and even though I don't want to close them because I'm afraid of what will happen—I do.

Suddenly, the physical pain doesn't feel so bad anymore...but the emotional pain becomes overwhelming...because I know I'm dying.

When you wake up in the morning, you never think the day ahead of you will end up being your last day on earth.

You never assume that simple things, like having lunch at school with a friend, will end in your death.

You never realize how trivial things really are...until you're struggling for your last breath.

Twenty minutes ago, my biggest problem was being jealous over Asher and Breslin's relationship—and now—it's that I'll never see them again.

I'll never get to tell them how much I love them—because your life can change with every heartbeat.

And while I wish I could spend my last few minutes alive thinking about all the good things I've had in my life...I can't.

Because I'm too busy thinking about the people I'm going to miss and the things I didn't get a chance to experience in this lifetime.

I don't want to die.

I want to graduate college.

I want to sit at my piano, creating and playing music that moves people to tears.

I want to take my girlfriend to Europe and see her gorgeous smile when we find that tent she loves so much.

I want my boyfriend to kiss me in public like he promised.

I want my second chance to live, so I can do it right this time.

But that's not the way the world works, people die every second of every day. And right now, I'm one of them, no matter how much I don't want to be.

Terror rushes through me when I see my brother Levi's face, and even though he's telling me not to be scared and that it's okay, I know it's not, because I'm not ready to leave.

Blood fills my mouth and my body shakes as my heart starts to pound out my favorite rhythm, followed by my favorite melody, for what I know is the last time.

I'm so glad they found each other once again, because their song is so beautiful. It soothes me as I start to float away and I never want it to end.

A wave of comfort envelops me with my last breath...because I know that where I'm going, it won't.

CHAPTER 50
BRESLIN

Everything is one big blur as Asher and I run through the doors of the hospital.

My heart is squeezing so hard, that for a moment, I think I might die.

And if my best friend is gone...I very well might.

The officer that I was on the phone with as Asher talked to Kyle wouldn't tell us what was going on after Preston's phone disconnected, and the entire Campus was blocked off by police and ambulances, apart from the dorms.

We tried to push our way through to the campus cafeteria on foot, but we were stopped—even after Asher started screaming that his brother was in there and I screamed for Kit.

A few officers were sympathetic, but no matter how hard we begged, they wouldn't let us past the courtyard, and when Asher started to fight one of them, we were physically escorted off campus.

A little while later Asher received a call telling him that he should head over to the hospital, so that's what we did.

Unfortunately, due to all the roads being blocked, it took forever to get here.

The emergency room is buzzing as we frantically make our way to the front desk.

"I'm here to see Preston Holden and Kit Bishop," Asher all but chokes out.

The nurse frowns. "I'm sorry, but I can't—"

"I was told to come here," he interjects and when she looks like she's going to argue he says, "I'm his brother."

Her eyes soften and she motions for us to follow her. "He was brought here as a precaution. Granted, I'm sure he's a little shaken up—"

I don't hear the rest of her sentence because as soon as we round the corner and I hear Kit sobbing, I run full speed ahead toward the sound.

If she's crying, that means she's alive.

I pull the curtain out of my way and when I see both her and Preston, I rush over and hug her so tight it hurts. "Thank God you're okay."

Out of the corner of my eye, I see Asher wrap Preston in a hug.

I focus back on Kit and my stomach dips when she starts crying even harder. I cradle her face in my hands, trying to reassure her that she's safe. "Kit, honey, it's okay. You're okay."

She's so upset she can't form words and the sick feeling in my stomach intensifies when I look over at Preston who looks like he's trying his hardest to keep it together.

There's an ominous vibe in the room and I know Asher feels it too because he whispers, "What's going on?"

I turn back to Kit but she looks down at the ground, sucking in deep breaths. The fact that my best friend can't even look at me causes my vision to blur.

"Kit," I say, harsher than I intended because her and Preston are scaring the shit out of me.

She curls her arms around herself. "Landon was in the cafeteria with us."

I stare at her, unable to comprehend what she's saying.

I called Landon right after I got the text message from the college, and although he didn't answer, I assumed he was at his apartment, sleeping from all the jet lag.

Plus, Preston never told us that Landon was there with them when he was on the phone.

I open my mouth but then Kit looks at Preston and he says the words that rip my entire world apart. "He was trying to protect us and Kyle shot him."

My muscles seize and my heart clamps, unable to beat.

Behind me, a strangled, guttural sound tears from Asher's throat before he runs out and I follow him, or at least I think I do.

It's like everything is happening in slow motion and I can't form or acknowledge any thoughts or feelings because if I do...

Then what they said is real...and it can't be real.

Because I won't survive it.

My heart starts to pound and everything sways. There's a deep ache in the center of my chest that keeps getting bigger and bigger with every painful breath I try to take.

In my peripheral vision, I see Asher yelling at a woman wearing bloody scrubs—and when I hear her say Landon's name, the deep ache in my chest bursts wide open.

CHAPTER 51

ASHER

The only thing I can hear is the sound of my heart cracking bit by bit as I make my way toward the room. I've been watching the nurses like clockwork for the last hour and I have exactly ten minutes until they do their next check.

According to the surgeon, Landon coded on the helicopter ride and he lost a significant amount of blood, enough that the medical team debated if they could even do the surgery in the first place. Thankfully at the last minute, they decided it was better to try than not to. Once in surgery, they were able to retrieve the bullet and repair the injury to his heart and the lower lobe of his left lung.

He then went into detail involving a lot of medical terminology that I didn't understand and when I stopped him and asked him point blank what my boyfriend's chances of survival were because that's all I cared about...he spouted off a slew of more medical terminology.

However, the look on his face told me all I needed to know.

Not good.

When I asked if I could see him, he declined...which is why I'm currently taking matters into my own hands.

My stomach knots as I slip through the door and when I see all the machines and tubes he's attached to, there's a sharp sting in my heart and it takes everything in me to keep one foot in front of the other.

He looks so fragile and helpless and I want nothing more than to trade places with him.

Landon wouldn't be fighting for his life right now if it wasn't for me...and that's something I will never forgive myself for.

I reach for his hand and when he doesn't return my touch and all I feel is cold skin, something inside my chest shifts and I lose it completely.

I run my thumb along his cheek and stare down at him with tears burning my eyes. "I'm so sorry."

Grief wraps around my heart, making it hard to breathe, because there's so many things I want to tell him. So many things that I need him to know.

Like the fact that I love him.

In all our time together, I *never* once told him.

And now, he may never know.

I kiss his forehead and a thick sob mangles the words until they're coming out in a hoarse whisper. "I love you." I squeeze my eyes shut, the pain of this moment sends shards of guilt through my heart. "You were never second best."

I am.

A wave of agony swells in my chest and I cup his jaw. "I need you to wake up for me, Landon."

I squeeze his hand again and when there's no response, the tears fall harder and I know there's only one more thing I can do.

Give him what I know he wants more than anything.

No matter how much it may hurt me, I love them enough to finally do the right thing. What I should have done all along.

Because if I had...this never would have happened.

I let go of his hand, the pieces of my heart knocking against my rib cage. "She's yours, Landon. I'll keep my distance. I'll—"

Fingertips brush against my hand and I still myself, certain I was only imagining it.

When I feel the flutter again and my heart jumps, I look down.

Slowly, his eyes open. "Don't leave me."

His voice is so faint and when he gasps for a breath and tries to speak again, my hands frame his face and I shake my head. "I won't," I tell him, because I'll do anything he wants. "I love you. And I swear to God you better fucking live so I can tell you that every day."

His lips start to curve into a smile, until his eyes dart around the room and his face falls.

I know who he's looking for.

Pain flashes in his eyes and he tries to speak again, but I kiss his hand and say, "I'm gonna go get her."

He nods, but the second I start to turn away, he grips my hand, concern marring his face.

"I'm not leaving you, nerd. I'm yours for however long you want me to be." I give him a smirk. "I'll be right back, I'm just going to get our girl."

The smile he gives me is luminous enough to light the darkest of rooms and a lump swells in my throat...because I'm so grateful that I get to see it again.

I run out of the room and down the hall, only stopping when I pass the nurses' station to tell them that he's awake.

I roam up and down the halls, looking for her everywhere.

When 15 minutes go by and I still can't find her, I walk out to the parking lot to check if her car is still here.

For the briefest of moments anger flares in my gut, but when I find her kneeling on the ground by her car, shaking like a leaf near a small pile of vomit, any animosity quickly disappears and I feel like shit for not checking on her sooner.

I drop down and pull her into my arms, "How long have you been out here, baby?"

It's like she doesn't even hear me.

"I wish Kyle shot me like he wanted to," she says through trembles. "It should have been me. I *wish* it was me."

My heart plummets and I run my thumbs over her tear-stained cheeks. "You and I both know Landon would never want that."

She clutches her stomach. "I can't lose him."

I kiss her temple. "I know you're scared, Breslin. But everything is going to be okay. I promise."

She blinks and stares up at me. "How can you be so sure?"

I can't help but smile as I lower my lips to her ear. "Because he's out of surgery and he's asking to see the girl that he loves."

She jumps out of my arms so fast she nearly head butts me before she starts running toward the hospital as fast as her legs can carry her.

I look up to the night sky and silently thank the universe for granting me not one, but two second chances in 24 hours.

I'll never take either of them for granted.

CHAPTER 52
ASHER

I watch from a distance as they lower him into the ground. My mother sits stoic on a chair near the front, large sunglasses framing her small face. The sounds of people weeping have my teeth grinding and it's all I can do not to walk over there and tell them all about the man they're wasting their tears on.

Turns out my father did us all the ultimate favor and passed away on his own the night of the shooting.

I didn't want to come here today, partly on account that Landon's still in the hospital, but Landon told me I would regret it if I didn't. He said I needed to say goodbye in my own way, not for my father, but for me.

And I suppose in a way he's right, I just can't bring myself to sit with a bunch of people mourning the loss of a man who abused his kids for years, sexually manipulated a mentally ill teenager, and then disowned his son when he needed him the most.

And had he not done the second—who knows how many unfortunate events could have been prevented.

I wait until everyone is gone and then I make my way over. A pamphlet from the funeral flaps in the wind until it lands at my feet. There's a picture of him smiling, but that's not what snags my attention.

It's the scripted print underneath his name that reads—*Beloved Father*.

Words that couldn't be further from the truth sit like a boulder on my chest and before I can talk myself out of it, I do a quick look around, unzip my pants, and let it flow.

"You know, if you shake it more than twice you're playing with it," my brother's voice calls out as I tuck myself back in my pants. "Then you'll really give that woman a show."

My eyes flit to a woman a few grave rows over, her mouth is parted in sheer horror as she gapes at me.

"Guess you didn't want to attend the service, either," I mumble as my brother sidles beside me.

He looks down at the ground. "I thought about it, but in the end, I couldn't stomach sitting there listening to people talk about how great he was and how much they're going to miss him."

"Same here." I dig my hands in my pockets, trying to decide how to approach this topic. "I received a call from Dad's lawyer this morning."

"Figured as much." He mirrors my stance. "I'm assuming he left everything to you?"

"Yeah." I shift my feet. "I'm not sure what to do about the football team, though. It's kind of a major conflict of interest when I'm trying to make it into the NFL myself. I think I'm going to sell it."

He rubs his jaw. "Makes sense."

There's an awkward shift in the air between us now and I decide to just get on with it. "I'm thinking about giving our mother a little extra seeing as he did renege on their infidelity clause."

He snorts. "I'm sure she'll love that, given he made certain their prenup was ironclad in the event of his untimely death."

I rub the back of my neck. "I'm donating a portion of it to a few charities."

"How very philanthropic of you."

"Preston." The serious tone of my voice has him turning to face me. "I want to write you a check, because this money is as much yours as it is mine...but I'm trying to be a good brother here."

I draw in a deep breath. "Bottom line—I'm afraid that if I do, I'll only be enabling you further. So, here's what I was thinking. Your tuition at Yale will be covered as well as your apartment and any other living and school expenses that you need. When you graduate, I'll give you half of dad's money...but only if you stop gambling for at least two years. This way, you can use the money to start up a business like you always wanted to and—"

"Yeah, I'm gonna pass on that, brother."

I fold my arms across my chest. "What?"

He looks over at his car. "I didn't come here to say goodbye to our father. I came here to say goodbye to you."

I shake my head, uneasiness surging in my gut as I fire off questions at him. "Why? Where are you going? What about Yale?"

He fishes his keys out of his pocket. "I dropped out."

"What the hell do you mean you dropped out?" I bark, my anger rising. "You need to graduate college."

He starts walking to his car and I'm right on his heels. "Look, I know what happened this week really fucked you up."

He opens his car door. "It's more than that."

"Okay, so start talking and explain it to me then."

"I can't." He checks his watch. "I really need to hit the road."

"I don't understand why—" I stop mid-sentence when I realize. "Fuck, you're in trouble again, aren't you?" I slam my hand on the hood. "How much do you owe?"

He slides into the driver's seat and sticks his key in the ignition. "Don't worry about it, Asher. You don't have to bail me out of this one. I got this."

Before I can say another word, he hits the gas and drives off.

CHAPTER 53

LANDON

I run my fingers through her hair as she sleeps beside me in the hospital chair. The soft red strands feel like silk and I can't help but skim her soft pale cheekbone next.

I don't realize my mistake until she wakes with a jolt and her eyes open wide. "Are you okay? Do you need anything? What's wrong?"

For the past six days Breslin hasn't left my side. She also hasn't slept, eaten, or talked about anything deeper than the weather or hospital food.

She thinks I don't hear her at night when she cries and sobs for forgiveness, but I do. And no matter how many times I try to tell her that she has nothing to be sorry for...it goes in one ear and out the other.

"Nothing is wrong," I tell her. "I'm sorry I woke you."

I just wanted to touch you because I miss you.

She waves a hand and stands up. "It's not a big deal." She leans over and kisses my cheek. "You look hungry. I'm gonna run down to the deli downstairs and get you some actual food. Do you want anything in particular?"

I open my mouth to decline but then Bertie the nurse walks in and Breslin waves at her before she skips off.

Bertie looks in the direction of the door. "That girl hasn't slept more than five minutes at a time since you've been here."

She motions for me to stick out my arm and tisks. "Poor girl is going to end up running herself into the ground."

"I know," I say as she starts to take my vitals. "That's what I'm afraid of."

Bertie sighs just like she always does whenever we talk. "On the bright side, I hear you're getting out of here in a few more days."

I give her a grin and waggle my eyebrows. "I walked around by myself today."

The first few days were the hardest, but I can feel myself getting stronger every day and I can't even pretend that I'm not ecstatic about it. I know exactly how lucky I am to be sitting here right now and it's something I won't ever forget.

She starts to smile but then lets out a whistle when Asher walks in the room, wearing a suit.

"Back off, Bertie. He's taken," I tell her and she laughs before leaving.

"Hey, you," he says as he strides over to me. Before I can return his greeting, his lips are on mine. My heart flips as he kisses a path from my jaw to my ear. "I love you."

I press my hand to his chest where his heart is hammering wildly. "I love you, too." When he plops in the chair next to my bed I say, "I take it you went to the funeral and said goodbye?"

A hint of amusement dances behind his eyes briefly before they turn sad. "I did."

I press the button on my hospital bed, raising it. "You okay?"

He leans forward, resting his forearms on his knees. "Preston skipped town."

"What? Why?"

"I think he's in trouble again. I tried to tell him I would take care of it, but he took off anyway."

"Shit," I whisper. "Maybe he'll come to his senses and come home soon."

He leans back. "That's what I'm hoping for."

I reach over to touch him but then Breslin walks in the room. "Sorry," she says, slowly backing away. "I'll give you two some space."

"Breslin," my voice comes out sharp and she stops in her tracks. "Come over here."

Asher's attention turns to her as she walks in and even though she tries to avert her gaze, there's a magnetic energy between them that's undeniable.

Asher sits up in the chair. "Hey."

She tucks a strand of hair behind her ear and places the bag of food on the table beside me. "Hey."

He gives her a small smile and I can sense the touch of sorrow in it. For the briefest of moments their eyes meet, like two ships passing in the night before Breslin looks away.

I scoot over on the bed and pat the spot next to me. "Sit."

This will undoubtedly be awkward—but sometimes you have to have the messy and complicated to get to the good.

When she's next to me, I tuck her to my side. "I don't forgive you for sleeping with Asher."

She stiffens and her eyes brim with tears. "I'm so sorry—"

I place my finger over her mouth, silencing her. "I know, Breslin. That's my point. You shouldn't be sorry and you don't need my forgiveness for sleeping with someone you love."

She looks at Asher and then back to me. "I never meant to hurt you."

"Me either," Asher whispers.

"I know," I tell them. "Things got out of hand between us before I left for England. But if I'm being completely honest—I was insecure about you two from the very beginning...and that was on me. I had good intentions when I first suggested that we should all be together. But the more time that passed, and the closer you two got, the more jealous I became. There was a huge problem in our relationship, and that problem was me."

"No," Asher interjects. "It wasn't all on you, Landon. I was just as much a part of the problem."

Breslin worries her bottom lip between her teeth. "Me too." A tiny wrinkle forms between her brows. "How do we make this work now? After everything that happened how do we —"

"We keep trying," Asher cuts in. "We don't give up."

The space between us all tightens and then sizzles with charged energy as we lock gazes, a silent agreement made among the three of us.

My hand finds the scar on my chest and immediately I'm transported back to that moment. "Do you know what I kept thinking about when I was on that cafeteria floor?"

Breslin's face contorts in anguish and I kiss the top of her head before shifting and looking at the both of them. "That I was never going to get a chance to tell you both how much I loved you again."

I suck in a breath. "I don't want to ruin my second chance and make the same mistake. When it's my time to go for real, I don't want to be thinking about how much time I wasted on being jealous or about all the things I never got to do." I reach for both of their hands. "When I die, I want it to be with a smile on my face— because I'll know that I spent my time making every moment count with the two people who mean everything to me."

My fingers find the spot on their wrists where their pulse is beating rapidly. I close my eyes as the beautiful rhythm and melody coarse through me, wrapping around my heart and squeezing.

"What are you doing?" Asher questions.

I look at them both and smile. "Listening to my favorite song."

EPILOGUE
BRESLIN

Seven months later...

I take a step back on the busy street that's bustling with people, appraising the small building from the outside.

My chest swells and my throat locks up as I take in the large glass windows that will be perfect for displaying art.

My art.

The slightest of breezes flows through the muggy summer air and I close my eyes and soak it in.

The past seven months have been a whirlwind.

Asher was officially drafted to New Orleans. And even though the current starting quarterback still has one more season left—which means Asher's on the sidelines for his first year—the coaches are practically bursting at the seams to get him out on that field.

And I know that when his time comes...he's going to take them all by storm.

I was petrified to move here, but now, I can't imagine living anywhere else. These streets are dripping with creativity and the only person who loves and appreciates it even more than I do...is Landon.

A few weeks after the school shooting, someone ended up uploading a video on YouTube of him performing Complicated Hearts at the Black Spoon.

It quickly ended up going viral, and people went nuts. So nuts, that not one but *two* major record labels approached him about signing with them.

He declined.

He said he was a musician, not an image or a package.

The meetings with those record labels prompted him to pursue music full time, though and he's quickly gaining traction and becoming extremely popular on the indie front. He performs once a week at a local venue nearby and every performance is so packed they had to start selling tickets and hire extra security.

There's no doubt in my mind that he's going to be performing in sold out venues around the world in the next year or so.

Watching Asher and Landon pursue their dreams made me want to pursue mine. Of course, I didn't just jump into it head first like they did. I actually managed to land a job as an architect after I graduated. And even though I hated every second of it, I kept at it. Until I just couldn't take it anymore. I needed to do what set my soul on fire.

Which is why I decided to open my own art gallery. It's costing me a fortune and I internally wince whenever I think about the loan I took out, but when you're no longer giving half of your paycheck to an addict father who uses you...things aren't so bad.

I give the building one final glance before I turn around and my gaze snags on Asher and Landon walking out of the ice cream shop across the street.

Right when they're about to cross over, Asher pulls Landon back, sweeping his thumb over the drop of ice cream on his lip.

A second later, my heart does a little flutter when he leans in and kisses him softly.

An elderly lady on the street makes a face and I'm about to run over there and tell her off, but she walks away, shaking her head in disgust.

Her rude behavior doesn't deter Asher who goes back for another kiss as soon as the first one ends.

The smile on their faces as they walk over to me ignites my own.

"So, is this the one?" Landon questions, pointing to the building.

"I'm signing the paperwork tomorrow."

He picks me up and twirls me around so fast my head spins. "I'm so proud of you."

I open my mouth but then his lips capture mine, causing butterflies to swarm in my tummy as I wrap my legs around his waist and kiss him like he's my lifeline. I rest my palm on the scar over his heart before tracing the new tattoo under it. A tattoo consisting of music notes from the song he wrote about me and Asher.

"I love you," I tell him when we break apart.

His hand slides to the nape of my neck and he holds my gaze, the heat in his eyes is so palpable my heart goes into a sprint. "I love you, too."

Two fingers tip my chin until my head lolls back and I'm staring at the bluest eyes I've ever seen.

"You're really doing it," Asher whispers, his fingers trailing over my neck, causing little shivers up my spine.

"I am," I tell him, my voice cracking with emotion.

"I always knew you could, baby," he says gruffly before he kisses me. His teeth tug on my bottom lip before he slips his tongue inside, tasting me. When I moan, the pads of his fingers dip ever so slightly inside my shirt, prickling my skin.

Thump, thump, thump.

I'm breathless when he draws back and gives me that cocky smile. "I fucking love that I can still do that."

A blush creeps up my cheeks. "Me too."

I squeal when Landon twirls me around again. "Hmm, should I carry the soon to be world-renowned artist home like this or make her walk?"

"Carry me," I say at the same time Asher says, "Make her walk."

I shoot Asher a dirty look and Landon kisses my temple. "Carry it is."

"So, a funny thing happened when I was looking at the gallery today," I tell them as we make our way down the street.

Landon and Asher exchange a glance.

"Oh?" Landon questions, his grip on my hips tightening.

"Turns out the gallery is already paid for." I raise an eyebrow. "The broker mentioned two anonymous donors."

"Wow," Asher says, the corners of his eyes crinkling. "Talk about some awesome luck."

"Looks like you have two people who really believe in you," Landon says.

I motion for Landon to put me down and I glare at them. "Guys, we talked about this. I told you I didn't want your money."

Landon feigns offense. "I had nothing to do with it. It was donated."

Asher grins. "Anonymously."

I shake my head and those dimples of his deepen as we approach our house.

Although house is a bit of a downplay. Asher purchased a farm for us to live in and it's so big it echoes.

"Close your eyes," Asher says when we reach the front door.

"Why?"

"We may have gotten you a little surprise," Landon says. "Just humor us and do it."

"And hold out your arms," Asher adds.

I do as they say and a moment later something furry and tiny is placed in my arms.

My eyes pop open and I stare down at the little golden puppy in awe. "You got me a puppy?"

Asher and Landon exchange another glance.

"We thought it was about time," Landon says and my eyes fill with tears. Tears that the puppy quickly licks and I can't help but laugh.

Strong arms wrap around my waist from behind. "We're not going anywhere, Breslin," Asher whispers. "Hold on to us."

I shake my head because I can't hold on...I can only do the opposite.

The room becomes blurry and my heart races, pounding out a rhythm that makes it hard to breathe as I feel myself free-fall for the second time in my life.

Only this time...I know they'll both be right there to catch me.

ABOUT THE AUTHOR

Want to be notified about my upcoming releases? https://goo.gl/n5Azwv

Ashley Jade craves tackling different genres and tropes within romance. Her first loves are New Adult Romance and Romantic Suspense, but she also writes everything in between including: contemporary romance, erotica, and dark romance.

Her characters are flawed and complex, and chances are you will hate them before you fall head over heels in love with them.

She's a die-hard lover of oxford commas, em dashes, music, coffee, and anything thought provoking...except for math.

Books make her heart beat faster and writing makes her soul come alive. She's always read books growing up and scribbled stories in her journal, and after having a strange dream one night; she decided to just go for it and publish her first series.

It was the best decision she ever made.

If she's not paying off student loan debt, working, or writing a novel—you can usually find her listening to music, hanging out with her readers online, and pondering the meaning of life.

Check out her social media pages for future novels.

She recently became hip and joined Twitter, so you can find her there, too.

She loves connecting with her readers—they make her world go round'.

~Happy Reading~

Feel free to email her with any questions / comments: ashleyjadeauthor@gmail.com

For more news about what I'm working on next: Follow me on my Facebook page: https://www.facebook.com/pages/Ashley-Jade/788137781302982

Thanks for Reading!
Please follow me online for more.
<3 Ashley Jade

ALSO BY ASHLEY JADE

ACKNOWLEDGMENTS

Yup, this will be long. Because each and every one of you are so important to me and there will never be a good enough way to thank you for all the support and generosity you've shown me. A simple acknowledgment in a book doesn't do it justice, but I hope it matters all the same.

Complicated Hearts was and is a gamble.

This duet isn't for everyone and a lot of people turn their noses up at this sort of story. They judge before they understand. Writing this duet was a journey...and it was...well, complicated.

I'm so incredibly humbled and grateful for each and every one of you. And truly, I thank you all from the bottom of my heart and the depths of my soul. I hope like hell I'm not leaving anyone out...and if by some horrible chance I did...just know that I'm sorry.

First off, I have to thank all of the amazing bloggers. You selfless, amazing people. I'm so incredibly thankful for you.

Tanya: I love you. The whole entire world knows I love you at this point. Cue: 'Wind Beneath My Wings.' Thank you for taking a chance and letting me corrupt you. Thank you for the amazing covers, teasers, and graphics that you do. Thank you for dropping everything to read the chapters that I sent you because I was freaking out. Thank you for being there for and with me every single step of the way.

Avery: I can't begin to tell you how grateful and thankful that I am for you. I know it wasn't easy staying up until 3:00 am with me going over every single word in a Google doc with a fine-tooth comb. You treated every paragraph, every syllable like it was of utmost importance and somehow, you made it bearable and even enjoyable. I honestly can't thank you enough.

Jamie: Thank you for being there and listening to me and my idea. When I told you about CH, you rooted for me, the characters, and this story. You wanted me to get it right as much as I did. Thank you so, so, so very much.

Michelle: Because this *still* applies and then some. I don't think I can ever express my gratitude for all that you do. From the big things—to the small things that always add up to big things. You keep me organized. You keep me sane. You keep me going when I want to throw in the towel. Thank you, babe. So fucking much. There is no way this could have happened without you.

Pennie: Not every author is blessed to have a guardian angel in the book world. Thank you so very much for being mine. You are such an incredibly valued soul to have by my side.

Erika: I love your face. You are the bestttt at what you do and I can't thank you enough. From being my cheerleader, to making me laugh, to being my pimp. I'm so grateful for you.

K. Webster: Woman, you slay me. On the bright side, now that it's finished. NO ONE can blame K Webster for Complicated Hearts being a duet and not a standalone. Thank you for being my unicorn and being someone that I look up to.

Amy: You *still* drive me crazy, baby. But I love you. Thank you so much for everything.

Tanaka: Thank you for believing in me and being so adorable and sweet. You make me all gooey inside. Thank you a million times over.

Crystal: You're beautiful. I love you. Thank you.

Shabby and Laura: Your support means the absolute world

to me. Thank you so much for believing in me and for all that you do. #CornForever

Michelle R: Or as my husband would say, my 'New York' friend. Hoped you liked a certain 'butterfingers' character :p Who knows, maybe he'll even have his own story one day. Thank you for being awesome.

Nico: Thank you for all of your encouragement and kind words. You're such a sweetheart with such a gentle soul.

Michelle McGinty: Hopefully you've now forgiven me for the senile science teacher in book 1. Butttt knowing you you're probably cursing my ass out about other things now.

Guess it's time to write a new book to cure it. I adore and love you, sexy.

My Bat Girls!!! OMG , MY BAT GIRLS!!!!: Jessica K, Belinda, Paula, Maria, Kim, Nik, Tammy, Di, Thai, Crystal, Jessica M, Danielle, Tijuana, Jadey, Melanie, Dee, Janie, Kim, Mari Ann, Hanan, Brandy, Janice, Nikki, Margie, Rose, Diane, and our other Bat Girl who gained her angel wings too soon- Heather Stanley.

I love you. I'm blessed to have the very BEST people in my corner. I will never, ever forget anyone of you. Because as far as I'm concerned- I don't shine without you all. Thank you for all that you do.

Ashley's Little Survivors Group: You babes' are my everything. Thank you from the very bottom of my heart for being one of the BEST groups in the whole world full of the very best readers out there!!!

The Complicated Hearts Arc group: Thank you for dealing with my crazy, and my teasers, and my 'Ahhh' moments. I hope it was worth the wait and it paid off. <3

Cassie- You were my very first 'fan'. Starting all the way back from the days of the 'Twisted Fate' series. I will never, ever forget that. Thank you so very much. You're my 'MVP' for life!!!

And last but not least...the person who makes my world go round'. My '**Hammie**'—My heart and soul. I couldn't do this without you, baby. My love for you knows no bounds...because we'd find a way to demolish anything standing in our way. You're my 'alpha', my strength, my weakness, but most importantly...my everything.

Made in United States
North Haven, CT
29 July 2024

55544204R00235